MATTHEW HART

SECOND HARVEST

BOOK 2 OF THE SERIES
THE LAST ITERATION

A CAPSCOVIL BOOK | GLONN | GERMANY

International English Edition
published by CAPSCOVIL, Glonn, Germany, December 2013
ISBN Perfect Paperback 978-3-942358-37-8
Copyright © CAPSCOVIL, 2013

Editor: Helen Veitch
Typesetting: Beth Flemington
Art work and design: Tom Jester

CAPSCOVIL® is an imprint and registered trademark of Britta Muzyk

Electronic editions are available for various reading devices and platforms.

Capscovil and their authors support several non-profit organisations.
For further information please visit:
www.capscovil.com

Attention: Organizations and Corporations

For information on exclusive editions or special offers for sales promotions, premiums or fund-raising, please write to:
projects@capscovil.com

About the Author

Matthew is the author of six technology books, the management book *Middlework*, and one previous science fiction novel titled *The Last Iteration of Dexter Maxwell* .

He lives in Kansas City with his family. *Second Harvest* is his second novel and the sequel of Book 1 of the Sci-Fi series"The Last Iteration".

Connect with Matthew through http://about.me/hartmatthew and visit www.matthew-hart.com or http://lastiteration.com/

Acknowledgements

Thanks to Britta Muzyk, for keeping the light on; to Helen Veitch, for understanding and improving, Tom Jester for another superb cover; John Hart for technical art and a beautiful map of Venus; Beth Flemington for double-checking and producing a good book.
Thanks to early readers Carl Knerr, Angela Fleischmann, and Martin Ingram.

Thank you for reading Second Harvest. An author is nothing without readers.

FOR BETH

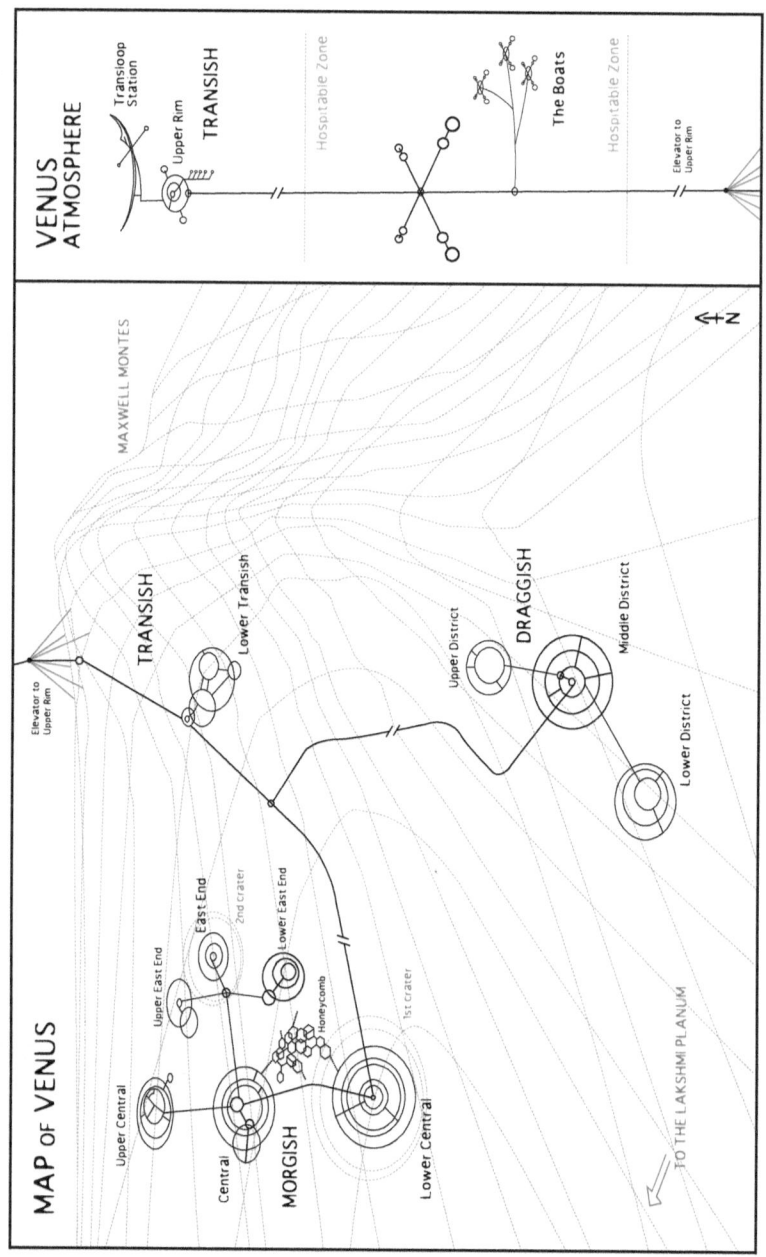

VENUS ATMOSPHERE

Transloop Station

Upper Rim

TRANSISH

Hospitable Zone

The Boats

Hospitable Zone

Elevator to Upper Rim

MAP of VENUS

MAXWELL MONTES

Elevator to Upper Rim

TRANSISH

Lower Transish

DRAGGISH

Upper District

Middle District

Lower District

Upper East End

East End

2nd Crater

Lower East End

Honeycomb

1st Crater

Upper Central

Central

MORGISH

Lower Central

TO THE LAKSHMI PLANUM

N

PROLOGUE

EARTH TRANSLOOP STATION, SEPTEMBER 19, 3027. DAY 5.

Once again, Thelonius Hollywood found himself floating alone in space.

He watched the junk-collecting spacecraft depart, carrying his old friend Dexter Maxwell to whatever fate waited for him on the surface of Earth. Out above the world like this, Thelo could gaze for hours. Things always seemed to be in slow motion, even if they were actually moving at thousands of kilos per hour.

Thelo hoped it was all worth it—the resistance had sacrificed everything to free Dex from Venus. What Dex could do on Earth, only Logos knew. And Logos was dead.

Thelo thought of Trance and the work she'd done on Venus. He hoped she was alright. She'd be living a double life, for the threads of the interconnected sensors of Venus. But she'd carefully find the outages, the dark areas, the off-cam places so that she could meet with the rest of them. To follow Fuel and his fight against the Families. All of that, just to put Dex on Earth and in touch with some old monks?

The space junk collectors were older, relatively speaking, than the garbage collectors he had driven for old man Newbury back in Grenver a thousand years ago. And they were even easier to hack. You could pull the tugged chip in about five minutes flat if you knew what to look for. That was the problem across the board for the Families of Venus: they hadn't updated their tech in centuries. You could manually override an expensive piece of space equipment, and they couldn't stop it. They acted all wealthy and superior, but in reality they had been slowly going bankrupt for three generations.

The junk collector was barely visible now. Soon, Dex would drop down into the atmo and burn towards the mountains outside of Grenver. From there, he would get himself to Longstown, in the Western Cawlrian Empire. And look for a couple of monks that worshipped crazy ol' Brody Jones.

Thelo closed his eyes against the bright white of Earth, the stark black of space, and swallowed back the taste in his throat. Part of it was his own blood. But mostly it was the bitter metallic sting of the Other. The one who calls himself Moses.

Millionaire's Disease. Thelo could not explain how he'd gotten it, but without Logos' chemical cocktail, it owned him. This was the only way to suppress the Other, a second personality trapped in his brain. And Moses hated Dexter Maxwell.

The rage of the Other beat against the quickly dissipating chemical blocker. Thelo began his cognitive exercises, just as Logos had taught him. He had a series of games he could play in his mind to keep himself in control—spatial exercises, mathematical proofs, even an old block game that he'd trained himself to complete without a threader.

When he'd gotten himself back under control, Thelo did a quick catalog of the situation. *Sublimated neurological disease? Check. Massive headache stemming from potential concussion? Check. Right arm broken, probably in a bone-sticking-through-the-skin kind of a way? Got it.*

Thelo opened his eyes and looked around. Taking stock wasn't helping. He took a long, deep breath and tried to think what he should do next.

Thelo had straight up lied to get Dex out the door. There was no backup plan for Thelonius Hollywood. The plan was: drop Dex off Earth-side, fly the untugged shuttle back to Venus, and check back in with Leshan for his next smuggling assignment. But the shuttle had been destroyed. And Leshan was probably dead from the cut Dex had given him. There was nowhere for Thelo to go now.

But here he was. Time to improvise.

Thelo was only a few kilometers from the Earth Transloop Station, floating in geostationary orbit above Earth and hidden from view by the massive solar collector. The entire station resembled an umbrella: a vast, curved surface held together with strong steel fingers, with a long line of space station components jutting away from the canopy like a stem. The surface of the collector was lined with hundreds of thousands of photovoltaic cells, and its outer surface, which was facing toward Earth, was covered with matte-black insulating foam. The cells concentrated energy from the sun to power the space station, while the cooling water was recycled back through the station. Unlike the Transloop Station above Venus, this station had no ready access to the fuel from the asteroids. It had to run on whatever could be passed over the Transloop and generated by the sun. The Earth Transloop

Station also had to be discreet. Thus the connection from the center of the solar collector went straight up and away from Earth: first to the command center, then the Transloop Ramp, and then to what was to be the new living quarters for the Family's imminent invasion. All concealed behind the matte-black canopy of the solar collector.

Surely, Thelo reasoned, he could find an infantry trooper that he knew. Someone who could smuggle him back through the Transloop to Venus. He squinted into the darkness of space, trying to get the math right for a jetpack burn toward the barracks.

That's when he noticed a few stars blink out, and then on again. He watched for a while before he saw the spacecraft approaching. It was a Family recon unit, matte black with no hard angles. They called them Slabs. He'd been briefed on their existence in his training, had even seen renderings, but had never been close to one in real life like this. At first all he could think about was its beauty. A real fighter shuttle, extremely maneuverable, with good zero-grav and full-grav flight capabilities. Functions just as well as a plane as a shuttle. Undetectable by all but the most advanced surveillance equipment. In fact, against the black of space, it was almost upon him before he even realized it was there.

As he gazed in admiration, the Slab made an uncomfortable change in direction. It was heading directly for him.

Thelo looked around. He was stranded. The barracks station was still a significant distance away—he could get there with his suit impulse jets, but there was no way he could outrun the Slab. Besides, the cannons mounted under the wings were pointed directly at him, taunting him, daring him to try and escape.

Remember your training, Thelo told himself. They will probe your mind, try to find out about the resistance. Thelo couldn't help but smile. Wonder what else they will find in this broken old brain of mine?

The recon shuttle switched to a gentle drift, somewhat awkwardly, and eventually settled into position above him. Who's driving the damn thing? Thelo wondered. I could give them a few pointers on piloting that beauty. Underneath the hull, a large cargo door opened. Thelo could see up inside the shuttle, it was so close. It was empty. No troopers came jetting out in formation. After a while, someone

13

in Family-issue flight gear descended from what appeared to be the bridge into the cargo bay. The lone individual zero-grav jumped down to the cavernous cargo door, and began waving madly, indicating that Thelo should move toward the Slab.

Thelo squinted. Who is that? He wondered. And why would I want to get on that thing?

The waving became frantic, and then stopped. The Family soldier performed a gesture at neck-level, very deliberately. Thelo couldn't make it out, but with nothing else to do, really, he used his jets to approach the ship. The trooper on board relaxed a little and kept moving his hand around. Thelo realized that this person was touching his right hand to his neck, touching it again, and then swiping it across his lower jaw. Over and over he did this: touch, touch, swipe. Touch, touch, swipe.

Thelo remembered that gesture—it was how he and his friends had engaged their communications back when they'd pulled that traffic-stopping stunt in Grenver. Everyone in the Urban Resistance League had a different set of gestures on the tab glued to their neck. Tap, tap, rub. That was one of the codes for a specific one-to-one conversation. Tap, tap, rub. But who was this?

Through the fog of his head, it came to him in a rush: *that's Dex.*

Thelo stared dumbly for a few seconds. Then, as a test, Thelo took his good left hand and did the same movement: touch, touch, swipe. The masked man threw up both arms in a mixture of frustration and excitement and began gesturing wildly for Thelo to get on the shuttle.

If Thelo squinted, he could still see the junk collector in the distance, making its slow descent to Earth with Dex in it. How could Dex have gotten on the Slab? But who else could it be?

Thelo's jets propelled him into the cargo bay, and the pilot pulled him on board. Through the transparent visor, Thelo saw that it really was Dex. Dex gave a tight smile, put a finger in the air as if to say *hold on a minute*, and then he was gone, up the ladder and into the bridge. Thelo held the grappling handles on the wall as the cargo door closed. He heard an overhead voice, Dex's voice, say, "Get up here and strap in." Thelo carefully pulled himself up the ladder one-handedly. There were three chairs in the bridge. One was occupied by Dexter Maxwell, pulling the recon shuttle away from the Earth-side Loopstation and the army barracks above it. Another chair was occupied by what appeared to be the shuttle's original pilot, roughly trussed to the chair with insulation tape, his mouth bound shut, and a wild look of fear in his eyes at the sight of Thelo. The third chair was empty. Thelo slumped into it and awkwardly strapped himself in.

No sooner was he in, than the shuttle's primary engines engaged. They were heading back down to Earth.

"Crackpipe, Dex, how did you get this shuttle?" Thelo said.

"I'll explain later," Dex said. "Do you think you could drive this thing?"

"It would truly be my pleasure," Thelo said, taking the yoke in front of him. He looked over the controls, switching to the secondary interface. "Gonna be tough with one hand. I'll need your help. Are you okay, eh?" Thelo asked.

"Been better," Dex said. "Just tired. The system has our coordinates for landing."

"I'm not meant for Earth, Dex," Thelo said. "This isn't part of the plan."

"Scrap the plan," Dex said, leaning back in the chair, and stretching his arms. "From now on, *I'm* the plan."

PART 1

FAMILY HIGH-ALTITUDE FLOTILLA SS *MONSANTO*, EMERGENCY MEDICAL FACILITY, DAY 4.

One.

Ashion backed away from the med-bed, letting go of Tano's limp hand. His mind raced through the timeline. He'd seen the iteration's shuttle explode, and now, minutes later, Tano returns, cut up by a skilled swordsman long before the iter could have made the Transloop. And how had he even made the loop? Because the shuttle had been destroyed.

Scratch that. Ashion knew the loop field had been growing. The iter must have been close enough to eject directly into the hot jump field. The SIN automatically allows anything through—for safety reasons. It all added up to one thing.

Dexter Maxwell is using the monks' shifting mech to attack my Earth-side troops.

Ashion turned to the closest White Scientist and pointed at Tano. "Stabilize that," he said.

The Whi-Sci did not look at Ashion. His frontal lobe connection, sprouting from the interface on his forehead, prevented decent eye contact anyway. "Sir, we require Family-privilege overrides to reconstruct him properly. All we can do is stabilize him using standard planet-side technology."

Ashion didn't hesitate. "Consider him a primary asset of the Family Security Council. I will override the Family controls to ensure critical information can be retrieved."

The Whi-Sci nodded. "I have recorded the override and will work to secure the asset."

The attendants began to plug Tano into numerous surrounding feeds. Ashion stepped out of the ER unit, but turned back to watch the Family-only med-tech go into motion. Massive robotic arms whirred to life and descended on Tano with a merciless efficiency. Needles extracted blood samples from every open wound, and his mouth was forced open and swabbed. Cameras were inserted. All the while, the

SIN was extracting more and more data, looping it through the network, building threads, analyzing them, comparing them, graphing probabilities.

"Initial data levels indicate Earth-born infection has taken hold," the Whi-Sci said.

"Increasing bacteriophage levels to counteract," replied his partner. "Expect bacterial infection at zero in thirty seconds." The surgical arms immediately began to emit a bacteria-destroying virus. Ultraviolet lights flooded Tano's body, showing where the robotic arms and blades were depositing the oozing virus.

"Faster, please," the first Whi-Sci said calmly. "SIN analysis demands we get to the damaged tissue now."

Ashion turned to leave, but found himself facing Exemplar Thadwick Lewiston, arms folded, a smug look on his doughy face.

"Trouble with your slave, slave?" Thadwick asked, glancing over Ashion's shoulder. From behind him, Ashion heard the dull tone of Tano flat-lining, and the Whi-Scis calmly but rapidly changing their strategy. Ashion pretended to ignore it, and gave Thadwick a thin smile.

"No more trouble than usual," Ashion said.

"Oh, it sounds like he's gone and had himself killed," Thadwick said with mock pity. But even as he spoke, the flat-lining was replaced by a rhythmical beat. Thadwick's smile slipped.

"If you will excuse me, Thadwick, I've got business that needs attending to." Ashion went to push past the large man.

When the clumsy hand grabbed at his arm, it took all of Ashion's efforts not to snatch Lewiston's hand and deftly break his wrist. Straight to the icer for that, Ashion thought. He remembered the last time he had been put down for attacking a Family authority. It'd been over a hundred years ago. Now wasn't a good time to get iced. Instead, he slowly turned to face Thadwick. The fat man's mood changed, his face cold and hard. It took Ashion by surprise; the likes of Thadwick Lewiston had not surprised him for decades. He had no idea what to say.

"The endgame is upon us, slave," Thadwick whispered, so quietly that Ashion could barely hear it. And then his tone was back to normal again. "The Governor keeps you around for her own reasons.

I don't pretend to know them. But let me tell you what *my* reasons for you will be."

Ashion shook himself loose. "If you don't mind, Thadwick, I have far more important things to do than listen to the unhinged banterings of a grundled middler." Ashion turned to leave again.

"I know who you seek in the plebeian caves of Venus," Thadwick said, talking quietly. "I know because the Governor knows. She's not told her Exemplar. She's not even told my father. I wonder why that is?"

Ashion said nothing, still facing away from Thadwick.

"But she decides to tell me. Pulls me aside, off-thread, and tells me straight. Then walks away."

Ashion turned around. He felt as if he was balanced on a thin blade, waiting for the wind to blow.

"So here I am, slave," Thadwick said, his face still stone cold. "I am delivering her message to you. Off-thread. As she must have envisioned." Ashion glanced up. The overhead was dead. Thadwick wagged his fat finger, and looked thoughtful. "But your reaction leaves me wondering who exactly is being played by the great and revered Governor Goldman. Is it you? Me? Or are we both mere pawns in a bigger game?"

Ashion still said nothing. Thadwick went on. "Nonetheless. I have a reason for you now. You should try not to confuse it with the Governor's. And you should come to my boat soon to discuss it in greater detail."

Without another word, Thadwick shuffled his oversized mass past Ashion. Ashion stood watching after him for a moment, unmoving. The overhead clicked on above him. Then he turned and stormed out of the med.

Two.

The cell in Ashion's private bunker was still hot with the sweat and energy of the prisoner. He was fresh off the ice, the mad look in his eyes betraying the chems flowing through his veins, burning his zombie flesh back to life. The prisoner's old skin shivered, his horribly disfigured face pulled into a pained grimace.

It had been a long time since Ashion had last tasted the pain and madness of coming off ice. Early on, after the first experiments, they had put him on and off ice, to test his mental capacity in the moments after the blood returned to his veins, after his brain was pulled out of its metastasis state. It chilled Ashion to remember.

By comparison, the waking process for a brand new body, fresh from the grow-tubes—that just meant a bit of the chills and a day's blindness. Hardly an inconvenience. But the icing mechanism was rough. Even these hundreds of years later, Ashion could look at Prisoner Six and remember vividly the burning pain in every pore, the searing agony of being heated back to life by the chems.

Then the memory disappeared, pushed deep, way back deep, and Ashion had Prisoner Six by the wrist and was slapping his face.

"Come to me now, Root," Ashion said calmly. The prisoner's maddened look didn't change. Ashion sighed in frustration, and slapped him again. "Come on, now, Root. Wake up."

It took a few minutes, but the prisoner finally sat up, still shaking. His face showed the kind of hatred and resignation that informed Ashion that he had regained his mental faculties.

"There now, let's talk," Ashion said.

"How...how long did you ice me this time?"

"Does it matter?"

Root closed his eyes and wiped the sweat from his brow.

"Let us speak of dear departed Logos," Ashion said.

Root nodded. "So, not long then. Not long this time. You bring me the same mysteries. The ice only as punishment. As punishment."

"Focus, Root. Tell me about Logos' visits."

"Did you consider your own predicament, when you gave him his turn? Who will take care of your fragile mind now?"

"I've been looking over your threads, Root. Someone's been tampering with them. Removing Logos from the feeds."

"If not Logos, who will make the next facsimile of you?"

"Answer the question."

"You are asking the wrong man about your precious threads. I sit in this padded cell, or in a freezer. Go bother someone else."

"Tell me about the deleted bits. About you and Logos."

"We play chess."

"Right. Got that part. And what do you talk about, while you play old children's games?"

"Earth."

Ashion sat down on the single chair in the room. "Now we're getting somewhere. Earth, that's a good start. What interest in Earth could the good doctor have possibly had?"

"He was interested in my stories. About what it is like there. To feel the sun directly on your skin. To know rain."

Ashion scoffed. "What do you know of these things? You never went to Earth during the First Harvest."

"I have not always been a prisoner."

"Guess that depends on which *you* we're talking about."

"Are we done yet? The chemicals are demanding to be pissed from my bladder."

"No. Why do you think someone would delete threads of two useless men gushing about sun and rain?"

"I do not know."

"Maybe because you spoke of more than chess?"

The prisoner shrugged.

Ashion's com pinged in his ear. He pulled the thread. "Ashion here."

"Armitage Holden, sir. Status report on the Earth-side mission."

"Let's have it then."

"Sir, the Slab team confirms heavy damages to the Earth-side team. Single survivor bled out overnight. Signs confirm a large-scale Transloop team was here. "

Ashion took a long, slow breath. "How many must I send back

to finish this?"

"Sir, the report confirms eighteen Knights shifted to intercept the combatant."

Ashion rubbed his eyes. *A steep price to pay indeed.*

Holden spoke up. "Should we dispatch the team, sir?"

"Yes! Now!" Ashion yelled. "I want them dripping nano-suits within the hour. Send the first three-by-three pre-dated to Tano's return chrono-tags, say at a thirty-point quant lag. Chaz, Boost, and Ni'ello to lead. Dope them for a full data retrieval so we get the data regardless of their health state on return. Then put the second three-by-threes at an alternate chronos, say, a six-degree lag, so they can recalibrate tactics as needed."

"Sir," Holden said.

"Out with it, Arm," Ashion growled.

"You send these men to their death, sir."

"For Venus. For the Families. Are you clear on your instructions?"

"Yes, sir."

Ashion could almost see Holden grimly threading the Transloop orders. Ashion glanced behind him. Root was shivering, his eyes closed. With the iter contained, perhaps this interrogation was not the same priority.

"Now," Ashion continued in his com, "let's get real-time soldiers back down there. We don't want to leave the front three alone Earthside. Let's get a full station-side team down there immediately."

"Sir, yes, sir. The front team has requested permission to perform a perimeter scan. There may be real-time combatants."

"By all means. Tell them not to engage without authorization."

"Yes, sir."

"And what is the status of Central Processing?"

"Room re-taken, no Family casualties." Holden paused. "Three guerilla survivors."

"I explicitly ordered extermination."

"Sir, I understand that. They wired the overhead to the threadcasts, sir. The room went live. Then they surrendered."

"What?"

"They surrendered, sir. Just the three of them. On live threads. I made the call to stay their execution."

Ashion was quiet for a moment. "Excellent decision, Holden. We don't need to be slaughtering anyone on the public threads. Smart move on their part to run the splice."

"Sir, after they went live but before the surrender, they claimed to be acting on behalf of the man they call Fuel."

"What? No, Fuel is dead. I ended him four days ago."

"Nonetheless, they said they had been sent by Fuel to liberate the people of Morgish. Fuel for the fire and all that, sir."

Ashion closed his eyes. "Where are the three prisoners now?"

"The Whi-Scis at the Draggish Security med-fac have their heads plugged in and we're doing a sift on them. They show signs of probe training."

"Not surprising. Those skills have been trickling down planet-side for decades now. Anyone useful?"

"I don't think so, sir. A rehabbed princess and other tunnel-muck."

A princess. Could it be *the* princess? Ashion wondered. "Let's start with what they know about Fuel and go from there."

"Yes, sir."

"And the Sinners?" Ashion asked.

"Father Morgish and the fat one are fine, sir, if a little indignant."

"Thank you, Holden. I will be by to see them shortly."

Ashion dropped the thread and turned back to the prisoner. The prisoner had fallen asleep, his body overwhelmed by the crash from the zombie drugs. He lay in a puddle of his own urine, and the pungent odor of the chems pierced Ashion's nose. He covered his nose and left. The process is easier when the body is fresh. How many livers had Root gone through?

He walked quickly past his Whi-Scis and their read-outs, heading up the lift.

Too many variables, Ashion thought. Did this attack on the old network room mean Logos was not Fuel? All the data supported the Logos connection. All the analysis. Was it just an attack that predated all this current mess? It seemed too much of a coincidence that the attack led to the iteration going free.

Ashion emerged from the lift at the Draggish township level, where two armed guards were waiting for him. He waited for the security identification to clear him, and then exited his bunker through the Family medical facility to enter the teeming hot avenues of Draggish. His two bodyguards followed at a slight distance.

And what was Goldman trying to do with Thadwick Lewiston? Or to him? Is it a threat to me, a warning that I'm getting sloppy?

Ashion walked calmly along the side avenues of the primary boulevard. Compared with Morgish, Draggish was cool, and quiet. It was a long, hard, multi-generational grind to work your way into a Draggish life, so folks didn't piss it away for nothing. In other words, Ashion was safe here.

And what did Thadwick Lewiston want with me? Ashion wondered. Other than the usual arms arrangements, Ashion and the younger Lewiston had little to do with each other. Thadwick's father, Salzon, well that was a different story. A very old, very different story.

Ashion felt his age lay down upon him like a heavy sedative, blurring his vision and shortening his breath. He leaned against the wall, his head beginning to spin. He had labored for so long. Killed, iced, battled, and finally earned this charade of freedom. And for what? To still get pulled into every petty play between these... these *children*? He had thought the last generation of Family oligarchs would be his last. But the bureaucracy chewed so slowly; the Second Harvest arrangements simply wouldn't proceed until the peril of annihilation was upon them. So here they were. The endgame, as Thadwick had called it.

Ashion's earpiece crackled to life. He checked the thread. Morgan Goldman.

No time to get the olds.

Ashion quickly threaded a chem dump to his brain. He kept an emergency supply locked tight in lipids that floated through his bloodstream at all times. He usually introduced pharmaceuticals from the drips installed in his living quarters, but for moments like this he always had a small supply at hand. He could introduce a low frequency impulse from his wrist threader that would begin the process of delivery. The perfectly architected nano-particles began their timed decomposition, starting with a calming cocktail. The dread vanished, his balance returned, and he started walking again before answering the hail.

"Hello Morgan," Ashion said.

"Greetings, slave," Morgan said.

"Wee bit busy," Ashion said.

"Charles is wondering why you've got an army of hit-men getting dunked for chrono."

"They are Red Masks, Morgan. If you continue to refer to them as common thugs I will—"

"Why is Holden loading data into the Transloop, Ash?"

"Tell Charles she'll get briefed with the rest of the Security Council."

"She's holding up deployment until you give *me* justification."

Ashion stopped in mid-stride. *Charles knows exactly why I'm sending all my best men to Earth. Why these games?* His chems had not fully released yet, so Ashion paused.

"Ash? Are you there, Ash? Working on an elaborate lie?"

Ashion said nothing. Finally, the nano particles that held his concentration chems broke through the blood-brain barrier and released the clarity-enhancers he needed. He continued working through the variables. Lewiston. Goldman. Fuel. Dexter Maxwell.

"Ash? Should I tell Charles your answer was a stupefied silence?"

Ashion began walking again. "Tell Governor General Charles Goldman that I am invoking Writ."

This time, Morgan was stunned. Ashion just kept walking.

"You can't possibly be invoking Writ for *this*, slave," Morgan stuttered out.

"If you are challenging my rights, Morgan, you can put them before the mediation board."

More silence from Morgan. Then, "I will invoke the Writ of Direct Confrontation. When will you have your audience?"

"Tomorrow morning. After the Governor has seen to her critical workload."

"I daresay, slave, you *are* the critical workload."

"Then fit me in at her convenience." Ashion dropped the thread and stopped in his tracks.

He'd arrived at the detention center where Father Morgish was being held. And it was chaos.

Ashion Goldman owned Draggish. This was common knowledge, from across the surface of Venus to the Family boats that floated above the roiling atmosphere. Morgish suffered from a certain amount of poverty, a haphazard layout based on its experimental origin, and an aging infrastructure that made the township tough to manage (and therefore required Leshan's help as Thug King). Transish was mostly 'roid slaves, one level below even the planet-side plebeians, and who the ruling Gregors could therefore treat however they liked; it was essentially self-regulating.

Draggish, it could be argued, had been molded into its current form by Ashion. Its rapid growth came after the Great Harvest, when optimism was high. The planet-side classes were trying to differentiate themselves from each other, and the Families were looking for a better approach to governing than the haphazard security measures used in Morgish. Enter Ashion, who created a more optimized state of monitoring and self-regulation. Less enforcement, cleaner avenues, better air quality, but just as long as you don't start any shit, right? The people of Draggish got the message and went along with it.

Which is what made the sight in front of Ashion's eyes so very hard to comprehend. He'd been on the com with Morgan and so hadn't registered the noise, but when he rounded the bend, not only could he hear, but he could also see for himself: there was something just short of a riot taking place outside the Security med-fac.

Hundreds of people were crammed into the already-tight space, yelling something about Father Morgish and the SIN. They were either screaming directly at the overheads, or in the direction of the doors to the med-fac, which six Red Masks where guarding, swords drawn. The crowd were keeping their distance on account of the swords, but Ashion could tell they were starting to think that it wouldn't be too difficult to take on just six Red Masks.

The fools.

If this was Morgish, Ashion would have gassed the lot of them and be done with it. But here in Draggish, there would be hell to pay if he knocked them out. He hadn't done it in, what, sixty years? Most people gathered here had likely never been gassed. Would serve their parents right for not raising them to know their place, Ashion thought. Since when were there this many Sinners in Draggish?

People had begun noticing his presence, and turned to face him. This was going to get ugly fast. He threaded his security override for tunnel microphone control. First he broadcast a screeching noise at max decibel, using his internal dampeners to protect his own ears. His own bodyguards and the Red Masks flinched and covered their ears. It had the effect of silencing everyone.

Ashion tuned the overheads to his com. "Please, let me through!" he said, his voice echoing through the tunnels. He raised his arms up over his head. He was aware of the presence of the sword at his back, but he left it there. "I am Ashion Goldman, chief of Family security. I want to ensure you that Father Morgish and his companion are safe after that horrible attack in Morgish."

Ashion walked toward the crowd. There were angry looks, but his name was enough to keep them at bay, and even had them making way for him. He kept talking.

"I share your outrage at this act! The SIN network room shouldn't be seen as anything short of a shrine and place of protection! We will punish these terrorists!"

Ashion was glad for the nano chems he had dumped earlier. The slow release mechanism kept him at an even, regulated state. He was on a knife's edge, the ambient rage ready to overcome individual fear at any moment.

"I will be releasing the good Father as soon as I can get inside. Please! Let's work together!"

Ashion scanned the faces, looking out for the one that would send the mob into action. He was only a few steps away...

And then he had passed between his Red Masks. He didn't hesitate, but walked directly through the double doors. He heard the mumbling rise behind him and then disappear into silence as the doors closed.

Four.

Father Morgish and the short, fat Sinner looked as comfortable as possible given they were in prison. It was a debriefing room, with sofas and low tables, but still clearly a prison. Family soldiers manned the doors and a special security mitt was required to come and go. Nothing to be done about that.

As Ashion entered the room, a soldier saluted.

"Sir."

"How many Sinners?" Ashion asked in a low voice.

"We haven't threaded a direct count sir," the captain said. "But it appears to be close to two thousand."

"What?"

"Sir, that is just an estimate at this time, it could be a bit more than that."

"Fire and hell. How long have they been here?"

"It started about three hours ago, sir."

Ashion closed his eyes. Not today. "Please issue a statement that Father Morgish is having his medical wounds seen to, and that he will be released within the hour."

"Sir, yes, sir."

Ashion turned to the Father Morgish and the Sinner, Jules.

"Hello, Father," Ashion said, indicating for everyone to take their seats again.

"Ashion the Dark," Father Morgish said. "How is the SIN? Did you manage to destroy it this time?"

"Now, now," Ashion said, clicking his tongue. "So testy. Your precious metal boxes are fine. A little gunpowder stain, nothing your little minions can't rub off with their tongues."

Father Morgish said nothing. Jules looked back and forth at the two men.

"So," Ashion said, "it seems you have met my little problem, face to face."

Father Morgish gave a cold smile. "Ah, yes, the iteration. An unauthorized copy of a copy. I hope your property is back in your hands?"

"Yes, yes, the iter has been destroyed," Ashion said dismissively. "But I wonder, what kind of conversation did you have with him?"

"My only words were to tell him that I was turning him over to the authorities."

"Yes, that is a matter of threaded record. But after the terrorists

30

took control of the network room, did he share anything with you?"

"No, I'm afraid I was swiftly taken from the room and deposited away with poor Jules here. I only interfaced with the princess they call Trance."

"And what did you say to her?"

"Get out, you fools, before you get yourself killed."

"This princess; is she the same one that brought the iter to you?"

"Yes."

"So, she was a part of the guerrilla movement?"

"She seemed to know them quite intimately. I daresay she was something of a *leader*."

"I see. And why did you call Leshan Gregor just before the attack?"

"He asked about the iter. Asked that I report anything. I found that the iter Leshan described was being brought to me at the temple. I merely did as he asked. It is a misfortune of living in Morgish that I must deal with thugs such as Leshan."

"Why did you turn your chest thread off before you called him?"

"I have the same unthreaded rights as the Father Morgish before me, and the one before him, granted by Family Writ in 2910 by Contessa Goldman."

"Yes, but in all your years as Father, you have never used your unthreaded rights."

"Judgment seemed to dictate its use."

"And what judgment was that?"

"The one that doesn't allow my followers to see certain... unpleasant truths. About keeping our position in Morgish."

"You make arrangements with Leshan all the time!"

"Not direct bargains for people's lives. Unlike you, Ashion, we worshipers of the Slave do not take human life for granted. Not even the life of an unauthorized iteration."

Ashion stood, and looked away briefly. Turning back, he said, "I want you to describe the terrorists to me. What did they say? What did they do?"

Father sighed, looking tired and suddenly much older. "I have made my statement to your people already. You can strum the thread."

"No. Tell me again, now. Then I'll compare it with the threads."

"Then we can leave?"

"Who's we?"

"Jules and myself."

"Jules does not leave until I've spoken to him."

"Then I will remain until you are finished with him as well."

Five.

Father Morgish and Jules emerged two hours later, exhausted, to a crowd of nearly three thousand, who roared at the sight of them. Father Morgish was quickly handed a cam necklace, which he kissed and put over his head.

Father had no choice but to provide an ad hoc sermon on the strength of the Venus people, and their relationship with the Singular Integrated Network. But this failed to calm their anger at the terrorists that had attacked the network room and at the security forces that had kept their leader in jail for nearly twenty-four hours. So, he gave another sermon, a homily about the SIN protecting a young child from wandering too close to a heat exhaust fan.

Hungry, desperate, and with nothing to do and nowhere to go, the crowd did not immediately disperse. Ashion's forces remained on high alert at the periphery of the crowd, but they looked bored. Father Morgish realized what those yawning soldiers already knew: there was no danger here.

Father finally said goodnight, and retired to his quarters. He pulled a quick thread from his analog threader to watch the crowd break up. It took only a few minutes, but he was heartened to see a few small kernels of followers take their time moving away. *There is still heart left in these broken souls.*

He changed threads, and began digging deep, going back to the network room attack. What he had seen at the First Term… those threads had seemed so alive, and he couldn't snoop the lines, or even construct a com bundle. They kept falling apart, degaussing into binary. In all his years, Father Morgish had never seen the Slave behave in that fashion. So now, as he tried to rub the exhaustion from his eyes, he wanted to see it again. But the threads were all perfectly constructed now; they showed no signs of having ever been pulled. No dust or age. No left-noise.

Did I imagine the whole thing?

The buzz of his door made Father look up from his threader. Not everyone had access to his personal quarters. He ignored it.

The buzz came again. With a sigh, he shuffled to the door, and pulled the thread of his outside overhead.

Jules. Father punched the lock, and opened the door.

"Heah, Sorry's to bother, Father," Jules said, looking down at his feet. "But I's can't sleep."

"I'm afraid I am having the opposite problem, Jules," Father said, yawning.

"I's sorry, Father. If you's sleepin, I's come back later, eh."

"No, no, please. Let's talk."

"Thanks, Father."

Father Morgish sat at his humble steel table, and Jules sat across from him. Jules looked longingly at Father's legendary threader, still engaged, with standard threads rolling past, weaving the day's recordings one over the other.

"You's lookin for it?" Jules asked. The event of threads falling apart had been of such significance that all Sinners knew about it.

Father Morgish's exhaustion disappeared. "Yes."

"Heah. It's is all reconstructed. I's guessin some high-end rebuilder algorithm was doin a parity thread at a high level, I's talkin *stratosphere* level, so we's don't see any traces at th' time. Heah, that's explains how th' threads is destroyed, and th' split and recombine weave that's is there's is zero trace of now. Heah sure, maybe it's is not a parity watcher at all, and instead we's gettin false thread impressions that's is so masterfully constructed we's can't tell th' difference."

Father waited for a moment before answering. "But you could tell the difference, Jules."

"Heah." Jules was looking right at Father now. "No parity watcher ever that's doesn't leave stains."

"It was coming from inside the thread," Father said.

Jules gulped, breaking eye contact with Father. "I's never see th' Slave, really, you's could say, just like that, tall, I's means, Heah, it's was an intelligence drivin th' thread reconstruction in th' network room..." Jules trailed off, looking at Father for help.

Father Morgish did not smile, did not offer Jules any comfort. "It is not just a myth, Jules. It is not just a story."

Tears rolled silently down Jules cheeks. "I... I's always loved th' Slave at th' systems level... but I's... I's never dreamed He was real..."

Father stood, walked around the table to Jules, pulled him to his feet, and held him as he cried.

Six.

It was ten minutes before Jules had cleaned himself up, whispered his goodbyes, and hurried out of Father's abode. Father pulled the threads to watch where Jules went. He watched him wander around Low-Cen Morgish without any clear direction. But slowly, he made his way toward the network room. Father Morgish pulled and tagged the thread, kept it available, while continuing with his search.

He could have used Jules' help, but Jules had been through too much, and above all else, Father needed Jules to believe. So, he would search alone. Search for whoever had hacked the threads, broken the interface encryption, and found a way inside.

Was it Ashion himself? It seemed unlikely. The threads were doing his bidding. But then, Ashion was doing the work of the SIN, expelling the terrorists. No, the thread rewrite was more likely an old Family secret. But was it a Goldman? The reign of the Goldmans had all taken place after the Primary Family Interface had been put into place. It could be Charles Goldman, but Father Morgish felt it was more likely to be a Lewiston.

That is where he began his low-level snoops. Father Morgish felt his own hunger eating away at his belly, but he turned the ache into energy, focusing his inner strength on his threader.

And for the second time in as many days, Father Morgish turned his camera off.

FAMILY HIGH-ALTITUDE FLOTILLA SS *VANESSA*, LOWER LIVING QUARTERS.

Seven.

Ashion finally found his way to his late-night pharmas. He pulled a thread to set the minuscule machines inside the drugs to immediate release. He almost felt his body react physically to the sight of the insert; he wanted to sleep so badly. While the drug drip loaded, he walked to his light box and started pulling security threads.

All quiet. But Ashion was not really looking for security problems tonight. Just waiting. Finally, a thread began circling up, snaking around his security feeds. The visualization rose to the surface.

CHARLES HAS POSTPONED YOUR WRIT OF DIRECT CONFRONTATION.

Ashion didn't hesitate. He fingered his response. *When will it be?*

AT THE SECURITY COUNCIL BRIEFING.

Ashion thought about this for a moment. Then he threaded, *What does Thadwick Lewiston want with me?*

HE HAS BEEN OFF-THREAD FOR FORTY-THREE MINUTES IN THE LAST THREE WEEKS. MORGAN GOLDMAN COMES AND GOES DURING THIS. SALZON LEWISTON COMES AND GOES. THAT IS THE DATA.

Enough data. I need analysis.

THE FAMILIES ARE LOOKING FOR A POSITION DURING THE UPCOMING TRANSITION.

Transition. I like that.

GOLDMAN'S TERM.

She always has had a way with words.

EARTH-SIDE IS ALMOST COMPLETELY DARK. WE ARE BLIND.

A small price to pay to end the iter.

DEXTER MAXWELL FOUND THE MAP AND USED IT TO SHIFT.
ALIVE, HE LEADS US TO IT. WE MUST HAVE THE MAP.

We know the map still exists in the future.

YES. WE MUST FIND IT. ALIVE DEXTER MAXWELL WILL HELP.

*Maybe. Prisoner Six is not forthcoming with details concerning the
lost transcripts. Who has deleted them?*

LOGOS.

Ashion sat up straight, and stopped glancing longingly at his
chem drip. *Logos? How did Logos get the PFI?*

I DO NOT KNOW THAT.

Ashion growled out loud.
What do you mean, you do not know?

WHOEVER PROVIDED THE PFI ALSO DELETED THE SAME FROM
THE THREADS.

That is impossible.

NOT IMPOSSIBLE. IMPROBABLE.

Ashion sat silently with his eyes closed, trying to focus. He felt
dizzy trying to realign what was happening with what he thought he
knew. When he opened his eyes, the thread had changed.

THE FAT SINNER IS ON PUBLIC THREADS TALKING ABOUT
DEXTER MAXWELL. THE NAME IS BEING THREADED FROM A HUNDRED
TERMINALS. I CANNOT BURY YOUR ORIGIN FOREVER.

Ashion threaded back. *Not forever. But for a little longer.*

He clicked the light box off, and headed for his chem drip.

Eight.

Despite all of the mistakes of the past week, and even his pending Writ of Confrontation with Governor Goldman, Ashion was still head of planet-side security. As such, a half-dozen skirmishes required a clean-up. There were also three investigations to deal with into where the guerrillas were getting their electricity and leadership—two resources that were tough to hide on Venus. Three days had passed before Ashion could get back to his underground bunker.

He headed down the lift to the training level. One of the toughest outcomes of the iter running loose over the past week had been the loss of over thirty Red Masks. Ashion had had to pull strings to get the next layer of guards into the elite training center immediately. And making sure that the training was done right was always one of Ashion's dearest passions.

But he would not be able to personally oversee the training this time. He'd have to leave it to the sims and his remaining elite guard. Which posed a new problem: with the elite guard in training duty, who was minding the planet-side plebs?

Thus began the downward spiral of small problems in Morgish and, surprisingly, in Draggish. He was even dragged into an interrogation in Transish, the most tightly run of the three encampments. It was quickly spinning out of control, Ashion realized. Of course, based on the last week, it would appear he was never in as much control as he had given himself credit for.

But he did not have to hold on much longer. *The endgame is upon us.* As Ashion made his way through the general training quarters, he tried to focus his mind on the remaining days in front of him.

I have infinite access to the past, but never the future.

He arrived at the door to his private training arena, threaded his passcodes, and entered into an enormous, open room, the kind of planet-side extravagance that only came to someone with a few hundred years of credit accumulation. Along the walls were an array of training modules, martial art towers, swords, and stun blasters of different calibrations. In the middle of the room, locked in a sword-fight with a masked guard, was Ashion's most prized possession.

She was wearing only the lightweight black dress of the elite guard, her hair recently cut military short, sweat dripping as she dodged and parried against the strength of the guard. *She has increased her quickness*, Ashion noted. *She could destroy the iter without blinking.*

But would she?

As he watched, she glanced over and gave him a quick wink. In three moves, she had the guard disarmed and lying on his back, the sword at his neck.

Ashion walked up with a grin. "Hello, Kat," he said.

"Heah, Ash," she said, between big gulps of breath.

"Are you alright, Gurn?" Ashion asked the guard on the floor.

"Sir, yessir," He said, pushing the sword away and standing quickly to attention. "I's is not a match for Kat no more."

"Do not worry, Gurn," Ashion said, "I do not think there is a match for her on this or any other planet."

Kat tried hard not to beam. *She's so young*, Ashion remembered. *What is it like to be that young? To have a mind so free of aged wreckage? To still be capable of receiving a compliment?*

I want it back.

"Gurn, I would like you to take charge of my Knight training program," Ashion said, not taking his eyes off Kat. She looked down uncomfortably under his burning gaze.

"Sir, yessir," Gurn said, barely hiding his own satisfaction.

"And given Tano's current state, I need a new special ops lieutenant. Your thread privs are waiting in your light box."

Gurn didn't budge. "Thank you, sir."

"That is all."

Gurn bowed slightly and turned to leave.

"Heah, Gurns," Kat said. Gurn turned back. "Congrats, eh."

Ashion could almost see the grin through the mask as he nodded curtly, and then sprang quickly from the room.

"Please, Kat, we've discussed this," Ashion said. "You may affect the speech patterns of the Tunnel Muck in your own time. But not in this room, and certainly not in front of me."

"Ever so sorry, dearest father," Kat said mockingly. "Perhaps we might retire to a more appropriate location for a little respite, then?"

"Always with the sarcasm," Ashion said, and he tried to throw his arm over her shoulder. But she moved too fast, grabbing his arm and twisting until she had him on his back.

"Always with the slowness," Kat said, her eyes sparkling with glee.

"There's a first time for everything," Ashion said, pushing her offered hand away, and standing.

"Better get used to it," Kat said.

"Yes. Have you made it to the Whi-Scis today?"

Kat looked down. "I don't like getting hooked up to those machines. It hurts my head. I have nightmares."

"It's for the best. It accelerates the training process that most men take their whole life to accumulate."

"But you just said it; no one can take me now. I don't need the burn-ins anymore."

"Just a few more weeks, Kat. I know it's uncomfortable. We can push it out to once a week, if you like."

"How about once every never?"

"Always with the attitude."

"I can't help it. I'm a teenager."

"That's no excuse. Come, let's get something to eat first."

Nine.

"I don't want to do it."

"Kat, it's for your own good. Your mind is too powerful, too full. You need to be closely monitored."

"I'm tired of it. I don't want to be powerful anymore."

"Lie still."

"Please don't."

"I'm sorry, child. This is not a choice."

"Can't you give me something to sleep?"

"We've been over this. We can't monitor you if your neural connections are being falsely amplified or stifled."

"I'm scared."

"Of what? There's nothing to be afraid of."

"I can feel it."

"That's impossible, child."

"Not the scan. The changes. To my brain."

"All the burn-ins are sub-cortex. They can't be perceived consciously."

"But I can. I have nightmares. I'm burning up in them. "

"Just relax."

"No, no, no."

"I'm sorry, Kat."

"No! Dad! NO."

Ten.

Ashion felt his heart rate returning to normal as he entered the monitoring room. It was a simple box, just the right size, as all White Scientist rooms were. Wires of different sizes and purposes were everywhere. White Scientists felt it was a ridiculous notion to hide the guts of a thing. Why conceal the glorious complexity of the mind's creations behind walls? Instead, they had everything exposed that could be exposed, making the room nearly impossible to understand.

But Ashion had been in this room a lot in the last few years. He had even garnered enough respect from the Whi-Scis that they had secured a permanent chair among the mess, just for him. He slumped down into it now, and let out a sigh.

A single scientist was plugged into the room at his frontal lobe. He did not acknowledge Ashion, but kept threading information. On the monitor was Kat, twitching with the tracer signals racing around her magnificent brain.

"She fights us more each time," the scientist said.

"I know. It's why I come down personally," Ashion said. He kept his eyes on Kat.

"Yes, only you can convince her to undergo the treatments."

"I understand. How close are we to having her mapped?"

"Ten more sessions. There is the possibility that we might have to do an eleventh, or even a twelfth. We are learning new things each day. Her brain is extraordinary."

41

"Tell me about it."

"As you wish. You see, she has a higher concentration of serotonin in highly specialized areas around the part of the brain we've come to know as the Sea of Time—"

"No, it was just an expression. From a long time ago. Forget it. Anyway, I told her that she only had to do it once a week."

The scientist turned toward Ashion, slowly, gingerly, keeping the wire plugged into his forehead. "That will be playing it very, very close," he said.

"But if we push her, she could refuse to do it at all. Then it will all be for nothing."

"You can convince her. You can always convince her."

"Is there any way to increase the rate?"

"If I had time to fully investigate a model brain, I could find out if perhaps the superior neural system we are looking at could afford us a higher voltage. However, on lesser specimens, an increased through-put will succeed, but also terminate the host."

"I'm not interested in terminating this host."

"Indeed not."

"You get eight more treatments. No more. Make them count."

"Very good, sir."

Ashion took one more look at his twitching daughter, and left the monitoring room.

Eleven.

Ashion's shuttle drifted slowly with the windy lilt of Thadwick Lewiston's boat. There was a messy security protocol for his computer to run through before the docking could complete. Part of the protocol required a complete blackout of all communication systems while the shuttle and the boat port negotiated encryption keys the size of entire visual threads. Ashion used to lament the time wasted during such a massive decryption process; of late, however, he had come to appreciate the docking lag as the day's only respite. These were two, perhaps three, precious minutes that belonged to no one—not even him.

From Lewiston's lower boat port, the shuttle's front window shield was threading the eternal sunrise of Venus. The distant sun was burning its way slowly into the western horizon, smeared by cloud and storm. The poisonous atmosphere whipped at the four stabilizer drums of the massive floating fortress, spinning them slowly around the center boat, drifting on top of the high-pressure atmo that separated Family life from the plebeian masses stuck in the rover-runs of planet-side existence. The shuttle rocked in the constant wind, and Ashion closed his eyes, listening to the deadening roar of complete thread silence.

It wasn't long before his shuttle cabin lit up again, sensors began threading data, outer cams whirred to life, and the thread viewer was blinking madly. A voice came through the com port.

"Ashion Goldman, you have been cleared for entry onto this private Family boat. All weapons must remain on your shuttle. Please proceed to the guest chambers at the mezzanine level."

Ashion pushed his door open and walked out onto the docking port, taking it all in. He hadn't been on the Lewiston boat since old Salzon had been at his peak—forcefully assuming control of the floundering Lewiston family, and putting them on the road back to respectability. Back then, Salzon and Ashion had been close allies. Very close indeed. But the Lewistons were stagnating again—and running out of time.

The shuttle port was run down, unused. There were not many visitors to the quarters of Thadwick Lewiston these days, and certainly none of any distinction. Ashion found that the path to his guest quarters had been lit up, with most of the bulbs still working. He was able to navigate his way to the mezzanine.

The reception room was a marked improvement over the dock. It was a large space, much larger than Ashion's own quarters, with a high ceiling that had been painted with fat children dancing in the clouds to match some sort of Earth-art ideal. Real leather couches, aging but in good condition, had been positioned at studiously askew angles throughout the room. Earth-side woven rugs decorated the floor. There was an analog threader the size of three grown men in one corner, in sparklingly perfect condition. Ashion gravitated toward it immediately.

"Do you play?" a voice rumbled from across the room.

Ashion turned to find Thadwick had entered the room. "I'm afraid I'm a bit of a hack. A functional threader, to be sure. But this is a beautiful specimen."

"It's a Maddali. An original. Handmade for my father."

"It is beautiful, and in excellent condition. A shame to keep it here in the guest room."

Thadwick was next to Ashion now, delicately fondling the taut steel of the feelers. He shrugged. "This is my favorite room. All of my dearest possessions are here."

"Why is it called the guest quarters, then?"

"I like to remind myself that I am only visiting."

"Venus?"

"Life."

"Ah. How introspective of you."

"Sneer if you like, slave, but we all have our little systems to keep us from spiraling into uselessness." Thadwick migrated toward the closest sofa, while a servant brought in refreshments. Ashion sat across from Thadwick in an overstuffed piece that enveloped his lanky frame.

"Quite a sofa," Ashion said, genuinely enjoying it.

"Not enough can be said for fine craftsmanship."

44

Earth-side wine was served, along with real fruit. Ashion kept his eyes on Thadwick throughout. Thadwick raised his glass, and Ashion raised his in the folksy cheers. Ashion let Thadwick take the first sip, and then he followed suit. The flavor was so strong, so complex, he almost choked, and his eyes watered.

"And to what do I owe this indulgence?" Ashion asked, trying to subtly wipe his eyes.

Thadwick shrugged. "We might as well drink it. There is little time left."

"Indeed."

"Besides, we have important business to discuss."

Ashion put a few grapes in his mouth, slowly popping them with his teeth. "And what business is that?"

Thadwick tilted his head back, draining the wine, and promptly poured another glass. Ashion had never seen such disregard for something so expensive. Thadwick reached into a fold in his long dressing gown and pulled out a minute threader. He gently strummed, waited a moment, and then looked at Ashion.

"We are off-thread," he said. The easy-going tone had disappeared. "Charles Goldman has made me aware of the iter that escaped planet-side. I have tried to find out how a copy of you could possibly be churned at a Draggish med, but the answer eludes me."

"The primary threads have all been deleted," Ashion said.

"How?"

"I don't know. But that is why you cannot find them. The records do not exist."

"Charles? Could Charles do that?"

"I do not know who has that level of access," Ashion said. "I can remove public threads, but med-facs? I have only rudimentary read privs there. For all I know, it was you that convinced the doctor to pull the iter, and then removed the records."

Thadwick thought about it. "Yes. It could very well have been. I cannot see an angle for me, though."

"To weaken my position on the Council. Or, more directly, to get me killed."

"Yes, that would be good use of an iter, particularly this one," Thadwick said with a smile. "But I did not order another Ashion be

45

unleashed on the people. I am not as foolish as that. You do not have to believe me, but I have not done this."

"It is immaterial who has done it," Ashion said, sipping his wine again. "What is material is containing the damage. And I have been stymied in my attempt to get this threat under control."

"What is *material*," Thadwick said, "is your lack of understanding of systems. You ask for resources, more and more resources, for your little set of interlocked circuits. But your concerns are nested in the larger network of circuits demanding resources."

"Thadwick, the iter is Earth-side. You have been told as much. What your father might not have told you is that the Earth-side Transloop station is dark. Stop blathering on about interlocking circuits for a moment, and explain to me if these two things are not interrelated. I can end this, but I need the freedom to act."

"I do not deny that you are causing problems on Earth."

"It is not me."

"You, not you. Details. But I agree that neutralizing your iterate is a top priority. But it is not everyone's top priority. The very fact that you are being stymied indicates that perhaps the iter is doing exactly what was intended when he was pulled off the bed. Have you considered this?"

"Of course I have. But it is in no one's interests to have the iter Earth-side."

"And who is preventing you from getting Knights to clean up the iter?" Thadwick continued.

"Charles. Charles has her hands on every thread right now."

"Yes. Charles. Always Charles." Thadwick looked into the distance, and gulped down another glass of wine. "There was a time when the Governor could not act without Family support."

"Did you bring me here to educate me on your view of court politics?" Ashion asked.

"No. I am burning valuable off-thread time. Court politics are useless now."

"Then what?"

"Charles told me about your little problem. Straight, with no demands. Just wanted me to know about your delicate situation. But why?"

"Perhaps she wanted to arrange a meeting between the two of us." Ashion said, "She wanted us to talk about this. Just like we are doing."

"Yes. And why do you think that is?" Thadwick asked.

"Charles' circumlocutions give me headaches, Thadwick. Why don't you simplify it for me."

"I honestly do not know, Ashion. I wanted you to tell me."

Ashion closed his eyes, trying to think it all through. See all the threads. The two men sat in silence for a few minutes, lost in thought. Ashion rose and began to pace.

"I helped your father, you know," Ashion said. "Back in 2945, after the asteroid wars. I arranged for him to take control of the Lewiston family."

"This is the worst-kept secret in Family history," Thadwick said.

"I called in a favor from your father at the Security Council two weeks ago. I bought his vote to keep my PFI's after I root deleted public records."

"This I did not know," Thadwick said, lost in thought. "My father was greatly agitated after the Council meeting."

"Yes. It was a tough call for him; it cost him much in the Council. The forces aligned against me were powerful."

"The Governor."

"Yes. Always the Governor. Charles would have already had me destroyed, if not for an old debt I called in. Your father did that for me."

"And you think it is related to our current condition."

"I am putting data on the floor to consider."

"Why are you trusting me with this, Ashion?" Thadwick asked. "I could have you and my father put up on collusion, take complete control of the Lewiston Family, and be done with two of my biggest obstacles."

"But that would leave you with only your largest obstacle."

"Charles."

"Right. And her left with none but you."

Thadwick looked up. "You are better at this than I gave you credit for, slave."

"I have been surrounded by this kind of ludicrous behavior for nearly three hundred years. I am not naturally good at it. I am just old."

"Who is Dexter Maxwell?"

Ashion stopped pacing. Started again. "That was my name. On Earth. In the 22nd century."

"Excuse me?"

"Are you playing dumb?" Ashion said.

"Calm down, slave. I do not know your history. You overestimate my interface privs."

Ashion stared at Thadwick for a while. Then he spoke. "I will trust you, Thadwick. This may turn out to be a tragic error on my part, but we are all of us running short on strategy downtime. And I am running out of options. So here's the short version.

"I was an orphaned child on Earth in the year 2113. I broke into a medical facility on a stunt, was captured, and put on purgatory freeze. For reasons that have been lost to time, my frozen body ended up on the off-planet medical facilities of those days. Those facilities housed the technology that came to Venus after the expulsion."

"Ah," Thadwick said. "I thought you were a natural born Venus slave. I did not know you were a de-iced prisoner."

"Yes. Well. All of that was a long time ago. But my name, once upon a time, was Dexter Maxwell."

"And now the iter goes by that name."

"Yes. An odd iteration of me for Logos to generate, I suppose, except that its neurals would be very prone to persuasion. So the wrong elements can easily mold him into whatever sort of soldier they require."

"As you were molded by the Goldmans, three hundred years ago?"

"We are done discussing ancient history," Ashion cut him off.

"Fair enough."

"I trust you can keep this information to yourself."

Thadwick shrugged. "I will say nothing, but information creep is sure to set in. The name burns across the threads like dry lightning across the Venus sky. No one says anything aloud, but everyone digs for its meaning."

"Yes, well. Time runs short."

"Indeed. To the business at hand: namely, is Charles attempting to get us to cancel each other out, or does she want us to align and thus make of us an easier target?"

"It all depends on if she wants the iter captured or not."

"Or perhaps she merely needs the iter to be a distraction for you, and desires it to be a distraction for me," Thadwick posited.

"If that is the case, she has succeeded on both accounts."

"Yes. She is good at what she does."

"State your intent, Thadwick. I need to know what it is you seek."

Thadwick stood and moved closer to Ashion. "I want the Lewistons safely on a boat to Earth when the time comes. And I want you to personally usher my son to safety."

"I did not know that you and Ingrid were expecting."

"We are not."

Ashion blinked. "Right. Of course."

"Now we have both revealed things. I want the Lewiston heir under your protection."

"That can be arranged."

"And I want to cut Charles Goldman's throat."

"Don't we all."

"I am not talking idly, and I do not mean this in the abstract. It must be me that kills the Governor. And it must be threaded for all to see."

LOWER-CENTRAL MORGISH, MEDICAL FACILITIES.

Twelve.

Ashion found himself inside one of the claustrophobic steel strong-boxes that passed for a sterile environment in Morgish. Leshan the Thug King had tubes full of rebuilder plugged into every available vein. He looked thinner and paler than usual, but he was still wearing sunglasses.

"Greetings, Leshan," Ashion said.

"How's is th' thuggery business?" Leshan said hoarsely.

Ashion smiled. "Business is good. How goes it for you?"

Leshan coughed. "Seen better times. I's got cut on by that damn iter you's lookin for."

"I was under the impression he'd killed you."

"Heah, you's a liked that, eh?"

"Don't suppose you got a good look at him?" Ashion asked casually.

"Heah, I's got a good look. He's is wicked wit a sword."

"So I've noticed. Anyone with him?"

"Heah. One of my drivers."

"Who was the driver?"

"He's goes by Orpheus. Good driver, too. Heah, stoles one of my boats."

"They did not make it far," Ashion said. "We shot them out of the sky."

"Where they's was headed?" Leshan asked.

Ashion shrugged. "No telling. They exploded with the shuttle-craft."

Leshan coughed again. "You's owe me shuttle, eh. That's not a cheapsy trinket."

Ashion smiled. "It was untugged. That's illegal. You're lucky I won't fine you."

Leshan smiled weakly. "I's will keep quiet if you's will."

"This driver of yours," Ashion said. "Would he be on our

threads?"

"Maybes. He's is an old 'roid slaver. Popped his hamstring, so they's send him planet-side, defective, eh. I's grab him from th' street, for his size. Big guy. Turns out he's can fly real good. So I's put him on cargo. All off-threads work, eh."

Ashion nodded. "He have any friends?"

Leshan shook his head. "Heah, a real loner. I's had him shadowed, like wit all my illegals. Make sure they's is on th' right team, eh. But Orpheus, he's just go back to his hire. Watch th' casts. Sleeps. Has nightmares, like all 'roid slavers. Comes back next day, drives cargo for me. Heah, that's is it."

"You have a picture of this driver anywhere?"

"What's is th' matter? Didn't you's kill him already?"

"Just trying to put all the pieces together."

"My heavies that's took me's to this med fac," Leshan coughed again, a deep, wet cough, "they's say, you's left me's for dead, eh."

Ashion shrugged. "I figured you can take care of yourself."

"You's figured right. But this time, I's takes a sword for you. That's mean anything?"

Ashion didn't blink. "Not anymore."

"Heah," Leshan said, closing his eyes. "Heah, nots anymore."

Ashion's com beeped in his ear, and he turned from Leshan to answer. "Ashion here," he said.

"Sir, it's Holden," the voice said. "Someone just tried to kill Tano."

51

FAMILY HIGH-ALTITUDE FLOTILLA SS *MONSANTO,* EMERGENCY MEDICAL FACILITY.

Thirteen.

I am spending too much time in medical wards, Ashion thought as he entered Tano's recovery room.

Compared with the dank hole that Leshan was recuperating in, Tano's Family-grade facilities seemed downright luxurious. The equipment had large, easy-to-follow threads pouring into a light box: heart-rate, neural patterning, oxygen saturation, bacterial and viral counts, nutritional counts, pH, sodium and potassium levels—every measurable biofeedback, and they were connected to the decision-support threader that Ashion was currently staring at.

The data then looped the SIN, passing through hundreds of thousands of nodes, polishing the facts, adding evidence, correlating to other biofeedback inputs throughout the integrated network, and then coming back with calibrations for treatment.

The Whi-Scis did not need to look at the light boxes. With their frontal lobes directly connected to the network, they themselves were nodes, consuming and producing data like everything else. The sensors in their foreheads gave them a front-row seat to the correlation data and treatment conclusions.

Gurn was also with Ashion, in full Knight uniform, including the mask. His massive size barely fit under the low ceiling. Ashion left the Whi-Scis to their work and turned to Gurn.

"Tell me what happened."

Gurn nodded. "As a precaution, I's puts an alert stamp on th' med fac threads. I's couldn't monitor all of them, but I's could get filtered bio-data. Anyone's not wired to th' fac, anyone's not Whi-Sci, and I's get they's blip, eh." Gurn pointed to his earpiece. "Heah, sure as anything, last night, someone's wit Family clearance blips into Tano's room. Overrides you's Security Asset tags. Heah, I's sends three Knights in. They's find this on Tano's drip." Gurn pointed to a clear bag lying between Tano's inert legs.

"Poison," Ashion said.

"Heah, slow death. Hard to trace. Anyone's could get th' substance."

Ashion turned to one of the Whi-Scis. "Any damage done?"

"The poisonous attack was precisely attuned to the medical state of the asset. The asset's recovery has been slowed, and we will need to keep his neurals sub-leveled for longer. No permanent damage."

"Who blipped the door?" Ashion asked.

Gurn shook his head. "It's is hard to say. No face on th' overheads. Male, average size. But th' blip's shows Family access. A Gregor."

Ashion looked up. "I'm sorry. Did you say a *Gregor*?"

"Heah," Gurn said. "Gregor."

Ashion shook his head incredulously. "The man would have known we'd be able to trace his blip."

Gurn shrugged. "Heah, I's is guessin he's is less worried about his identity, more worried 'bout Tano bein not all dead."

Ashion walked over to Tano. Someone had put a new patch over his bad eye. "Why would a Gregor want you dead?" The Gregors have not made a meaningful political move in decades, Ashion thought. Is this some kind of message? It was certainly a feeble attempt at murder.

"Sir, I's will investigate," said Gurn. "Tano is my's *brother*, eh. My's blood. I's will find th' fool, and end him."

"Gurn, I understand. But, no. More than ever, I need you training my new Knights. We have lost many brothers in the past three weeks. Go now, and double your efforts. The more Knights we can train, the more we will be prepared for the war that is coming. See if we can cut out some non-battle training. Skip languages, customs, that type of thing. Hack out all the subtle stuff. I want swords, silence, and shifting."

Gurn did not reply. His eyes lingered on Tano, then he gave a short bow and left without a word.

Ashion threaded his com.

"Sir, Holden here."

"Holden, I am afraid I have not spent enough time lately thinking about the Gregors. Short of digging the threads, what can you tell me?"

"They align with Governor Goldman, of course. They do the Governor's dirty work on the asteroid mines, keep the fuel flowing, and take their profits; that's about it. Very active in the slave trade, of course. For the labor. The primary Gregor family is led by Gram Gregor, who has a single son, Mash Gregor. They race tricked-out shuttle crafts in the outer rim, burning expensive fuel for races that the planet-siders love. They have a nice gambling racket out there on the 'roids. Nothing out of the ordinary. They do not keep permanent residences on the Family boats."

"How old is the son, Mash?"

"In his late forties. No wife, no children. Plenty of mistresses."

"Right, it's coming back to me now. Had twin sisters… dead now?"

Holden paused, clearly strumming his threads. "Twin sisters, dead for sixteen years. Killed in an asteroid explosion." He paused again. "The same one that took the life of Kat's mo—"

"I remember that explosion," Ashion said. "What were the sisters doing on that rock?"

"It was never known. Gram did not know. Mash did not know. Or at least, they always claimed not to know."

Ashion was pacing. "The Gregor's Consul, who sits on the Security Council; Holden?"

"Gram's wife, Thula. Gram Gregor is in the twilight of his life. He may die at any moment. So representation was passed to Thula."

Ashion snapped his fingers. "Thula. Daughter of Junta Lewiston. I knew Thula's father—Montigo's brother and our friend Salzon's uncle." Ashion paused. "But, Thula is Gram's second wife. He was married to… Trianna. Planet-sider. Hot gossip at the time. Now dead, most likely by Thula's hand. Trianna had a son by Gram."

"Right, of course," Holden said, searching his own memory now, not the threads. "Leshan Gregor, firstborn son of Gram Gregor. After Trianna's death, Thula pushed hard for Leshan's exile from the Families."

Ashion nodded to himself. "She wanted to ensure that her son Mash was the sole heir to the Gregor Family patriarch title."

"Yes, that's right, sir," Holden said.

"I need time to look into all of this. More loose threads to sort." Ashion stopped pacing finally. "Nothing connects this to Tano yet. I need him awake, and lucid. I want soldiers posted at this door around the clock. No one is let in or out other than the Whi-Scis. And even they get escorts. No exceptions. And let's work on a way to get him to a safer location."

"Yes, sir," Holden said, "Sir, there's one more thing."

"Arm, unless it's something no one else can manage, just handle it!" Ashion yelled, and closed his com.

He turned to leave, but in his head he recalled the last conversation he had had with Tano, before Tano had drifted into unconsciousness.

Tano, what are you sorry for?

My betrayal. I was so angry, Ash, and how could I have known?

Known what, Tano? Ashion asked himself. How have you betrayed me

FAMILY HIGH-ALTITUDE FLOTILLA SS *GREGOR* IV, GRAND MATRON'S QUARTERS, DAY 10.

Fourteen.

"First you meet with Salzon's son outside your dying slave's medical room," Thula Gregor said to Ashion by way of greeting as he entered her bedchamber, "and magico-presto, the conversation is not threaded. Next you fly all the way out to young Thadwick's ship, and he burns forty-two minutes off-thread again."

"Thadwick is not so young, anymore," Ashion said, bowing to the old matriarch.

Thula waved her flabby arm dismissively. A slave was slowly rubbing all kinds of preserving oils into her naked body as she spoke. "He is much younger than me. And much younger than you, I might add."

"Yes, but he sees the threads in their entirety now. There is a lot that the older generations miss."

"Yes, well, and then you go and call for a Writ! Ha!"

"I am glad you are finding my, um, predicament so amusing."

Thula snorted, rushed her slave out, threw a robe on, and strummed her overheads off. She squinted at Ashion. "You are here because I attempted to kill your slave Tano."

"Someone blipped into the med-fac as a Gregor," Ashion said delicately, sitting on the chair next to Thula's bed. "I could not say if it was you."

"Me, my guard, doesn't really matter. It should be pointed out that if I actually wanted that soldier dead, he would be dead."

"Then what did you want?" Ashion asked.

"Of what will you be speaking to the Goldmans about off-thread?"

Ashion shook his head. "I have no time off-thread with the Goldmans."

"Your Writ, you ninny! Your Writ!"

"Ah, that. Just looking to get certain rights restored."

Thula squinted again. "If you are speaking to the Lewistons and the Goldmans off-thread, what kind of ruling Family would the

56

Gregors be if we did not have something to say to you in secret?"

Ashion smiled tiredly. "I suppose you're right." He got up to leave.

"Sit down, slave," Thula said. "Just because it's a political game doesn't mean I don't have something to say."

"Excuse me, Madame," Ashion said. "I am old, and very weary."

Thula sniffed at this. "I know what most of Goldman's court thinks of the Gregors. Just a bunch of rich children using their fuel monopolies to stay near the surface of power. Wasting their resources, racing around the 'verse in oversized rockets. They say we are not important. That we are nothing but the purpose we serve: Fuel Merchants." This last phrase came out like an invective spat at a hated enemy. Ashion waited for her to continue.

"They are not all wrong. My addled husband indulged himself in the body's pleasures, and spent no time on his own longevity. Now he rots in a puddle of his own senility."

Still Ashion waited, saying nothing. Thula continued. "The Gregors have not been well-served by the last three generations of patriarchs. But, I am not interested in the past. I think now only of the future.

"I have watched the med threads from when you went to see your slave Tano. When he arrived back from the Transloop. He has betrayed you, but you do not know to whom."

"I was wondering when that would come to the surface," Ashion said.

"I am not part of the conspiracy you seek. All the more reason for me to want Tano alive. Let's all find out what Tano has to say, shall we? Then, let us find out why he has suddenly changed his tune," Thula snorted and shook her jowls in disgust. "But yet you leave him unprotected! A mere security asset! Phah! As though he were of no interest to those he conspired with! You can see now, I hope, that I had to get your attention. To get you to put someone in that room before he really does wind up dead."

"Well played, Thula."

"I'm not finished yet. Tano did not come to me. But that is not to say the Gregors are above suspicion. My son Mash..." Thula trailed off. "My biggest failure. I tried to pry him from his father's lazy habits...

He cannot be trusted, Ashion. Not at all."

"Are you fingering your son in some kind of plot against me?"

"I am saying he is not above suspicion, you fool," Thula said. "You must interpret that all by yourself."

"I will take this under advisement," Ashion said. "Is that all?"

"Let us find a way together to keep your slave out of harm's way, yes?"

Thula reached for a small handheld, and Ashion heard the overheads whirring into operation. She pretended to fumble with the buttons some more as she said, "And if you ever accuse someone in this Family again, I will take you before the Security Council and lash you myself!" Finally, Thula made a grand show of turning the threads back on, even though they had been running before she began this non sequitur.

Ashion played along. He stood quickly, knocking over his chair. He looked up at the cam angrily, and said, "You keep your 'roid-crazed offspring away from my Knights, and we won't have a problem." Then he stormed from the room.

FAMILY HIGH-ALTITUDE FLOTILLA SS
VANESSA, LOWER LIVING QUARTERS.

Fifteen.

The call scratched him awake shortly after he had chem'd himself to sleep. Ashion quickly tapped into his thread.

"Ashion here."

"Sir, there is a situation that requires your attention: Morgish."

Ashion was already out of bed and at his light box. "Drop the thread."

He watched a thread bundle slowly rise from his box, then a single thread coming into focus. It was an overhead from a main avenue—the old type in the old part of the city, with a low ceiling but a wider central area. It was a channel connecting two of the larger living quarters and the first merchant center, which had been mostly abandoned except for a few small black-market vendors.

But today, it was teeming with the same guerrillas that had taken the SIN network room the week before. There must have been three dozen, grappling with the local security forces using antiquated stunners and - was he making this out right?—swords.

"Are those swords, Holden?" Ashion asked.

"Sir, yes, sir. Makeshift swords and a few old stunners that must be older than I am. It started out as a protest against the imprisonment of the Sinner priest, but when the forces arrived, they revealed their weapons."

"Holden. The guerillas. They are... winning."

"Yes, sir."

"Who's local?"

"Gunner. He's deploying now, sir."

"Let me study the threads, and I'll get a strategy plugged. Standby for a one-fiver."

"Yes, sir."

Ashion pulled the thread, and began analyzing the skirmish from the beginning. He put his hands inside his light box and began pulling his strategy-builder code to assemble his counterstrike. When it was done, only moments later, he pushed the thread up into a buffer and strummed his security.

"Holden. Planning is up. Resourcing reqs are there... now."

"Sir."

"If you don't mind, Holden, I'd like to get some sleep. Big day tomorrow, what with the Writ of Confrontation."

"I understand sir, but—"

"Let me know the blood toll tomorrow. And try to get me some leaders alive."

"Sir, I must -"

"Holden. Plans are on the security thread. What else do you need?"

"Sir, I'm getting word of another isolated situation."

"What? Fine, what's the niner? I've still got my threader up."

"It's in the Draggish med quarter."

Ashion pulled his hands out of the light box. "Did you say med quarter?"

"Yes, sir."

"In Draggish?"

"Yes, sir."

"Pull Gunner out of Morgish. I want him protecting the guerrilla prisoners at the med-fac. Who's local in Draggish?"

"Sir, it's Malthorn, sir."

"Good lord, Arm. He's just a kid. Get him threaded. And drop me the visuals from the med quarter."

"No visuals, sir. There's an override."

"They are jamming the cams?"

"Yessir. And with a sophisticated method at that."

Ashion was already at his closet throwing his clothes on, reaching for his scabbard. "I'm headed to Draggish. Move ops to my onboard shuttle system."

"Sir, yes, sir."

Sixteen.

Ashion showed up at the Ceremony of the Writ of Direct Confrontation in his military garb. He had thought of being late, and changing into something less, well, bloody, but ultimately he decided it set the conversational tone. He did leave his gloves in his shuttle, brown with dried human insides. But his spattered black fighting garb would have to do.

He made a stir even as he entered the main hall of SS *Contessa*, where the lower Families had gathered for pre-meeting gossip and information trading. There was a general hiss of whispers as Ashion walked confidently through the crowds toward the Governor's courtyard, where he would go through the ceremonial motions required to get access to Goldman. Ashion had not been on the Governor's boat in a long time, and had forgotten just how large the rooms were. What a luxury, he realized. After spending the last twelve hours in the confines of planet-side boxes, engaged in a surprisingly fierce bid to take one of the med facilities, the immensity of the open space made Ashion feel almost agoraphobic. Where would he defend such a ludicrous space? How could he protect his own back? He played out the strategy as a focus exercise as he rippled through the Lower Family courtesans.

He needed focus. He was exhausted. The guerillas in Draggish had put up an excellent fight. They had brought three different waves of fighters from three different avenues. Then, after the local officers had established themselves around the perimeter, the terrorists had ignited fuel cells and used a fan hack to push the smoke down at Ashion's soldiers. They had then unleashed a fourth set of guerrillas in a circular fashion.

It was a great play, he had to admit. If they'd had weapons that didn't short half the time, the sheer audacity of the plan would have probably enabled them to succeed before Ashion could arrive with his remaining Red Masks to break them up.

It was over just in time for Ashion to make his Writ. He'd had to push Holden and Gunner back to Morgish to finish the clean up by themselves.

When Ashion arrived at the entrance to the courtyard, two soldiers pushed the door open. They gave him a brief nod of approval and recognition. Ashion murmured their names quickly without looking at them. He did not want to give away this lowly familiarity to the Family members who were standing watching this ragged slave-who-is-not-a-slave swagger around their precious open spaces. There were murmurs of disgust as they figured out what the stains on his clothing were.

As the Upper Family courtesans pushed to get out of the way of the smell of death that rose from Ashion, he was finally able to make out the Governor's chair, all gold and old-Earth wood. Sitting upon it was the beautiful Charles Goldman herself, elbows resting on the animal-skin arms, gesticulating lazily at her Exemplar, Morgan, and shooting Ashion an amused sideways glance that affirmed her control of the situation.

She is still the most beautiful woman I've even seen, Ashion thought. She is aging well.

Ashion slowed to a stop at the ritualized distance from the Governor, and the Family around him finally buzzed into their specific locations, before coming to a dead silence. Charles whispered something to Morgan. Morgan did not move or acknowledge in any way what Charles might have said. She simply stared at Ashion with naked hatred and disbelief.

Ah, the power of youth, Ashion thought. To be so straightforward with emotion.

Charles sat in silence. It was upon her, as Governor, to begin, but she was making no effort to do so. Ashion waited, his legs stiff with exhaustion, and his shoulders aching from hacking at human limbs. He kept his eyes locked on Charles, and felt the moment slow—almost like it used to do for him. He could sense the hundreds of eyes glancing nervously back and forth, between slave and owner, trying to fathom their relationship, trying to learn something new, trying to see the angle.

At last, Charles spoke.

"The Writ of Direct Confrontation is the right of all *free* men

62

and women who are citizens in good standing in the Open Democracy of Venus. The Writ was established after the introduction of the threads to provide an avenue of open discourse with the Governor of the free world when recriminations upon a person's reputation and property have occurred. To clear one's name, one can provide evidence of injustices to the Governor in an unmonitored situation, with no threads, and no outside influences.

"For the privilege of such a time with the Governor, a deal has been established by law and practiced as tradition. By agreeing to the confrontation, the Governor agrees to hear the demands of the confronter. At the end of the session, the Governor must meet the demands of the confronter. If the Governor sees no merit in the demand, then the Governor has no choice but to have the confronter executed immediately with extreme prejudice."

Charles let this sink in over the crowd, relishing the speech.

"Ashion Goldman, semi-free man in accordance with the description of post-ten-twenty-oh-one, has asked for a Writ of Direct Confrontation on this day of September 25 in the year 3049 of the Earth calendar. Do you so ask, Ashion Goldman?"

"On this day, I so request the Writ," Ashion said.

"Very well, Ashion," Charles said, her eyes twinkling. "In front of representatives from each of the Upper Families together with their Exemplars and children, we will begin your Direct Confrontation."

"As you wish, Governor Goldman," Ashion said with a bow.

"As you know, Ashion, the Writ of Direct Confrontation has been invoked only three times during my rule as Governor. Each case ended in execution."

"I understand very well," Ashion said. "I performed all three executions."

"Yes," Goldman said. Her eyes were dancing, her half-smile barely contained.

"Shall we retire to your private quarters, then?" Ashion asked.

"Ah, ah, patience, Ashion," Charles said with a slight wave. "First, you must publicly declare who has wronged you."

"It is not in the Writ to do so," Ashion said.

"Ah, but it is tradition, young man, it is tradition. And who is this court to defy tradition?"

"As you wish, Governor," Ashion said. "I have been wronged by Governor Charles Goldman, and am seeking recourse by the Writ of Direct Confrontation."

The room burst into a hushed buzz of people trying desperately not to talk. Charles appeared to lose control of her façade for a fraction of a second, before regaining her composure, laughing loudly, fully, and sincerely.

"Ashion, you are, by far, the most entertaining slave I've ever had."

"I am not a slave."

Charles waved her hand distractedly as she stood. "Details, Ashion the Dark. Come. We will see to your confrontation now."

Seventeen.

The door closed on the room. With its genuine marble floors, it felt cool underfoot even through the soles of his boots. In the center was a hand-woven rug that must have been twice Ashion's age. There was a small table, for two, in the middle of the rug. The two large windows angled down toward the swirling mess of the Venus atmosphere, letting in the sunlight through the drawn gauze curtains. Paintings so old they could barely be made out adorned the walls. At the back of the room was an enormous bed, larger than the entire quarters assigned to Ashion's soldiers.

"How long has it been, Ash?" Charles said, following him in.

"I was just trying to remember," Ashion said, looking around. "You've put new paintings up. And the café table I do not remember."

"Twenty years? More?"

"I've stopped counting."

"Nonsense, Ash. No one is more aware of time than you." She was slightly taller than Ashion. She leaned down, placed her hands around the back of his neck, and kissed him. Ashion felt her tongue in his mouth, and he answered, hungrily, pulling her close, pressing into her.

Charles pulled away. "Mmm, now you must remember *that*," she said. "But you smell of your vocation. Please, do us both a favor and use my bath tub before we decide your fate."

Ashion pulled his crusted shirt off as he walked toward the bathroom. He could not remember the last time he had taken a proper water-shower, but he was looking forward to this one. It could be his last. His actions had forced a few hands, and it was just as likely he would be executed on this day as it was that he would walk away with what he needed: his Knights down on Earth exterminating a single iter.

He kicked his light infantry boots off, dropped his breeches, and stepped under the hot shower. Two heads pulsed hot water onto his chest and back, beating the fatigue out of his muscles. He rinsed his long hair, letting the water pour over his head. He took a deep breath and relaxed, in spite of himself.

Charles was in the shower with him before he even noticed. When did she learn to be so quiet? He wondered. But then he had her in his strong arms, her mouth at his hungrily while Ashion lowered her to the tub floor.

"There, now, that's better," Charles said quietly, gasping as he entered her. "If I must execute you today, I will at least be satisfied one last time."

Eighteen.

Real coffee and pastries had been brought in. Ashion marveled momentarily at such luxuries before tearing hungrily into the meal. Charles sat across from him, slowly brushing her long grey hair. They had not spoken since their shower.

Charles looked at the nylon necklace around Ashion's neck. Hanging from it was a battered and worn metal key.

"Does that key open the door I think it opens?" Charles asked.

Ashion nodded. "A reminder of where I come from."

"Everyone calling you a slave all the time isn't enough?" Charles said.

"Those are everyone else's reminders," Ashion said. "This one is mine."

Charles nodded, sipping her coffee. "What I can't figure out," she said, tilting her head slightly, "is what you had on old Salzon that convinced him to vote for you after you deleted the threads."

Ashion shrugged a little. "It was an old favor. Older than you."

Charles nodded. "Of course, he may have voted out of his own interests, with the guerrilla forces taking over Central Processing."

Ashion leaned back. The match was on. "Would you like to know why Salzon owed me something?"

Charles smiled. "I love history lessons. Pray, tell."

"This was back in 2945, back when the Lewistons were hitting rock bottom, as far as the Families go. Thrown off the Family Council, and all that."

"By my mother," Charles put in.

"Yes, Contessa Goldman, may she rest in peace. Your mother was one of a kind. After she and Trace Gregor pushed the Lewistons off the Council, Salzon comes to me. He must have been, what, sixty-four years old? A mere child. But he understood the politics of the time. Understood them like some children understand math: without meaning to. Salzon comes to me, off-thread of course, back then it was much easier, and he's concocted this foolish plan to restore order to his Family."

"Murder his father, brother, and uncle?"

Ashion's smile was cold. "Something like that, yes."

"You really are evil," Charles said.

"No one starts evil. But we all end that way."

"Live long enough and that's what it looks like."

"Anyway, we were talking about Salzon wanting to murder his father," Ashion took up the story again.

"Which he did, in quite public fashion. Worst-kept secret in family history. Why did he come to you?"

"Boy had no experience in the murder business. Needed some guidance."

"I'm not sure I see how training a boy for patricide deserves a called-in favor at the Security Council, nearly one hundred years later."

"Right next to the worst-kept secret in family history is the best-kept one," Ashion said with a grin.

"Oh, tell me," Charles said with genuine delight.

"Salzon did not kill his brother, Arvura. His father and uncle, yes, but not his brother."

Charles wrinkled her brow. "It was threaded. Everyone with Primary Family access saw it happen. Watched him do it."

Ashion gave his shrug. "DNA was the same. That's about it."

Charles closed her eyes for a brief moment, then opened them wide. "I did not know the Lewistons were experimenting with flesh iterations back then."

"Nobody did. Salzon, being untrained in the politics of information, let it slip. I know good intel when I see it. So, I kidnapped Arvura. Cut up his face for a while until he told me where his brainburn facilities were. I liberated an iteration of Arvura, dropped a brain dump down into it, and let it go back on its merry way. Even the clone thought he was Arvura."

"But the brain dump would have killed him," Charles said. "The process only works for that mutant brain of yours. All the Families tried."

"Details," Ashion said mockingly. "It only had to work for a few hours. The neuro burnout did not have time to kill the iter before Salzon so eagerly did."

Charles nodded, a far-away look in her eyes. "I take it you keep poor old Arvura locked up in your private prison, then."

Ashion nodded. "But he is near his end. And quite mad, at this point. Still, the mere threat of him still alive keeps Salzon in check."

"But now, Salzon will expect you to turn him over? For this favor?"

"That is the expectation."

"You will not do this, though."

Ashion shrugged again. "The future on Venus is short, but murky. Even my own actions seem unknown to me."

"Actions such as demanding the Writ?" Charles asked.

Ashion ran his hands through his still-wet hair. "I need those Knights Earth-side. We both need this problem cleared up. It is one thing for the problem to exist on Venus. But on Earth, it threatens all our interests."

"Do not assume you know everyone's interests," Charles said with a smile.

"Fair point."

Charles stood and walked toward the window. "First of all, I want to thank you for the history lesson," she said, facing the window. "And I admire that you have made a dangerous gambit, this close to the end." She turned to face Ashion. "Executing you today would erase a lot of my problems."

"You won't execute me today," Ashion said.

"Tell me why not."

"Thadwick Lewiston."

"Salzon's man-child is barely less trouble than you are."

"You would not have arranged our meeting if you did not need us to watch after each other."

Charles smiled her approval. "You are getting much better at this."

Ashion bowed sarcastically. "I learned from the master."

"Tell me about Thadwick."

"He means to cut your throat."

"He will have to get in line," Charles said.

"He has the means," Ashion said. "And a very good plan."

"He has the means, Ash, but who gives him his plan?"

"Thadwick and I have put your assassination in motion. Very public. When the Second Harvest is announced."

"Good!" Charles said, clapping her hands. "The boy is predictable, like his father."

Ashion waited, sipping coffee, as Charles remained lost in thought. Finally, he cleared his throat, "I need my Knights Earth-side. I need you to release my forces."

Charles blinked, coming back to the task at hand. "The Dexter Maxwell problem. Yes, it is a sticky situation, now that he has the big wide Earth to roam. However will you find him?"

"I will send forces to eradicate the iter at the one time and place where I know he will be."

"A time shift to the moment your Red Mask Tano was attacked last week."

"That is correct. End this with extreme prejudice. Reports indicate the team has done just that. The problem is already cleaned."

"Then what are we doing here? Wasting valuable time?"

"That's the funny thing about manipulating time. Chronology isn't what it used to be."

"So, if I execute you, will those troops still go back in time?"

"Release your grip on my forces. Leave me to do my job."

"That is your demand for the Writ?"

"That is it."

"Consider my grip loosened. You have won your Writ of Confrontation. There will be no execution today." Charles sighed. "You will be given a wide berth, for now, Ashion the Dark. But you have called in all your favors. You have served all your purposes. The next time I get the opportunity to execute you, I will take it." Charles turned and walked back toward the shower. "Now leave. And take your dirty laundry with you."

Nineteen.

Artificial night descended on the Family boats, and the threads were quiet. Ashion sat in the comfortable chair at his light box and strummed the threads absentmindedly, waiting. He idly fingered the worn key that hung around his neck. Word from the Earth-side mission would not be available for a few more hours, but until then there were still things to be done. He built a cocktail for alertness, injected it into his bloodstream, and pulled two threads simultaneously. This was not the best way to concentrate, he knew, but sometimes there were just too many things happening at the same time.

First thread: Tano's recovery room, boat-side. Gurn had stationed two Knights outside the door, and one inside. They stood at attention. Ashion watched the inside and outside cams closely.

Second thread: The neurals on the prisoner named Trance, strapped in tight under a Whi-Sci tube, three shivs stuck into her skull at different angles. She was perfectly still, her body drugged into complacency. But her mind was racing. She was being interrogated by a hundred sensors, all connected to each other and to the millions of other sensors all around Venus, precisely and rapidly correlating and building postulations about who, what, when, where, and why.

First thread: The Red Masks outside of Tano's door had walked away. Two new men were standing at the door now. Ashion checked the time. One more minute.

Second thread: The White Scientist in charge of Trance's interrogation was strumming Ashion. Ashion responded. "Tell me."

"We've planted the name Orpheus, and are getting excellent peaks on her synaptic transfers. The name clearly has been imbedded artificially, but we should break the code in just a few more minutes. We'll have correlating outputs on thread shortly."

"Very well. The minute you get anything that matches, chord me."

"Yes."

First thread: The Red Masks inside Tano's room opened the door, and the two new guards walked in. Ashion checked the time. One of the guards disconnected the body from the med box, and an alarm was sounded. The other two picked up Tano gently, and all three left the facility. Ashion pulled the threads to follow them out of the facility and into a waiting shuttle. Ashion dropped the thread even as Holden hailed him on the com.

"Sir," Holden said, sounding tired, "Alarm at Tano's med bed. He has been disconnected. It would appear he has been… kidnapped, sir."

"I want a full investigation," Ashion said, trying not to sound bored. "Let's find out who did this!"

Second thread: The Whi-Sci was saying something. "... we have the matches and need to make a reasonable assessment. It will take just a few seconds to thread the analysis. If I may be so bold—"

The Whi-Sci had been cut off by the blaring of alarms. Explosions could be heard, and the interrogation room was all smoke and noise. As Ashion watched, black and grey guerrillas began carefully extracting the mind probe equipment from the princess named Trance.

Ashion left his threads up. He was running from his command room, reaching for his sword, and communicating with Holden at the same time. "Arm, we'll find Tano later. The princess is being liberated at the Draggish med-fac! Get forces in a perimeter immediately!"

71

MIDDLE DRAGGISH TOWNSHIP, DAY 13.

Twenty.

Ashion sat silently at the makeshift table in the med room, a light box in front of him. Next to him, staring into the same box, sat Armitage Holden. The general looked older than Ashion remembered, but then, it had been a long time since they had actually looked each other in the eye. Holden was so much more useful connected from his boat. But the situation in Draggish had cobwebbed Holden in as surely as it had Ashion. It was important in Draggish to show the faces of authority.

A successful attack on the medical facility, only days after Ashion had quashed a similar attack. That had made a lot of people nervous. And nervous people made life hard for Ashion.

But that wasn't what Ashion and Holden were looking at right now. The Transloop data from the Earth-side mission had arrived while they had been cleaning up the mess in Draggish. This was the first chance they had found to review the information. Ashion strummed his security clearance and waited for the SIN to make the link to the massive quantum nightmare they called the Transloop. Once connected, the SIN would start to recreate the scene based on the vitals and uploaded data that came from the nanos that lived in the blood of the time shifters, as well as the nano-suits they wore. The scene could then be understood as something that roughly took place in chronological order.

"There," Holden said, pointing in the box, "There is Tano's arrival. And… wow, that can't be right."

Ashion was moving the thread back and looking at the data again. "Is that a simultaneous shift by the iter? Tano… Iter. Tano… Iter. Fascinating. I've never seen that before…"

"Then Tano goes down," Holden continued. "Grievously injured."

Ashion pulled another thread to the surface, spinning the data around and around. "Second team comes first, chronologically, hundred-and-eighty seconds. They put themselves in defend position.

Boost, Chaz, Ni'ello came in ninety seconds prior. They cannot expect the simultaneous shift, so they are defeated. Blip back."

"The data seems to indicate a speed that is a near-physical impossibility!" Holden said. He couldn't resist rewinding the thread. "Is the iter still shifting somehow?"

You've really outdone yourself this time, Logos. "Second three-by-three comes in immediately, trying to use time advantage. First team circles."

"By the SIN…" Holden whispered, watching the threads bundle and unbundle. "It's a massacre."

Holden glanced up at Ashion, who felt the gaze but did not meet it. "Last Transloop shifter blips back at five-hundred-and-sixty-six seconds into the shift. No survivors." Ashion grabbed the pile of strings and watched it again. And again. Holden could not keep up, and he leaned back. Ashion kept watching.

"There is no indication of a mortal wound to the iter," Ashion said. "Where did that report come from?"

"There was a real-time survivor from the down-room," Holden said. "He called in the report, but did not last the night."

Ashion continued to pull the threads. "There are no soldiers apparent in the data. No witnesses." He let the thread bundle fall into the background. Do we have cam feeds from Earth-side?"

"Never installed, sir," Holden said. "Your orders."

Ashion closed his eyes. *Dexter Maxwell is not dead.* He looked over to Holden. "What is the current status Earth-side?"

"Sir, Earth-side is back to full-force. We are on high alert at all times. We are bringing more Knights and soldiers down with each favorable weather pattern." As Holden said this, a soldier entered and stood at attention.

"At ease, soldier," the general said.

"Sir, Exemplar Morgan Goldman has arrived, sir," the soldier said. Even as he spoke, Morgan came into the room.

Twenty-one.

Holden stood erect, unmoving. The presence of Morgan Goldman next to Ashion was clearly making him nervous. Ashion just felt annoyed.

"Can we get to the business at hand?" Morgan asked.

"Of course, Morgan," Ashion said. "The reason we are here. Interrogation room breach, last night, 2300 hours."

"Sir," Holden said, "it would appear that we have underestimated the firepower of the guerrillas."

Ashion nodded. "For starters. But I recognize those bolt guns in the cams. Last week they were in the hands of Leshan Gregor. I will speak with him about the matter. But those bolters all require charging. Plug them into the grid, and the SIN reports their location and how much juice they pull. Why don't we have that data? Where are they getting their juice?"

Holden shook his head. "It must be the same place where they are training. But no such place exists. We have eyes and ears in all locations."

"We should be focusing our primary investigation on following the electricity," Ashion said. "Find the syphon they are using, and we break Fuel's army."

Morgan spoke up, "More distressingly, might we have underestimated the guerrilla's intel?"

"Sir?" Holden asked.

"The princess was kept in a Family-held facility in Draggish," Morgan said, walking to the light box on the table. She strummed a security chord and pulled a schematics thread. "It was unmarked for military or medical duty. Up until now, the guerrillas had attacked highly visible targets only. This had led us to believe they operated wholly independently. But how did they know where the princess was being held? And how did they know the interrogation had begun?"

Holden looked back and forth between Morgan and Ashion, not sure whom to address. He chose Ashion. "Sir, I will pull all privs for that site and get a list created."

"Yes," Ashion said, "That will do, Holden. Send in the scientist."

Holden gave a short bow and nearly tripped on his way out. In his wake, the quiet certitude of the White Scientist was calming. He was older than most of the scientists that Ashion worked with down in his secret labs. But here in the Family-run facs, the scientists had been plying their trade for much longer. They were a different group

74

entirely.

"Tell me about the interrogation," Ashion said.

"An unfortunate affair, in retrospect," the scientist said, with a deep bow, "that we did not start the interrogation in earnest until but a few days ago."

Ashion understood the implication. *Had you told us from the beginning she was important, we would have taken action sooner.* "There will be time to second guess decisions at the next Council meeting, I'm sure," Ashion said. *Your actions will be put under the review of the Security Council.* "For now, tell me what you were able to find out."

"The neural interrogation is highly complex, as you know," came the response. "Your pioneering work in the forties has helped us refine our processes over the last hundred years. We started by doing a deep neural topology, nothing fancy, just the broad strokes of the subject's pathways. Then, we attached thread feeds. To jog the neurology to life. Get a sense of how she thinks. At first we were feeding broadcast threads from planet-side sources. To get a feel for her connectedness. Figure out where she lives, how she survives, et cetera.

"As you have been made aware, this proved to be difficult. She has had probe training. Her neural paths have been habitually trained to throw off our networking feeds. We were getting only garbage data."

"Skip to the part where you were about to break her," Ashion said.

"Yes. At your request, we planted the word Orpheus, along with all known threads of the Central Processing occupation. Her neurologies went off the charts. Deep new lines were unearthed. Some of the heaviest protections were laid down against this name. We began to iterate and tweak the feeds. When the attack came, we were just beginning to hypothesize some simplistic emotive matches."

"What matches?" Morgan asked.

"Love. Devotion. Trust. One might think they were mates."

"It is not out of the question," Ashion said. "Any linguistic cross-references?"

"We found one, deeply buried. Hard to shake free. But we have re-capped some statistical matches, and the word Orpheus would appear to be an alternative for the word 'Thelonius.'"

"Thelonius?" Ashion and Morgan responded simultaneously.

"That is correct. An uncommon name. A rudimentary analysis would suggest that Orpheus and Thelonius are one and the same person."

"Anything else?" Ashion asked.

The White Scientist shook his head, and was dismissed.

"The name Thelonius mean anything to you?" Morgan asked.

"Not a thing," Ashion said, returning to his own light box. "Let's start threading it. See if we can get something from it."

"It's an inside job," Morgan said suddenly.

Ashion said nothing.

"The intel on this jailbreak. It's precise. Specific. We have a Family mole."

"What we have to ask ourselves, Exemplar Goldman, is how much do the guerillas know."

"And whom can we trust," Morgan followed on.

"You're new to this, Morgan," Ashion said, without looking up. "So let me give you the only answer to that question you will ever need: no one. Not one damn soul."

Morgan stood and left, and Ashion kept his eyes fixed on his light box. He wasn't really looking at anything, just pulling random threads and letting them drop. His mind was spinning in circles trying to get a grip on the name. Thelonius. There could be more than one Thelonius, Ashion thought. But there was only one that matters.

Thelonius Hollywood and Dexter Maxwell were back together.

Twenty-two.

Holden had left. Morgan had left. Ashion sat alone at the table, staring into the portable light box. He did not have to wait long.

PROBABILITY OF DEXTER MAXWELL SURVIVAL IS CLOSE TO 95%.

Ashion leaned into the box and threaded quickly. *He lives.*

HIS USE OF THE MONKS' SHIFTING TECHNOLOGY IS UNIQUE.

76

WE MUST FIND THE MAP. THE ITER CAN LEAD US THERE.

How did he get to Earth?

The thread dropped, a new one came up, showing the schematics of a functional orbiter shuttle.

JUNK COLLECTOR WAS REDIRECTED TO EARTH ON SEPTEMBER 19. EXTRAPOLATED COORDINATES PUT THE CRASH NEAR LONGSTOWN, CAWLRIA. PAST THAT, THE DATA CANNOT ASSIST.

We must follow the final two monks in real time. No more trips to the past. The monks will lead us to Dexter.

AGREED. FREEDOM AND JUSTICE ARE THE FINAL TARGETS.

I will retrieve Tano and get answers.

THERE IS SOMETHING ELSE HOLDEN FAILED TO TELL YOU. THE RECON SHUTTLE THAT YOU SENT TO EARTH. IT SITS IDLE.

Where? What is the report from the Front Team?

IT SITS AT THE STATION PERIMETER, 2.5 MILES NORTH BY NORTHEAST.

The exact coordinates appeared in the light box.

THAT IS JUST THE TUGGED DATA. THERE ARE NO OTHER DATA FEEDS. THE FRONT TEAM IS NOT RESPONDING TO HAILS.

I'll send a team to look into it.

THEN FIND THE MAP. FIND IT.

Ashion dismissed the thread and closed the portable light box. He stood and stretched his back. He'd find the map. But first he needed to clean up this mess.

He had business to deal with in his least favorite place on Venus.

Twenty-three.

Ashion avoided spending time in Transish. He could argue that there was so little political activity; that it was so stable there was no need for security forces; that the economies of Venus required that he turn a blind eye to the place. But actually it was none of these that kept him away.

It was the smell.

He could grow accustomed to the sulfur burn of Lower Morgish. He could handle the aggressive hyper-clean detergents they used to douse the Draggish vents. But the smell of Transish was one of spent fuel, burnt and raw, stuck in the artificial atmosphere like unprocessed profax in shit.

All of which was an aside to Ashion's situation—unable to navigate to his destination because he did not know where it was, he had had to submit his shuttle to the autopilot and the nav-prog provided by Thula Gregor. As such, he was merely a spectator of his own arrival at the shuttle docks at the far southern end of Transish.

Unlike the Lewistons, Goldmans, and dozens of other Lower Families currently cannibalizing each other for position, the Gregors took no interest in permanent settlements in the congregation of Family boats that floated off-planet. Sure, they still had one of the originals up there, a real ancient beauty, and in excellent condition, attached to the Goldman court. But it was unmodified, and thus small. It still resembled the original transport vehicle it was built as, rather than a grand residence. However, Ashion knew that Thula spent more and more time at their boat, now that her husband was slowly rotting.

The bulk of their money and interest had been channeled into the huge underground complexes here at the southern end of Transish. This kept them close to their financial pursuits. And if anything could be said historically for the Gregors, it was that they valued commerce above courtesans.

Ashion's shuttle eventually arrived at the final shuttle dock location in Transish, as located on his read-outs. However, his shuttle did not slow, stop, and dock. Instead, his read-outs all indicated that such things were occurring, but the shuttle itself continued to fly over the surface of Venus.

Ashion panicked for a brief moment, thinking he had allowed himself to be ushered to his own death. Trapped out in the wilds, his shuttle's heat protection would finally give out and the entire contraption would melt in the super-heated atmosphere.

Too late to think like that, Ashion muttered, and waited to see where he would be taken. His equipment assured him he was already landed, so there was no way for him to know where he was, exactly. Thula's nav-prog was an extremely useful hack, Ashion thought. He should have spent more time with the Upper Rim folk. He absent-mindedly opened his portable light box, threaded into the nav and started poking around, trying to get a look at the nav-prog code. It was protected, deeply, but with a few swipes he broke through the copy protection and made a version for himself. He pulled the threads apart and began searching.

His shuttle finally slowed about ten minutes later. Ashion was still threading madly with the nav-prog hack when he felt the craft land. His shuttle went dark for the security blackout. Ashion closed his threader, and waited for the door to open.

Thula Gregor was waiting for him, alone, and clearly uncomfortable on her feet. She was not accustomed to walking. When she saw Ashion descending from his shuttle, she motioned for him to follow and shuffled through a doorway. Ashion followed her to a lift, and they began their descent.

"Everything went to plan?" Thula asked.

"I had to relieve the guards of their duties, for the lapse," Ashion said. "But they are already on their way to Earth as foot soldiers to help out with repairs and security."

"Morgan believes that you were responsible for the kidnapping of Tano," Thula said, and snorted. "But she cannot figure out where you've put him."

"All that matters is that he's down here," Ashion said, "in this interesting bunker of yours, out in the middle of nowhere."

"We Gregors have always liked a touch of privacy," Thula said.

"How do you sustain atmo without the SIN?" Ashion asked.

"Do you think the SIN is constantly connected to long-haul spacecraft that we send off to mine the asteroids?" Thula asked.

Ashion nodded with understanding. "This is a ship that left Transish and never returned."

"That's right. And not a cam in sight."

"I gathered that. Nice navigation hack."

Thula snorted again. "Having shuttle racers in the family has a few perks, I suppose. Here we are."

They had arrived at an unmarked door, with no clear entry mechanism, at the end of an unmarked hallway. It was thin, low, and simple. Purely functional. Ashion admired it greatly. It reminded him of his own secret bunker. Thula placed her hand on a stainless steel plate next to the door, and they heard the electric lock release. Thula shoved the door open with her shoulder.

"They stick a little," she said.

Inside, the room was well lit, clean, and large. The ceiling was still low, but the room had plenty of space. It was filled with the three sizeable bodies of Tano's kidnappers, standing at attention, now, around three sides of a bed that was set against the far wall. In the bed, propped up with pillows, sat Tano. He was awake, but looked drugged. His gaze shifted slowly toward the door, but he seemed unable to focus on who had just walked in.

Huge pieces of medical equipment either lined the walls or sat around the room on makeshift tables. Wires had been taped to the ground, to the ceiling, anywhere that would allow them to connect to the patient, and then to the electricity and network interfaces. Ashion turned to Thula.

"I appreciate your help in all of this," he said. "As per our deal, I will speak to him alone. Then I will tell you who he has been leaking information to."

Thula nodded. "And then he stays here. As collateral."

Ashion gave a bow, and Thula shuffled out of the room, taking with her the three Red Masks that Ashion dismissed briskly. Ashion made sure the door was closed, and then pulled up his sleeve to reveal a portable. He strummed a few commands, and waited.

"Ash, I..." Tano started.

Ashion put his finger to his lips, and watched the information on his portable. He walked slowly around the room until he found what he was looking for. He pulled a tiny, coin-sized piece of metal from underneath one of the medical boxes and crushed it between his hands.

"She's has bugged us?" Tano said with a dull smile.

"Wouldn't you?" Ashion said.

"Heah," Tano said. "Wouldn't be family still if she's didn't, eh."

"I have been underestimating Thula Gregor for too long."

"Ash, I's would already be dead, done myself's in, but I's wanted you's to do it," Tano said.

"First things first, Tano," Ashion said. "Tell me what happened on Earth."

"I's shifted for th' final monk, eh. Just like the Transloop orders: kill th' man named Faith, heah, the monk Freedom's lover, then put Freedom to th' grill. Sees if she's know th' map, eh. But then someone's open th' door, comes in. It's look like you's, eh, but th' iter, he's is freshy in my minds, all I's could thinks about Earth-side. I's realize, dis ain't Ashion, it's is th' damn iter. That's is when I's realized, it's was him, th' other time."

"What other time?"

"When I's lost my eye. I's was set to kill th' imposter child, eh, named Jase."

"You were interrupted," Ashion said, remembering. "Attacked by Chadwin's guards. It was just the imposter, so we did not return. One of the guards took your eye."

"No, nots a guard. Th' iter. Iter's stab me in my's eye."

Ashion let the implications sink in. *The iter has been tracking our actions against the Earth-side timeline.* Tano had been alerted to this months ago. "Fire hell, Tano, why didn't you tell me?"

"Heah, four months ago, I's didn't know there was goin to be an iter of ya, attacks me in th' past. On Earth. Heah, that's is tall, eh."

Ashion closed his eyes. *Live by the sword, die by the sword.*

"You thought it was me," Ashion said.

"Heah, I's thoughts it was you. Th' whole time I's is in loop recovery, I's is thinkin, why's is Ash trying to kill me? He's know somethin I's not know? Way I's sees it, it's was some you from th' future.

81

Tryin to accomplish some new goal. So I's start makin my own plans. Gets my own future worked out."

"Who did you go to?" Ashion asked.

"No one's, at first. I's just start gatherin."

"Useful information. About me." Ashion said.

"Heah. All kinds of things, maybe I's not even know it's is useful. I's start puttin threads into security mitts. Things like Second Harvest." Tano gulped. "And Prisoner Six." Another pause. "And Kat."

Ashion imagined himself putting his sword through Tano right now. In the stomach, so he could die a slow death lasting days and days. He imagined cutting fingers, toes, eyes.

"Who did you give it to?" Ashion asked evenly.

"Solds it. I's had street contacts, back from before. I's had old habits I's went lookin for, eh."

"Gambling, drinking, that sort of thing?" Ashion asked. He knew where this was going.

"Heah. Shuttle races. Upper Rim."

"You sold me out to a Gregor."

"Heah," Tano said. "Mash Gregor boughts all my's mitts."

Twenty-four.

Ashion let the three Knights back in to protect Tano. Then he closed the door behind him, and turned to face Thula. She appeared nervous, which made her even harder to look at.

"Don't worry about the audio threader," Ashion said. "I would have been remiss not to look."

Thula nodded, composing herself. "Did you find what you seek?" she asked.

"Yes," Ashion said. "It was your son. He's been buying locked mitts from Tano."

Thula frowned determinedly and turned to leave.

"Wait, Thula," Ashion said. She stopped.

"Let us continue our trust, for a time," Ashion said. "Let me speak with Mash first. If I have come to understand your relationship with Mash correctly, I might be a better... interrogator."

Thula stared at Ashion. "This serves your purpose very well. I am not so sure it serves mine."

"I will take an audio threader," Ashion said. "You will have a real-time feed of the entire conversation."

Thula thought about this. "If I lose the feed, I will interrupt the conversation immediately, and expose your treachery to Mash."

"Deal."

Thula nodded. "I have much to gain by seeking the specifics of what your slave in there knows about you. What Mash knows. But I am old, the world is about to change dramatically, and I have other purposes. The minute you no longer serve my purposes, we are done and I will terminate your mess in there." Thula pointed toward Tano's door.

"Understood."

"Mash will be racing his precious shuttles in thirty-six hours. You should be able to get there by tomorrow evening. I will provide the coordinates to your shuttle's nav." Thula turned and left.

Ashion walked back to his shuttle. As he waited for the nav system to disengage from Thula's latest coordinate loader, he went over the conversation with Tano.

Kat's training, feeds from you's cams. Cams of Whi-Scis doing they's things with her mind.

Not even Tano knew who Kat was. But his indiscretions could still compromise the entire project.

I's gives anythin on Earth-side ops. Anythin I's can find. Knight training. Security strategies. Anythin that might help Families destroys ya, Ash.

What was the last thing you gave to Mash?

Th' planet-side threads of th' iter, eh. Copies before they's deleted. Just after I's brought them to ya, heah, I's dropped them with Mash.

How did you move the mits?

Takes it to a wage pit, eh. Different table every time, eh. I's put the mits into th' pot. I's lose th' bet. Walks away.

Okay. You can sleep now, Tano.

You's not gonna end me's?

No, Tano. I need you now more than ever.

I's never doubts ya again, Ash. Nevers.

I believe you, Tano. But I need you healed. So sleep. Oh, and Tano?

Heah, sir?
Get yourself a new eye put in. No more scars.
Heah, sir. No more scars.

Twenty-five.

Ashion had to switch shuttles at the Transish docks to get one that was deep-space ready, which was fine: his current shuttle still stated it had never left the lower docks. The upper Transish docks sat tethered up above the atmo, hovering over Venus at a distance that didn't come with any gravity. Easier to launch shuttles to and from the 'roids. The Upper Rim.

It would take some time to get there. As Ashion sat back in the new shuttle, he pulled up his interface and began threading the Family interface for Mash's privs. Ashion shook his head. *How could this child be a threat?* He barely had read privs on low-level Family data. He had access to higher level data, by birthright, that he had merely to ask for. Yet, he had never requested security privs, med privs, anything.

Would he even be able to open the mitts that he had bought from Tano?

Ashion pulled the threads higher, trying to get a more detailed view of the young Gregor. Born in 3001, making him a youngster of forty-nine. Still, old enough to have married, by Family tradition— even among the alienated Gregors. Yet Mash was single, and with a clear disinterest in Family politics or in any sort of power in the political sense. But he was loved in Transish. Hundreds of threads documented his success in the shuttle races that had been a mainstay of the Upper Rim for a century. Ashion found threads speaking to his engineering prowess—he had been involved in one of the key innovations in shuttlecraft that allowed them to get significantly more burn out of the same amount of fuel. This pushed his interests even farther out into the 'verse, as smaller ships could now go farther and longer. Ashion pulled an interview thread from an old broadcast. Mash Gregor was good-looking, in the grand Gregor tradition: pale skin, blue eyes, blond hair. Ashion had forgotten that the Gregors took pride in their natural features. Mash had a square chin, cleft, and a crooked half-smile that always alluded to an inside joke he was sharing with the world.

"What led you to spend ten years of your life on the new Gregor Engine?" the interviewer asked. Ashion checked the interview date: Day 301, Year 3044.

"Are they calling it that?" Mash said, almost blushing. *Really?* Ashion thought.

"The Gregor Engine," the interviewer said. "That is what they call it."

"Well, I'll be honest with you," Mash said, his smile gone, leaning in toward the interviewer. "After the death of my sisters, I was a mess. We hadn't had an accident on the rocks in two decades. And never on my watch. They said it was unavoidable, but I blamed myself."

Ashion whistled. *This guy was good.*

"So, I turned control of the rocks back over to my guys, and I hid from the world. Buried myself in the engineering threads. I was looking for an escape. The next time I looked up, it had been eight years and my team had the new engine prototyped."

"Will you be outfitting all of your shuttles with the new systems?" the interviewer asked.

"Absolutely," Mash said, sitting back up, putting that smile back on. "The only thing better than the efficiency is the improved safety."

"Mash, what we really want to know," the interviewer said conspiratorially, "is will you be racing again? And will you be using the new engine?"

Mash's half-smile turned into a mega-watt smile. "I'll be racing. And as for the engine, well, if you take away the safety throttle, it goes fast. Really fast."

The interview cut to an interlaced thread of a shuttle blasting across the cam view. Ashion dropped the thread, and it settled into the pulsing glow of the millions of other threads. He pulled his hands from the light box, and the display disappeared. *A hotshot space 'naut with a mind for engineering,* Ashion thought. *With no security privs and no presence anywhere near the nexus of power. What does he want with my secrets?*

Twenty-six.

"This is all my mother's doing," Mash yelled again.

He was quite drunk. Ashion could see it in his unfocused eyes. He had his arm over a beautiful brunette who, by all estimations, was wearing only just enough clothing to prevent her from being classified as naked. She was pouring more of the hot liquor that dominated the bars out here. Red Hot, they called it. The overall noise of the bar was such that when Ashion finally spied Mash from across the room, and came and sat at his table, he had to shout just to get Mash's attention from the cleavage of the girl. Mash had given Ashion the insider grin. Then the comment about his mother, which Ashion had asked him to repeat.

Through a series of elaborate hand gestures that he had to use multiple times, Ashion convinced Mash to follow him out of the bar. The bar was located on a large shuttle that was currently blasting, top speed, from the Gregor stronghold on the rim to the racing platforms on some unnamed rock that had been fired into high orbit around Venus, like a new moon. Ashion had bought his way onto this exclusive shuttle, which was taking Mash Gregor and his racing entourage to some great race that was taking place at some hour sometime in the near future. As far as Ashion could tell, most of the people on this shuttle either owed Mash money, or were owed money by him. He was, therefore, the absolute magnetic force on board, bending all toward him or repelling them away.

Mash staggered down the hallway after Ashion (shouting at friends and foes alike the whole time), and into his private quarters. Inside, there was another brunette waiting, in the same semi-clothed garb as the one Mash had just abandoned at the bar. Mash dismissed her with one hand; she pouted, but left. Mash still had not said another word to Ashion. He ambled up to his private bar and poured another shot of the Red Hot. With a hand gesture he offered some to Ashion, who shook his head. Mash shrugged, and took both shots.

"You know, I expected you sooner," Mash finally said, sitting at a stool. Ashion walked over and took the stool next to him.

"I am a busy man," Ashion said.

"Well, when that rover-bitch tried to set me up for murder, I thought you'd be knocking down my door, eh."

"You mother set you up?" Ashion said.

Mash laughed. "I saw the threads. Dunno who she got to look like me, but it was enough. Goldmans have been all over me like flies on shit."

"Morgan Goldman is very interested in my people these days," Ashion said.

"Self-absorbed runt." Mash then did a spot-on impression of the Goldman Exemplar: "'What do you know about Tano? Why would a Gregor want him killed?' On and on and on."

"Mash I need to talk to you off-thread," Ashion said.

Mash snorted, and pointed up at the cam. "You think that thing up there works? Where do you think you are? The Family boats? We don't live on the threads out here, Ash."

Ashion thought of all the laws that he had seen broken already on this boat, up to and including the unthreaded life. I could bring you in right now, Ashion thought.

"You've got a nice little racket out here," Ashion said. "Gambling, racing, liquor. Reminds me of your brother Leshan's work down planet-side at Morgish."

"That mongrel half-breed is not my brother," Mash said through gritted teeth. His hand reached for his tunic reflexively. A knife, Ashion thought. Or a bolt gun.

"Tell that to your father and the planet-side whore he banged up back in '91."

"Only decent thing my mother ever did," Mash said, "was kick that rot out of the Family."

"Still," Ashion said. "He presides over his own little fiefdom now, just like you. Makes his own rules. Has his own thugs."

"What is it you needed, *slave*?" Mash asked, looking at the door.

Ashion smiled. "Tano tells me you've been buying illegal mitts from him."

Mash took another shot of the liquor. "Dumbest thing I ever did," he said quietly.

"You gave the information to Logos," Ashion said.

"Who?" Mash asked. "I don't know anyone by that name."

"Sure you do. Doctor down in the Draggish med facs."

"Unlike you and the Goldmans and all the dripped Family crazies on those antiquated boats, I don't go in for the self-mods. Gregors don't get artificially extended. My father will live a normal life length. My father's father did the same. So will I. No need for all the preservatives. No need for *your* technologies. So I don't go to any med facs. Ever."

"How very noble of you," Ashion said. "But I'm not talking about the medical facilities for life preservation. I'm talking about the skin trade."

Mash shrugged. "I deal with a lot of doctors that pull iced crims. Don't ever learn any of their names. It's better that way. Besides, I didn't sell your precious threads to a doctor. It's way worse than that." Mash threw back another shot. "I sold the mitts to Salzon Lewiston."

"*Sure* you did, Mash."

"I don't care if you believe me or not. I'm just the middle man in this transaction. What the hell would I want with your dirty laundry? Besides, I couldn't decrypt the damn things. I'd have had to make a trip to the boats, request a bunch of privs I don't need. So I just put the threads back onto the market place. Salzon was the highest bidder."

"Who else made offers?"

"A couple of Goldmans. Salzon's son Thadwick. Some clueless middlers. Salzon really iced the cake, though. I've got three class-C transport cruisers thanks to his money." Mash poured another shot and mostly missed the glass. His speech was becoming slurred to the point of incomprehensibility. "Still, I'd give it all back to be rid of you and all your damn people. I thought I was just playing an angle, right? Some eye-patched lunatic's given away stolen security threads? It's jis easy money, right? Goddamn Family, though. Always the Goddamn Families. I shoulda left well enough alone."

"I need specifics, Mash," Ashion said. "What was on the mitts?"

"I'm telling you," Mash said, "I couldn't open them."

Salzon Lewiston, Ashion thought.

"Listen, Ash," Mash said. "You tell that ice-ball mother of mine, if she wants to drag me into Family nonsense, she can do it herself.

If she wants to take the Gregors back to those damn boats, that's her goddamn problem. Not mine. You tell her, no more sending *slaves*. I'm done. Done. If anyone asks me about all this shit, I tell 'em the same thing I told Morgan. I didn't try to kill Tano. And then you can go stick yerself and leave me alone. I gotta race the win."

With that, Mash stumbled away from the bar, steadied himself against the wall, and fell into his bedroom quarters. Ashion took the last shot Mash had poured, and drank it, letting the heat burn down his throat and into his belly. Then he headed back to the bar to negotiate a ride back to Transish.

Twenty-seven.

Charles Goldman did not attend the next Security Council meeting, a pointed remark that, according to the Governor General, everything was under control and running smoothly. The Lower Families took quick note of this, and settled into the usual court politics and intrigues. As Ashion made his way through the groups, he kept hearing the same excited whispers: *A Second Harvest! Is it true? When will we go?* Ashion did nothing to quash the rumors. The moment was close enough. The decision would be made today.

The Lower Families made their way out of the Security Council room, leaving the primary Council members: Ashion, Morgan, Salzon, Thadwick, and Thula, as well as the militarians: Mars, Cheltin, Warship, and Dante. Morgan brought the meeting to order.

"Ashion Goldman, please update us on what is happening Earth-side," Morgan said. "The rest of our day hinges on Earth-side preparations."

"Yes, sir," Ashion said. "Twelve days ago, a single enemy combatant attacked our forces at the Earth-side station. This combatant took out every soldier and Red Mask in a matter of minutes."

There was a hushed silence. Ashion continued. "After the Writ of Confrontation, I authorized two bands of Red Masks to neutralize the threat via time shift. While completely devastated, an eye witness confirmed the combatant was mortally wounded. However, upon being so wounded, the combatant blipped."

"What do you mean, blipped?" Thula Gregor asked.

"Apologies, Thula," Ashion said. "It is a term we use when a time shifter is pulled back to their present chroneographic coordinates."

This was allowed to settled in for a moment before Salzon spoke. "Our understanding is that all Earth-side shifters had been neutralized."

"They have been," Ashion said. "But we have never found and

neutralized their mapping technology."

"How could they have found the Earth-side station?" Morgan asked.

"That is a mystery for another day," Thula said with a cough. "What we must ask ourselves is whether the Earth-side guerrillas continue to pose an ongoing threat?"

Ashion nodded curtly. "The answer can only be yes. Those that enabled the attack have not been located, but we have a few leads."

"What kind of leads?" Salzon asked.

"There are only two remaining monks of the Order of Brodius that have any knowledge of the shifting disciplines. We will monitor their whereabouts and this will lead us to any Earth-side resisters."

"You are already moving troops back down to the Earth-side station?" Morgan asked.

"Yes. We have set up a heavily fortified perimeter. We will not be taken by surprise again. I have begun moving larger numbers of infantry troops in to support my Knights. We have over one-hundred-and-fifty troops on stand-by at the Loopstation above Earth. Fifty of them have been deployed."

"Only one question requires consideration today," Salzon said. "Are we ready to commence with the Second Harvest? Time runs short, and we need recruits to begin moving goods across the Transloop for the invasion."

"Our understanding of the Earthlings' time-travel technologies is not complete," Ashion said. "We still have not located their chroneography machine. There is evidence of an extremely advanced mapping system, but we have not yet located it."

"But you have clearly destabilized the region," Mars said. "The western Cawlrian region is nothing but bickering warlords. The eastern Amrikan Empire is gripped by a succession crisis, and no longer cares for the backwaters to the west. Our time travel work is done."

"Yes, Mars," Ashion said. "But the paradox of what we have done is that all our hard work could be compromised if there is any chance of someone shifting back to undo it all."

"The possible presence of time travelers on Earth is a cause for concern," Morgan said. "But you have eliminated all of those capable of using the technology, correct?"

"We thought so. Every known person with shifting capabilities has been erased from Earth-side history. It is only the two monks who have knowledge of how it used to work. But someone is shifting. We need to find the chroneograph."

"Its existence does not prevent us from proceeding," Morgan said.

"I would request one more week to complete the investigation," Ashion said. "Based on the latest shifts, we have excellent intelligence on who to interrogate. New leads on where to look."

"Ashion," Salzon said. "Do you remember why we blocked your request to allow time travel on Venus?"

"Yes, sir," Ashion said.

"Quite right," Salzon said, turning to face Morgan. "We cannot control the side effects of our time manipulations, if the manipulations affect us as well. The only way to use time travel to meet all of our needs is to limit it to Earth. Yet here we are considering launching hundreds of ships and sending many Family members to Earth, where the two worlds will have their fates intertwined. Can we really continue to allow time manipulations when there will be direct consequences for our own people?"

"Salzon is right," Morgan said. "The time manipulations have been a delicate, complicated process. Any more missions might hinder us more than they help."

"If I may—" Ashion started, but Thula interrupted.

"The question put to you has not been answered," she said. "Is it your opinion, as head of security and Earth-side lead, that we are safe to proceed with the Second Harvest?"

Ashion spoke with icy calm. "I am requesting of this Council seven days to continue my investigation, with no time manipulations."

"Request denied," Morgan said, "speaking as the Exemplar for the good and just Governor Charles Goldman."

Ashion was quiet for a moment before he spoke. "Given the immutability of our deadline here on Venus, then, I would say we have little choice but to proceed. Conditions have been primed in western Amrik. Our invasion will be swift, and our occupation will be in place before any of the power centers of Earth can complain about their good old Venus pals returning."

"Then it is settled," Morgan said. "The Second Harvest can be initiated. Real-time troops will begin their deployment Earth-side. Ashion, do you have a leadership team in place already?"

"I have six Knights Earth-side who are overseeing operations," Ashion said. "My leadership team will be made up of Tano and Gurn."

There was a moment of silence.

"Ash, last we knew, your slave Tano had been kidnapped," Morgan finally said.

"He is safe, and recuperating. I insist that he lead Earth-side operations."

"But where is he!" Morgan scoffed, incredulous.

"As head of security, it is your choice," Salzon said. "But choose wisely."

"My resolve in this matter is firm," Ashion said.

"Very well," Morgan said. "Salzon, you will be in charge of information operations planet-side. Your family's handling of the First Great Harvest has become something of a legend. The legend will count for a lot in achieving our goals with the planet-siders."

"I have been preparing my threads for this day," Salzon said. "The Lewistons will once again rally the people to the Harvest cause."

"How soon can you begin making the announcements?" Thula asked.

"Tomorrow," Salzon said. Everyone nodded.

"Good, then. Next order of business, though not quite as *epic* as the Harvest," Morgan said. "Planet-side security matters. Primarily, the emergence of an organized, well-armed resistance force in Morgish." Morgan looked around for effect. "After the attack on Central Processing two weeks ago, we have been subjected to an escalation of outbreaks from a group that, for all practical purposes, acts like a resistance army. They dress in uniform. They show signs of training tactics used by our own security forces,"—an icy glare at Ashion—"and they have illegal weaponry.

"At Charles' insistence, I took a primary role in the investigation, as Ashion has seemed a little distracted by other matters lately. I started with the easiest topic: the weaponry. Threads have given us clear visibles on the bolt guns they are using. They are from our own infantry, an older model that has been retired. The underground arms trade has moved them out to the layer of thugs, such as Leshan Gregor, that we tolerate because of the purpose they serve. However, they have since moved them from Leshan to the guerrilla forces. Leshan Gregor can account for every weapon he has sold. Those he has sold them to are currently under investigation.

"Past the weaponry, the guerrillas have turned out to be exceptional at hiding themselves. After they have been killed, they turn out to be regular planet-siders—working whatever menial position, they have families, interests. But as we began to review the dead guerillas, we indeed found that they all have small pockets of their time spent unthreaded. How this is possible remains one of the big mysteries. But, we have begun to build the algorithms to compare on-thread and off-thread time for all citizens, so that we can begin to understand just how many possible suspects we have."

"Are you doing random sweeps?" Salzon asked.

"Against my recommendation," Ashion said. "The home sweeps were ordered by Morgan two days ago."

"Why are you opposed?" Thula asked.

"Politics, sir," Ashion said. "The level of unrest is already extremely high planet-side. These guerillas did not appear out of nowhere. They are dissatisfied citizens. I do not believe that at this critical juncture we need to give them any more reason to hate us."

"This from a man who once condoned the public execution of thirty women," Morgan shot back.

"Different times," Ashion said.

"I started the sweeps as part of a comprehensive response to the integrity breach that occurred two days ago at the planet-side interrogation facility," Morgan said.

"When the guerrilla escaped," Salzon clarified.

"Was rescued," Ashion corrected. "They sent in their troops and rescued her."

"And they left behind the other two captured guerrillas?" Salzon asked.

"That is correct," Morgan said. "And we have broken them. The information has proven to be quite valuable. But, we have suffered from losing the third. Clearly, she was one of the leaders. We have marked her hot on the threads. If she shows up, anywhere, anytime, we will find her."

"In all my years as head of security," Ashion said. "I have never seen a resistance force this well trained, this organized, and this invisible."

"Not even the asteroid rebellion?" Salzon asked.

"The asteroid rebellion was a labor dispute," Ashion said. "It had been on the brink of disaster for decades. This... this is different. They have an unmetered electricity source. The SIN cannot account for where the bolt guns are being charged, or when. Or where the training is taking place. These are planet-siders. It's not like the asteroid rebellion, where there were miles of unused mining tunnels. Where could they be going to train? To plan?

"For these reasons, I will send Tano to Earth in my stead. I would that this Council continue to concentrate its efforts on hunting down and exterminating this resistance force before the Second Harvest." He paused. "I do not believe we can fight a war on two fronts. If we lose ground too soon on Venus, the Harvest will be lost."

There were murmurs of approval all around, until it came to Salzon. He looked at Ashion carefully before he spoke. "You have a short leash, slave. We have suffered an unseen failure at the Draggish medical facilities—one of the most important strategic assets for the Families. You lost Central Processing for a few hours. And then Earth. The most precious of our plans hinges on Earth, and we go dark for weeks. I cannot analyze the data as you can, but there remain many unanswered questions." He paused for effect. "Now, I will approve your plans to continue this resistance investigation. But the minute anything else goes wrong, this Council will not hesitate to remove you from power. Remember that."

Ashion kept his face impassive. "Yes, sir."

Thula, looking sweaty and uncomfortable, spoke up. "Someone needs to tell me where we are at with this Fuel nonsense. I thought this little cult would go away. Why are the guerillas aligned to this character? Is he real?"

Morgan spoke first. "The person that is being referred to by the name Fuel could actually be real. Two weeks ago, I would have doubted it. But given how little we know of the resistance forces, we have to rethink that position."

95

"Here, Exemplar Goldman and I are in agreement," Ashion said. "There was a high statistical probability, based on a full SIN analysis, that the person known as Fuel was the same person as Logos, the med-fac doctor from Draggish. When he was killed over two weeks ago by my Red Masks, I was confident the cult of Fuel would slowly die away. But given Salzon's highlights of recent events, I would say the cult has only escalated."

"The threads burn with the name and his catchphrases," Mars croaked. "We ran an analysis for positive and negative emotive captures. He grows in positive mentions, and shrinks in negative. He is quite popular in Morgish, and Draggish is growing warmer."

"Let's keep our eye on those trends after we announce the Second Harvest," Salzon said confidently. "We will give them something more exciting to dream about than a make-believe guerilla hero."

"Let's watch it indeed," Thula said. "My experience tells me that the cult of personality is usually stronger than governing bodies expect."

Twenty-eight.

Ashion was at the docks, idly overseeing the preparations of his last Red Mask contingent. There were three dozen of them heading through the Transloop toward the Earth-side Station. From there they'd make their way to the occupation headquarters near Longstown.

Morgan Goldman appeared next to him, out of nowhere. "We have word that Tano is on his way," she said. "Coming from Transish."

"Yes," Ashion said.

"Not sure where you managed to hide your precious slave in Transish," Morgan went on. "Not that big of a place, really."

"Not very big at all," Ashion said.

"Made me realize, maybe you have more friends than I thought."

"I have no friends."

"Still," Morgan said. "Do you have any idea what she seeks, Ashion?"

"What who seeks?"

"Thula Gregor."

"It is of little importance to me."

"Well, well. There are still some things I know that you don't."

"Salzon Lewiston murdered Thula's father. Her motives are naked," Ashion said.

"I would make the same assumption, but I have heard other whispers."

"Why are you here, Morgan?" Ashion confronted her.

"You put a lot of faith in Thula. But you should know that she seeks something more obtuse than revenge for a dead father. Thula wants to transform the Gregor Family from a patrilineal line to a matrilineal line."

"That is interesting, except for the funny fact that she has only one son and zero daughters."

"But what of her son? What of Mash Gregor?"

"I do not know much of him, except that he holds no Family of his own."

"Yes, that is what we all know of Mash," Morgan said. "But then, is that what Thula knows?"

The shuttle arrived at that point, putting a stop to their conversation. Tano emerged, and saluted first Ashion and then Morgan. Morgan gave her Family orders to Tano, winked at Ashion, and left.

Ashion watched her go, lost in thought. After she disappeared from view, he and Tano returned to Tano's shuttle to wait for the encryption codes to run. Tano had his new eye in already, and looked to be almost back to full strength. Ashion had to hand it to Thula's med team; they had their craft down very well.

The shuttle went dark, and Ashion turned to Tano. "The iter is shifting, that much is for sure. It means that he has found the monks. All evidence points to the two at the monastery."

"Heah, Freedom," Tano said. "Th' other's is Justice."

"Seek out the monks. They will be at the churches, but they should return to the monastery. If we find the monks, we find the iter. If we find the iter, we find the map."

"Heah, I's will not fails you, Ashion," Tano said.

"Gurn can defeat the iter, I am sure of it. Leave that to him."

Tano smiled coldly at this thought.

"There is something else," Ashion said. "The iter was helped off-planet by a smuggler that worked for Leshan. A really big guy. White skin. Red hair. Goes by the name of Orpheus. He was an illegal slave, damaged on the 'roids and bought by Leshan. I fear this man is on Earth, assisting the iter. Be wary of him. He is extremely dangerous. While on Earth, he may answer by the name Thelonius. Keep alert for him as well."

"Heah, sure," Tano said. At that moment, the shuttle finished its security handshake, the overheads turned back on, and they set off for the Transloop station.

"You will proceed directly to the monastery," Ashion said. "Gurn will join you in three days. Only travel in twos or threes, on horseback. If the monks are there, I do not expect they will put up much resistance. There is plenty of space, and room for exercises so Gurn can continue with the training.

"Once you have the Knights assembled, we can begin to move

out to the satellite positions we discussed in the briefings with Morgan. The infantry will begin making its way to the monastery at the same time." Ashion turned to Tano. "Move swiftly. We want to be in position in two weeks' time."

"Heah, sir," Tano said. "We's will makes it in time."

Twenty-nine.

Ashion had to hand it to old Salzon Lewiston: the man was a master of the broadcast threads.

The day of the Security Council meeting, the 'casts were flooded with nostalgic interlaced threads about the glory days of the Great Harvest. Ashion found himself absorbed by the masterful touches: the first Earth invasion forces landing; the common infantry herding scared but unharmed men and women into camps while their goods, their animals, their livelihoods were loaded on shuttles and sent back to the Transloop station.

Never mind the nasty little details of murder, destruction, and rape.

Other threads showed the Venus townships flush with the influx of new goods: dogs, goats, and ravens. Wine, water, and mead. Leather furniture. Wood. So much real grain wood. Tree after tree, loaded onto the logger shuttles, brought up to the loading docks, and pushed across the Transloop to Venus.

Salzon edited out all of the mistakes: the infiltration; the explosion that almost destroyed the supercomputer that was keeping everyone alive on Venus. The explosion that nearly prevented the entire First Harvest from fulfilling its promise of guilt-free looting and robbing.

All in all, the broadcasts capped what had been a long couple of years of stoking the planet-siders into a mood of pliable readiness. Ready to hear it: the official announcement of the Second Harvest.

"The projections clearly indicate that the galaxy conditions now exist for a second fold," Salzon announced. The audience, hand-picked in the comfort of northern Draggish, cheered. Salzon held up his hands to silence them. "The SIN has run all the scenarios. We will have another window of twenty-three years on Earth. We will again bring what we can to Venus. We will take from them what they stole from us, those nine hundred years ago. With the resources we gather, we will restore life on Venus to what our ancestors promised: a true utopia, free of the constraints of the inferior classes of Earth. We will begin accepting volunteers for the first wave tomorrow, right here in Draggish."

More cheering. Ashion dropped the thread and pulled his hands from his interface. It had begun. He knew the rest of Salzon's speech: the folding mechanism was already constructed at the Transloop station. The illustrated projections were on the public threads for everyone to review. The Great Governor Goldman had made this all possible, but left the administration in the hands of the capable Lewiston Family, who had been so successful with the First Harvest.

Ashion had studied the First Harvest over the last two decades enough to understand the grand charade that had just been undertaken. The Transloop had been envisioned by its inventors as a means of moving the Venus population back to Earth. At the time, Venus was considered by many to be a failed colony. To muster the computing power to drive the calculations for the plaeonic organizations, all the different processors and computers on Venus had been connected: the Singular Integrated Network was born and the Transloop turned on.

But the politics had changed. They always do. Those in power who had wanted to abandon Venus had been overruled by the Nativists, who had fought for a continued presence on Venus. The Nativists had proved to be better at politics, which really meant that they were better at murdering their opponents or crushing them by any available means. With the Nativist movement came the discovery that the Transloop could do something quite remarkable: turn back time.

Ashion had used the Transloop to travel back in time so frequently he didn't think about the physics of it anymore. But whenever he tried to wrap his head around the folding, it made his brain ache. Somehow, with the SIN at their disposal, the original engineers had discovered that the Transloop could be used to turn back time for the whole of planet Earth. Ashion could still picture the conical cross-sections and four-dimensional models; still, he could not make sense of how the membrane of reality could be retracted, permanently, for such a large body.

But understanding the science didn't stop the Nativists from publicly floating the idea of rolling back time for planet Earth. First, they suggested, let's go get a bunch of their resources, and bring them back to Venus. After we've had our fill, we'll blink them back in time twenty-three years. For them, nothing will have changed, but Venus will have a whole load of great new stuff. Ashion tried to put himself in the position of the people of Venus at the time. He could see that this must have sounded like a good idea, but he still could not figure out how it could have been better than just going back to Earth.

Nevertheless, the plan was put into action. On September 21, 2656, of the Earth calendar, the invasion was launched. Secretly at first, and then less so, the Family shuttles began to land in old North America, where civilization was holding on by a thread. It all went well for ten years or so. But then things started to go wrong. There was no viewable data on exactly what happened, but it was clear that a counter-force from Earth made it to Venus and attacked the folding mechanism on the Transloop station. The fold still took place, Earth was shifted, in its entirety, right back twenty-three years to September 21, 2656, when it had all started. The folding mechanism was destroyed immediately afterwards, along with a significant chunk of the SIN.

And now, the Families had announced a Second Harvest. Second verse, same as the first. It meant Ashion had a hundred things to do simultaneously, and none of them had anything to do with Dexter Maxwell, or the mysteries of Logos' scheming. Ashion had to focus on getting his Red Masks ready for deployment to Earth. He met with Gurn, prepping him for the mission. Then there were meetings with Holden, Mars, and the militarists. The Security Council demanded daily briefings. There was a pile of strategy scenarios to review.

There were smaller details as well, such as the list of infantry troopers that needed their security privs cleared for the first mission. Ashion barely even bothered with it. None of these troops would be given the truth. They were just place holders. Their future would be brighter than that of their families, but nothing else would really matter.

Ashion had yet to dig into his discoveries concerning Mash Gregor and his information trade. What did Salzon know? Did he know the true identity of Prisoner Six? Or worse, Kat?

All of this weighed on Ashion's mind as he made his way down to see her in his private bunker. She had been refusing her neurals.

He hit the training floor to find Kat and Gurn in a heated discussion. When Gurn saw Ashion, he stood at attention. Kat turned away and walked toward the weapon wall.

"Sir," Gurn said. "She requested my presence."

"You have a relationship with her," Ashion said, as he walked by Gurn, headed for Kat. "Perhaps you have an allegiance. But now your mind must be occupied with only one thought: our forces on Earth. Your presence is required Earth-side. Get there."

"Yes, sir," Gurn said, but didn't leave. "If I may, sir."

Ashion stopped, just past Gurn, but did not turn toward him. "Speak."

"She has requested that I... help her escape. Run away."

Ashion nodded. "Thank you, Gurn. You are dismissed."

Gurn trotted to the door. Ashion headed for Kat, who was pretending to study a set of throwing knives.

Ashion saw a flash of motion, and his instincts told him to drop. He felt the two knives sail past his face as he hit the training mat. He rolled to a fighting stance just in time to see Kat coming at him with a short sword drawn.

Ashion pulled his sword from his back just in time to parry the first attack. He was concentrating only on preserving his own life. After seven attack swings, Kat swung her leg under Ashion's, sending him dropping him to the mat, and in the same movement used her short sword to disarm him and brought it to his throat. She stopped short of beheading him.

"Let me out," she said, breathing hard.

"I cannot do that," Ashion said. The sword pressed harder against his throat.

"I want to go back to my home in Draggish," Kat said. A bead of sweat fell from her cropped hair into Ashion's eye. He blinked it away, trying not to move and force the sword into his Adam's apple.

"Your destiny is on Earth, not some rover-hole in Draggish," Ashion said.

"I don't want a destiny," Kat shouted. "I want a life!"

Ashion heard the footsteps of his personal guard entering the room. He could almost feel the bolt guns aimed at her head.

"Hold your fire!" he shouted, without taking his eyes off Kat.

"Kat, you can kill me now, but all that will accomplish is to ensure that we both die today. It will not give you back your life, and it will not take you back to Draggish."

Kat's eyes flitted out quickly to survey her situation, and came back to rest on Ashion's gaze. "I might as well be dead, being cramped up in this place." As she said it, tears began to seep from her eyes. Ashion waited. She removed the sword from his throat, and slumped down onto her knees, sobbing. Ashion took her in his arms in what he hoped was a warm embrace.

Kat pushed him away. "Get away from me," she cried.

Ashion sighed, and grabbed Kat to pull her to her feet. She tried to engage his hand and throw him onto his back, but Ashion was ready, twisting her arm until he had the wrist and elbow locked and she was bent over at the waist. Kat was shaking with rage, her tears forgotten.

"Leave us," Ashion said to the guards. They looked uneasy, but slowly lowered their bolt guns and left the training facility.

"I could kill you," Kat said. Her eyes were darting about madly.

"Focus, Kat," Ashion said slowly. "You need to focus. It is easy to lash out at me as the enemy. I would appear to be your captor, yes? Keeping you locked up in this facility, yes?"

Kat said nothing. The tension in her arm was loosening. Ashion knew the ploy. Instead of loosening his own grip, he gave her arm a twist, and with a yelp she stood up straight to keep her arm from popping out of its socket. Ashion pressed his shin into the back of her knee and she dropped face-down onto the mat. He had her pinned.

"You need to grow the hell up," Ashion said. He was leaning over her head and breathing down the back of her neck. "If you walk out of here and head for Upper Draggish, you'll be tracked by Family soldiers and thrown in a real prison faster than you can say 'I miss my poor 'sider Family in Draggish.' Listen up, little girl. You have only one future, and that future is on Earth. You start walking around Venus and you will be *ended*. This is not your fault. It is mine. Go ahead and blame me for it. It is the truth."

Kat wasn't struggling anymore. Her eyes were closed.

"I am preparing you to take control of your own destiny. Providing you with all the skills you will need to live a long, healthy, and independent life *when we get to Earth*. Earth is your ticket to freedom. Draggish is the past. No one is waiting for you there, despite what your fantasies tell you. So, here is what will happen right now. I am going to stand up, and you will stand up as well. Then I will escort you to your neural treatments. After that is all done, you can continue to hate me if you like. Am I clear?"

"Yes," Kat whispered.

Ashion stood up, letting go of the girl. When she eventually rose, she quietly walked toward the door to the treatment facility. She did not look back to see if Ashion was following.

Thirty.

Ashion found Prisoner Six sitting at a table with two chairs, a chess board painted roughly onto the surface. The old man was staring at the configuration of old chess pieces. He did not notice Ashion come in. "Check," he said, then stood, walked around the table, and sat at the other chair.

"Playing against yourself works better for you than anyone else, doesn't it?" Ashion asked.

The prisoner looked up. "Ashion," he said. "Come to torture your pet?"

"Perhaps," Ashion said. "Last time we spoke, you were still strung out on the zombies, I couldn't keep you awake."

The prisoner's face darkened. "I remember."

"It's interesting, to me, that Logos would ask you about Earth. You've never been to Earth."

The prisoner smiled a wide, toothless grin. "Depends on which me you're talking to, now doesn't it?"

Ashion shook his finger at the prisoner. "Right you are, Root. I have a question for you then. Which you are you now?"

"A complicated question, Ashion," the prisoner said. "Who are you?"

"Don't play games," Ashion said.

"It is not a game," Root said. "Who I am depends largely on who you are. Sometimes when you come to talk to me, you want me to be Arvura Lewiston. And so that is who I am. Your pet Lewiston, down here on ice for all these years. Sometimes, you want your pet to be someone else. Sometimes you want your pet to be *you*."

"You'll never be me, Root," Ashion said, sitting down at the empty seat across the table. "When was the last time you saw Salzon?"

The prisoner tried to think. "You have burned my brain so many times, and left me to rot in your freezer for so many years, I've quite lost any sense of time. When is today? When was yesterday?"

"You know how to answer the question," Ashion said.

"I'm afraid I don't. I don't even know what year it is. What decade. What century."

Ashion stood, and touched his com. "I need to move the prisoner back to cryogenics."

Prisoner six flinched, and waved at Ashion. "No, no. Sit down."

"Hold that order," Ashion said, and sat down. "Talk."

"I have seen Salzon. Since my imprisonment as Avura Lewiston, my brother came to see me once, with you. He needed to know it was really me, yes? I did not know why I was being tortured, my face cut up, my fingers broken. I was half crazy. I begged Salzon for my life."

"I remember," Ashion said. "I was there."

"I was left to rot, except for those times you wanted my precious brain for your little tests." The prisoner paused, took a deep breath. "I was not lying, about time. I have no sense of it passing, other than my body slowly wearing out, waiting for its turn. But Salzon came to see me. Many years after the first time. Perhaps recently? I do not think it was long ago. Let me count it this way: I have been frozen twice, since then.

"It was during a visit from Logos. We were playing chess. The door opened. I expected to see you, or a Red Mask. But instead, in walks Salzon. Alone."

"Be careful here," Ashion said. "Are you telling me that Salzon Lewiston came into *this* prison cell, alone?"

The prisoner's eyes were out of focus. "Have I ever been anywhere but here?"

"No," Ashion said.

"Then here, he came to see me. Logos saw him, and left without a word. Salzon spoke. Then he left."

"What did he say?" Ashion asked.

106

"I cannot remember."

Ashion was seeing red. "Try harder, or by the SIN I'll fill your pores with ice. I won't even put you to sleep!"

"I'm trying! I'm trying!" the prisoner said. "He said that he had already killed me. And that being alive, it was an insult? Yes, something like that. Yes. Like that. Something like that. An insult. Insult."

Ashion reached across the table and slapped the prisoner. "Keep it together, Root."

Root was rocking back and forth. His scarred face twitched under the white beard. "He told me that he wanted me alive now. Just that. Just to be alive. Alive. Then he... he left."

"Did he speak with Logos?"

"I don't know."

"Remember!" Ashion got to his feet, looming over the prisoner.

"I can't! I can't remember!" the prisoner was screaming, falling backward, knocking the chair down, trying to hide from Ashion.

Ashion was breathing heavily, staring down at the quivering mess he had made of this man. Of these men. He turned in disgust. "You have escaped the icer for now, Root."

Then he was gone. The prisoner sat huddled on the floor, against the bench that was his bed, for a few minutes. Finally, he stood, wiping the tears and snot from his mutilated face. He picked up the chair slowly, and sat back down at the table. He put the disrupted pieces back in their proper positions, just as they had been before the interruption. He stared at the table for many minutes. Then he moved the queen across the board.

"Checkmate," he said.

Thirty-one.

Ashion watched his light box as the different-colored threads of the Security Council circled up, slowly, until the cam views of each of them came into focus. He ritualistically pushed the threaded views into positions that matched where everyone sat when they met in person. Morgan was the last to arrive, and then Ashion spoke.

"Tano, everyone is here. The thread is secure. Please provide your update."

"Heah, sir," Tano said. The feed was low-quality, and had a delay, bouncing from the portable sat-unit at the monastery, up to a telecom sat, down to the Earth-side station, over a secure signal to the space-side station around the Transloop, and then down to a threader at the Family military boats. "Our's number grows daily at th' monastery, heah, and th' locals blinds to it. Longstown Earth-siders, they's tall distracted by news from King Mastiff. Th' day I's land at th' Earth-side station, King Mastiff's nephew Travin's was murdered."

"You have verified this?" Ashion asked.

"Heah, sir. There's attacks on the castle. Mastiff's caught th' assassins, heah, and is sure it's was King Grawl, from the Nor'east deserts."

"Was it?" Morgan asked. "Was it Grawl?"

"I'm not sure it matters," Ashion said. "A distracted Mastiff plays to our hands."

"Travin's was an easy mark, heah," Tano said. "We's paid him to avoid th' Earth-side station."

"We've used shifting to position him as Mastiff's successor," Mars said. "We need to think about how that impacts our long-term position."

"Meanwhiles," Tano went on, "I's established quarters at th' Brodius Monastery, as planned. When we's arrive, heah, th' place is empty. But we's see that th' monks has been here, plus a third, maybe one or two days before us. So we's proceed, eh. We's moved th' Red

Masks into th' compounds in twos and threes. We's keeps a close look for anyone's comin our way. That's is all, for now."

"Thanks for the report, Tano," Ashion said. "Does anyone have questions?"

"The loss of Travin will affect our occupation," Morgan said.

"I think we are better off without him," Salzon said.

"I agree with Salzon," Ashion said. "Travin was not trustworthy. He was a little too interested in playing the angle."

"Tano, what is the estimate for full occupation of the monastery?" Morgan asked.

There was a pause as the question made its way to Tano. "Heah, I's gives it seven Earth days, eh. Eight at th' most, dependin on how long we's can moves at our's current pace."

There was a pause. "No more questions?" Ashion asked. Still the pause. "Then this meeting is done."

The Council members quickly dropped away, and the secure thread to Tano was destroyed. Ashion leaned back from his display for a moment, and took a sip of water. He was in his private quarters again, and looking forward to some good sleep, but he was also waiting for his display. So he began to prepare his chem drips. By the time he was done, he turned back to his display, and found what he was looking for.

SALZON HAD HAD AT LEAST FOUR OPPORTUNITIES TO VISIT THE GOLDMAN MEDICAL FACILITIES IN DRAGGISH IN THE PAST FIVE MONTHS. OF THOSE, ONE CORRESPONDED TO A DELETED THREAD OF LOGOS AND PRISONER SIX. FOUR MONTHS PAST.

Ashion put his hands into his interface and threaded. *How did he get in?*

CHARLES GOLDMAN LET HIM IN. THEY HAD BEEN INTERFACING FREQUENTLY REGARDING PRESERVATIVE TECHNOLOGIES. BRAIN-BURN TECHNOLOGIES WERE BEING TRADED BACK AND FORTH.

Ashion thought about this. Charles and Salzon discussing trade secrets about their brain-mapping technologies—this was news indeed. Charles had kept that type of thing to herself. Until now. And

109

it could mean that Salzon knew more than he was letting on. Ashion looked up to see his interface had changed.

Tano said there were three people at the monastery.

Ashion threaded, *Yes, three. I assume it was the monks Freedom and Justice, and the iter.*

You should be searching the churches.

I must move carefully.

There is little time left for caution. We need the map.

We have the monastery. Patience is required.

I have been patient for too many years.

Ashion ignored this last bit. *Tell me about Thula Gregor.*

There is strong contextual evidence that Mash Gregor is keeping a secret child in Morgish. There are shuttle visits that are obfuscated, but if Mash Gregor's known whereabouts are compared with the shuttle visits, there are enough matching holes for the implication to set. This has also been compared with other data points concerning hospital births, both legal and illegal. There is a statistically significant indication that Mash Gregor has been responsible for 1.2 children over the last eight years.

Any idea where all 1.2 of them are?

That cannot be extrapolated from the available data.

Does Thula know where the child is?

Unknown. But it seems that Thula has been taking Gregor assets under her control. Her husband's senility clearly has helped.

So the transfer to matrilineal succession is real.

It would appear that it is one workable hypothesis.

Ashion considered this for a few minutes. He rubbed his eyes, and turned his chem drip on. The slow calm spread smoothly across his mind. Then he threaded again.

Show me the thread of 286 being opened.

The interface was blank for a moment, then a thread rose into view from out of the teeming, roiling bundle. On the display was an old cam overhead, grainy, showing a single door, ancient in its design. On the simple metal door was the number 286. Nothing was happening. Ashion plucked the string forward, and a man approached. He had a key mechanism in his hand, and he mashed it against the door sensor. The man, Ashion knew, was Logos, even if his face was obscured from view. The door opened, and Logos walked in. Ashion plucked the next thread, and the view changed to face Logos from inside 286. The ceiling of the room was a story and a half above Logos' head. He was looking up at a wall of small doors. The only other feature in the room was an examination table and the accompanying equipment. The room was cold; you could see Logos breathing, short and labored. Scared.

Logos took his key, and placed it next to one of the interfaces. He connected a few wires, and began to thread quickly. Ashion strummed the thread, and the view sped up, with Logos convulsing in that way that people do when they are standing still in high speed. Finally, the examination table lifted itself up on its own hydraulics, and positioned itself in front of one of the small doors on the wall. The door opened, and a long cylinder slid out onto the table. The hydraulic lift lowered itself back down again next to the doctor. Ashion slowed the thread to normal speed, as Logos began plugging feeds into the

111

cylinder. Then, Logos unclasped the cylinder, opening it at its halfway point. There was a man inside, a huge man, naked and shivering. Logos helped him sit up, and he vomited a violet-colored liquid.

Ashion froze the thread interlace and pulled the thread closer, focusing on the face of the man in the cylinder.

Thelonius Hollywood.

It had been seven years since the good doctor had pulled Thelo off the icer. Ashion had been on assignment, off-rock, out in the 'verse, cleaning up some mess or other. By the time he had returned, Thelo had already been sold, and was digging rock at the bottom of some 'roid hole. There had been no way to track him, at that point. The entire skin trade was based on the slaves disappearing.

Logos had never said anything, and Ashion hadn't either. But they both knew that both of them knew. From then on, Ashion had spent more time watching after his good doctor.

Ashion pulled the auxiliary thread, and the view spun backward at breakneck speed. He stopped the thread for 286 again, nine years before Thelo. It was the same vault, the same floor-to-ceiling doors. There were two men inside the room this time. One was Logos. The other was obscured, dressed plainly, and never allowed his face to be viewed by the overhead. Ashion had always disliked seeing himself on thread.

There was a large cylinder already lying on the examination table, and Logos was opening it. Ashion watched himself pace nervously. Finally, he pushed Logos aside, and peered into the cylinder. Then he clapped Logos on the shoulder enthusiastically, turned, and left. Logos completed a few more procedures on the interfaces, reached into the cylinder, and pulled the person out. She was shaking and groggy, and he carried her toward the door.

Ashion paused the feed to zoom in.

"Rest in peace," Ashion whispered. He left Mallory's face, scared and disoriented, on his interface for a long time before he dropped the thread and allowed the calm of his chems pull him into a dreamless sleep.

Thirty-two.

Father Morgish rubbed his beard, and wondered when he had last slept. Or even emerged from his quarters. He couldn't seem to wrap his head around time. He put his hands back on the threader, to see if he could make it happen again.

He just had to pull all the thread manipulation times, and order them chronologically. Then add the thread deletions from the med facilities, the ones that lacked a deletion record. And if he created a thread pile, and then went to move them—

There it was again. The message.

It only appeared for a brief moment, but he saw it again. He'd done it enough times now. He'd seen all the numbers. Knew they were not an illusion of old age, or lack of sleep. He'd constructed the same bundle, again and again.

Someone had found a way to keep some kind of SIN interface from before the threads. A thread manipulator that existed below the Primary Family Interface. And this person was systematically cleaning up after themselves. Threads were missing, leaving no trace of how they were deleted. Just gone.

It was like the interlaced threads they had seen in Central Processing. With Jules, and those other people that called themselves the resistance. But those threads did not fit into the same pattern. They had not served the same purpose as all the other manipulations.

That is why he had kept pulling the threads. That is how he had discovered the numbers. That is why he had been awake for nearly forty-eight hours. And that was why he was now feeling a numbness, an awe, that he could not shake.

The Slave is real.

And he is asking for my help.

Father Morgish read the numbers, did the math, and heard the message.

I am alive.

Ashion will save me.

I will walk among you.

Find the woman Trance and we find the resistance.

Father Morgish dropped the threads. He fell to his knees and prayed to the great and all-knowing Singular Integrated Network, the Slave of the people, the King of the people.

"I will do whatever you ask," he whispered.

Two words appeared on Father Morgish's threader.

USE JULES.

Thirty-three.

It was two days later that Tano put through a secure thread: the monk Freedom had returned to the monastery and been captured. Tano had already begun interrogating her. It was decidedly barbaric, Ashion knew, but there was no other way to get the investigation equipment to the monastery. Ashion had seen Tano work his ancient arts before, on many monks just like Freedom. She would break, sooner or later.

It took less than one Earth day. Tano put a secured emergency thread through directly to Ashion.

"Heahs, we's got him, eh," Tano said. "Been to th' churches, eh? Been havin some funs in time, eh?"

Ashion knew who he meant. "Do we have his location?" he asked.

There was the com lag. Then, "Heah, three locations, over three days, we's know where he's haunts. We's gots a sixer back at Earth-side, we's could dispatch them now to th' shifter."

Ashion thought about it. "No reason, yet. With his location in space and time, he is in our cross-hairs. Let's give it time. Better to get him in real time, instead of looking to the shifting. We are too close in space, and too close in time. What about the other monk? Any leads?"

"Heah, sir. Justice gots pulled into th' Travin murder mess. He's was sent to Longstown to do rites for th' condemned."

"That's too close to Mastiff for my comfort. We leave him be for now."

Pause. "Heah, sir. There's is something else. Th' monk speaks of someone named Lynia, connected to th' iter. You's ever heard that name?"

"It's common, Earth-side. What has the monk told you?"

Pause. "Nots a thing, eh, 'cept th' name. Moment of delusion, she's yells at me's, 'you'll never find her!' and so I's begin to ask who? Who I's not find? So far, I's only get th' name."

"Let me know when you have more on this Lynia."

Pause. "Heah. I's thread you straight away."

Tano blinked out. Ashion felt himself moving away from the edge of the abyss. Slowly, he was pulling his nets back together.

Thirty-four.

Tano reported later that day to the entire Security Council. They had taken the time to gather in person again, although there had been much grousing, particularly from Thula. Since it was not a regularly scheduled Council meeting, a lot of the Family courtesans had been unable to make it. A few arrived, but were summarily ignored by Council members. Ashion initiated the thread to Earth as soon as everyone was seated.

"Heah, King Mastiff's has assembled his warriors," Tano said, "and puts out a march northwest over th' mountain pass toward Telonia. He's call war on Grawl and th' Telonians. Revenge for th' murder of Travin. So he's got hisself a war party. Marchin hard and fast."

"He's gone completely mad," Salzon said.

Ashion looked at Salzon and shrugged. "Perhaps. But this is good for us. Mastiff off to avenge some death or other suits our purposes."

"I agree," Thula said. "Can we bump up our timeline to align with this news?"

"Let's not get ahead of ourselves," Morgan said. "Let's make sure Mastiff gets out of town safely before we start marching legions of troops across the Longstown flats."

"Restraint is in order," Warship croaked. "Mastiff might be marching out of town, and that certainly is good news. But he has also rallied his troops to him, which is not such good news."

"Point taken," Ashion said. "Let us proceed with the deployment as already outlined. Anything else?"

"I have something," Morgan said. "But first, listen to this." With that, Morgan played an audio thread.

Heah, we's gots him, eh. Been to th' churches, eh? Been havin some funs in time, eh?

Do we have his location?

Heah, three locations, over three days, we's know where he haunts.

We's got a sixer back at Earth-side, we's could dispatch them now to th' shifter.

Ashion's vision went dark. The abyss rushed to meet him.

Morgan turned to Ashion, but spoke to Tano. "Did you hear that correctly, Tano?"

Pause. "Heah, I's heards it."

Morgan did not take her eyes off Ashion. "Tano, be a dear and tell us who you have found that we should be dispatching Family Knights to dispose of."

Pause. A longer pause. Morgan held Ashion's gaze, the slight smile of victory on her lips.

Ashion felt the knife-edge of his plans shifting underneath him. How did she get that secure thread? Ashion would have to make a wager. He was cornered. So he dug back into his old bag of slave acts. He slumped his shoulders and broke his gaze with Morgan. "Tell her, Tano."

Pause. "Th' iter. Gots hisself Earth-side. He's is th' third from th' monastery, eh."

"Wait, the same iter that killed over thirty Knights, here on Venus?" Salzon asked.

Pause. "Heah, that iter."

Ashion could feel all eyes on him. He kept his gaze averted, his look defeated. Playing the part.

"How long have you known this?" Thula asked. All eyes were on Ashion.

Ashion spoke. "We forced the information out of the monk Freedom."

"Come now," Morgan said. "You knew before then. Who attacked the Earth-side station? Who destroyed all your Red Masks there?"

Ashion looked up and met her gaze. The abyss opened. Ashion walked its edge. "It was the same iter."

"Why have you lied to us?" Salzon asked. He was as calm as the executioner's blade.

"Cleaning up my own mess, Salzon," Ashion said. "I had the opportunity to end this back at the med fac, and failed. I take full responsibility for the release of this threat into the wild."

"Tell us Ashion," Morgan said. "Who is Dexter Maxwell?"

Thirty-five.

Ashion took a deep breath. "That is the name of the escaped iter."

"But who is it?" Thula demanded. "I've heard that name a lot lately. Who is Dexter Maxwell?"

Ashion looked from face to face. No friends left. No favors left here. *The endgame is upon us.*

"Dexter Maxwell is my name," Ashion said, watching their faces. Thula's surprise was visible, as was that of the militarians. Morgan's eyes bulged, but with the smell of opportunity. Salzon was unreadable—an expert at this part of the game.

Mars was the first to speak. "Am I to understand that the escaped iter, all this time, was a copy of you? A copy of our own security lead?"

"Not only our security lead," Salzon said quietly, "but the only human who can survive a brain-burn."

Thula snorted. "How can we not know this name? How can a man who has lived three hundred years in servitude to the Families have a secret name?"

"With all due respect," Warship said, "how this occurred does not concern me so much as the magnitude of the security risk. I've seen Ashion fight. Having a version of him on the loose is a very frightening thought."

"What does he know?" Salzon demanded.

"*That* we do know," Ashion said. "He is an original copy of the earliest version of me. He was burned with fighting, shuttlecraft, and subterfuge. But there were no security burn-ins. Nothing from the past three hundred years in terms of knowledge."

"We need this threat neutralized," Morgan said. "Now."

"In light of Ashion's indiscretions on this matter," Salzon said. "It is my recommendation that Earth-side operations be handed over to Morgan Goldman, and Ashion's PFI be revoked."

"Revoked?" Morgan asked. "I appreciate your trust in me, Salzon, but we are talking a security lead that has lied to the Security Council. Hidden details that have led to the destruction of so many of our resources. At the very minimum we should strip him back down to slave status, where he belongs! I would have him publicly executed!"

Salzon turned to her. "Your passion on this subject is noted," Salzon said. "And I share your sense of betrayal. Perhaps we should end this here."

Cheltin, the oldest of the four militarians on the Security Council, cleared his throat. While the other three generals, Dante, Mars, and Warship, remained to some degree or other engaged in Family politics, Cheltin was famously obstinate and only interested in military strategy. He rarely spoke at Council meetings, so whenever he did the room went quiet.

"Lying about the details of the risk is inexcusable," Cheltin said. "But I look at the actions Ashion has taken. Would we have done anything differently, had we known? Or have these facts you now know become simply political tools that you would like to use against him?"

Ashion kept his eyes down. It took all of his effort not to smile.

"That is preposterous to claim this is purely a political—" Morgan started.

"I'm not done yet," Cheltin interrupted. "I agree that it is time to split duties. I suggest that Morgan, you take the command of Earth-side forces. Instead of revoking the PFI, we continue to monitor his use—as you so clearly already have been." Cheltin looked straight at Morgan. She kept her cool, but said nothing.

"Agreed," Thula said. "To the vote then. All in favor of putting Earth-side command in the hands of Exemplar Goldman?"

The vote was unanimous. Ashion kept his contrite look, even as he raged internally. He imagined putting his sword through all of these Family pukes. How much longer? How much longer would he be ensnared in their webs?

Not long now. Stay focused. You have survived for today.

"I will take over Earth-side command, then," Morgan said. "So, my first question, Ashion: why do you not send your Red Masks to neutralize the threat, if you know where your copy is?"

"I do not think a rash decision is in order," Ashion said. "I have not been able to compute the Transloop success projections on such a mission."

"I beg to differ, slave," Salzon said. "This iter poses an immediate threat to our operations. The sooner we end this copy of you, the sooner we can move forward with confidence."

"I agree," Morgan said. "I will send the Red Masks to clean up the mess."

"With all due respect," Ashion said, "attempting to adjust the current time-like curve with a shift into the past can lead to unknown consequences. We have ways of determining the success, of checking to see if we have already manipulated the past—"

"We all know what the Transloop does for us," Thula interrupted.

"Yes, but do you understand the implications?" Ashion shot back.

"Ashion, you are no longer in charge. This is my decision now," Morgan warned.

"Then make it!" Ashion said, his anger flaring. "Look, we can use the Transloop. Hell, we have a woman in our custody who saw the iter only five days ago. We can ask her if she saw us take down the iter. By all estimations that appears not to be the case."

"We haven't done it yet," Thula snorted.

Ashion looked at her madly. "If we did it in the past, we've already done it."

"Nonsense. I say we put this to a vote."

"I second the motion," Salzon said.

"All in favor of deploying the Red Masks?" Morgan asked. Salzon, Thula, Thadwick, all voted in favor. The four generals looked uncomfortably at each other. They knew a foregone conclusion when they saw it. Dante put his vote in, closely followed by Mars and Warship.

"I defer to Ashion on this matter," croaked Cheltin. "No other of you has ever so much as set foot in the Transloop."

"That is not enough votes, I'm afraid," Morgan said to Cheltin. "Tano, are you still there, dear?"

Pause. "Heah. Sir." The hatred was bubbling at the surface.

"Order the six Red Masks that are currently equipped for a shift to mount up, or engage, or whatever it is they must do. Let's put them on a mission to intercept this iter at the first location we have for him. And send a dozen foot soldiers along with them, just to make sure we get it right this time. All those swords and no bolt guns, it just can't be a good idea. We will have the tactical advantage and we will destroy this Dexter Maxwell for good." Morgan stared at Ashion with this last bit, eyes twinkling.

There was a pause from the com before Tano replied. "Heah, equippin th' infantry for th' shift will take more time. Th' nanos, after injection, take time to replicate. Gettin th' nano-suits ready we's need customizations."

"Why?" Thula asked.

"The shift requires passing outside of the membrane of our dimension," Ashion explained. "This cannot be accomplished without firing an electron beam at a chemical layer on the surface of whatever object passes through. This chemical layer needs to correlate to machines inside the human's cells so we know how to mark the bits for reconstruction—"

"How long it takes doesn't matter," Morgan said, "since they will be traveling *back in time*. Besides, the infantry will simply stand back and fire their weapons from a great distance. So, please, be a dear, and get to it."

Pause. "Heah, yessir." Tano dropped the secure thread.

Ashion shook his head. "You are making a mistake. This is a fight we should be having in real time."

"Which fight, exactly, are you referring to, slave?" Morgan asked.

Thirty-six.

Ashion had only just left the Council chambers when his ear piece crackled. As he climbed into his shuttle, he wanted nothing more than to ignore it. But the crackle echoed again, and he answered. "Ashion here."

"Sir, it's Holden," the voice said.

"Talk."

"Sir, a report from the Earth-side station. Infantry patrol found the recon shuttle. It was a few miles out."

Ashion paused. "I am not running Earth-side ops, Arm. Loop Morgan into this thread."

"Sir?"

"You heard me, Arm. Get Morgan on."

"Yes, sir." There was a pause. Ashion sat and stared out of his shuttle window, thinking. Finally, his com cracked again. "Sir, Morgan is on."

"Out with the report, Holden," Morgan said.

"The recon shuttle we sent Earth-side three weeks ago. It went missing soon after that. We've found it, sir."

"Anyone with it?" Morgan asked.

"Infantry reported three dead Red Masks. Food, meds, emergency supplies gone. But nothing else. Plenty of fuel left on board. Doesn't look like it was flown much. Infantry is requesting that it get looped back to Venus for full investigation. They are short-handed right now."

"They have my authorization," Morgan said. "Anything else?"

"No, sir. That is all."

"Take a look at the shuttle, Holden, and let me know what you find."

"Yes, sir."

Morgan dropped, and Ashion threaded his shuttle for Draggish and his bunker.

FAMILY HIGH-ALTITUDE FLOTILLA SS *VANESSA*, LOWER LIVING QUARTERS. DAY 32.

Thirty-seven.

Tano made a point of ensuring the line was a secure Council thread, requiring everyone's presence. Ashion sat calmly in his quarters, watching them all join the thread. He had finished his breakfast and chem'd for alertness. As before, he positioned everyone in the right place as they joined. Once they were all there, Tano spoke.

"Heah, we's got words from th' Earth-side Transloop station's recovery room. We's got six dead Read Masks, twelve dead infantry."

There was silence.

Tano continued. "All soldiers doped for full retrievals, eh. So we's look through th' data. They's find th' church at th' right time, heah, according to th' captured monk. They's waits until sundown, watch carefully as th' churchgoers finish their singin and left, eh. Monk and iter's do not leaves, eh. Wit th' church empty and sun goin down, th' Knights goes in. Infantry's surround th' place. Red Masks go up top, breach th' upper chamber from th' top. Heah, that's is it. Next, we's haves eighteen soldiers, ended. Probability of destroyin th' iter's is nearly zero."

Ashion said nothing. No one said anything.

"Morgan, we wait for your guidance," Cheltin croaked. Ashion smiled.

"Who else do we have there, prepared for shifting?" Morgan asked.

"We have an entire battalion down there," Salzon said.

"I think I am now firmly in the caution and restraint camp," Thula said. "I would like to hear Ashion's opinion."

There was a pause, as everyone waited.

Finally, Ashion spoke, "Perhaps my men have not died in vain. It was after this ill-conceived attack that Freedom returned with haste to the monastery, where she was promptly captured. Perhaps the iter is not far behind. Let us put our faith in Tano and Gurn and the good men and women of our front team. Let us wait for events to unfold in real time."

Morgan looked around the Council before speaking. "There is no harm in holding our position. We will continue to grow our numbers at the monastery. We will be ready."

The meeting ended. Ashion dropped the thread and took a few seconds to gather himself. He threaded again.

"Charles Goldman, please. Yes. No. I understand. I have posted my privs, you can pull them from this thread. Yes. Do you know when she will be available? Of course that's fine. She can thread at any time, I'm waiting for her. Emergency, and all that. Thank you."

Ashion dropped the thread, and strummed another.

"Thadwick. Ashion here. Yes. Something of interest. Yes. Certainly. Tomorrow sounds fine. See you there."

Dropped the thread. Charles' thread was up on his light box.

"Ashion the Dark," she said. She always had a holo of herself when she threaded, and it smiled wickedly at mention of his planet-side nickname. "To what do I owe the pleasure of your call?"

"Sorry to bother you, Governor," Ashion said. "I understand these are busy times."

"All times are busy," she said. "Isn't that why we've been doing so much work in the past?" The holo laughed, and it made Ashion's skin crawl.

"Your Exemplar on the Council just cost us six Red Masks and a round of infantry."

"She's young, Ash. She needs to make some mistakes. So that she can learn."

"An easy mistake to avoid," Ashion said.

"Compared with your body count recently, she's just getting started."

"After the Writ, you committed to leaving me alone!" Ashion yelled.

"I am leaving you alone," Charles said. "Morgan may be my Exemplar, but she is also her own woman. And a Goldman by birth. You should have cleaned up your mess by now. I let you free to do so, and you failed. Events will play out as they will. Unless," she smiled wickedly, "you would like to invoke the Writ again."

"I need you to put Morgan on a leash so I can do my job."

"Your job is security on Venus," Charles snapped. "Not cleaning up after Dexter Maxwell on Earth."

"I don't understand where you are at, Charles. We are all on the same team here."

"That is either a desperate ploy or hopeless naivety," Charles said. "Yes, our goals have aligned quite frequently lately. But what you are up to down in that bunker, or your unending desire to own the Earthlings' shifting technology, these goals align to nothing."

"I'm just trying to get everyone through this," Ashion said. "The Second Harvest will not be as simple as the broadcasts make out. I need Morgan off my back. And as for my compound, that is my right as a free man."

"You are free only as long as I allow it!" Charles snipped. "Do not forget that you may walk as a free man, but I can own you with a word." Charles' holo paused, calmed down. "So, here we are. Morgan has made a critical error. If my memory serves me, you have made at least two critical errors yourself, recently. Let's say she's a faster learner than you, and you are all even. Let's see who makes the next mistake, shall we?"

With that, the holo was gone, and the thread was dead.

Ashion left his quarters and headed for his shuttle. He needed to get to his compound. *What does Charles know about Kat? Was she in league with Salzon? Or was Mash lying about who he sold the mitts to?*

His com piece crackled in his ear.

"Sir, it's Holden," said the voice. "I've got a critical thread coming from the monastery."

"It needs to go to Morgan," Ashion said, sitting down in his shuttle and threading coordinates quickly.

"Sir, it's Gurn. He's asking for you. I will continue to hail Morgan and bring her on when I get her."

"Put him through."

There was a pause, crackle, and then fuzz as the thread quality dropped to inter-planet communication.

"Heah, Ashion," said Gurn. "We's have him. We's have th' iter."

LOWER-LOWER MORGISH.

Thirty-eight.

"I's see you's mades it safely," a female voice said.

Jules squinted into the darkness. "Heah, I's mades it," he said. "I's never been this deep before. Where's is this place?"

"It's doesn't exist," she said. "Heah, we's is not just off-thread. Off-SIN."

"That's is not possible," Jules said, looking around. "SIN provides th' atmo we's breathin eh. Still SIN. Stolen, but still SIN."

"Heah, true." She leaned forward into the small glow of the LED lamp.

"Heah, Trance," Jules said.

"Heah, Jules," Trance said. Even in the low light, Jules could see she had shaved her head, lost all her piercings. She was wearing a plain grey shirt. She could have been anyone, now.

"I's heard you's escaped," Jules said. "I's not believin it, but heah, you's here now."

Trance looked away. "I's could show ya th' scars."

"Heah, that's is ok." Jules shifted his weight. "What you's need? I's can't stay long, eh. You's wanted, eh. Sinners been in enough stinks lately."

"I's sorry you's buried in this, eh," Trance said. "For real. But I's needed to talk. About th' threads. Back at Central Processing."

"Heah, that's was tall."

"Heah. I's think we's know what it's is, Jules."

Jules straightened up. "It's was th' Slave, eh. *The Slave.* I's saws it."

Trance nodded. "Maybe's. Jules, I's need ya help. More than ever."

"You's attacked th' Slave. Put it's in harm's way."

"Th' Family's been lyin to us, Jules."

Jules said nothing.

"You's know when th' Primary Family Interface was first deployed?" Trance asked.

127

"Yasure," Jules said. "Three centuries ago, eh. After th' First Harvest, eh. Too many systems, th' Slave's spends all its time reinterpretin commands and puttin information backs out in readable form. Insufficient. Better interfaces required, eh."

"That's is right," Trance said, impressed. "Heah, back then, Lewistons is runnin th' Families. They's enforced th' interface across all systems. All equipment, no matter how menial or complex, it's has same interface, eh. Sophisticated enough for Sinners, heah, even's Jules." Trance smiled; Jules looked away. "But simple enough that th' slowest common man's strums it. Watches it. Consumes it."

"Heah, th' threads," Jules said, reverently. "Th' Father Morgish of th' times, he's invented it, eh. He's says, it's come to his in a dream, eh. Inspired by th' Slave itself, eh."

"Inspired by th' Slave, implemented by Father Morgish," Trance said. "Deployed by th' rulin political power."

"Heah, it's was a good day for th' Slave, eh," Jules said. "Th' increased throughput at each corridor repeater jumped thirty-two percent after th' threads were enforced at all interface points. Heah, ingenious. Sensors on ever'thins, eh. It's turns every shuttle, every toilet, every door into th' same data source. Always talkin to each others. Everything's speaks, an' ever'thins speaks th' same. After that's, ever'thins can talk to ever'thins else. No more reinterpretations. No more data conversions. Ever'thins is accessible from th' same interface. Now, th' toilet's knows about th' door. Door's knows about th' threader. Threader's knows about th' overheads. Overhead's knows about th' air processors. All of it's is electricity. All of it's is censored. Data, data, data."

"And it's is all cycles through th' SIN," Trance added.

"Heah," Jules said.

"Jules, we's not just jawin," Trance said. "I's talkin 'bout the PFI to reminds you of two things: First, system's is buried in th' SIN that predate th' threads. Th' threads dominate; no way's anymore to interface wit'out them. Seconds, th' last person's to use any other system to interface with th' SIN was Lestan Lewiston, who himself turned th' final lever that put th' threads, th' Primary Family Interface, online."

Jules swallowed. "You's want to speaks of th' self-destroyin threads. At Central Processing."

"Heah."

"You's thinks it's not th' Slave."

"Haps not."

"You's think, 'haps th' Lewistons keeps themselves another interface. Maybe's been passin it's down, like family heirloom."

"Heah, that's is what I's thinkin," Trance said. Seeing the look on Jules' face, she continued. "I's do not think th' Slave would be so callous to destroys its own threads, wit those threads currently pulled, and to serve th' purposes of th' someone's like Ashion th' Dark."

Jules was silent.

"I's needs ya help, Jules," Trance said. "Th' Lewistons is manipulatin threads outside th' knowable system. I's think you and me's, we's can uncover th' truth. But I's need ya hands to help me's." Trance paused. "Will you's help me's?"

Jules glanced down at his hands. He took a deep breath, and then offered them up. "They's are yours. Tell me's what's you's need them to do."

"Thanks, Jules," Trance said with a small smile. "I's knew I's could rely. First, I's need you's to meets a friend."

Trance turned behind her. There had been someone sitting in the shadows throughout this whole conversation. On cue, this person emerged from the pitch blackness. Jules started in surprise.

"No need to be afraid," the woman said. She had greying black hair, tied behind her head, and was dangerously thin. "I've heard so much about you, Jules. I need you to teach me about the Slave." She put her hand out. "My name is Lynia."

DRAGGISH TOWNSHIP, NORTH END.

Thirty-nine.

"Where did you find him?" Ashion asked. He mashed his shuttle into autopilot, and pulled his interface up while he waited for the com lag. He was already pulling three threads at once when Gurn finally spoke.

"Heah, th' iter's shows up at th' monastery. Gots hisself inside. Tryin to save th' monk, eh. He's was trapped. Tano's want to know if you's want th' iter terminated."

"Yes, Gurn. This is the kill order. Terminate the iter. End him until he is confirmed ended. Now."

Pause. "Heah, yes, sir." The thread dropped.

"Sir, you don't have the authority to make that call," Holden said. "That's Morgan's call."

"She can dock my pay when she gets on the com," Ashion said. "While you hail her, get the rest of the Council on. They will want to hear this news."

"One moment, sir."

Ashion had his shuttle away, heading down the long stretch to Draggish. His sense of elation was matched only by the anxiety of Charles' easy dismissal of his bunker rights. He had just begun the shaky ride through lower atmo and into the Venus winds when his earpiece crackled.

"Holden, sir."

"You have the Council members already?" Ashion asked.

"Not all of them, sir," Holden said. "I have another emergency dispatch from Earth, sir."

"Do you have Morgan yet?"

"Not yet."

"Patch it through."

Another crackle, and then the hiss of the inter-planetary com. Ashion recognized the sounds of warfare in the background. Explosions, yelling, chaos.

"Sir, it's is Tano!" came the yell. "Heah, th' monastery's is under attack. Repeat, we's under attack. Sir, we's thinks it's is Mastiff, sir.

Mastiff. He's is circled around from th' north and east." It sounded now like Tano was talking to someone else. "We's got to get th' monks outta here." The line went fuzzy again, and then it went dead. The thread dropped.

"Tano!" Ashion shouted into his shuttle. At himself. "Tano! Tano!"

"Sir," Holden said. "I have the Council on thread. Would you like me to patch them through?"

Ashion sat at his controls for a moment. Then he dropped the yolk, full throttle toward his Draggish compound.

"Sir?" Holden said. "Are you there, sir?"

"When you have them all, including Morgan, please share the news from Gurn and Tano," Ashion said, and he dropped his com. Charles' last words came back to him. *Let's just see who makes the next mistake, shall we?*

Ashion mashed the coordinates of his planet-side compound into the shuttle interface and strummed the autopilot as he leveled off on the Venus plain toward Draggish. He dropped the shuttle interface thread and began pulling from his private thread pile, loading a mitt.

His earpiece crackled, and toned. Emergency tone. Ashion tapped the thread. "Ashion here."

"Sir," Holden said. "I have the Council on. They requested your presence."

"By all means, proceed," Ashion said.

"Tell us the latest, General," Morgan said.

"The Earth-side station is under attack as well."

"Details, Holden," Morgan said.

Ashion pulled a second thread, dropped it onto the mitt. Then a third. His hands moved as quickly as the interface allowed.

"Siege engines, sir," Holden said. "Tossing boiling tar. Infantry, no cavalry. Outer defenses are holding. Our soldiers are holding with some ease. But there are a lot of them."

"How did we not see this coming?" Morgan demanded.

Ashion dropped two more threads into the mitt.

"Sir, I don't know, sir."

"I'll tell you why," Ashion said, still threading. "Morgan Goldman sent the people in charge to their doom three days ago!"

"Ashion, this is your failure!" Morgan yelled. "How dare you attempt to pin this on me!"

"The war has officially begun," Salzon said with disgust. "After all our hard work, we are not on the offensive, but rather stuck defending an old monastery and a goddamn shuttle dock!"

"I want the attacking forces at the Earth station annihilated," Morgan said.

"Yes, sir," Holden said.

"I am ordering a full frontal assault on the attacking forces," Morgan said. "Confirmed?"

"Confirmed, sir," Holden said. "I will—" he stopped. There was a pause. "Sir, I have an emergency secure thread from Gurn, sir. At the monastery."

"Patch him through," Morgan said.

Ashion's shuttle was moments away from his dock.

"Sir, Gurn here. Tano's is dead, by th' iter's sword. I's nearly had him. But an explosion. Th' iter's escaped. I's saw him ridin east by horse." He paused. "We's losin, sir."

"Morgan, would you like my advice?" Ashion said. Nearly there…

"What could you possibly add to this situation?" Morgan spat.

"Order a full retreat. The monastery is compromised. The Earth station is compromised. Deploy coms to all remaining Red Masks. Put one at every prayloop church you can find. Send Gurn after Dexter Maxwell. Pursue the iter until you kill him."

Ashion's shuttle set down at the dock. He had completed his mitt. He dropped his com and turned it off with no overrides. He threaded his new code and his shuttle went dark, initiating a security reboot. He jumped up and ran from the shuttle.

One of his soldiers was waiting for him. "Keep her warm," Ashion told him. "I won't be long." The soldier nodded and began the refueling protocols.

Ashion dropped down the lift, tapping his foot impatiently. Finally, he hit his compound level, and practically burst from the door. The first Whi-Sci he saw, he threw the mitt to him. "I need you to secure all P6 and P7 data on that encryption key." The scientist said nothing, but slid his hand into the mitt and engaged in an elaborate set of threading exercises.

Ashion did not stop. He sprinted to the cryo, where he had Root iced and de-iced, and grabbed a Whi-Sci. "I need two cans, prepped. No zombies, just empty." The scientist turned to get the cylinders prepared. Ashion turned and ran down to his prison cells. He met the salute of the guard on duty, then pulled the stunner from the guard's hip and opened the door to Prisoner Six's cell.

The prisoner was staring at the chess board, but looked up immediately when Ashion walked in.

"I am just beginning a new game," the prisoner said. "Would you like to play?"

Ashion walked up and pushed the stunner into the prisoner's side. He flailed for a moment and then was still. Ashion dropped the stunner and threw the surprisingly light body over his shoulder.

"Sorry, Root," Ashion said. "No time for chit-chat today." He carried the old man out of the cell and down to the cryogenic labs, the prison guard following him. The first cylinder was ready. Ashion dumped Prisoner Six into the can and turned to the guard. "Put this in a fuel crate and get it to my shuttle immediately. Then come back. I will have another cryo can for you."

The guard nodded and began moving the cylinder from the room. Ashion headed for the training facility, one more level down. He found Kat there, watching threads of Earth from the First Harvest. She turned and saw him, and pointed at the thread.

"Isn't this so tall?" she asked. "The Second Harvest is going to be amazing. I can't wait to go."

"You will get your turn," Ashion said. He recalled Prisoner Six's use of that word, and his stomach flipped. "We have to leave, Kat. We have to leave now. People will be coming for you. They know who you are. Worse, they know *where* you are."

Kat stood. "Where are we going?"

"Not we," Ashion said. "Just you, for now. You will be well cared for. I will join you when I can."

Kat nodded. "I can do it. No problem."

"You will need to leave in secret. I will put you in a cryo can."

Kat looked at him in horror, and backed away. "The hell you will."

"Kat, no drugs. No ice. Just the can. It is equipped to sustain life, for a bit. Long enough to get you where you are going."

She looked at Ashion, then nodded firmly. "If it's the only way."

"It's the only way, Kat."

She walked with him to the cryo, and stepped into the can herself. He smiled at her as he closed the lid. Then he patted the outside in an attempt at reassurance. The guard appeared, and took Kat's cylinder.

"The shuttle is programmed for its destination," Ashion said to the guard. "It does not require a pilot. Just launch it."

"Yes, sir," the guard said.

"One more thing," Ashion said. "I need the arms depot cleared. All bolt guns, blast poppers, anything that can fit on your security shuttle. I need this done in less than two minutes. Then fly the shuttle to Morgish, to these coordinates. Drop them. Someone will be waiting."

"Yes, sir." The guard sprinted away.

Ashion went back to the first scientist. "You are done?" Ashion asked. The Whi-Sci nodded, and handed the mitt back to Ashion. Ashion dropped the mitt into the nearest incinerator. He watched the flare as it burned. Then he walked to his private quarters, sat down, and pulled the threads for the overhead cams at his docking station. His heart raced, but his mind was like ice.

And he waited.

PART 2

EARTH-SIDE STATION,
SEPTEMBER 19, 3027. DAY 5.

Forty.

Early morning light streamed through the barricaded windows of the shuttle launch station. Dex looked around again at the devastation he had brought to the Earth-side station after chasing Tano through the breach. Tano had escaped, but not much else had. While most of the dead bodies had blinked forward to whatever future they had come from, the dead soldiers from the present remained, lying in drying pools of their own blood. Dex's rage had disappeared into exhaustion, closely followed by sleep. He woke to the lingering aches and bruises of the combat.

And the bodies.

Dex wasn't sure what to do with them. So many dead at his hand. He felt the dizziness, the small breakfast he had scrounged rising at the back of this throat. He walked back to the mess hall and tried to think. There, tied and gagged, was the one surviving soldier. He was missing most of his right hand. Dex had used the available med kits to stop the bleeding. The wound was healing, but he would never use it again. Dex recalled his own mashed up hand, chopped into little pieces by Dr. Johannsen at the orphanage. So long ago.

The poor soldier had proved useful. When the station above Earth had demanded a status update, Dex had hauled him to the com.

Everyone's is deads but me... th' iter was mortally wounded, heah, then shifts back to his future... heah, sure... I's can secure th' station pendin reinforcements.

They had called to confirm that a single investigation shuttle would be coming in twelve hours. Then the com had gone quiet. That was eight hours ago.

Dex looked at the soldier, undid his gag, and asked him, "You hungry?"

"Y-yes, sir," the soldier replied. "I's need to drip, eh."

Dex looked at him closely. He couldn't be more than twenty years old. Dex untied the bonds at his hands and feet. The soldier tried

137

to stand, but fell forward. Dex instinctively reached out to help him, and the soldier grabbed Dex by the arm and twisted.

Dex was exhausted, but he didn't need the moment to go into high-jack. A momentary sense of vertigo gripped him as he twisted to avoid breaking his arm. He leaned forward, pushing his right foot back to connect with the soldier's knee. The soldier cried out, but before he could make another sound, Dex had pulled Judas from his sheath and, without extending it, lopped the man's already-damaged hand clean off.

The soldier grunted and fell to the ground, his legs at the wrong angle. He stared at his bleeding stump, his eyes rolled up, and he passed out.

"Crackpipe, you idiot!" Dex screamed at the unconscious man. "That was your plan? That's how you were going to escape?"

Dex did not try to save the soldier this time. He left the mess and headed back to the launch area. He sat, put his head in his hands, and cried.

Forty-one.

Why can't I do it? Am I permanently stuck in my own past?

Dex had done something new, something that wasn't from the altar rooms. He had re-written the patterns, used them to chase through a breach without an anchor. He had gone back in time with no rope to pull him back. It wasn't supposed to work like that, but he had changed it. And now he couldn't see it again. Whatever he had done, it had come from a place of rage and frustration—a cold, calm, deep ocean within himself.

Dex tried to shake his head clear and think about what to do.

They will be coming for me. Ashion knows—all those dead Red Masks blipped back to wherever they come from. They will send more. But there was an even worse realization: *They know I am traveling through time.*

He looked around, out of instinct. He stood up and walked around, staring at the dead soldiers as if they held the answer.

Think! Why hadn't they just kept coming? Why aren't they trying to kill me now?

All Dex could see was the damage he had wrought after shifting through Tano's breach point. Was this what he had become? A weapon of some larger battle? Some larger war? Who was the war between? Why should he care?

A stupid question, and Dex knew it. He need only peel back the thin layer of self-protection he put between himself and his memories and take a look at Freedom's broken body. Or deeper, and see how Tano and Ashion had tortured and murdered all those other monks.

Tano. It had been foolish to chase him, to try to change something that he had already known would fail. *If I had killed Tano just now, he would not have been alive for me to kill at the monastery.*

Dex found a door to the outside and burst through it, a heavy weight pushing on this chest. He needed some fresh air.

Forty-two.

Dex didn't realize he had been sleeping, but when he woke, two things happened immediately.

First, he realized: Ashion is not in a hurry. He sent soldiers from the future, and he thinks I have returned to the future as well. He doesn't know if I'm dead or alive. Or when in the future I came from.

Second, he realized: A shuttle was landing.

He could see the shuttle descending slowly, blasters on full landing power even though it was still hundreds of feet from the landing dock. He slinked back inside, his heart rate elevating, the moment slowing. It was as though the sleep had finally brought the clarity he needed. He watched the shuttle on its slow descent, and he knew his plan. He headed for the supply closet, and grabbed the biggest spool of industrial tape he could find. He put a large run of synthetic strap over his shoulder and headed for the landing dock.

The roof of the dock was open, coolant spraying in all directions to protect against engine burn, and enormous vents churning up to clear the air. Dex looked up, the moment crawling, and figured he had about ninety seconds. He surveyed the room until he found what he was looking for, and ran at top speed.

The landing pad must have been at least three hundred feet wide. The ceiling curved into a conical nose that jutted up to about one-hundred-and-fifty feet at the highest point. The two slabs of insulated steel forming the top dome would slide open whenever a shuttle was departing or landing, such as now. Maintenance ladders ran up both sides of the curved walls, but disappeared behind the slabs of steel. There were cooling vents near there. There was a certain degree of risk, but it would have to do. Dex began hauling himself up one of the hundred-foot ladders as quickly as he could.

The heat from the engines of the shuttle burnt against his back, and the noise was deafening. The cooling vent offered some relief, before he made it to the steel roof, pulling himself up on top of it. He was surrounded by loud, hot chaos. The coolants fogged the area, and Dex had to hold his breath against the chemicals. The whole building shook.

Then came the echoing clang of landing gear against the burnished metal floor, and the sound of the engines cutting off. The coolant and vents remained at full force, but Dex allowed himself a quick breath and a look over the edge of his vantage point.

The shuttle was an upright model, meaning its nose was pointing straight up. It had a glass cockpit, and fifty-foot wings that spread in each direction. It was matte black, and seemed to be covered in some kind of foam that had burned off in many places. Even as Dex watched, something seemed to be oozing out, and the foam appeared to be expanding and growing back into shape.

It almost looks cuddly, Dex thought. He squinted through the cockpit window. There was a single pilot there, examining dials and pushing his hands into one of the threader interfaces he had seen on Venus.

One pilot. But they will send Red Masks.

Even as Dex watched, he saw three assassins emerge in formation from below the shuttle and begin a rapid perimeter sweep. He watched for others to emerge, but so far, it was just the three of them. Once they had secured the area, the first two headed through the launch-pad door, while one remained behind, guarding.

Three Red Masks, split into two parties. One pilot. Perhaps more on board. Dex maneuvered the webbing straps off his shoulder and reached over to the curved ladder, tying what he hoped was a good knot.

Within a minute, the roof began to close, sliding up and away from the ladder. Dex didn't have long. He looked into the cockpit window. The pilot had disappeared from view. Dex looked to the floor—one hundred feet below, and rising—and picked out the lone Red Mask, sword drawn, still standing at the door.

With the moment still creeping, Dex did the calculations. He could still see the steam rising from the soft outer surface of the black shuttle. After he finished tying the webbing around his waist, he began wrapping the insulating tape around his fingers and palms. He glanced down and saw that he was moving directly over the top of the shuttle craft. He could look straight down into the cockpit. Still no pilot.

Then the moment came. The Red Mask was out of sight. Dex was about to get squeezed into pulp. He pushed himself off the top of the metal roof and dropped.

The strap caught his waist after a few feet and he was swinging straight for the shuttle. Dex put his feet out and made impact with the craft. Whatever the substance that was covering the outer hull, Dex noted, it was not as soft as it looked. His feet slammed into it, he absorbed the impact with his knees, and he put both hands out to steady himself against the hull. He slid down until he came to rest on one of the wings.

Dex could feel the heat of the surface eating at his boots, and his hands were burning. Balanced on the edge of the wing, he undid the knot of webbing at his waist, letting it swing out and hoping that it would simply look like a part of the overall chaos. The roof clanged loudly shut, and bright lights slowly clicked on from every angle. Dex could see windowed decks at his eye level. He needed to get inside the craft soon or he would be seen by the Red Masks doing their sweep.

Dex looked down. There were no footholds until the base of the shuttle. There, the braking panels remained opened, but even as he watched, they began to close. Without hesitating, Dex flattened himself against the shuttle's body and let gravity pull him over the top of the wing and down. He hit the braking panel and nearly fell backward. He regained his balance by hugging into the shuttle. The panels were about to close. Dex crouched, grabbed the edge, and swung underneath the shuttle and into the complicated landing gear.

There were no Red Masks visible. The one at the door had disappeared. Dex slunk into the open cargo-bay door and entered the shuttle, Judas out and at the ready.

Inside, he found that the cargo bay was meant to be primarily utilized from the bottom of the craft when it was in flight, so it was oriented to his side. He climbed up the ladder, and silently moved into the bay. He found a closet housing conventional space suits. These were big enough for men to step into, disrobe, and gear up, but only when the shuttle was horizontal. At this angle, he could not stand up. Still, he clambered inside and shut the door.

Then he waited.

Forty-three.

Dex felt his alertness waning in the stuffiness of the closet. Suddenly, the ship shuddered back to life, its grav thrusters roaring to attention. He couldn't make out what the Red Mask team had been saying to each other, but he knew that they were back on board. After a few minutes, the engines were fired up and they were heading back out. To where, Dex did not know, but he imagined back to the space station. He would have to act before then.

He felt the push of g-force against his skull as the shuttle rocketed up, but was surprised when it lasted only a few moments. He felt the craft leveling off, and slid down from what was actually the wall to the floor. He felt the dip as the ship made a slow arc to the right. Dex took a deep breath, gave Judas a shake, and burst from the door.

The adrenaline rushed up to meet the moment slowing, and Dex took in the room. The three Red Masks, still strapped in for the launch, were looking his way and trying to wriggle free. Instantly, Dex sprung across the small cargo bay and put Judas through the first Red Mask's heart. He pulled the sword free, spinning it toward the neck of the next.

But the second assassin jumped out of the way, his own sword now in hand, allowing Judas to sink into the seat where his head should have been. Dex pulled Judas free just as the third Red Mask took aim at his head.

Without thinking, Dex unleashed the patterns of the shifting altars into the space around him, ensnaring the moment and everything around him. As the microseconds piled up, he found his next motions readily and began his counterattack. Even as he pulled together his offensive, he could see the imminent arrival of the pilot, coming down to talk with the Red Masks. *I need the pilot. But I cannot let him send a distress thread to the space station.*

Dex ducked the strike even as he swung Judas up and into the chin of the second assassin. Without stopping, he swung his leg into the chest of the third, knocking him backward. Dex launched himself up the ladder toward the bridge, just as the pilot entered, eyes wide, taking in the situation. He turned to run but Dex grabbed him by the ankle, and pulled.

The pilot cried out as he hit the ground and fell the six feet straight backward onto the floor of the cargo bay. The flyer pattern spun around and around the body of the final assassin, while the halo followed the falling body of the pilot. Dex yanked Judas free from the second dead assassin's skull even as the third flipped backward, sword aimed at Dex's chest.

Dex rolled to the side, the halo identifying the pilot trying to rise shakily after hitting his head on the floor. Dex grabbed him by his head and banged it hard against the ground again. Dex then watched as the rock swung the rope across the flyer, predicting the final Knight's next move. Dex waited for a fraction of a second, and then swung from the side. The Knight caught the attack, but Dex slid Judas down and under, coming up into the Knight's chest.

The assassin dropped to the ground. Dex spun around and pointed Judas' tip at the throat of the pilot, who was again trying to rise to his elbows. He froze and stared at the sword at his neck.

"We need to pick up a passenger," Dex said, breathing hard.

The pilot nodded. "Yassure," he said. "Whatever you's need."

CAWLRIAN HIGHLANDS, WEST OF LONGSTOWN. SEPTEMBER 20, 3027. DAY 6.

Forty-four.

"Is *this* part of your plan?" Thelo muttered, glancing over at Dex. Dex had fallen asleep after they'd breached the atmo, and even the rough landing had not disturbed him. (The heavier grav of Earth is making this harder than I thought to fly, Thelo realized.) Dex was still strapped in, but Thelo had removed his helmet after the cabin had decompressed, and opened up the shuttle to let in some cold mountain air. He needed to do his mental exercises, someplace where Moses wasn't raging against Dex.

Thelo finally found the Slab's med kit. Where was the sense in bolting it down under a large plate at the back of the cargo bay? In an actual emergency, you would be dead before you could even get to the meds.

Dex had insisted they land near Grenver, while he tried to figure out his next move. Thelo did not want to be too close to anything, so he had coded coordinates for a position that was probably a little farther to the west than Dex had been thinking. But with a prisoner, even a compliant one, it made sense to keep a safe distance so that if he ran, he couldn't get anywhere for weeks. He had parked in a high mountain meadow, in the dead of night, with a new moon obliterating the mountains in darkness. The shuttle was capable of making a heli-landing, straight down.

Now he was finally able to put a shot of painkiller into his left arm. It was swollen, and not looking very healthy at all. He would need to set the bone before he could inject the mender nanos. Thelo sighed. *Not the first time I've set my own break.* He thought back to the asteroid mines, and the rock coming down on his shin. He tried to remember how it felt to push the bone back into place before the overseer arrived and canceled him as useless. But he could not remember the pain. Nor could he remember the pain of walking on the break for the rest of the day until he could fashion a makeshift brace out of the steel bars of his bed.

144

At least this time I've got pain meds and menders, Thelo thought. He braced his arm against the side of the shuttle, feeling for the outline of the bone, and pushed.

Forty-five.

The cry woke Dex with a start, and he winced with the crick in his neck. He looked around. The pilot was still taped to his chair, his mouth bound, and he was looking straight ahead. Thelo was gone, but he heard some cursing coming from the direction of the cargo hold. Dex went to unbuckle his restraints, and it took all of his effort as his fingers were so cramped from gripping the sword for so long. He slowly stood, and climbed down the ladder and out through the cargo bay. The cold night air bit into his exposed skin.

"Crackpipe, it's cold out here," he said.

Thelo was just pulling a needle from his arm. "Sorry about the noise. Trying to set the bone. Must not have put the painkiller near the right nerve. Hurt just a touch."

"S'okay. I need to be awake," Dex said, trying to stretch out his shoulder.

Thelo had put a long sleeve over his arm, and then pulled a tab. The sleeve inflated around his forearm, immobilizing it. "You mind telling me how the hell you ended up with three dead Red Masks on this here shuttle?" Thelo said, pointing back up at the open cargo bay.

"It's a long story," Dex said. "Can we go inside the shuttle and warm up?"

"Dexter Maxwell," Thelo said. "I have not taken a breath of mountain air in ages. Grab a blanket. I'd rather hear your story out here."

Forty-six.

Thelo realized, slowly at first and then with advancing relief, that he had no choice but to believe it all.

He had settled into Dex's recounting of the last four weeks with that vertigo that comes with the retelling of dreams. With the belief that it would end with Dex saying, "And then I woke up. How weird is that?" But instead, it ended with Dex trying to remember Thelo's old URL call handle from the traffic stunt. Touch, touch, swipe.

The sun was almost up, and Dex had finished. He was staring into the slowly brightening eastern sky.

"Man, that's tall," Thelo said.

"Tall," Dex said. "I'm not even sure I've processed it all. Or if I can."

Thelo looked at his feet for a while. "So. Time travel. Ashion hunting for you. What's next?"

Dex shook his head and kicked at the gravel below their feet, shivering. "Not quite sure. I am about to relive the same twenty-eight days all over again. Somewhere over that mountain range, there's another me, stranded and wandering by himself. Dying of thirst. Do I go help? Have I changed things from how I experienced them? I mean, I'm having a hard time wrapping my head around it all."

Thelo nodded and stood. "You need food. There are plenty of emergency rations on the shuttle."

"Food," Dex said. "That sounds divine."

Thelo began crawling back up into the cargo bay, and then stopped.

"You sure they made Jones into a saint?" he asked, looking back over his shoulder.

Dex smiled. "Yeah. A saint. How weird is that?"

They both tore into the freeze-dried profax as if it were a feast. They ate until they could not put any more down, and drank cold water from a nearby stream. Then Dex crawled back into the shuttle and went to sleep. Thelo began fiddling with the equipment in the bridge, trying to make sense of it all, find out what everything did. When he didn't understand, he would rip the tape off the mouth of the napping pilot and ask him. Once he was satisfied, he tracked down the power wrench he had used to get to the meds, and started pulling panels off.

In less than an hour, he had found what he was looking for. He noted the wiring configuration coming out the back of the little box, and quietly lowered himself into the cargo bay, and back into the engine room.

The engine room was not engineered to house a human, but rather it was meant to be serviced by the bots up at the Family military complex. Still, Thelo managed to squeeze his huge frame in just enough to begin tracing the circuit boards. It wasn't long before he found the specific pattern he wanted. He tore at the board until it broke loose, and used the wrench to pinch the wires free. He returned to the bridge, and started to compare the chip placement with the small box he had located earlier. After cutting the pilot free, walking him down to the latrine, feeding him, and taping him back up again, Thelo pulled himself back up to the bridge and set to work.

Forty-seven.

Thelo squinted into the light and looked around. It was late afternoon, or early evening, depending on how you looked at it. He looked at the mountains in the distance. It was still hard to believe he was back on Earth. In Colorado, no less. He had the wiring in piles around him, and had been sketching schematics directly on the floor of the bridge with a large pen he had been able to locate. He stood and stretched, and looked down into the cargo hold.

Dex was not there. Thelo dropped down the ladder, and then out to the ground below. He found the three bodies of the Red Masks piled up. Thelo scanned the horizon, and finally spotted Dex, sitting a few hundred yards away, on a rock that looked down into the valley. Thelo decided not to bother him. Instead, he found some rations to chew on, and went back into the bridge to continue his work.

He was slowly starting to put the systems back together when he realized Dex was standing in the bridge with him. It made Thelo jump.

"Crackpipe, Dex, you scared me."

"Sorry," Dex said, looking at the mess. "You do realize we're gonna need this shuttle to get out of here, right?"

"Yeah, sure," Thelo said. "But I figured you probably didn't want it to be tuggable."

"Tuggable?" Dex asked.

"Capable of being remote tasked to a pre-defined safe-point," Thelo said. "Put on autopilot and returned to its owner."

Dex laughed. "Like the old garbage trucks back in Grenver?"

"Right," Thelo said, smiling. "Except this is a bit more

complicated."

"You sure you know what you're doing?"

"Just one of the benefits of being a smuggler, eh."

"Thelonius Hollywood, smuggler. A nice ring to it. How close are you to being done?"

"Why, you got somewhere to be?"

Dex nodded. "Yes, I do. Let me know when she's ready to fly."

"Where we headed?"

"Back to the Earth-side station. I need a horse."

"A what?"

"You heard me. And a spare sword."

"You think it's safe at the station?"

"No. But I don't think we'll be noticed. And you need to stock up on supplies."

"Supplies for what?"

"For waiting."

OUR MOTHER OF BLEEDING REDEMPTION CHURCH, SOUTH OF LONGSTOWN. SEPTEMBER 24, 3027. DAY 10.

Forty-eight.

Dex looked out west, at the rugged red rocks shooting up into the sky. They reminded him of the rock gardens of south Grenver. The Garden of the Gods, it was called back then. Who knows what it's called now, Dex thought. The rocks were similar in color and shape, though not quite as dramatically cut against the sky.

Dex found himself, once again, sitting on the roof of an octagonal church. He had stumbled across it on his long horse ride from the off-landers' station.

Not exactly stumbled upon, Dex knew. The patterns were always around him, now; on the edges of his vision. As he had made his way on the back of the brown mare he had found at the station, he had kept trying to fix the shapes and motions, somehow turn them back into the instinctive change he had made when he followed Tano through the halo. But there was something missing. Something elusive and hard to reproduce.

It was in this state, riding at a trot along an old road, that he felt the math change. Like a gravity pulling, modifying the patterns, moving them in a different direction. He had changed his route to Longstown. That was when he arrived at the church.

It had been mid-afternoon, and Dex had meekly introduced himself to the local priest as an oldkeeper. He'd made it clear what old he kept, and the priest had welcomed him to the church.

Now, the church was in session below him, as the sun crept slowly down toward the mountains and the red rocks. Dex could hear the drums picking up speed. His vision almost blurred as the flyer and halo raced past and around each other, diverging and reconnecting over and over. He tried to shake it out of his head but couldn't. Instead, he opened the trap door, kicked the rope ladder over the edge, and slowly edged down into the darkened chamber.

The heat rose from beneath as the drumming increased. This was not a strong loop, Dex realized. The energy was barely sustaining the patterns in his mind. If this had been his first loop, Dex would never have made the shift. But now, this would be enough for the breach. The rest would be up to Dex.

The floor dropped out. Dex spun around, arms extended, as the window slats clicked into place, the late sun hitting and splitting time and space at the intersection of Dex and his unspooling patterns. The surface rose to meet him, and Dex welcomed the burning, breaking, eating release of the shift.

Forty-nine.

It was dark in Terran's chamber. Dex took a deep breath, and tucked the patterns back into the corners of his mind. The spinning subsided, and he sat down in the dark. I needed that, he realized.

He stood slowly, and groped his way to the door. His eyes adjusted, and he was able to let some light into the octagonal room by opening the door a crack. Carefully, drawing on his Red Mask training, he snuck out.

There was no sign of Terran or Mal. He had tried to time his arrival for a few days after his last visit to 2667, to see if they had made any progress with their study of the Judas sword molecules. The nanomessage or whatever.

They could be anywhere, he realized; it's not safe for me to be here.

Dex crept around, looking at the devices and the few books that lined the shelves. There was a hyper-clean smell that made him think of Dr. Johannsen's examination room back at the orph. His skin crawled. Just as he made to head back to the darkened room to wait, he heard someone enter, humming a tune. Dex slunk behind a shelving unit and watched through a crack in the books.

An older woman was pushing a cart up the aisles, putting a few items away while she hummed. Dex squinted in the dim light. It was Terran's wife. What was her name again? He couldn't place it.

He quietly shadowed her as she worked her way toward the room from which he had emerged. She stopped ten feet from the door Dex had left open and stared at it for a moment.

"Am I in the presence of the great and mighty Dexter Maxwell?" she asked, a grin spreading across her face. She glanced around, scanning the room, before settling on the shadow Dex had concealed himself in. Her grin widened.

"I have forgotten how good you are at that," she said.

Dex emerged from the shadow. "Do you know me?" he asked.

The woman broke eye contact. "Yes, I know you," she said. "Do you remember me?"

"Yes," Dex said, walking toward her. "You knew the origin of my sword."

She nodded. "Yes, the sword. One of the Arachnar classics."

"I have forgotten your name," Dex admitted.

"Thrina," she said, reaching her hand out. Dex took it, thinking she wanted to shake. But she grasped it firmly, surprising Dex with her strength. She reached her other hand out to hold his hand in both of hers. She looked deeply, warmly into his eyes.

"You mean so much to so many," she said. "Sometimes we all forget you are human, too." And then, without provocation, she pulled him into her and hugged him.

It took Dex so much by surprise that he didn't know what to do. But since Thrina just kept hugging, he decided to hug her back. When he did, he felt the tension release from his body, and from hers.

"Thank you," Thrina said. "I've always wanted to say that to you. Just, thank you."

"Um, you're... welcome?" Dex said.

He had to admit, it was an excellent hug.

Fifty.

"Let me have a look at you, then," she said. Her eyes were misty, but she did not cry. "Not too damaged, then."

"You should have seen the other guy," Dex said with a smile. "But it's been a long month."

"Oh, things are just getting started, dear," Thrina said. She turned and walked toward the octagonal room. "You seek Terran and Lynia, yes?"

Dex followed her. "Are they here?"

"They are not. Lynia is back in her real time. Terran had to voyage to the Southern Archives to find the equipment required to unravel Logos' cypher. He will be gone for three months."

Dex nodded dumbly. He really hadn't thought this through very well. "Really I just need to talk to Lynia."

"If I were you," Thrina said, "I would leave a message with me.

I can tell Lynia the exact time you will shift back to, and ensure she's back in 2667 at that time to talk with you."

"That's a good plan," Dex said.

Thrina tapped her temple with her finger. "I've a head for this time travel nonsense. So?"

"So, what?"

"So, what time will you be back?"

"Right. Tomorrow sound good?"

"Tomorrow it is. You can, of course, choose a time before now, if you want."

"Right. I think I'll just stick with tomorrow."

"Good, then. I already thanked you?"

"Yes."

"Right. Well, then, off you go. I need to clean."

Dex looked at the madly grinning woman. "Seriously, do I know you?"

"If only, Dex. If only."

Dex nodded, and let his anchor pull him back. "See you tomorrow," he said, as the breach opened and pulled him back.

Fifty-one.

Dex could not remember the last time he had felt this well rested. Sure, he had found sleep, a few times, over the last six days. But it had not been that satisfying. But after the visit to Thrina, he had spoken briefly with the priest, who had enthusiastically encouraged him to spend the night at the church. He had spread out his bedroll in the warmth of the stable, and fallen quickly into a deep sleep.

The good news, he supposed, was that he did not have the dream anymore. The burning surface did not threaten him as it used to. Instead, the unspooling mathematics of shifting now occupied his dreams.

When he woke, the knife, the rock, and the flyer swept over his vision, attacking his horse as it chewed its breakfast of grass. He slowly mastered them back into the corners of his mind.

He was getting used to the constant pressure of the shifting geometries. He felt the itch at the back of his mind, like he had lost something and needed to find it. But then he would be in the shifting room of the church, and the floors would drop out, the windows open, and the itch would be scratched, the shapes unspooling out, their power overwhelming him, sending him out of the universe, knifing back in, the annihilation of it purging him, renewing him. He would do his homework, always lingering a bit longer, not wanting to go back. Trying to remember the hack that had let him remain in the past.

He had developed an internal clock of magnificent precision, capable of keeping track of the chronological loops and his place in them. He no longer had to think about time; it was like breathing. Maybe it was living the same loop again that allowed him to remember so well. Remember exactly when he had landed the junk collector shuttle. Remember when Mebda had found him, starving, along that creek bed. Remember Travin attacking them. Remember Medba running west with the Judas sword strapped to his small back. Remember Rolink hogtied to the horse in front of him, stumbling as he was dragged through the streets of Longstown.

The thought of Rolink spurred Dex into action. He needed to get his horse ready to travel to Longstown. And he needed to find another church.

Fifty-two.

Back in the octagonal chamber in Terran's library, the room was brightly lit this time. Dex was met with the smiling face of Mallory.

"Hey, Dex," she said.

"Mal," Dex said. He rose and they hugged. "It sure is good to see you."

"Thrina gave me your message," she said.

"That was fast," Dex said.

"Actually, she had to wait nearly a year before she saw me again."

Dex smiled. "Right. Time travel."

"Never ceases to amaze."

"Chronology ain't what it used to be."

Mal smiled, but her gaze burned into Dex. "Are you alright? What is going on that you need me for?"

Dex shook his head. "I barely know where to start," he said. "I think I just need to tell you what has happened since we last talked."

He told her everything. When he came to the attack on the monastery, he choked up and couldn't continue.

Mal took his face in her hands, tears in her eyes. "They killed her, didn't they?"

Dex nodded. He felt the anchor tugging at him, and for a moment he almost let it pull him back. He didn't want to see Freedom again, the broken, dead Freedom.

Mal wiped violently at her cheeks, as though angry at the tears. "Are you tempted?"

"Tempted?" Dex asked.

"To go fix it. To save her."

Dex looked at her. "I won't try that again."

Mal nodded her assent. "Tell me the rest. What happened after they murdered Freedom?"

Dex tried to describe how he managed to follow Tano through his breach, but he couldn't reconstruct the math in his head. He told her about Thelo, and about where he was headed. When he was finished, they sat in silence for a few moments.

"So, you have done the impossible," Mal said.

"Seems like it," Dex said. "Not sure what that means."

"It means, we haven't even scratched the surface of what's locked in that brain of yours," Mal said.

"Mal, I... need to ask you something."

Dex looked at her. She was ten years older than him, now. Her hair was greying, and her face was wrinkled, her hands too. But she was still Mal, the girl he had taken to his secret place in the sewers all that time ago.

"Am I turning into Ashion?" he finally asked.

"What?" Mal asked.

"I've killed so many people," Dex said. "Watched people die. I'm letting Freedom die even though I have the power to save her. Is this what made him... is this why he's—"

"Dex," Mal said. "Let me tell you how I see things. Every person makes choices, every day. These choices lead to consequences. Some of them we expect, some of them we can never foresee. It is the consequences of our actions that define us, for better or for worse. But if we can't know all the consequences, how can we be good people? This question strips us down to our base principles. It tears us down to the core things that make us who we are.

"You just told me a story, the story of Dexter Maxwell since he woke up and found out that the world was a crazy, messed up place. It's the story of a world that needs Dexter Maxwell to care for people. And you, you crazy, dripped, wonderful man, you are being guided by a greater good. You have made a decision to act, not for yourself, not for power, but to protect people. To change the world. Make it safer. More just."

"But why do people keep dying?" Dex asked.

"You are not protecting a person," she said. "But a people. It's different. Ashion has allowed his actions to be guided by choices that destroy thousands of lives, choices that disregard the integrity of a person, a community, a people. He sees only power and self-preservation. Is that what you see?"

Dex was silent for a while. "I don't know much about all that," he said finally. "Choices, consequences, what does that even mean anymore? Logos made me who I am. I didn't choose this. You didn't choose to get pulled off the ice a thousand years later." Dex paused. "All I know is that people like Freedom, like my friend Rolink, they don't deserve a world that treats them this way. Same goes for the preacher that saved me back on Venus. His name was Booker. Or Trance. There are kind people in the world. I'm not one of them, but they deserve better. So I choose them."

"Then you are not Ashion," Mal said.

"I don't know what to do," Dex whispered.

"Sure you do," Mal said. "There's a jailbreak that needs your help."

Dex smiled. "I know what the consequences of *that* will be. I've already seen it."

Fifty-three.

The south road into Longstown was not hard to miss. There were a lot of people, most of them living off very little, streaming toward Longstown. Dex had joined the stream, and found that it was not that difficult to blend in. The only problem was his horse.

Until he told people his profession. This drew people to him—mostly children—wanting to hear a story. Dex recalled Mebda, and would sit around the fires in the middle of the nomadic shanties and talk of Grenver. This earned him food and acceptance. It also allowed him to get information about what he was walking into.

King Mastiff had been reinforcing the old, crumbling city walls. They had originally been built hundreds of years earlier, during the construction of Longs Castle. The Castle and its keep had been constructed for protection against the invading horse tribes of the plains. Tribes that had long been vanquished. But now, Mastiff was spending tax income on reinforcing them. And this meant there were only three gates into and out of Longstown.

"It is said he believes the pontiffs to the south intend to attack," one teenage boy told Dex with a laugh. "Like those great civilizations care about a dried-up, shriveled old place like Longstown."

The castle itself, which Mastiff occupied, had been built in the 28th century, and had never been conquered by force. It was a great military position to hold, Dex was told by a young girl who spoke in a reverent whisper. "Anyone who occupies Longs Castle cannot be defeated."

Dex sat his horse a few hundred yards from the south gate. Along the sides of the avenue leading to the gate were dead trees that had had all but one of their branches hacked off. On these single sturdy branches that stuck out toward the road hung a hangman's noose. And from a few of them, bodies swung slightly in the wind, neck broken, ravens circling.

"Enemies of Mastiff," Dex was informed by a teenage boy from his entourage.

"What makes someone an enemy of Mastiff?" he asked.

The boy looked away. "Just about anything, oldkeeper. There are new laws all the time and he only posts them in writing. He knows that we can't read them because, as Cawlrians, we believe that writing is the devil's work."

Dex nodded. "Thanks for your help."

The boy nodded. "Thanks for your story, oldkeeper."

Dex had to keep reminding himself that he was not returning to Longstown as a fugitive; this was, chronologically speaking, the first time he had ever been here. No one would recognize him. This time, he entered as a free man. It didn't stop his heart rate advancing, threatening to send the moment into high jack. When Dex had last entered this town, he had been dragged by a horse. He had been so exhausted and hurt he barely remembered which gate he had come in, or where he had been. It could have been the south gate, although from the conversations he heard it was more likely to be the west gate. The south gate, upon approach, was not all that interesting; just a wide entrance through the wall with a walkway overhead, guards standing duty with crossbows. They checked everyone as they entered, which had caused a slowdown and left a crowd of folks waiting to get through. Eventually, Dex and his small retinue made it up to a guard. He took note of the horse before looking up at Dex.

"State your business in Longstown," the guard demanded.

Before Dex could say anything, the teenage boy answered for him. "He's an oldkeeper, from the times before the Reconstitution!"

The guard didn't take his eyes off Dex. "You don't look like an oldkeeper."

Dex shrugged. "I didn't know I needed to look a particular way. I keep the stories of times long past. That is where I live in my mind. I don't care for the present or your fashions." He kept his gaze on the guard, a steady, bored look on his face even as his heart raced and he could feel the weight of the sword on his back. *I don't want a confrontation. Not yet.*

The guard finally shrugged and motioned Dex past, turning to the small boy that had spoken up. Dex didn't wait around to hear any more. Time to find Charla, wife of Rolink.

Fifty-four.

Dex had never experienced human chaos of this order before. Sure, he had been present when Salomon Salazar opened his penny shop down in the tunnels of Grenver, when the sewer folk would begin the daily process of haggling for their essentials. But that was nothing compared to the street he was looking at now. It was lined on both sides with handcarts, tipped down toward the road, the goods inside visible to all who might walk the narrow byway. The people selling the goods were all yelling at the top of their lungs. Mostly at each other, but sometimes at someone who was genuinely trying to purchase a tomato, or jugs of what Dex assumed was goat milk, or strips of dried meat, or freshly killed rabbit.

Dex squeezed his way down the avenue, and noted that behind the handcarts were buildings that were actually doing business: the money. The banks. When he found the door he had been told of, he shuffled between two handcarts, declining offers of strange balm and brightly colored cloth.

Inside, it was less chaotic than on the street, but only by a few decibels. The large room had a low ceiling, with people sat at round tables around the edge manipulating piles of wooden disks. A long counter divided the room into two, and it was across this table that most of the yelling took place.

It took Dex a few tries to find someone who could point out Charla. She was a sturdy woman with long, black hair pulled tight in a braid, and was engaged in an animated discussion with someone over the counter. They shook hands, and she shouted to a woman at one of the tables behind her. The wooden disks were shuffled.

"Charla," Dex said.

She looked at him inquisitively. "Yes," she said. "Do I know you?"

"No, you do not know me. I know your husband, and your son."

Worry flashed across her face. "Are they alright?"

"I need to speak with you," Dex said. "Privately."

Charla followed Dex out of the building, and they found a narrow alley.

"What is happening?" Charla asked. "Who are you?"

"I am an oldkeeper," Dex said. "I met your husband, Rolink, and your son, Mebda, in the mountains. I helped them with their goats."

"Which mountains?" Charla said. "What is your name?"

"Dexter Maxwell," Dex said. "We came from the west. There was a river, at the bottom of a steep ravine. They were returning from the summer grazing fields."

"They should be back today, or tomorrow," Charla said, looking back toward the trading room. "I am not finished selling our milk futures. The best prices have been hiding until today."

"Your husband has been taken prisoner by a man named Travin," Dex said. "Does that name mean anything to you?"

"The King's nephew," Charla said. "Why would he arrest my husband?"

"This Travin attempted to steal his goats," Dex said. "They were going to harm Mebda. There was a swordfight."

Charla scoffed. "Rolink has no sword."

"Listen to me," Dex said. "Rolink was victorious. He sent Travin and his goons away limping. But they returned, with soldiers. Rolink gave Mebda a sword. A sword like this." Dex reached over his shoulder and carefully pulled Judas out for Charla to see.

Charla swore, and pushed the blade down, looking around. "It's illegal to possess that, you fool," she hissed. "Where did you get it from?"

"Charla," Dex said, putting Judas away, "I will get your husband out of jail. But your son is in danger. He is carrying a sword, and he is being chased by Travin's goons. Rolink told your son to go to a secret smithy. From back when he was a blacksmith. Before the goats. Do you know the place I speak of?"

Charla did not move. She nodded.

"Good. You should go there. As fast as you can. Make sure your son is safe. I also need you to get the sword. Can you do that?"

Charla nodded again. "It will take a day, or more, by foot."

"I have a horse. Do you know how to ride?"

"I can ride... a little. It has been a long time."

162

"No matter. Enough to get you to the smithy?"

"Yes."

"Good. Now, have you collected money on your goat milk?"

"I need only go in and exchange the chips for gold."

"Then do so. Your goats are lost to you, so the sooner you take the gold, the better. And I will need a new horse, before the night is done."

"Oh, I see," Charla said. "I run off after your horse, but first I give you all my proceedings for the year's milk?" She turned to leave.

"I know about the smithy, Charla," Dex said. "Please, you must trust me."

"I will go see if my son is in danger," she said. "But I will not give you my money."

Dex looked up at the sun. "Get your gold. Then meet me outside the King's prison quarters in an hour. Do you know where that is?"

"Yes, I know the prison," she said.

"I will have the horse for you and I will show you that I am not lying. Then you can give me the money, or not, whichever you decide."

Fifty-five.

Charla was a few minutes late, but she came, hooded, with a small pack on her back.

"Well?" she said. "What have you brought me here to see?"

"Wait a minute. You will not be able to miss it."

Charla shrugged, and sat down on the hitching log.

"Your son is exceptional," Dex said. "He is an acute listener. Good with the goats. And an excellent weather guide. Rolink is very proud of him."

Charla looked up. "We are both very proud. How long did you spend with Mebda?"

"Only a few days," Dex said. "But those days have changed me forever."

Even as he spoke, there was a mess of noise coming from down the street, headed for the prison. First came Travin, leading the horses at a trot. Behind him were the crossbow soldiers, followed by two more soldiers on horseback. Tied to the horses, stumbling along, were

163

two dirty and bloody prisoners. Four more soldiers brought up the rear. The entire entourage pulled up at the prison, and Travin went inside. The two prisoners slumped to the ground, their chests heaving. Travin's second-in-command untied them and put chains on their wrists. They were too tired to protest.

Dex and Charla were close enough to recognize them. Charla did not move. Not a muscle. She sat, perfectly still, as the two prisoners were cuffed, forced to their feet, and dragged through the prison door. The soldiers and Travin then remounted and road off, in the direction of Longs Castle. Only after they were out of sight did Charla move. She turned to Dex and threw a heavy money bag at him, which clinked when he caught it.

"Give me your horse," she said to Dex. A little awkwardly, she took the reins and mounted the horse.

"Rolink and I will ride this night to meet you at the smithy," Dex said. She nodded, her jaw grinding, and rode off.

Fifty-six.

The moon was waxing, a half-circle lighting the night sky. The street outside the prison was quiet, at this late hour. Dex was shivering, but thankful for the cold: it was keeping him awake. He hadn't realized how boring it was to wait in the shadows for hours.

Finally Dex saw him, shuffling quietly down the street, his large frame impossible to mistake, the robes of the Order hanging loosely from his tall shoulders. Dex waited until Justice had passed, and then quietly walked up behind him, and put his hand on his shoulder. Justice jumped in fright, and let out a small yelp.

Dex grinned, and put his finger to his lips. "You are going to rescue Dexter Maxwell," Dex whispered.

Justice looked at him in disbelief. "I recognize you," he said. "You are down in the prison. The future bakes in the sun like new adobe."

"Shh," Dex said. "You still need to help me escape. I will take care of the front door distraction. You should go around the back to the kitchen window. Dexter is wounded and tired, and will need help crawling out."

Justice continued to stare at him. "You are in two places at the same time."

"That's right."

Justice looked at him strangely, then nodded. "A curved time-like paradox. What are you plotting, for the prison?" Justice asked.

"I'm going to save a goat-herder from his hanging," Dex said.

Justice just looked at him, before heading for the back alley.

"Justice, wait," Dex hissed, almost forgetting. He took the wrapped bundle from his shoulder, and gave it to the monk. "Be sure Dexter gets this." Then Dex turned and made his way back to the prison.

Dex pulled a small container of liquor from his pocket, and swished some around his mouth, before spitting it out. He put a little on his clothes for effect. He wanted badly to drink it all, but he had a long night in front of him. And a less familiar sword sheathed at his belt.

It was the closest to Judas he could find among the arsenal at the Earth-side station. It had less length than Judas. A different weight. Dex had taken enough swings to understand how to fight with it, but he was nervous, rushing into inevitable combat without Judas. But it was the only way to get Judas to his former self. And then Dex had to get it back from Mebda.

He finally reached the door of the prison, took a deep breath, and then staggered through, liquor in hand.

"Izzziss where I sign up fer th' infrantry?" Dex slurred, leaning against the doorframe. He looked around as drunkenly as he could, and found what he was looking for: a man at the front table, quietly enjoying a meal, and two guards at the back doorway. Past that, Dex could see the archway through which his other self would limp in a few moments.

The man at the table spoke, but did not stand. "This is the prison, man," he said. "We can throw you in here, but that won't get you in the infantry." The two guards snickered.

"A prison?" Dex said, staggering into the middle of the room, toward the seated man. He was looking for keys. "No, I don't wanna go to prison. I wanna join the King." He was at the table. He saw the keys, on the man's belt. "I'm with joining. Look, I brought m'own sword." Dex fumbled with the scabbard on his belt, awkwardly removing the short sword and swinging it dangerously close to the man, who jumped back, keys jingling, knocking over his chair. Dex leaned on the sword against the wall.

The two guards were already drawing their swords. The key holder held them back with his hand. "Carrying a sword will get you thrown in the stocks, you fool. Now turn over that weapon to me."

Dex waved the sword around, still stumbling. "But I'm to be a guard to the King. I'll need this sword."

One of the guards tried to disarm him with a quick swing of his sword. Keeping up his drunken act, Dex pretended to block the attack by accident, allowing it to knock him back. Two more guards had appeared and were slowly surrounding him.

"Izzziss some kind of test?" Dex said to his attacker, who laughed.

"Yes," he said. "We're testing you out for his highness's royal guard."

Dex made a show of raising his sword. "Then let the test... begin," he said, stumbling. The guard took a quick slice at Dex's right arm. Dex managed to knock the guard's sword out of his hands. The key holder laughed.

"What's the matter, Ketch," he said. "Can't disarm a drunk?"

The guard shot the key holder a look, and fumbled for his sword.

"What the hell?" yelled another guard.

All four guards were now in position, surrounding Dex in a three-quarter circle, with the key holder at Dex's back. Dex was still staggering about but in actual fact the moment was in high jack, held even tighter by the unspooling, shifting shapes.

"Jaggard," the key holder said. "Lock the door." The guard dropped a bar across the front door. "I don't know who you are," the key holder said, reaching for his own sword behind the table. "But you are a dead man now. No one attacks *my* prison."

Dex took a deep breath, and exhaled. The door was locked. The one called Ketch had risen from the floor and retrieved his sword. He was surrounded by five armed men.

Dex feinted toward Ketch, who jumped back a little, and Dex turned and met swords with the key holder. He swung twice, feeling a sword coming at him from his back, then spun quickly, putting the short sword into the key master's fat hip. The man gasped, dropping his sword. Dex brought his sword around, cutting the belt off as it exited the man at the hip. Dex reached down with his left hand and grasped the keys and pulled as he continued his spin around to the key holder's right side. He was left standing with the keys in his left hand and the short sword in his right. The key holder crumpled to the floor, holding his bleeding hip.

Ketch took another swing at Dex, over the slumping body of the key holder. Dex threw a quick defensive blow at the blade, catching the full weight, feeling the man's strength pressing down. The flyer chose the direction, and Dex pushed his blade and that of the attackers to one side. Dex saw shadows moving past, toward the kitchen, behind his attackers. Dex let out a roar and attacked, but not in a way to end the conflict. With the moment jacked, he replayed his escape as it was occurring at the back of the prison. He needed to give the monks a few more minutes.

Ketch and Jaggard were now looking nervously behind Dex, at the one and only door that led out of the prison. Dex kept himself squarely in front of the exit as he took a swing at the man on his left, then swung around and clashed swords with the one on his right. Ketch felt emboldened by the opening Dex had created and lunged forward, swinging quickly. Dex had seen it coming. He turned sideways and dropped his sword down his back to stop the blade from biting into him. Before the man could recover, Dex brought his sword around and put the hilt into the man's temple. Ketch crumpled to the floor and didn't move.

Dex unspooled the patterns around him, and they grabbed and held his attackers in place. The moment was crawling, and Dex could feel the time of his escape had come already. He would be through the window, with Freedom behind him. Dex spun again and brought his blade efficiently, but lightly, down on the leg of Jaggard, who cried in pain. Dex dropped the final two guards in a quick series of blows. These were not soldiers. They were barely even trained.

The whole thing took less than two minutes. Dex still had the keys in his hands. He stood and walked over to the key holder, who was gasping for breath on the floor, trying to crawl to safety. Dex rolled him over on his back.

"You will not die of your wounds," Dex whispered. "But I will kill you," he let this sink in, "unless you tell me where the goatherder has been locked up."

The man's eyes looked toward the back of the prison. "Second story down. Third door."

Dex jangled the keys in front of him. "Which keys open the doors?"

The man's shaking hands picked out two keys. "This one... first. Then...." he trailed off.

Dex turned to the groaning men. There were still three who could stand.

"Grab your friends here, and carry them in front of me," he ordered. The men quickly moved, dragging their unconscious colleague and the key-holder. It took longer than he wanted, but Dex didn't intend to kill these men.

Outside of Rolink's prison cell, a guard was laid out asleep. Freedom's doing, Dex realized. He put the key in the third door, and pulled it open.

"Rolink," Dex said.

"Who... who's there?" Rolink rasped.

"It's Dexter Maxwell," Dex said. He turned to the guards. "Everyone in the cell. Now."

The men slowly shuffled into the small cell. Dex followed them in, his eyes adjusting to the dark, and he saw Rolink trying to stand next to the cot. The sight of him made Dex's heart leap.

"Come, let me help you up." Dex put his arm under Rolink's shoulder, and helped him from the room, locking the guards in.

"How did you..." Rolink tried.

"Not now," Dex said. "We must hurry."

He gingerly helped Rolink up the stairs, and toward the front of the prison. Rolink glanced into the main guardroom, seeing swords strewn on the floors, blood, and the table overturned, and gave him another look. Dex nodded as if to say, *yes, that was me.* Once outside, Dex led them to the stable and his two horses. They were already saddled, with supplies in the saddle bags. Before Rolink could protest, Dex pulled a shot of nano-rebuilder from his pack, popped the top, and injected it into Rolink's thigh. Rolink grimaced and gave Dex an angry look.

Dex found a skin of water and gave it to Rolink. "Drink," he said. "Then wash up. We need to look somewhat respectable if we're going to clear the north gate."

GRAVITON, WEST OF LONGSTOWN.
SEPTEMBER 29. DAY 15.

Fifty-seven.

With Rolink's current condition, the ride to the smithy at Graviton turned out to be closer to a full day. After they had made it clear of Longstown, they had ridden all night and well into the next day. When the sun hit its low autumn apex, they finally stopped and Rolink slept. Dex injected another dose of the rebuilder against Rolink's protestations.

They had taken a long way around, to put out of Longstown to the north, in case they were tracked after the escape. Then they had headed into the mountains, due west, at a gallop.

It was near dusk when they saw the small, squat building, set back against the steep north side of the valley. Rolink spurred his horse into a trot. Dex followed suit, and in minutes they were upon the place.

Rolink gave one of his goatherder whistles, one that Dex remembered him using to call Mebda when they had been separated by a mass of goats. They waited, but no one came forward. They dismounted, tied their reins to a tree, and went inside.

It was empty, but the place looked destroyed. A small table was on its side in a corner, and a chair smashed. Rolink flew into a frenzy. "Mebda! Charla!" he yelled.

Dex went over to survey the damage, trying to reconstruct what he saw. In the failing light of the dusk, he saw something that he recognized under a demolished chair. A long set of black straps. Dex pulled them out.

"Mebda was here," Dex said, holding up the black scabbard that had housed the Judas Sword.

Rolink's eyes bulged from his head. "What has happened?" he said, looking around. "Dear God, what has happened to my family?"

"We do not know," Dex said. "Nor do we know when."

They looked at each other, and the room, for a moment.

"Would Medba have come up the valley, the same as us?" Dex

asked.

Rolink shook his head. "From where we were when we were arrested, he would have come over the south ridge. There is an animal trail we use if we come from the south."

"Why don't you go take a look up there, while the sun still shines on the ridge," Dex said. "I'll stay here and keep watch."

Rolink nodded, and set off at a run. Dex watched as he disappeared into the pine trees.

Fifty-eight.

The sun had set, and Dex had found feed and water for the horses by the time Rolink returned.

"Horse tracks," Rolink said. "All along the ridge. They must have been able to track Mebda from the gorge."

Dex nodded. "The struggle was in the residence," he said. "There was a broken chair. I don't think Mebda has enough weight to break a chair. But I met someone in Longstown who does."

"Charla," Rolink said. "She tried to defend Mebda."

"She drew the Judas from its hilt," Dex said. "But there is no blood. I could find no blood."

"They have taken them back to Longstown," Rolink said. "We must go back."

"We do not know this," Dex said. "And we are now renegades. We've attacked the nephew of the King, been charged with treason, injured four guards, escaped from prison," Dex took a breath, "and taken payment on goats we don't have anymore."

Rolink watched Dex warily before he spoke. "State your intent, oldkeeper."

"Let's not jump before we know what we jump into," Dex said. "So far, it seems that Travin's men were able to track Mebda to this location. We know Mebda was here because my scabbard is here. We can assume that Charla was here by the damage done. But, where are Travin's men now? Where is Mebda now? And Charla? Let's consider where they could be."

"Longstown," Rolink said again. "Captive to that swine Mastiff and his half-breed relatives."

"Where else?"

Rolink closed his eyes. "They could be at the ranch."

"Where else?"

"I do not think they would be any other place."

"Good," Dex said, standing. "Because there are only two of us. I do not know where your ranch is, but I do know where Longstown is. So, you go to the ranch. Discreetly, of course. Find out if anyone is there, or has been there. I will go to Longstown. Make inquiries. Find out if your family has been imprisoned."

"How will you get into Longstown?" Rolink asked.

"I think I still can use my reputation as an oldkeeper, if I enter from the south."

"There is a Brodius church not far outside from the south gate."

Dex nodded. "I know the one," he said. "Our Lady of Bleeding Redemption."

"I will meet you there, in two days," Rolink said, already heading for the door.

"Wait," Dex said. He went to his pack, and pulled out a nano-rebuilder shot. "Take this."

This time, Rolink did not protest.

They both rode by night, not certain who they might run into. Rolink had fetched himself a sword from a secret armory dug into the ground behind the smithy, and was headed north. Dex was headed east, back the way he had come. Dex watched Rolink fade into the dark. He closed his eyes, feeling the pressure of the halo, the flyer, the rope banging against the inside of his eyelids. He pushed his mind out, feeling the time, remembering where he was, the first time around. Healing, as Rolink was now, only slowly without the meds. Wandering the monastery. Finding the first altar room.

Thoughts of the monastery brought images of Freedom to the front of Dex's mind, and his stomach lurched. She was still alive, right now.

Why do I not rush to save her? But he knew why. It made him sick, but he knew why. With the weight of his decision pressing on his chest, he pushed his horse into a careful trot, heading back to Longstown.

Fifty-nine.

Dex stared at the bright, staring eye of the full moon. Or at least full enough that you could see a man's face clearly, even in the dead of night. For Dex, this was not a good thing. He tried to sink deeper into the cowl of his cloak. A few clouds lingered across the sky, their edges illuminated by the cold moonlight. Dex paced again, and his horse stamped its feet against the cold, letting out a snort.

"I know, I want to get moving, too," Dex said quietly, patting the mare's nose.

The south gate stood in the moonlight a quarter mile to his north. He had hitched his horse to a hangman's tree, and had been making the same sort of praying motions as he had seen others making at the feet of other dead folk hung on the other trees. He felt uncomfortable, and not just because his possible fate hung above him, smelling and attracting all sorts of monstrously sized flies. He was also uneasy about the southern passage into Longstown. Much hinged on his entering that gate for the third time in a week, without attracting the attention of the authorities. Dex went over his plan again. And then again.

A party of farmers, their carts full of goods to be sold at first light, ambled past Dex. As they passed, a lone rider at their tail broke away and rode up to Dex. He pulled his hood away: Rolink. He dismounted.

"I received your message at the church," Rolink hissed. "I am not sure what could come of being this close to the gate and its guards."

"You found nothing at the ranch," Dex said.

"Nothing," Rolink confirmed. "And what of your inquiries in Longstown?"

Dex took a deep breath. He was still unprepared for this. "I have found your wife and child."

"You have?" Rolink said. "They are here? In Longstown? In custody?"

"No," Dex said. "They are not in Longstown."

"Where are they?" Rolink said.

Dex pointed across the street. In the bright moonlight, Rolink saw the two corpses, one adult and one child, hanging from the same tree. He made a groaning noise that Dex would never forget in all his days. He dropped the reins and stumbled across the road. Rolink looked up at them, and then collapsed, sobbing.

Dex picked up the reins of Rolink's spooked horse, but did not go to the man. He stayed right where he was. And then, finally, he cried, too. He cried, thinking of Mebda's innocent smile. Dancing and spinning in the first snow of the season. Dex tried to blink the tears away, but he couldn't. They streamed down his face, blurring the bright eye of the moon as it stared down impassively.

Sixty.

Dex walked the horses over, and put his hand on Rolink's shoulder. The broken man looked up, his eyes red, a wild look on his face.

"We cannot stay here," Dex said. "There are eyes on us."

Rolink nodded mutely, but did not stand until Dex put a hand under his armpit and raised him. They both mounted their horses, and Dex led them south away from Longstown. They road in the moonlight for over an hour before Rolink pulled on his reins, and his horse stopped.

"I have nothing," Rolink said. "And I am nothing. This dog Travin has taken everything I am."

Dex waited, but kept quiet.

"I now want only one thing," Rolink said. He turned his eyes northward, toward Longstown. "I will kill Travin, nephew of Mastiff," he said. He looked back at Dex. "This is farewell. I do not know who you are or where you are headed, but I wish you more peace ahead then you have had behind."

"I am coming with you," Dex said.

"That is not wise," Rolink said. "I go to my doom, oldkeeper."

"I am not an oldkeeper," Dex said. "I'll tell you what I am, though: a weapon. I am an arrow and I am launched. Now, you are an arrow, and the bow is taut. I think that our trajectories will take us

174

to the same target." Dex paused. "You seek Travin. I need my sword, and I need it to be at King Mastiff's neck."

Rolink considered this. "You are an assassin? Sent to kill the King?"

"I am a warrior that misses his blade," Dex said. He nodded back toward Longstown. "The crimes listed at your family's feet include treason, and illegal ownership of a blade. My blade."

Rolink looked at him warily. "You are a reader?"

"I am a lot of things," Dex said. "One of them is your friend. And we must lay siege to Longs Castle together. It will take both of us."

"I do not know if that is all it will take," Rolink said.

"What do you think I've been doing for the last two days?" Dex asked. "Picking my ass? I have a plan."

Rolink looked at Dex, his piercing gaze cutting through the moonlight. "Tell me your plan, Dexter Maxwell."

"I will, but can we talk and ride at the same time? We need to get back to the church."

"Why the church? Shouldn't we be headed to the castle?"

"I need to visit the chamber above the church. There are… preparations to be made there."

"You must pray first, oldkeeper?"

Dex nodded. "You could call it that."

Rolink stared up toward Longstown for a minute more. Finally he spoke. "Tell me again why I am trusting you, Dexter Maxwell."

Dex gave a tired smile in the moonlight. "You don't know me that well yet," He said. "But if there's one thing I'm good at, it's fighting the authorities."

Sixty-one.

Dex took stock of the situation through ragged breaths. The sun was just rising over the plains of the east, putting that orange of morning on everything through the leaded windows of the castle tower. The soft glow was barely glinting off Dex's short sword, held, with an ever-so-subtle quiver, at the neck of one Travin Cutter, nephew to the great and terrible King Mastiff.

Travin, being dull but not completely daft, stood perfectly still and stared only at the bloodied blade that rested against his Adam's apple. He was trying hard not to let his deep, pained breathing push his neck any closer than necessary to the blade. He chose this moment to drop his saber to the floor with a clatter.

King Mastiff, for his part, was suffering the indignity of being in a one-piece sleeping tunic, buttoned under his crotch, and wearing hastily thrown on boots that had not been properly secured with lace. He had not yet dropped his own blade, and was apparently weighing up the worth of his nephew against the joy of slaughtering these two invaders.

The other invader, Rolink, was on one knee, bleeding at an alarming rate from his many cuts. His sword had been knocked wickedly from his hand, and he stared at Travin Cutter with a merciless rage that did not go unnoticed by everyone else in the room.

Surrounding Rolink in a semi-circle were the four remaining Royal Guards, long sabers all pointed more or less directly at his neck and face region. They, too, were breathing hard, lending to the increasingly stuffy air in the room. Two of their colleagues lay in a bloody slump next to Dex.

The room was not large by kingly standards. It is where Mastiff took his sleep, now that his wife had passed, because it did not remind him of that demonic witch, and because it was closer to his horses, his dogs, and the dining hall than the majestic upper residence of the castle. It also afforded Mastiff a better morning sun, and Mastiff had always been a morning person. The door to his sleeping chamber was one of thick oak, built to keep out both invaders and the cold. Right now, it was barred from the inside by a large armoire that had been toppled in front of it by Rolink only moments ago. On the other side of the door, there was more than a little clamoring to get in by what everyone inside the room assumed were dozens more Royal Guards, whipped to a fever pitch by the possibility of two assassins in the sleeping quarters of King Mastiff.

After the clatter of Travin's sword falling to the floor, there had been a moment of dogged silence. Dex looked to King Mastiff. He had seen him before, briefly, at the monastery when Mastiff had attacked. Then, he had been in full battle regalia, and in firm command of the situation. Here, his hair was tussled from sleep, and he was in pajamas.

"Good plan, oldkeeper," Rolink said, breaking the silence. The guards inched their swords closer to him. "End this!"

"You overestimate the worth of my nephew's life," Mastiff said to Dex, narrowing his eyes.

Dex glanced to the King, then back to Travin. "Either your men remove their swords from my friend's face, or I open this pig's neck and take a swing at you," Dex said evenly. "I'm guessing I'll get to you before they do."

This got the guards' attention, and one of them made a move to stand between Dex and Mastiff. Dex pushed his sword into Travin's neck, drawing blood. Travin gasped, and Mastiff threw his hand up.

"Lower your swords," he said to his men. "You have called my bluff, assassin. What is it you seek?"

"This hole you call family strung up a woman and child south of town," Dex said, his eyes on Travin. "Charges of treason and weapon ownership. I'm looking for the weapon."

"Travin," Mastiff said. "Do you know of what he speaks?"

"Yes, uncle," Travin said, minding the blade. "It is a toy sword. I liberated it from the treasonous wench only two days—ow!"

Dex had slapped Travin in the nose with the flat side of his sword. Without stopping, he took one long step and brought his sword around until it stopped, inches short of Mastiff's neck. The move was so fast the guards did not react until Dex was already at the

King. Dex wagged his left finger at Travin. "Speak with respect for the dead," he said, putting the blade at Mastiff's cheek. Mastiff seethed, his eyes popping.

Rolink rose slowly. The guards kept their swords low, but the tension remained in their bodies. The banging on the door was getting louder and more focused.

"I require this sword," Dex said to Mastiff. "My colleague here seeks satisfaction for the unjust hanging of his wife and son." Dex paused. His stomach tightened. The moment had finally come. He offered a silent apology to Rolink, then continued. "But those are idle concerns. King Mastiff, I am here this morning to save your kingdom."

"What?" Mastiff, Travin, and Rolink asked simultaneously.

Sixty-two.

"I have appeared as an assassin at your bed," Dex said. "And I could in fact kill every man in this room before you could spit."

"You are not so skilled," Travin said. "I had you on your knees in the moun—"

Before Travin could finish his sentence, Dex had spun, slapped the flat side of his blade against Travin's face, knocking him to the ground, and was then back to Mastiff before anyone else could come to attention.

"You will keep your mouth shut," Dex said, and turned back to the King. "You are running out of time, Mastiff. An army is organizing to the south. They are infiltrating Longstown. They will use the Brodius Monastery to the north as a station."

"That is nonsense," Mastiff said. "Who would dare attack me? The Undas are weak with their succession crisis, and fight among themselves. The Telonians are too busy marrying their own sisters. And to the south lies only the pontiff and his foofers."

"Nine months ago, Travin returned from a secret scouting expedition to the southwest mountains. Why did you send him?"

At this, Travin came alive. "How could you have known of that trip?"

Mastiff considered it. "We had heard stories."

"And Travin told you that a wandering nomad group from the plains had set up a cult altar to some pagan god. They were dressed strangely, but Travin has exterminated them and sent them running back to the plains."

The banging on the door had turned into a rhythmic thud as a battering device had been employed. The sound of wood splintering syncopated the conversation.

Mastiff now looked only at Travin. "How does the assassin know this?"

"I... I do not know, uncle," he stuttered. He was looking wildly back and forth between Dex and Rolink.

"I know this because I was there," Dex said. He hand grew tired with holding the sword. "I saw his scouting party. I saw what they scouted." Dex looked again at Travin. "He met with a single man, dressed curiously in black and red. This man handed Travin a bag of gold and a very nice new saber. Travin then said, 'Consider these mountains clear,' and left. His scouting team then spent the rest of the week at a whorehouse in Sunsertown."

"Uncle, that is a lie," Travin started.

"Shut up, pig," Dex said. "Here are my conditions. I will spare you and your nephew this morning. But you will tell those at the door that Travin has been grievously injured. Then you will lock Travin and me in the same prison, hidden from all prying eyes. You will send your most trustworthy scout with my friend here to a location I will provide, so that you can hear of the coming invasion from your own sources. When the scout returns, if what I say is true, you will declare Travin dead, his assassins caught, and an investigation underway. Then you and I, Mastiff, will plot your attack on the invaders."

"Uncle, this is madness," Travin said. "I checked the region. The pagans were ejected!"

The armoire was shaking visibly. Mastiff was looking at Dex. "And if my scouts find no army?"

"Then I am in prison, ready to be hanged," Dex said. "But Rolink walks free."

"I do not want freedom!" Rolink yelled. "I want Travin dead! Dexter, what are you doing?"

"I am sorry," Dex said. "That will have to wait."

179

Mastiff took one more look at Travin. Dex lowered his sword from the king's neck. Immediately, Mastiff yelled at his guards. "Move the damn dresser! Tell those fools to desist breaking down my favorite door!"

Mastiff kept his eye on Dexter. "You have put yourself in an impossible situation. I can kill you whenever I want."

"You are a man of your word," Dex said.

"I am a man who runs a kingdom," Mastiff said. "That's not the same thing."

"Then for your kingdom, delay killing us for a few days. See if I am telling the truth. I am not the gravest danger you face."

The door was finally opened and guards poured in. Rolink was knocked to the floor. Dex did not resist as he was thrown to the ground by a guard who put his knee into his back. Mastiff put his boot on Dex's face and leaned down into his ear. "You should have killed me when you had the chance, boy," Mastiff growled.

"Trust your instincts, King!" Dex yelled. "I have no reason to lie!"

Mastiff pushed his boot down, grinding Dex's ear into the stone floor. Then Mastiff moved his foot and let loose a loud yell. The room fell quiet, except for Rolink's tears of grief and anger.

"Listen carefully," Mastiff said, as he picked up Dex's sword. "The assassins have been apprehended. Travin has sustained a grave wound. Get a doctor, and wrist irons. We will execute these assassins after their interrogation." Mastiff turned to Dex. "If my men find nothing, you will be tortured and hung from a tree like the goatherder's family."

Dex relaxed into the hands of the guards on his back. "I need you to go to north and get a monk named Justice for me, too."

Sixty-three.

Dex was more comfortable than he had been in a month. He was warm, being decently fed, and had a real bed. The iron cuffs on his wrists chaffed, and he was getting a nasty itch, but these were minor details. Even the obligatory beating that Mastiff's men had given him after leaving the king's room had resulted in only a temporary set of bruises.

Travin, on the other hand, did not stop complaining. For someone who was dead, he was making quite the racket in the cell next to Dex. At first, it was all death threats thrown at Dex. He had clearly spent too long coming up with interesting ways to kill a man, and now he had been given an audience and a reason. But, by the end of their first day of imprisonment, Travin's monologue turned to mystification over how Dex had found out about his dealings with 'the cult,' as he called it, operating in the southern mountains. Dex said nothing, he was content just eating his meals, pissing in the provided pot, and sleeping.

Day two was Travin complaining about the prison. About the bed, the food, the space, the light, the cold, the guards, and Dex. Sometimes he would mix it up a bit, and focus on the light, the food, the bed, and the cold. Then he would start at the beginning and do it all again.

So it was with great relief that Dex welcomed the robed visitor to his cell, late on the second evening of his captivity. The visitor shuffled into the cell, and closed the door. The guard threw the lock behind him.

"This is an interesting turn of events," Justice said.

"I have murdered Travin Cutter," Dex said.

"From the sound of things," Justice said, "you did not do a very good job."

Dex grinned. "It is good to see you, Justice."

"While I am happy to see you, I am mystified," Justice said.

181

"How long have you held this shift? You have been down here for nearly two days, to hear of it."

Dex shook his head. "Something happened, Justice," he said. "Something I did not learn from the altar rooms. I... modified the knife. I cut the rope to my anchor and reworked the code. I followed an off-lander through his breach."

Justice gave a low whistle. "That's impossible. There is no way to maintain the halo. You would be obliterated."

"I didn't need to maintain the halo. I came through the off-lander breach one way. I came through permanently."

"But that's impossible. This is a practice going back over five hundred years. You simply cannot permanently shift."

Dex tapped his chest. "I am here. It happened. I have been here for sixteen days. I am not going back."

"But how? What did you do?"

"I cannot remember. It happened so fast. I was so angry..." Dex looked at Justice. "Much has happened. Or, I should say, much is about to happen. I know the future."

Justice stared through the small barred window, then back to Dex. "I daresay that is as much a curse as a blessing."

"Yes. But I have had time to think about your time-like curve, and its paradox. The strange permanent destiny I have created. Everything that I do now, it has already been done. Every choice I make, I have already made it."

"Does that make the choosing less important?" Justice asked.

"Far from it. I already know the outcome of my actions, but I must still carry them out. I am what makes the future possible. I am baking the adobe bricks."

"Indeed," Justice said, sitting down finally on the cot.

"Your coming here," Dex said. "I did that. I need you with me. I need you safe."

"What about Freedom?" Justice asked. "Is Freedom safe?"

"No."

They were quiet for some time. Dex spoke finally. "If I had come back in time and saved her, she would have been saved. But I did not come back and save her. I will watch her die, in eleven days' time."

Dex felt the guilt threatening to overwhelm him. Justice put his hand on Dex's shoulder. "Tell me what you are doing, here in your past. Tell me what keeps you from saving Freedom."

Dex took a deep breath. "I'm convincing Mastiff to attack the off-lander forces. I will succeed. Then Mastiff will save me from the off-landers. If I had changed that outcome, I would be dead already. It was…" Dex choked up, his eyes tearing up. "It was Freedom or me."

"You have made the right choice," Justice said. "Freedom knew the risks, and she was at peace with God. She made her peace long before she met you. She died for what she believed in."

"Yes," Dex said. "I will not let it be in vain."

"But to throw our lot in with Mastiff is a dangerous ploy," Justice said. "He has done nothing but rain destruction on the Order of Brodius since he took the crown."

"He is a pawn in the off-landers' plans," Dex said. "Do you still have the game called chess?"

Justice nodded. "I know the game. Do you play?"

Dex smiled. "Not even a little. But I remember the rules and pieces. And when you walk a pawn all the way across the board…"

Justice nodded. "You reclaim the queen."

"That's the metaphor. Right now, what Mastiff needs and what we need is the same. I have already seen it. So we move him across the board."

"Does that make him the queen, or just your pawn?" Justice asked.

"Only Brody knows," Dex said.

"You are a remarkable man," Justice said. "When I saw you absorb the altar room patterns so quickly, I thought you might be different. But I could not have predicted this."

"Yeah, well, I'm just full of surprises," Dex said. "One more thing. I need you to do something. I need you to find Lynia. She has been trying to decode a message in the past. I had some time. Before all this siege-the-castle. I did some shifting. Research on Mastiff and Travin. I also spoke with Lynia, but I did not know everything that would happen. But I need you to go get her. Bring her to Longstown. After Freedom is… broken, Lynia is no longer safe in the past. She must not go back to her hiding place."

Justice nodded. "I can bring her here. It will take a few days; she

183

does not stay in the same place long."

Dex gestured around the cell. "I'm not going anywhere."

Sixty-four.

Dex knew exactly who was coming to visit him by the change in tone and type of complaining coming from the adjacent cell.

"Uncle!" Travin yelled. "Uncle, it has been three days! *Three days*! I beseech you; let me free of this cell."

"Quiet," growled a voice. "Or I will make your death permanent."

Dex heard his lock being thrown, and he stood. In walked two guards, who by their stance and size alone filled the entire width of the cell. Dex recognized them from the king's sleeping quarters. Behind them, Mastiff entered.

"You'll excuse me if I remain back here," Mastiff said.

"I have recently held a sharp piece of metal at your neck," Dex said. "I understand."

"Yes, well," Mastiff said. "My scout and the goatherder have returned. My scout confirms the facility that you described. They found the entire hillside crawling with bumbling fools carrying strange weapons and grumbling non-stop."

"They are not used to your terrain," Dex said. "Or any terrain, for that matter."

"As you predicted, they are sending three at a time, by horse, dressed as men of the cloth, north and east toward my kingdom."

"They are converging on the Brodius Monastery."

"We will confirm that tomorrow," Mastiff said. "I have announced the death of my nephew. And I've set about looking like a sentimental fool, prattling on and on and sending people on mad missions."

Dex nodded. "You're good at this."

Mastiff growled. "Let this army think I am otherwise occupied. Then I will crush them before they see it coming."

"Confirm first, with your own eyes, that this army is accumulating at the monastery. Then let's talk strategy."

Mastiff's eyes narrowed. "So far, assassin, your words have been true. But I will make my own war plans. I am not king of this land for my good looks."

"I do not doubt your prowess on the field," Dex said. "But make no mistake; I will prove to be the key to your success at the monastery."

"Perhaps," Mastiff said. "Or perhaps I will leave you to die in this prison." He turned to go.

Dex spoke to his back. "If you could get that nephew of yours to shut up, that would be all I ask."

Mastiff said nothing, and knocked on the door. The guard opened the cell door, and Mastiff and his two guards left. As the door was being closed, Dex heard Mastiff growl, "Gag Travin, except when he must eat."

Sixty-five.

Dex lay on the cot, eyes closed, but awake. He had been using the idle time in prison to try and reconstruct what had happened when he had followed Tano through the breach. He was going over the shapes in his mind, trying to see the modified knife again. Seeing if he could do it, again.

Since parting with Thelo, Dex had shifted four times. He had gone back to find Mal, and he had done his research on both Travin and the fortifications of Longs Castle. Each time, when he had unspooled the flyer and deployed the knife, he could feel the absence of his new code, his new geometries; but he could not fill in the blanks. He could not rewrite them.

He opened his eyes as Rolink stepped into the cell, alone. The door closed quickly behind him, and the guard relocked it. Dex sat up, and Rolink found the lone stool near the door. It was the first time they had seen each other since the siege on Mastiff's sleeping quarters.

Neither of them spoke for a minute. Rolink was staring through Dex with that gaze that still made Dex uncomfortable.

"You betrayed me," Rolink said.

"Yes," Dex said. He couldn't see any reason to elaborate.

Rolink nodded. "You needed my help to get you close to Mastiff. That I understand, now. I do not understand why you sent me with the scout."

"I spoke to you, when we first met in the mountains," Dex said. "I mentioned a coming invasion. I sent you so you could see it. So you would understand why I did what I did. I wanted you to know why Travin still lives."

Rolink cocked his head. "I saw them. It was just as you described. And I believe Mastiff will find the monastery to be as you said it would be."

Dex said nothing.

Rolink went on. "You know much of this army and its ways. You seem to know their strategies and their numbers. Are you one of them?"

"I am more like them than I am like you," Dex said. "I come from their world. But I am here, in this prison cell with you, because I would like to keep you more like you. I will not have this army succeed. I will not have them come down here and destroy your world, your people, your customs, and your ways.

"The coming battle, between Mastiff and the invaders, it is a small skirmish," Dex said. "There is a larger war at hand, and larger battles coming. And I am fighting on your side. But your side includes Mastiff, now. It includes Travin. These enemies of yours, they are nothing compared with the enemies that now descend upon Cawlria. So, I used you. I used you so that we can win this battle. And so I can go and fight the next one."

Rolink said nothing, just stared through Dex again.

Dex looked down. "I don't expect you to forgive me. You told me once, never lie to you again. And I did. Thank you for helping me to get inside Longs Castle. I wish I could save your wife and son. But I can't."

Rolink's eyes misted. "You are changed, since we herded goats," Rolink said. "I can see it in your eyes. You see your own future now. Before, you could only see your past." Rolink gave a tired smile. "You are no oldkeeper," he said. "But you speak the truth. And I have nothing. I am nothing. Except you. I have your war. You must give this to me."

Dex looked at him strangely. "You can have my war. It is all yours, my friend."

Rolink nodded gravely. "They will put me in the cell next to yours. I will wait for you to determine our fate."

"Seriously, Rolink, you don't need to do that."

"I have nothing. I—"

"You are nothing," Dex said impatiently. "Right. Got that part. Fine. The prison food isn't that bad, anyway."

Rolink knocked on the door, and the guard came to open it. He turned to Dex one more time. "Good to see you, Dexter Maxwell."

Dex nodded. "I am glad you will be with me, Rolink the goat-herder."

"I think I will be Rolink the blacksmith, again," Rolink said. "I have no goats."

Sixty-six.

The wind whipped down from the western slopes and bled through Dex's coat. He could not help but shiver. He clasped his hands together and blew on them again, staring up into the night sky. More covert operations, he thought. More secret meetings at night. He and Rolink were at the bottom of a natural amphitheater. The rock slope had been carved into seats, many years before, and then been overgrown.

Rolink was checking on their horses, when they both heard the pounding of hooves coming from the lone trail that led to this place. Two horses trotted into view, and the two hooded riders dismounted, tying their exhausted horses next to Rolink. The horses bent to drink from the creek that ran by.

The first traveler pushed his hood back. It was Justice.

"You received my message," Justice said.

"Yes," Dex said. "This is a good place to meet. I would not have found it without your detailed instructions."

The other traveler pulled her hood down.

"Hey, Dex," Mal said with an exhausted grin.

Dex gave Mal a long, tight hug. "What took you so long?"

Mal smiled. "I had to say goodbye to someone."

Dex smiled back. "Right. Lynia, this is Rolink. Rolink, Lynia. Justice, I think you met Rolink at Longstown prison, already."

Justice smiled and shook Rolink's hand. "It is good to see you alive," Justice said. "I was giving you last rites last time we spoke."

"I barely remember that, Brother Justice," Rolink said. "I was not well."

"You look in good health now," Justice said.

"King Mastiff's dungeon is of a different standard altogether," Rolink said.

"The king should be joining us shortly," Dex said. He turned to Mal. "Did you figure out the message from Logos?"

Mal nodded soberly. "Terran spent ten years working out the

chemistry, but we finally got it. Ingenious, really. I can't believe Terran was able to do it so quickly."

"Ten years is not quick," Dex said.

"It is when you are starting from scratch," Mal said. "There were two separate and distinct messages. The first was a long series of mathematical equations, along with a series of proofs. A lot of time-travel chroneometry. Looked to be just huge number crunching gobbledygook to me. And then, one date: April 29, 2656. Do you know that date, Dex?"

"Yes," Dex said, thinking. "It's the first possible point of shifting. It's the date of the Great Schism. The date that Earth fell behind by twenty-three years."

"21.26 years, to be exact. And Earth didn't *fall* behind," Mal said. "It was *pushed* behind. When you were on Venus, did anyone tell you about the Great Harvest?"

"Never heard of it," Dex said.

"Wait a minute," Rolink said. "Did you just ask him about when he was on Venus? What is Venus?"

"Second planet from the sun," Justice said.

"I'll catch you up later, Rolink," Dex said, keeping his eyes on Mal. "Tell me about this Harvest."

"You know the Transloop?" Mal asked.

Dex nodded.

"Well, the off-landers were able to use it to roll back time for planet Earth."

"Come again?" Dex said.

"They literally turned back time. But just for Earth. No other heavenly body in the galaxy was affected."

Dex shook his head in disbelief. "Why would they want to do that?"

"To wage a secret war," Justice said, beginning to understand. "The twenty-three years of the Great Schism gave them enough time to harvest Earth, and then erase the evidence."

Mal nodded. "21.26 years. They came down here and took everything they could. I heard some of the stories. It was a slaughter. By the time Earth began to put together a resistance, it was over. The Families flipped a switch, time rolls back, and no one's any the wiser."

"And now they want to do it again," Dex realized. "But this time, Ashion eliminates the resistance first."

"No, it's not another Harvest," Mal said. "At least, if Terran and I figured out Logos' message correctly. It's way worse. See, we kept looking at the math of the time-folding event. An amazing engineering feat. They took advantage of the natural irregularities in the expansion of the universe. They stuck the Transloop into the membrane of the expanding dimension, and the loop stretches out like a rubber band, aimed at Earth. Then, as soon as they are done harvesting, pop goes the rubber band. Inside-outskie," Mal said, crisscrossing her arms. The three men looked at her dumbly. She shook her head and went on. "Anyway, that's what the first message told us. The second message was more math, but a completely different proof. It describes what happens after you pop the rubber band the first time. There's an echo effect when you trigger the fold back in time. The event isn't over yet."

"What do you mean, not over?" Dex asked. "Are we folding back still?"

"The time-based side effect has already been achieved," Mal said. "But the energy force the off-landers unleashed hasn't come to rest. Not yet. But the whole thing gets settled in about a month."

"I don't really understand," Dex said. "Just tell me what's going to happen in a month."

"The Transloop is a matter vacuum, and it won't stop looping until the vacuum is filled. Its field is uncontained and drifting toward the surface of Venus. It will begin to collide with the Venus atmosphere in thirty-three days. Twelve hours later, Venus will have all of its matter pulled into the Transloop."

"Like Earth was?" Justice asked. "Sent back in time?"

"No, back then, there were systems in place to manage the effect," Mal said. "This time it's an unprotected event. If the proofs are correct, the matter of Venus will be pulled through the Transloop, and spat back out. Venus, or what used to be Venus, will be put back into place in the universe. But it will be reorganized into a big globby mess of inert deadness."

Everyone was silent for a while, taking it in. Except for Rolink, who was looking at the other three as if they had all gone mad. Dex, who had been pacing, now stopped.

"So, the Families have not been planning a Second Harvest," Justice said. "They've been planning a homecoming."

"Right," Mal said.

"But why would they come here?" Justice said. "Cawlria is the middle of nowhere. The end of the world. Why not go after the grand civilizations to the south? Or to New Europa?"

Mal shrugged. "First, I think they want Cawlria for sentimental reasons. This continent is their old stomping ground. Second, Cawlria is home to the only remaining shifters."

"The timeline manipulations," Dex said. "They needed the threat exterminated."

"Yeah," Mal said. "Finally, I think they want it precisely *because* it's the backwater of the world. Maybe they can come in, not make a big splash, and get themselves established before anyone really notices."

"How could they not notice? You told me there are hundreds of thousands of off-landers. How would you not notice them descending from space?" Justice said.

"There won't be hundreds of thousands," Mal said. "Just thousands."

"Come again?" Dex said.

"The Families are going to abandon the planet-siders," Mal said. "They will bring only their armies, their servants, and themselves."

Sixty-seven.

Into the silence following Mal's proclamation came the sound of approaching horses. All four turned and watched as three more hooded riders left their horses at the creek and walked over. One put his hood back, revealing the braided grey hair of a travel-ready King Mastiff. The other two remained hooded, but by their size, Dex surmised that Mastiff no longer went anywhere without his bodyguards.

"Here is a cabal I wish never to see again," he said.

"King Mastiff," Dex said, "Thank you for coming." All four bowed. "How go preparations?" Dex asked.

"My troops set out this afternoon for northern Cawlria," Mastiff said. "King Grawl is beside himself. This will take months of diplomacy to explain." Then he smiled a grim smile. "It is good to be on the warpath again."

"You will be at the monastery, six days hence?" Dex asked.

"We'll be there," Mastiff growled. "The question is, assassin, will you?"

"Your scouts will be able to see me, from the position I gave you, in the tree above the monastery," Dex said. "I will enter at the back. You will see me in the courtyard. The Knights will gather around me. That is the distraction you need."

"I know the plan," Mastiff said. "I made it."

Dex nodded. "After your victory, you will provide a horse for me to leave the monastery."

Mastiff waved his arm. "We have been over and over this."

Dex nodded. "The four of us head south for the enemy base."

"We do?" Justice asked. Mal frowned.

"We do," Dex said. "And we would appreciate it if your guards left us alone."

"Consider it done," Mastiff said, and he gave a short, low whistle. "You may want to know that I have peeled off an attacking force toward the enemy's south fortress as well."

Dex frowned. "You already have my opinion on that decision."

"I will repel this force once and for all," Mastiff said. "Why do you head south?"

"I have a companion near the base that we need to find," Dex said.

"You will have time to return to the monastery in time?" Mastiff asked.

"I'll be there," Dex said.

A scout materialized next to Mastiff, and the king whispered into his ear. Then both of them mounted their horses.

"After the siege on the monastery," Mastiff said, "I do not want to see you ever again, Dexter Maxwell."

"You won't," Dex said. "You have my word."

"Good," the king said, turning his horse to leave the amphitheater. "I'll sleep better." With that, the king and his men rode off at a trot.

"Why are we headed for the Earth-side station?" Mal asked.

"Ashion's forces will be destroyed at the monastery," Dex said. "The rest of the invasion will then be funneled through that station. Thelo is waiting near there with an armed shuttle. We can help the fight with him."

"What about the people of Venus?" Mal asked.

"They are doomed," Dex said. "You said it yourself. But I won't let Ashion and the Families come destroy this place or this people."

"Do you think that is what Logos fought for?" Mal asked.

"We should consider the people of Venus," Justice agreed. "They are all God's children."

Dex threw his arms out. "Look around, people. It's just us. How would we get back to Venus? What would we do when we get there? I was there for four days. *Four*. I barely made it out alive. What do we get by going back?"

Dex mounted his horse without waiting for an answer. "We can protect Cawlria. We can protect Rolink's people. Venus will have to fend for itself."

Sixty-eight.

"We walk the rest of the way," Dex said. His three traveling companions looked exhausted. Just a mile or so on foot. Dex was tired, too, but he could feel the pieces falling into place. He had not felt this sure of what to do ever.

During the journey, Dex had tried to explain everything to Rolink. He had tried to break it down into digestible chunks, but Rolink had still shaken his head in confusion. The best he could do was to convince Rolink to wait and see. The enemy comes from outer space, Dex had assured him. Just you wait.

And you can travel through time, Rolink had rolled his eyes.

It was late in the day when Dex looked down into the short valley, and saw the shuttle. There did not appear to be anyone there. The cargo bay was open, and there was a line tied from the cargo door to a tree nearby. There were clothes hanging from the line. A closer look revealed a makeshift fire pit, currently unused.

Dex was about to walk down toward the shuttle, when a shirtless man stepped out of the cargo hold, stretching. Dex smiled at the sight of the big man. But when the man turned toward him, he realized that it was not Thelo, and he put his hand up for his companions to stay low. As he watched, the man walked over to the fire pit and made preparations to start a fire, throwing a few small logs in.

Off-lander soldier, Dex realized. Thelo has been taken. Dex turned and beckoned for Mal to come and join him at his perch. She crawled up quietly and took in the view.

"That's not him," Dex whispered.

Mal nodded. "What should we do?" she asked.

"We wait, for now," Dex said. Even as he said it, he saw a man approaching the shuttle from the west, walking up the dry creek bed. He was dressed in the fatigues of the Family infantry troops, including the black crash helmet. The shirtless man hailed the trooper, who waved back. The trooper began to disrobe, and handed his shirt and the helmet to the other man, and then went to the laundry line.

That is Thelo, Dex realized. "What the hell is he doing?" he whispered.

"My god, it's really him," Mal whispered, a smile on her face. Her eyes were welling up.

"What, he gets tears?" Dex asked. "I didn't get tears."

Mal gave a sad smile. "I was expecting you. But never, ever Thelonius Hollywood."

"Why is he play-acting as a soldier?" Dex wondered.

"Why don't we go ask him?" Mal said. "The other man is leaving." She stood, and began walk-trotting down the hill toward Thelo. Dex took a deep breath, beckoned for Rolink and Justice, and then followed Mal down the hill.

He caught up to her just as Thelo saw her. He froze. He blinked. Then a grin slowly spread across his face, reaching both ears. Mal was at a dead run. She threw herself at him, and he picked her up and spun her around.

"How can it be, eh?" he said. "You were dead! Exploded off a 'roid!"

"Thelo," Mal said. "Thelo. You look the same, absolutely the same."

"And you have aged beautifully," he said. He saw Dex, now, and he whooped. "You still running with this runt?" he asked her.

Mal laughed, and the three of them hugged each other, Thelo's huge arms around everyone. Then he released. "How did you get here?" he asked Mal again.

"Logos," Mal said.

"Logos," Thelo confirmed. He turned to Dex and hit him, hard, in the arm. "Why the hells didn't you tell me she was alive?" he yelled.

"Sorry about that. She was a secret. If you were captured... it was just too risky for you to know."

Thelo nodded, and saw Justice and Rolink shuffling into view. "Friends of yours?"

"Thelonius Hollywood," Dex said. "This is Justice, of the Order of Brodius. This is Rolink, late of goat herding and again of the smithy." Dex turned to the others, "Justice, Rolink, this is Thelo. He will be our pilot." They both nodded, and then bowed slightly to Thelo, who bowed back.

Thelo turned back to Mal and Dex, putting an arm over each of them. "I can't believe we're back together, eh. Come, I've got decent food now. No more of that emergency crack."

"What's with the Family soldier clothes?" Dex asked.

Thelo turned. "Oh, you saw that? Isn't it fantastic? I tell you, the Families will hire anyone to be infantry." He was rooting around for something in the cargo bay. He found it, and went for the fire pit. "An old smuggling buddy. Worked the loader on my boat for a bit, few years back. I was doing recon on the station, last week. I saw him setting out. Decided to reacquaint myself."

"That is so reckless I can't begin to see why you would—" Dex started.

"Relax, Dex," Thelo said with a grin. "Jordan there, he's one of Leshan's men. It's not an idle distinction. I can trust him faster than I can trust any of you." Then he had the fire lit, and was putting strips of fresh meat onto sticks.

"Let's eat a real meal, cool our heels, and you can tell me all about what you've been doing for the last three weeks," Thelo said. "I've got some incredible beer, too. You've got to try it."

Sixty-nine.

Thelo stuffed them full of food and drink, while he quickly recounted his exploits since Dex had last seen him.

"Poor folk, they are the same no matter where or when," Thelo said. "The soldiers are here for the start of the Second Harvest. So, they figure, why not get an early start on the harvesting? So they've already set to trapping for game, collecting anything that even resembles something edible. They've already hit the closest village. Started bartering for beer and wine." Thelo raised his cup at this. "So, I run into Jordan. He says everyone's got their panties in a bunch over this here shuttle. So we've made arrangements. I dress up like him, head out, I get to walk a free man for a bit. Get a close up of the Earth-side station. Not too close," he added, noticing Dex's nervous look. "But close enough to see that things are ramping up. They are bringing a lot of supplies down. And a lot of soldiers. A gaggle of Red Masks, looking all superior and bossing everyone around." Thelo shook his head in disgust. Then he smiled. "But enough about me! What have you been up to?"

Dex tried to encapsulate his experiences over the past few weeks of his life. Everyone went quiet when he came to the part about Charla and Mebda's death, then cheered during the siege on Longs Castle. Finally, Dex deferred to Mal.

Mal explained to Thelo about the coming apocalypse on Venus, and how she theorized that the Families would abandon the planet-siders. Thelo's mood darkened.

"They are telling these soldiers that it is the Second Harvest. Jordan tells me that Second Harvest talk is blanketing the threads. But I agree, Mal. It is what Logos feared. The Families are talking Second Harvest to distract the 'siders while they get themselves looped and set up Earth-side."

"We need to hold the armies here," Dex said. "Can you operate the weaponry on that shuttle?"

"Right," Thelo said. "What about the 'siders on Venus?"

"I don't want to have this conversation again," Dex said, closing his eyes.

"Dex, we can't abandon them," Mal said.

Dex thought of Booker, on the train. He thought of Trance. "There's nothing we can do," Dex said. "There's no way to even get there."

"I can get us there," Thelo said. "There's an army there that could use our help. I don't think they know about Venus, you know, dying."

Everyone looked to Dex. He stared at the fire. The shifting patterns flew around his periphery. Dex couldn't control them. They itched for a shift.

"How can we go undetected?" Mal finally asked. "I don't think we can just fly ourselves back to Morgish on that recon shuttle without someone noticing. And by someone, I mean Ashion."

"Mal, m'dear," Thelo said, "Leave that to me. Already got us three tickets back to Venus, if we need them." Thelo pointed to the shuttle. "We'll use the low-toll booths."

"What?" Mal asked.

Dex smiled. "The low-tolls. From the highway job, back in Grenver?"

Thelo nodded, grinning. "Yes, my friend, Jordan needs a way to smuggle Earth-side goods back to Venus. The market will be hot for goods coming in before the supposed Harvest actually starts."

Thelo pointed over his shoulder at the massive shuttle craft. "That thing is big news to Ashion. He'll clear its return to Venus. And he'll expect three body bags to be on board, for his dead Knights."

"And Jordan will arrange our safety when we get to Venus, smuggled off the shuttle along with their contraband," Mal finished. "Well done, Thelo."

Thelo beamed. But Dex shook his head. "It's risky."

"Since when did Dexter Maxwell calculate risk?" Thelo asked. "You said yourself that this Mastiff will be bringing the pain to Earth-side."

"Even if it is not successful," Mal argued, "It will hinder their operations. Slow things down. Give us time to mount an offensive on Venus."

"We can do more good disrupting Ashion from Venus," Thelo said. "I, for one, will be heading back. I owe it to Justine. To everyone I fought beside. Logos. Fuel."

"Me too," Mal said. "I'm going back."

There was silence. Everyone stared at the fire. Dex felt the math pressing against his mind, the flyer pushing away from the fire and into the darkness to the north. The weight of the Judas sword pressed against his back. Finally he spoke.

"There's only one hitch. We need passage for four."

"What? Who?" asked Thelo. "One of them?" he pointed at Justice and Rolink, who had been talking to each other for much of the night.

"Rolink must come with us," Dex said.

"I don't see where that's a good idea," Mal said.

"She's right," Thelo said. "We've got easy passage for three."

"Rolink is coming," Dex said. "He's a blacksmith."

Blank stares from Mal and Thelo.

"He makes *swords*," Dex said.

"Ahh," Thelo said, thinking.

"I'm not sure that's worth the risk," Mal said.

"It may be," Thelo said. "We've been trying to make weapons for our fighters, but we are working without a playbook. The swords turn out more like clubs. We're getting slaughtered in our close-quarter combat. With a legitimate blacksmith guiding them, our manufacturers could make the difference. It could turn the tide."

Mal nodded. "But how do we get four of us to Venus?"

Thelo was rubbing his chin thoughtfully. "I'll talk to Jordan. It could be that I can suit up as a pilot. My face will be on threads, but that might not jingle any bells. At least not right away."

Dex rose. "We head to Venus," he said. "We take the fight back to Venus. We fly this shuttle right up to the loop and grab a ride."

"It's decided," Thelo said, clapping his hands. "To Venus we go."

"If you'll excuse me. It's been a while since I had a beer." Dex stood, and teetered away from the campfire. He closed his eyes. Ever since the sun had dropped, the fire was lit, and alcohol was in his system, the shifting patterns had been exploding in his vision, with an energy that he had never felt before outside of an actual shift. The flyer and the anchor kept jumping into his vision, pushing toward a certain place on the periphery of their camp. Dex relieved himself, but instead of going directly back into the camp, he went into his assassin-trained mind, and quietly, quickly made his way around the darkness that encroached on his friends, laughing quietly and talking still. The patterns went crazy, and then did something they had never done: they made a perfect outline of a human, crouched in the shrubs, peering into the fire.

Dex quietly pulled the Judas sword from its leather sheath, and in one quick motion he shunked it to its full length and swung.

The interloper was faster than Dex could have expected. The person pulled a sword and deflected Dex's initial swing. Dex pushed his advantage, feeling his strength weighing on his opponent. The speed of the other frightened Dex; he had never seen anyone move a sword that fast. But the intruder was not taking the offensive, and fell backward into the light of the fire.

For their part, Dex's friends had stood at the first clink of sword-on-sword violence, and peered into the dark. When the intruder tumbled into the fire circle, they backed up a bit, but held their ground.

Thelo pulled a bolt gun from his belt and aimed it.

Dex could see the opponent now. She was young, a mere teenager, small, thin, with close-cropped black hair. She had a telescoping short sword like Judas, and she held it like a master. She was glancing at Thelo's gun, and at Dex's sword. Without hesitating, she smashed her fingers against an interface on her sword arm and leaped into the blazing fire.

Dex saw it happening. He knew what she was doing with her interface. It was the reason his patterns had danced around her. She was shifting. She was holding a breach. And now she was jumping back through that breach. The moment slowed to a crawl.

She will inform them. She has heard everything.

"No!" Dex shouted, and he unspooled the knife, recoding it, trying to rebuild the hack that had let him through Tano's breach. He knifed into the breach of the young girl, chasing her into time.

He tried to halo into the space, but there was no space. There was only the burning surface. He could feel the girl's anchor, pushed out, not too far away. He could feel her real time, the shape of it. But it was across the surface. The knife was shattering against the surface, not cutting, and Dex was burning up, burning, his anchor weak at his back, the breach closing and his rope failing.

This is not it! I can't do this!

With all his energy, he concentrated on the rope and his anchor at the breach hole. He used the flyer to pull himself back and free of the breach.

He landed in the fire, and screamed with the pain of burning coals.

Seventy.

Thelo jumped in, dragging Dex out of the fire. Mal and Rolink were at his side quickly. Dex did not look to be seriously burned, but he couldn't focus his eyes, and he was having some sort of seizure.

Thelo slapped him. Then he slapped him again.

Dex finally settled down, his eyes came into focus. He looked at his concerned friends' faces.

"What just happened?" Thelo asked.

"I saw her. I saw her shifting," Dex said. "I followed her into her breach."

"That was amazing," Mal said. "How did you do that? See that she was a shifter? There is no anchor. There is no map."

"I – I don't know," Dex said, sitting up. "I could see her. The patterns—they found her in the dark. But I couldn't follow her. She was from our future. I didn't have the math right, or maybe without the map..." Dex trailed off. "But I saw where she was from. I mean when. I could feel the shape of the time."

"When was she from, Dex?" Mal asked.

Dex could still see the breach patterns when he closed his eyes. The great crashing ocean of time. He could see her halo, and feel the time and space. "November 4," Dex said. "Twenty-four days from now."

"They know we're coming," Thelo said, slumping to the ground. "They know where we are."

They all sat in silence, allowing the realization to sink in.

"No they don't," Mal said. "Not for twenty-four more days. We need to get up there and disrupt their plans, so they don't send someone else to finish us off." She stood up. "Come on. No time to waste."

PART 3

DRAGGISH TOWNSHIP, NORTH END. DAY 32.

Seventy-one.

Ashion was surprised, ultimately, by how long it took. If it had been him, he would have done the raid first. But clearly Morgan and Salzon had felt compelled to review all the threads. Get all the security levels cleared. Check with Charles. Gather a team. Get sign off from every Family bit-player. Then, and only then, would they raid Ashion Goldman's Draggish compound.

What naivety.

When they did come, Ashion had to acknowledge Morgan's flare for the dramatic. Four shuttles worth of infantry. Instead of just downing the cams from the SIN, they shot them out one by one as they moved closer so that Ashion had to keep rethreading the view from the threader in his private quarters. Instead of using security data to overwrite the sensor privs on the door, Morgan had it blown open with a bunker buster. The infantry poured in, looking for someone to shoot. But Ashion had cleared all his guards out, leaving only the Whi-Scis and himself behind.

The infantry moved quickly from room to room, ignoring the scientists, who did not look up from their work. They placed sensors everywhere, Ashion noted. A typical step to ensure they had direct access to room data—oxygen, heat, movement—without it potentially being manipulated. Once they had secured the floor, they would take the lift to the next floor down. In this fashion, they reached Ashion's private quarters and prison cells in about ten minutes. The soldiers were excited when they saw him—someone to yell at, finally. Ashion kept his hands in the air, not giving them any reason to fire. They threw him to the floor clumsily, and Ashion almost laughed. He put his hands behind his head, and waited.

He did not have to wait long. He was picked up by the soldiers and taken to his lab-viewing chamber. The chamber where he had watched Kat getting her brain mapped and burned. There, sitting in Ashion's seat, was Salzon Lewiston. He was pointing a blaster at Ashion. There were no White Scientists in sight.

The soldiers cuffed Ashion's hands behind his back, and chained his feet. Then they left. Ashion stood there, and Salzon sat. They were alone.

"Where is he?" Salzon asked.

"Who?" Ashion said.

"My brother, you fool," Salzon growled.

"Poor old crazy Arvura Lewiston," Ashion said, staring into space. "He is dead, Salzon."

"Don't play games," Salzon said. "It does not suit you."

"You have me cuffed and a gun pointed at me. Perhaps you should dispense with the games."

"Is Arvura with the girl?" Salzon asked. "The one you call Kat?"

"She is safe. I cannot say the same of your brother."

"Cute. She even calls you Daddy. How romantic. A father and his daughter. Tell me, doting father, why do you map her brain? Why do you spend all your energy looking into the dark crevices of a child's mind? What do you think you will find?"

Ashion said nothing.

"Or perhaps you are building something," Salzon said, pointing around the room. "All the technology you have used, to burn your own brain into these shells of your body, over and over again for... what? Three hundred years now? That about right?"

"More or less."

"What then for the girl? Burning military training, languages, stealth... to what end?"

Morgan Goldman burst through the door. She looked at Salzon, before turning to Ashion. She was apoplectic with rage. "Tell me how you did it," she managed to splutter.

"Did what?" Ashion asked.

"How you encrypted your threads so that my PFI cannot read them."

Ashion shrugged and looked at Salzon. "Stick around three hundred years. You learn a few tricks."

"Unlock them," Morgan ordered.

"I will not," Ashion said. "And Salzon here is not going to shoot me. And I won't be arrested."

"You have achieved nothing but massive failure on Earth,"

Morgan said. "For that alone I should have you executed."

"There have been setbacks. But I'm afraid the Families still need me."

"Setbacks?" Morgan yelled. "The monastery is lost. Your Knights are out chasing ghosts at churches. We won the fight at the Earth-side station, but the facility was nearly destroyed, and its position compromised."

"Compromised by your incompetence!" Salzon yelled at Ashion.

Ashion's earpiece cracked. "If you'll excuse me," he said. "I'm being hailed."

Morgan turned and tapped her own earpiece. "Get me Charles," Morgan said, leaving the room.

With his hands secured at his back, Ashion had to lean his ear into his shoulder to engage his com. "Ashion here," he said.

"Sir, it's Holden."

"Speak."

"Sir, I have been reviewing the recon shuttle threads, as you requested. I have found some data points that I think you might be interested in."

"Let me hear it," Ashion said.

"First, about the infantry man that piloted the shuttle back to Venus. He matched a description that—"

The thread had gone dead. His privs had been revoked. Again.

Salzon looked at him, cocking his head. "Morgan finally get your rights revoked?" he asked.

"Sounds like it," Ashion said.

Morgan entered the small room again. "At the urging of Thula Gregor and the military board of the Security Council, your presence at future Security Council briefings is required. You have been relieved of all security duties, but will report to the briefings to assist with the hand-over for a new security lead."

"Which would be you?" Ashion said.

Morgan did not have to say anything. The smug look spoke to her new powers.

"Unlock my shackles," Ashion said.

"Not until we've escorted you from these premises," Morgan said. "This compound is no longer yours. All sensors have been rehomed to my thread privs. For security reasons."

Morgan and her soldiers took Ashion to the docking station, and loaded him onto a security shuttle. Morgan pointed at a soldier, and spoke to Ashion. "Tell this soldier where you want to be dropped off."

Ashion looked at Morgan, and said quietly, "Enjoy it while you can."

"Any time you want to talk about your encrypted threads, you just hail me," Morgan said. "We'll negotiate." Then she tapped the door, and left.

"You have nowhere left to go," Salzon said.

"We all end up in the same place, in the end," Ashion replied.

MORGISH TOWNSHIP, LOWER-LOWER DISTRICT.

Seventy-two.

Dex crawled slowly in almost-complete darkness, squeezing through the narrow tunnel that had been carved into the bedrock of Venus by mining bots. It was so hot he could barely breathe, and the close walls gave him a panicked sensation that he realized was probably the beginning of claustrophobia. In a way, it reminded him of the second shifting altar in the mountains above Longstown. He remembered holding onto Freedom's hand for dear life as she dragged him through the blackness toward the shifting patterns. Lost in memories, his sheath on his back caught on a rock, pulling him to a stop, and the person behind him bumped into his feet.

"Crack, Dex, let's move it," Thelo said irritably.

Dex thought how much harder it must be for Thelo to squeeze through this hole, and kept his snark to himself.

It took another ten minutes of crawling and scraping their hands and knees before they came to a flat iron wall. Dex gave the secret knock Thelo had taught him. A knock came back, and Dex had to concentrate to remember the response that was required, based on his unique identification. A small hole opened and Dex inserted a simple stone—carved into a loop and hanging from a wire cord around his neck—through the hole. Moments later, the entire iron wall groaned on old hinges and swung open. It was, by far, the most rudimentary two-factor authentication Dex had ever used.

The shaven-headed guard stared impassively past Dex. She was thin, all muscle and bone, dressed in the black and grey of Fuel's army. She had a blaster in her hands, and it was pointed squarely at Dex's chest. When Thelo had finally unfolded his huge frame and dusted off his knees, the soldier saluted him and led them to the next door. She passed both Dex's loop-stone identifier and her own through the next gate. There was another knocking sequence exchanged and then the door opened. The three of them did this again, not speaking the whole time.

Finally they emerged into a wide but low room full of equipment. Dex would never get used to seeing all the people walking on the long treadmill below them. He could see the turbine they were turning, and the transformer it led to. From the transformer, thick wires snaked over to a makeshift table where a row of men and women sat, their hands in dim light boxes, strumming away at any number of threads.

"How deep do we need to go this time?" Dex muttered. He'd only been back on Venus for a few days, but he couldn't get used to these secret tunnels. The sweat dripping down his back made his skin crawl.

"He can't be too safe," Thelo said.

They entered a long, narrow walkway that was illuminated by lights at each end, but pitch black in the middle. Thelo tapped Dex's shoulder and pointed up. Dex saw holes drilled into the ceiling at five or six-foot intervals, about the size of his head.

"With a manual crank, those can be opened to the outside Venus atmo," Thelo said. "It's not the poisonous gas that kills you. The heat melts you first."

"Thanks for that image," Dex muttered. He hurried faster down the corridor.

At the other end, there was a single metal door, and the corridor widened just enough to allow two people to stand side by side. There was no fancy knocking pattern this time, just a loud rapping of knuckles from their escort. Finally the sound of a large metal bolt being thrown echoed down the corridor, and the soldier stepped out of the way. Dex needed Thelo's help to push the door open, and then to close it behind them. They heard the bolt re-enter the door from the inside, and an overhead light flickered on.

"Welcome to the Honeycomb," said a voice. Dex and Thelo turned. A lone man stood on a treadmill that was linked up to the overhead lights. There was a small table on one side of the small room, with eight chairs around it. A map lay across the table.

"My name is Fuel," the man said, and he smiled. "Or anyway, that's what everyone down here calls me."

Seventy-three

"Get over here and help me run this generator," Fuel said. "It works better with two or three people on it."

Dex and Thelo walked over and stepped onto the tread. It was at a slight angle, and they had to push down to make it move. But with the three of them, the overhead light certainly was a little brighter.

"Sir, it… it's an honor to finally meet you," Thelo said. Dex looked at him. *Is this the first time I've ever seen Thelo nervous?* "It's you. I mean, it's *you*…"

Fuel threw up his hand. "Enough of that. It doesn't matter who they think I am up on the boats. Down here, we all play our part. I'm just a man, like both of you. Although," Fuel looked Dex up and down, "from what I hear, you may be more than just a man."

Dex shrugged. "I had a few upgrades," he said.

Fuel laughed a deep, belly laugh. It was infectious, and Dex and Thelo both found themselves grinning.

"Upgrades," Fuel finally said. "I love it. So, you two know why you're here?"

"Fuel asks to see you, you show up," Thelo said.

"Yes, well," Fuel said with fake modesty. "But just meeting isn't a good enough reason. I needed to ask, again: was this Lynia correct? Is the end so soon?"

Thelo nodded. "Logos provided the math."

"I have been too long out of touch with the Families," Fuel whispered to himself, lost in thought.

Thelo cleared his throat. "Sir, we're outmatched. There's not enough time. We don't have the people. I just came back from the training arena. We sacrificed much on the Central Processing attack. Then on the rescue of Trance that you approved."

"That was necessary."

"Sure," Thelo said. "But now we're short."

"Perhaps," Fuel said, his grin returning. "But now we have all kinds of secret weapons."

"Like what?" Dex asked.

"That sword-maker of yours, to start with," Fuel said. "We already have him hard at work. Combined with your training of our fighters, we should make faster progress—"

"Hold up," Dex said. "My training?"

Fuel tapped Dex's temple with his finger. "You know the tactical methods of Ashion's Knights. We can't match them, but we can defend against them. We can find holes in their techniques. You can teach my soldiers."

Dex shook his head. "I've never taught anyone anything."

"Well, no time like the present. Second secret weapon: That beautiful woman Lynia."

"She's good with the networks," Thelo said.

"Indeed. Trance has enlisted her Sinner friend to help teach her how to thread. So we can discover how to hack it."

"Why do you need to hack it?" Dex asked.

"All kinds of reasons, but the most important comes from our final secret weapon: we know the future."

"What do you mean?" Thelo asked.

"Only a few hours ago, Ashion's goons on Earth suffered an embarrassing defeat by the backwater King of Cawlria. Dexter is there, and here, at the same time."

"They can't suspect what we know," Dex said with a nod.

"Correct. They are preoccupied with finding Dexter on Earth," Fuel said. "And we know the exact date when they discover that you are, in fact, not on Earth, but rather here on Venus. And that, my friends, is the day we invade."

"Invade what?" Thelo asked.

Fuel grinned, slapping Thelo on the back. "The Family boats, of course."

MORGISH TOWNSHIP, LOWER-CENTRAL DISTRICT.

Seventy-four.

"That's is it," Trance said, pointing. "Did you's sees it?"

"Heah," Jules said, threading madly. "That's was it."

Trance was at an auxiliary threader, hooked to a cam that was monitoring Jules' light box. They had made a small prog together that captured the light box and then ran quick modeling to a mitt.

"It's matches th' pattern," Trance said.

"It's is not a prog," Jules said. "We's sure of that, now."

Mal had her own light box, but her movements were slow. She did not have the hang of this interface, yet. She spoke up. "You need to stop thinking of it as below the threads, and start thinking of it above the threads."

"Heah?" Jules asked.

"The threads are made up of code, or whatever you want to call the carrier information. That code is impenetrable by us. We only have code that is based on the thread construction. But make no mistake; the thread is constructed of *something*. The SIN has been given a pile of construction bits so that it can build, monitor, loop, and ultimately destroy the threads."

"Heah, sure," Jules said. "I's been at this for a longs time, Lynia, I's don't need lessons."

"Sorry, Jules," Mal said. "Just hear me out. When code is constructed of something, the construction is an information set in itself. It is a metaset. It is above the set. Now, what we are watching happen here isn't an action. It's not underneath the thread. It's part of the thread's metadata. Part of the construction itself."

Jules nodded. "Heah."

"Someone built themselves a backdoor into the metadata. A thread definition that acts upon the data. So that a thread can react to its own construction, and disintegrate simply because it is defined as a disintegrating thread."

Jules finally looked away from his light box. "Who's are you, again?" he asked.

Mal smiled. "When I was a kid—this would be back in the 22nd century before I got iced—I was really good at programming. One of the best. I burned my way through the schools as fast as I could, and then found myself working on this team of other savants like me. Working for Luckey Corporation. They asked us to create an equivalent of the SIN, or what it looked like back then." Mal closed her eyes. "It was going to be so great. New, simple, inclusive. Engineered for communities and stringing them together. Make the open net understand them. The first thing we worked on was huge medical structures. Medical data, streamed from millions of hospitals. We worked on ways to integrate the data for individuals, as a way of knowing a person exactly. Correlate that information to the massive genome mapping projects taking place in China. Get it right—no mistakes. Every piece of medical data, for every person, without errors. We were going to save so many lives."

Mal stared down at her hands, still inside her light box. "Then, Luckey took our system live. Rolled it out. But instead of adding to the existing net, it went on to replace the other. Turned ours on, then slowly phased the open net out. All they had to do was turn off the backbone step by step, successively replace it with the one that we built. Used our medical data as a way of ensuring they knew who was on the net, and who was off. And just like that, they had control. Most people barely noticed."

Mal shook her head. "The final step when you want total control of a system is to ensure no one knows how to break the system. All my friends on the project started disappearing. I was scared. That was the first time I faked my own death."

Mal looked up at Jules and Trance. "Anyway, they didn't change the code I built. How could they? And a lot of us, we'd put backdoors into the code. We'd built in metadata definitions so we could poke around. So I could go hunting for people on the Charts, as we called the new net. It was a game. I'd go see where my friends were—if they'd been arrested, or were in hospital, or just tagged by a camera or something."

"Heah, what's has this to do with th' Slave, eh?" Jules asked.

"I'm getting there. After I was dead, and hiding in the sewers of Grenver, I could still access the Charts. Because of the traffic definitions themselves. I wasn't hacking them. My access was part of the Charts itself." Mal pointed at the light box on Jules' fat stomach. "Someone else has done the same thing, here."

Trance shook her head. "I's not sure I's gets it."

"You's sayin, someone builts a secret door to the SIN b'fore it's is rolled out?"

"Probably not the SIN," Mal said. "But definitely the Primary Family Interface. We won't be able to see it from a threaded interface. It's outside the threads."

"Heah, but where's that thinkin end, eh?" Jules asked.

"There's no telling how deep the layers go," Mal said. "It's like the layers of an onion."

"A what?"

"Never mind," Mal replied.

Jules looked away from Trance and Mal, staring into space. "I's knows where we's gets a look outside th' threads, heah."

"Where?" Mal asked.

"First Term."

Trance shook her head. "That's is too dangerous. Not after th' stunt we's pulled." Trance reached up to the healing scar on her forehead where the probe had been inserted.

"If it's the only way, it's the only way," Mal said. "We need to get past the thread decoiler before we can..." she trailed off.

"Before we's can what?" Jules asked.

"It's is nothing," Trance said, shooting Mal a warning glance.

Jules looked back and forth between the two women before speaking. "I's gets you in."

Trance looked at Jules. "Heah? It's is tall!"

"Heah. Just gives me's a few days, eh." Jules touched his ear. "Father Morgish," he said reverently. "He's wants me's to visit. Heah, day after tomorrow."

Jules stood immediately, and paced back and forth before finally leaving, without another word. Trance looked at Mal. "He knows too much," she said.

Mal shrugged. "We're out of time. If we can't get the threads to behave, Fuel's plans will fall apart. We have to trust him."

215

MORGISH TOWNSHIP, CENTRAL DISTRICT.

Seventy-five.

Where everyone goes, in the end, Ashion thought bitterly. Some call it hell. Here, we call it Morgish.

The world of power and influence drifted quickly away from Ashion, like a boat riding the Venus atmo untethered. His com dead in his ear. His credit suspended. All his material goods lost to Morgan.

He'd walked out of his Draggish compound a free man, in word only. His actions were tightly constrained by the meager resources at his disposal. The guard at the door had loaned him enough credits to take the transit from Draggish to Morgish, plus a bit for basic supplies. On the train, it was clear to Ashion that nearly everyone recognized him for who he was, and therefore pretended not to see him and left him alone. For now.

He disembarked and started the hike up. His destination was close to the surface, in the older parts of Central District. Not quite the same pit of Low-Cen, but still. Nothing like the *Vanessa* and her cooled air and cold water. After two flights, he found a small street vendor, and bartered for a small bundle of profax to chew on and a well-used LED bulb. He then continued upward. When he arrived at door 126, he reached under his shirt and pulled the nylon necklace over his head. The old physical key was black in the low light. Ashion inserted it into the door and turned. Nothing happened.

It took him ten frustrating minutes to finally get the key to unlock the deadbolt. He pulled the door to the side, and it slid with a metal groan into the wall. The overhead light did not turn on, but a fan kicked in with a loud ticking noise. He left the door open, and reached up to replace the dead bulb in the socket. Then he closed the door, threw the bolt, and stared around the room. It was about twenty feet by seven, and there was a single cot with an old mattress on one side. The toilet was pushed back into the wall, and there was a bare, fold-down desk on the other side. All in all, it was hardly as large as the cell Ashion had kept Prisoner Six in.

"Welcome back," he whispered to himself.

Seventy-six.

Jules shuffled nervously from one foot to the other. He was more nervous than he could remember ever having been. Father Morgish was still speaking into his reflected threader cam to a congregation of Sinners. It was a sermon on knowing all about the technology surrounding us.

"The heart of a man pumps, day in and day out," Father Morgish was saying. "And the man does not consider how it pumps. He does not consider the purpose it serves, or how to better treat it. The man dies an early death, for he did not care for his heart." A pause. "The power of the Slave is harnessed by our ingenious civilization, day in and day out. It pumps cool air throughout our townships. But do we consider how this heart pumps? Do we consider its purpose? Do we care for it, or shall we die an early death?" A pause. "It is fortunate for us that the Slave is no dumb muscle, doing the same thing over and over in our chests. Instead, the Slave cares for us. It cares for us individually, and as a whole. Sometimes, it must make decisions for the whole. Other times, it will find it necessary to look after an individual. But more than a heart that pumps, the Slave is our collective soul, our collective belief that we can continue to live and prosper on this world, century after century, its caring warmth flowing over us. All we need is faith. To trust in the Slave. And then, we must care for it. Feed it, nourish it, and thus, it will nourish and feed us. All of us."

Jules had heard this one before, or some version of it. Father Morgish could deliver one hell of a sermon. Jules had pulled the threads of every sermon he had ever delivered, cross-referenced them, and pulled a palimpsest of the primary themes. It was an amazing topography of passionate belief and stunning practicality. Always, it came back to worship and service. Always.

Jules shifted his weight again. Father Morgish had summoned him, but Jules did not know why. They had not spoken since the attack on Central Proc. Not since his meeting with Trance down below.

Further down below than even Father Morgish knew about.

Father Morgish finished the sermon, and dropped the broadcast thread.

He turned to Jules. "Thank you for coming."

Jules gave a slight shake, meant to be deference. "Heah, it's is always good t'see ya, Father," he managed.

"Relax, Jules," Father said, smiling. "I call upon you because I need your assistance."

Jules brightened. "Helps, eh? Heah, somethin on th' threads?"

"Indeed," Father said. "You have done some amazing work, lately. I have been watching you closely. So has the Slave."

Jules deflated. "It's is not th' Slave, eh. We's figured it out, eh. Lewiston's gots an old interface. Pre-threads. Rots the threads. No trace. Trance showed me's where's to start. We's found th' patterns. They's all over the place."

"So, you've seen Trance since the attack?" Father asked.

Jules looked up in alarm, his face flushing deep red. "I's... it's is..."

Father reached over and touched Jules arm. "Relax, son," he said. "I wish her no harm. I wish you no harm. Perhaps this... movement is part of the Slave's plan."

Jules took a deep breath.

"Do you doubt the Slave is real?" Father Morgish asked delicately.

"I... I don't know." Jules sounded miserable.

"Jules," Father said, putting his arm over his shoulder. "The Lewistons do have a trick up their Family sleeve. I discovered it as well. But as I looked through the records, it came to me: who would tolerate such an invasion? Such a thing is immoral and abhorrent. That path leads to chaos. It leads to the loss of the Slave's ability to watch over and protect us. Why would the Slave allow such a thing?"

Jules was silent, but Father Morgish knew he was waiting.

"I'll tell you why," Father continued. "Because there is a larger purpose behind it. The Slave cannot be doubted. It knows more about the world than you or I could ever grasp. That is why we bow at its interfaces and praise its imminence."

"I... I's thought she's was right," Jules said. "The Lewistons..."

Father Morgish patted Jules' shoulder. "Jules, I discovered something else. Something deeper than the Lewistons. I found something. Something I would like you to see. Will you join me?"

Jules nodded. Father smiled. "Come to my threader. Let us commune with the Slave."

Seventy-seven.

What Ashion missed most were the chems. The beautiful, laced sleep he could get up on the *Vanessa*. In his magnificent old-world bed, made of cotton and springs. A world away from the small mat he lay on now, rolling over again and again, trying to escape the heat of Morgish.

He was not upset, then, when his door blipped weakly. He stood, happy to no longer have to pretend to sleep. There was no threader to view the visitor, so Ashion pulled the door open a crack and looked.

Thadwick Lewiston, sweating and glancing around madly, looked back. "Open that door, fool," Thadwick said.

Ashion moved aside for Thadwick, and noted that the Lewiston had already disabled the overhead before he entered.

"Burning more off-thread time?" Ashion asked, closing the door.

"How are we to meet our goals now?" Thadwick asked loudly. "Your privileges are revoked. You are squatting in this...this *hole* in the ground. You are nothing! You are nobody!"

"Good to see you, too," Ashion said, sitting down on his cot. Thadwick looked like he felt trapped in the small space, and kept looking back at the door.

"This is unacceptable," Thadwick said.

"The plan has not changed," Ashion said.

"How are we to proceed?" Thadwick asked.

"With patience," Ashion said icily. "We will proceed with patience. Your moment will come, Thadwick, make no mistake. But that moment will be late in the endgame. You are the final strike, not a premature feint."

Thadwick looked at Ashion warily, "How can we strike, from a place such as this?"

"Everything is temporary," Ashion said. "This included."

"I need only wait, is that what you are telling me?" Thadwick asked.

"Correct," Ashion said. "The chaos of the coming weeks will consume everyone, including Governor Goldman. But we must not show our strategy too early."

"I need assurances," Thadwick said.

Ashion smiled slightly. "We are pawns in the same game. We are in this together, to the bitter end. That is all the assurance I can give you—that our goal is the same. We will see Charles Goldman dead."

Thadwick looked at Ashion in silence, wiping away the sweat that threatened to drip into his eyes. "Do you need anything?" he asked.

Ashion gave him a searing look, and gestured around the small cabin. "Look around me," he said. "I want for everything. But, if you're asking, a light box would be much appreciated. Any old model will do."

Thadwick nodded. "I'll have someone bring one by." Then he left without a word.

A moment later, the overhead outside whirred to life. Ashion lay down and pretended to sleep again.

FAMILY HIGH-ALTITUDE FLOTILLA SS *CONTESSA*, SECURITY COUNCIL BRIEFING ROOM. DAY 36.

Seventy-eight.

Ashion closed his eyes against his own nervous energy. He had flown his own shuttle craft for over fifty years now, and was familiar with every shift, every shimmy, and every sound. To be stuck in the rear of a shuttle, a mere passenger, made him feel as though he were spinning into a vortex of despair.

Maybe he was. So much had been set into motion. So many mysteries remained. Ashion had tried to play this one as well as he could, but he had still had ended up back where he had started.

I have not played all my moves yet.

The shuttle landed at the docking port of the SS *Contessa*, near the Security Council chambers. The consolation prize for having been the security chief for the past two centuries was that the sane minds of the generals insisted that Ashion remain on the Council, in a consultative role, during the transition to Morgan Goldman as the new chief. This must have made Morgan's eyes do that bulging thing, Ashion thought, with a smile.

So here he was, waiting in the blacked out transporter for the handshake to verify, at the onset of the briefing. He would walk in and listen to the Council make decisions without him. Perhaps they would ask his opinion. Perhaps not.

The shuttle sprang back to life, and the door hissed open. Before he could even move to the door, someone was pounding up the steps into the passenger hold. Ashion recognized the snorting and huffing.

Thula keyed the door shut, and used her Family Interface to down the overhead. She slumped into the seat next to Ashion, catching her breath. They both stared forward into the featureless wall that separated them from the bridge.

"I have visitors," Thula said, finally.

"I hope they have not been making pests of themselves," Ashion said.

"How did your shuttle find my retreat?" Thula asked.

"Your nav prog was not too hard to crack," Ashion said. "I've been flying these craft for years. I may not be a Gregor, but I can hold my own."

Thula nodded. "Please come and collect your goods," she said.

"Salzon is much annoyed at their disappearance," Ashion said. "I thought you might like to know that."

"Anything that makes that man uncomfortable suits me," Thula said. "But not enough to house your fugitives any longer." She stood. "I am sorry, but you are Ashion the Fallen, now. This is our last conversation."

"I need them to remain with you," Ashion said. "I had hoped we could negotiate a lodging fee."

Thula snorted. "And what could you possibly have to offer?"

"I know where to find your granddaughter," Ashion said.

Thula looked at him closely. "Keep talking."

"My lodgers for your granddaughter. Straight trade."

"When?"

"I will need some time."

"Time is what we all lack, these days."

"Two weeks, no more."

Thula slowly worked herself back to her feet. "I will keep your guests for ten days, at which point you will deliver my progeny. Any care and feeding instructions?"

"The old man will need a chess board, or you will find he goes quite mad. For the girl, find something for her to hit repeatedly."

Thula nodded once, and clicked the overheads back on. "Come, I have been ordered to escort you to the Council briefings."

They walked in silence. In the antechamber, the Lower Families made a specific point of ignoring the existence of Ashion the Fallen. With his removal from the Council, Ashion had effectively been bankrupted at Goldman's court—all debts null and void, either direction.

They entered the Council chambers proper. They were the first to arrive, but slowly the militarians made their appearance: Mars, Cheltin, and Warship. Salzon followed the generals in and did not look at Ashion. They all waited for Morgan. She finally arrived, late, smugly enjoying being the center of this universe. Ashion gave her a solemn bow. He was here to play a part. And that part was one of deference and shame. It was not a new part for him; he was just a touch out of practice.

"Right, then, let's get started," Morgan said as she sat down, as though she had been waiting on them all along. "Let's start with our Earth-side operations. As you all know, and as this Council will now make permanent, Ashion Goldman has been relieved of all duties related to security chief. He is here only to facilitate the transfer of information and duties."

"So it will be," Salzon said.

"So it will be," Thula said, followed by the generals.

"The acting commander from Earth-side, Tano Down, is now dead. Ashion, this happened on your watch. Care to illuminate us?"

"After this Council's failed attempt to destroy the iteration at his shifting location," Ashion said, "the iter behaved as we expected and returned to save the captured monk, Freedom. We had him trapped until Mastiff attacked. Tano was killed by Dexter Maxwell, as reported by Gurn to this Council."

"What about Mastiff?" Warship asked. "Could this iter have collaborated with Mastiff?"

"We cannot rule it out," Morgan said. "One thing is for sure, we can no longer anticipate or count on Mastiff's actions. He must be considered a hostile element, to be dealt with upon Family arrival on Earth."

"Do we know where Dexter Maxwell is now?" Salzon asked.

Morgan nodded. "The captured monk provided intel that the iteration was frequenting churches in the region," she said.

"Remind me about the churches," Warship croaked.

Morgan looked to Ashion, who gave a short nod to her and spoke. "Before we eliminated the practice, the churches were involved in the Cawlrians' time-travel process. But we were never able to link them to the underlying technology they used for shifting. We have always operated under the assumption that they had deployed a wireless bandwidth system to push the map into the church chambers, to allow the chroneographical coordinates to be downloaded into the travelers."

"You think the iter is attempting to time travel," Salzon said.

"I know it," Ashion said. "And the way to prevent him from succeeding is to keep watch at the churches."

"This is wise," Warship said. "But do you believe this iter has already shifted?"

Ashion shrugged. "It seems likely. Even though the Earthlings' technology typically takes two to three years of intense mental training. I cannot imagine how the iter could be doing it already."

"The iter has shifted," Morgan said. Everyone turned to her. Ashion stared at her. She smiled. "My first officer Gurn tracked the iter to a church. This was the day after the monastery loss. Gurn attacked him, and they fell into the upper chamber of the church. The iter shifted. He took Gurn's arm at the elbow along with him."

"How long did the shift last?" Ashion asked, his curiosity overcoming his politics. "How did the iter take the organic material with him? I've never seen Earthling technology do that before. There's no nano-suit dip. Sure, we know the electron bath is there—"

"The details are immaterial at this point," Morgan interrupted. "Gurn is on his way back to the Family boats for his new arm. At this point, we have secured all shifting locations. We have Knights at all possible church locations. If the iter tries to shift, we will have him."

"And what about Mastiff?" Warship asked.

"We must operate under the assumption that the iter has been in contact with Mastiff," Morgan said. "That Mastiff has some idea of our intentions. This changes our plans to a slash and burn operation. More infantry, more weapons. No more sneaking around. No more finesse."

"Agreed," Salzon said. "Earth-side station repairs are already well underway after the attack. It will be housing more... *conventional* weaponry and craft."

"If there is nothing else concerning the Second Harvest," Morgan said, "I would like to discuss the matter of Ashion's Draggish compound."

"What compound?" Thula asked.

"Salzon Lewiston discovered, and revealed to me as acting security chief, that Ashion Goldman was keeping a securely threaded facility in Draggish. After his colossal failures on Earth, Salzon and I invaded this compound. We found a team of Whi-Scis conducting secret experiments. Private training facilities. Private living quarters. Private prison cells."

"It would appear that Ashion had been constructing this facility using Family resources over the course of the last century," Salzon added.

"Most distressing," Morgan said, "was that Ashion had employed illegal encryption on massive amounts of threads he produced in his private dungeon."

"It is not a dungeon, and the threads are not encrypted," Ashion said firmly.

"Only because they are too new for laws to exist!" Morgan said. "As soon as you strum them, the threads fall apart. It violates the intent of every threading law that has ever been put into place by Governor Goldman and her parliamentary advisors."

"I have broken no laws," Ashion returned.

"Do you forget that this Council represents Governor Goldman herself on such matters?" Salzon said, his face going red. "We are ordering you to decrypt the threads and reveal how you manipulated the threads."

"I am well aware of this Council's scope," Ashion said, "having served on it for longer than any of you. The Security Council can enforce the law. They can do anything in their power to enforce security, even outside of that law. But this is not within your power. There is nothing illegal. There is no encryption."

"But the interlacing technique obfuscates their matter!" Morgan shot back.

"Then refine your techniques," Ashion said. "But my thread patterns are not a matter of national security."

"As the Exemplar for Charles Goldman, I am ordering you to provide theinterlace decoding mechanism!" Morgan shouted.

"Only Charles Goldman herself can order me to do anything," Ashion said. "And only then if she revokes my freedom."

"Are you tempting the Governor to turn you back into a slave?" Salzon shouted.

Ashion bowed deeply. "Charles knows where to find me."

MORGISH TOWNSHIP, CENTRAL DISTRICT.

Seventy-nine.

He was back in his hovel in Morgish when the cheap light box Thadwick had loaned him crackled to life. A secure thread. Charles Goldman.

That didn't take long, Ashion thought. He threaded his security codes and waited.

"Ashion here," he said. Charles' hologram appeared.

"Ashion," Charles said. "Are you there? In your old room?"

Ashion nodded. "Want to come join me? For old times' sake? We made good use of this old cot."

The hologram wrinkled her nose. "The vagaries of youth no longer grip me, I'm afraid."

"I do appreciate you leaving it for me," Ashion said.

Charles shrugged. "The least I can do for an old Family slave."

Ashion said nothing at this. He waited.

"Morgan is quite upset," Charles said. "And I cannot blame her. She is just trying to do her job, you know."

"Poor, picked on Morgan," Ashion said. "It must be ever so hard on her."

"It's a nice trick, what you did to your threads," Charles said. "I've never seen it done before."

"Did you like that?" Ashion asked. "I call it Schrödinger's Cat."

"Who is Schrödinger?"

"Doesn't matter."

"I wonder, where did you learn that technique?"

Ashion laughed a bit. "I am old, Charles. Older than you. I still know a few things that will surprise you."

"I do not care for this surprise," Charles said. "Reveal your threads to Morgan."

"I will not," Ashion said.

"Then you will be executed, slave."

Ashion closed his eyes, his vision going red. *Try it, bitch. It would feel good to fight instead of playing these games.* "Then you will never

227

know my secrets, or the people I keep them from."

Charles smiled. "Do you trade secrets for your life?"

"I merely imply that my life is still valuable to the Great and Good Governor Goldman."

"Start with the people, then."

"Salzon Lewiston," Ashion said.

"Ah. He knows many of your secrets, now. Have you figured out how?"

"Yes. Tano has been indiscreet. What has he told you?"

"Oh, a thing or two. We have grown close in this final play. Lewistons and Goldmans will be very good together, after the move."

"Who needs enemies when you have friends like that?"

"Tell me a secret I don't already know. Tell me what we will find when your threads are decrypted."

"Arvura Lewiston," Ashion said.

"That you told me during your Writ of Confrontation. Have you not turned him over to Salzon yet?"

"The prisoner is more than just Arvura."

"More than Arvura?" Charles asked.

"I have been honing the brain burn technologies. Arvura holds many things in his mind. Not all of them are his. And I need his brain to unravel the threads you want to see."

"You are using Arvura Lewiston's brain as a decryption key?"

"Something like that."

"You really are a fascinating creature. Tell me about the girl," Charles said.

"She is an ongoing experiment," Ashion said. *Careful, now.*

"Keep going," Charles ordered.

"She can accept the burns."

"Interesting. But why fight for that secret?"

"Because it's *mine*. Salzon has been poking around the mind transfer technologies for years. He would not hesitate to take my property."

"Perhaps I will not hesitate, either."

"I thought you were out of that business."

"I am. I am not interested in living forever. Where did you find her?"

"One of the unknowns, pulled off the old-world icer. I needed some testers. It was dumb luck."

"There are all kinds of wonderful secrets in that old freezer full of criminals. First you, and now this Kat. I wonder what other great minds we've wasted on the asteroid mines."

"I suppose we'll never know," replied Ashion.

"You have given me no reason not to let Morgan summarily execute you."

"Hells, Charles. Because the house always wins?" Ashion said.

"What?"

"You ever go up to Transish? Place a few bets?"

"Not since I was a very young woman," Charles said.

"But you know why gambling is so lucrative for the Gregors."

"Win or lose, they make money," she said.

"Right. The house always wins. So, I figure you are realizing how empty your threats are. It puts all your bets on one horse. And I've known you for too long, watched you since you were a child, and I've never seen you play only one side. Ever. What you are asking yourself right now is whether Morgan is going to be able to take you all the way to the end of this?"

Charles was silent. "I am not so predictable."

"No. Not predictable, just smart."

"I'm tiring of this."

"Planet-side operations have been all wrong," Ashion said, playing a face card. "It's not military action we need. We need to be hunting data."

"Data? What data?"

"Stop fighting, and start looking where the air is going. Where the electricity is going. Put the Second Harvest aside for twenty-four hours and let the SIN focus on life-support anomalies. The resistance has found a way to hide their connection to planet-side systems. But the civilizations of Venus are closed systems—they have to be if they are going to work. All the sensors talk to all the other sensors to calibrate temperature, humidity, air quality. Every little bit of electrical current is accounted for, every drop of water carefully monitored. They've hidden their usage for this long, so it's going to be subtle. The SIN can't manage that and the Second Harvest at the same time."

Charles was silent for a few moments before she spoke. "You will reveal your threads to Morgan."

Ashion nodded. *Charles always did know when to move on.* "I will reveal the Arvura threads. But she will have to wait until I get him back to, how did you say, decrypt them."

"Yes, where *are* you keeping him and the girl?" Charles asked.

"Come now, Charles," Ashion said. "If I told you that, it would ruin the mystery."

Charles smiled. "Arvura is an interesting man. I knew him before Salzon murdered him. Have you spent much time with him?"

"Only a little."

"The Second Harvest was his passion," she said. "Arvura Lewiston had all the modeling down for a Second Harvest before Salzon murdered him. He wanted to go to Earth so badly."

"I'll have to ask him about that," Ashion said. "Are we done here?"

"Oh yes. We are finished. You live to fight another battle, Ashion the Fallen."

Eighty.

For the first time that day, Leshan, Thug King of Morgish, cursed Morgish. More specifically, he cursed the wretched med facs he was forced to frequent, the med facs that had sewn up the huge gash across his torso. No rebuilders, no nanos; just plain old stitches and 'try not to bend over' advice. Not like up on the Family boats. Not like before he fell planet-side and chose his current profession.

What was interesting about this particular curse directed at this particular med fac was that he had made it through the majority of the day without denouncing Morgish to the seventh level of hell. Leshan had to admit this probably meant he was mostly healed.

The reason that he had made him curse his medical choices today also meant that he would have to be a bit more forgiving of common Morgish medicine: his chest had hurt because he had been laughing. Not just at anything; but at Ashion Goldman, leaving his slum apartment in Lower Morgish, and taking the transit – *the transit!*– to meet Leshan. The former security chief, coming to visit Leshan, without a single Knight accompanying him. Without a shuttle.

Leshan looked over at the massive crates that were piled carefully in the corner of his private office. He had managed to open one of them, no problem. The other four were locked with some type of encryption Leshan had never seen before. And this was coming from a man that took great pride in picking locks.

Leshan walked over to the open crate and pulled one of the bolt guns from its carefully shaped foam protector. Family issue. New, no older than two years. Kept a charge for three hundred blasts. Semi-automatic, laser mounted site. He'd seen them a hundred times on Ashion's peace officers. Now he was holding one, and looking at twenty-three more of them in this crate. Not to mention four other, larger crates, containing other mystery spoils.

Leshan had been waiting for Ashion to arrive for almost a week now. Ashion had some explaining to do. Or, more than likely, a deal to close. Clearly, Ashion needed something. Leshan suppressed another gleeful laugh as he aimed the bolt gun at the shutdown cam on the ceiling.

"There is no better hand-held weapon around," Ashion said from the door. Leshan turned to see one of his heavies closing the door behind him.

"Heah, but I's need th' code to fire them," Leshan said, pointing the weapon at Ashion. "I's could be th' man who killed Ashion the Dark."

"Oh, have you not heard my new name?" Ashion said, sitting down at Leshan's desk.

"Heah," Leshan said. "But as someone who's is fallen, I's thought I's show some respect."

"Suit yourself," Ashion said, looking over Leshan's threading equipment idly. "You want the guns?"

"Heah, I's want th' guns," Leshan said. "But th' question is, what's you's want?"

"An untugged boat," Ashion said. "Like that one of yours I shot down the night you got yourself cut on by my iter."

"Heah, tall cut," Leshan said. "Still I's can't move right. A shuttle for bolt guns? Seems steeps to me. What's is in th' other crates?"

Ashion smiled. "That is for a different transaction. Tell me if I've got a shuttle, then we can talk about the other goodies."

Leshan glanced at the other four crates. They were larger than the bolt gun carrier, rounded, tougher. "I's give you th' shuttle for th' guns," he said. "And to know what else you's bring me, eh."

"Shuttle blasters," Ashion said. "Quick mount to any surface: threadable, guidable shuttle blasters. With access to direct solar, they recharge themselves. I saw six direct hits from these things vaporize your shuttle."

Leshan whistled. "Th' hell I's do with shuttle blasters?"

Ashion shrugged. "I finally took the time to meet your half-brother, Mash," he said, changing the subject. "Hell of a racket he's got up there in Transish."

Leshan growled. "That foofer's is no brother of mine," he said. "He's tries to kill me's mores than you, eh."

"Still, I bet he'd pay plenty for military-grade shuttle blasters."

Leshan was still looking at the crates. "Families will know where's I's got them."

"By then, it won't matter."

"The Second Harvest?" Leshan asked.

"The Second Harvest."

Leshan looked at Ashion. "What's you's want?"

Ashion stood. "That's the best part. I do need a little spending money. But in the end, you get to stick it to your hated kin twice on this one."

Leshan narrowed his eyes. "What's you's want?"

"Mash Gregor has a daughter. A bit hush-hush and all that. I guess he's got a touch of his father in him, couldn't keep it in his pants. Anyway, she's slumming it planet-side in Draggish." Ashion pulled a mitt from his tunic. "I've got a pile of leads but no resources to expend. Bring me Mash's daughter and I unlock these crates."

Eighty-one.

Thelo and Mal walked on a self-powering analog threader, side by side, cramped into a small underground room of the Honeycomb. They stared into the light box in front of Mal, watching a live feed of Leshan and Ashion.

"It's weird," Mal said, watching Ashion entering Leshan's compound.

"I suppose I've gotten used to it," Thelo said. "I've been able to detach the iteration of Dex that has been warped into Ashion from the Dex I knew in Grenver. From the Dex I know now."

Mal nodded. "Still, I can see Dex in him. In Ashion. I can see his sarcasm. He still has the same sneer when he thinks he's won something." Mal shook herself. "It's weird."

"As weird as meeting Dex again, only he's the same age?"

"No, that's weird, too," Mal said. "I still kind of have feelings for him. But I also kind of feel protective of him. Like his mother, now."

"Now *I'm* weirded out," Thelo said.

"I'll shut up now."

"You really think this is going to work?"

"Absolutely. It's the same kind of hack I used on the 'roids to hide."

"But this ain't the 'roids. This is Morgish."

"The rolling blackout will work. I learned more about the thread interface with Jules than I could ever have imagined. The man is a walking database of information."

"And he's not afraid to tell you everything he knows."

"He is verbose. I'll grant you that."

"I don't like him knowing you. Knowing about you."

Mal sighed. "It's a necessary risk. Trance wasn't making any progress on the thread hunting. Jules will do anything for her. So I come along, play third wheel, and voila. Shit gets done. We figure out the thread destruction."

"Are you sure it's safe?" Thelo asked. "Heading to First Term, I mean."

"We have to. It's too big an opportunity to miss if we want to get inside this SIN. The overhead cam hack you're about to drop is just the beginning. If we can figure out this thread anomaly, we could be dropping threads, not just killing cams."

"Speaking of which, it's ready."

Mal checked her threads. "Any time now. Just throw the switch."

"There is no switch, Mal."

"You know what I mean. Strum the thread."

"Let's wait for Ashion to leave."

"Sounds good. You hear anything from Dex?"

Thelo shook his head. "No com from him or his team. We just have to trust that he and that goatherder friend of his know what they're doing."

"I've seen some of the recruits. Dex is rising to the challenge."

"He's been doing that a lot, lately."

"Yes."

There was silence for a moment. Then Thelo spoke. "I've been having those hallucinations again."

Mal looked at Thelo. "From the Millionaire's Disease? I thought you had a serum."

"Logos provided it. Monthly shots. But I'm out. I'm overdue by two weeks already."

"Crack, Thelo. What are you going to do?"

"I don't know. Logos gave me a series of exercises to go through in my head. Cognitive games. Training my mind to focus on the puzzles keeps the deterioration at bay. I can do long division, or go through some of the navigation calculations required for space travel." Thelo smiled. "You remember Tetris?"

Mal laughed. "Wow, that's a blast from the past."

"I've trained myself to randomly generate blocks. Playing Tetris helps. So I haven't had any blackouts yet. But it feels like… it feels like…" Thelo shook his head. "It feels like it's waiting for something."

"Can you understand its intentions?" Mal asked. "When you are Moses. Do you understand why you act a certain way?"

"No," Thelo said. "After I come back to me, I can remember what I've said. I can remember my emotions. But I don't know why. It's like I'm watching a movie of someone else. It's so deliberate, so specific. It doesn't feel like a disease."

"If I can get into the SIN, I'll see what I can find."

Thelo put his hand on hers. "Thanks. For now, I just need to stay away from Dex. He's a trigger."

"That won't be hard," Mal said. "Dex is buried in Fuel's bunker. Teaching people how to fight Ashion's army."

"And I'm going to attack the boats," Thelo said, shaking his head. "It's lunacy."

"Not if we figure out this thread anomaly."

"Wait, did he just say shuttle blasters?" Thelo asked, watching Ashion.

Mal ignored Thelo's question, watching the conversation intently. "Did you hear that? About Mash Gregor? Should we ask him about the daughter thing?" Mal asked.

"Who, Fuel?"

"Who else?"

"Send him the thread," Thelo said, jumping off the treadmill. He pointed at Mal's display. "Ashion is leaving. It's time to throw the switch."

Eighty-two.

"I's is a popular man, today, Orpheus," Leshan said.

235

Thelo walked up to Leshan, and the two men hugged tightly. "I'm glad to see you are alive," Thelo said. "That was a hell of a cut you took."

"You's don't have to tell me's," Leshan said, sitting back down at his desk, and pouring over his interfaces. "Heah, it's has to looks believable, eh? Can't makes it's look like I's helpin th' iter and ya's, eh."

"Well, I'm still glad he didn't kill you," Thelo said, sitting down. "Ashion give you the codes to those guns?"

"Heah," Leshan said, then he swore. "What's th' hell is wrong with my's interfaces, eh? Threads are blackin out all over th' place."

Thelo grinned. "It's not your interfaces. It's us. Our new secret weapon."

"Th' iter?" Leshan asked. "Th' iter did this?"

"Even better," Thelo said. "The iter's old girlfriend."

Leshan stared for a moment, then let out a belly laugh, which immediately made him wince and stop. "No's laughin, eh. Ouch."

"Sorry. Anyway, she figured out a way to get localized, traveling blackouts. They are programmable, untraceable, and long-lasting. With the SIN occupied on Second Harvest work, it doesn't have enough cycles to crack the blackout code."

"That's is tall, eh."

"It's all part of the final phase."

"Heah?" Leshan raised an eyebrow.

Thelo nodded. "We need to get our hands on the threads. That means we need the boats."

Leshan whistled. "You's needs more than rollin blackouts for that's, eh."

Thelo pointed at the unopened crates. "It'll be a lot easier with those shuttle blasters."

Leshan nodded. "Guess I's needs to finds a little girl in Draggish, eh."

Eighty-three.

Dex spun the Judas sword down, easily blocking the brute attack from the front. He then turned and swung quickly at the attacker behind him, who had no choice but to throw her sword up to block, leaving her legs exposed. Dex kept spinning, bringing his leg around and tripping the attacker before coming around to parry the next swing from the first attacker. There was a shing of sword blades sliding down each other, then Dex pushed the combatant back away and held up his hand. The attacker paused, wiping sweat from his eyes.

Dex reached back and helped the second attacker back to his feet. Then he turned to the two dozen people watching.

"Do not ever believe their defensive ploys," he said through ragged breaths. "Not ever. The Red Masks are always on the offensive. It is the philosophy they live by."

There were many nods, and a few less-terrified looks than yesterday. Dex knew he couldn't teach these soldiers to readily beat Red Masks. But he could help them survive an onslaught. Even just two weeks later, they were already defending themselves better, and using their numbers to attack successfully. He wasn't sure they had enough time, but he'd do everything he could.

He walked around the training room, watching the Resistance trainees. The room they used was part of the Honeycomb, and close to Morgish so that the freedom fighters could get here and back home again without having to navigate deeply into the maze of tunnels. The room was a long, rough-cut rectangle with two doors on opposite sides of the room: a single iron door to the north that led to the poorest, least-used parts of Central Morgish; and a south door, which burrowed deeper into the Honeycomb. Training equipment hung from the walls, and makeshift mats covered most of the floor. Dexter had come to know the room very well as he trained soldiers that now clashed with blunt training swords. Swords fresh from the smelter. Fresh from Rolink.

These training blades were like the men and women that wielded them, Dex thought. Not ready for real battle yet.

There were now twelve groups of soldiers, and they arrived in shifts around the clock. Most of them were ordinary planet-siders, living normal lives, using the series of hidden tunnels and back avenues with broken cams to sneak down into hidden Morgish to join in battle against the Family hegemony. Dex had set up sessions at all times of night and day, and would sleep in ninety-minute intervals in between. It was all he did.

He found no solace in sleep, anyway. Not with the dream, and the constant shifting math.

It had started with the trip back to Venus. He had braved the Transloop again, terrified of what was coming, and it had happened again. The dream. He could not shape how he shifted, and the patterns beat against the surface, across his mind, but careened uselessly against the loop.

Dex shuddered a bit to think of it again. Since then, nearly every time he slept, the dream had boiled up, angry and aggressive, daring him to find a breach point and use his newfound patterns to help him. But in the dream, the knives didn't help. He had to do it himself. He couldn't find the patterns. They were wrong, somehow. Broken. The surface came at him, and he woke, sweating, unrested.

If I could just shift once more, he realized. I just need the release of one more shift. Maybe then I could fix it.

Instead, he grabbed a sword and got back to work training the planet-siders so they could attack the Family boats on a suicide mission meant to wrest control of the threads away from the Families long enough to convince people to rise up and escape.

Dex patted the young man on the back. Patrix, that was his name. He was one of Dex's favorites—passionate, determined, a natural with a weapon. Part of the oh-six-hundred team. Dex spent more time with him than others, and it was showing in his improved skills. But it was oh-nine-hundred hours, and Patrix and the rest of his group had to get back to their lives. Dex watched them sneak back in ones and twos, and then he left through a different tunnel, turning off the lights as he went and closing the doors.

The Honeycomb. That's what everyone called their nest under

Morgish. No one knew how far back it dated, but parts had collapsed, and it had taken a stolen asteroid tunneler to reestablish a hole big enough to get through. The fact that the Families did not know they existed spoke to either how old, or how new, they were.

It was not technically underneath Morgish, but from a view of Morgish that oriented to the Venus north pole the Honeycomb was to the south of the rest of the township. Dex had seen a rough drawing of the known tunnels and rooms, and if you looked at them in their entirety, it was clear to any mildly militaristic mind that these were built for hiding from and defending against an attack from Central Morgish.

Dex was walking one of the main corridors, but that only meant he didn't have to duck, and you could perhaps stand shoulder to shoulder with one other person. Otherwise, most corridors acted as choke points that would never allow a large number of people through. The entry points into Morgish existed at five places, or so Dex had been told. He'd only been made aware of four of them. And that was because he was Dexter Maxwell; most of the Resistance knew of only one, or perhaps two.

The best kept secrets on the planet, Thelo had said.

Thelo. Dex shook his head. He wanted to talk to his old friend. Be near him. But Thelo had to avoid Dex. Whatever it was about his disease, it was worse when Dex was around. Since their audience with Fuel, Dex hadn't seen him again.

And Mal was off learning how to use the computer interfaces so she could help them find a way to get to the Family boats.

That left Rolink.

Dex finally came to the door he was looking for, and pushed it open. An unbearable heat burst from the room and took his breath away. Inside was a long hallway, like the one he and Thelo had used to meet Fuel, but this one had been modified recently. Modified into a smithy.

At the far end of the room, Rolink had a thick lead apron and gloves on, and was pushing a steel blade into water. At the groan of the door, he turned and looked at Dex. His eyes were bloodshot and half-wild. His frame was wiry but muscled from swinging a hammer. When he recognized Dex, he gave a short smile, before returning to work.

Dex walked closer, but kept his distance from the burning work surfaces and materials that surrounded Rolink.

"Can't sleep?" Dex asked.

Rolink shook his head. "Sleep is a worse nightmare than waking."

Dex nodded. "Same here. How's it going?"

"I'm starting to make real progress, finally," Rolink said. "It has been many years since I made a blade. And it took some time to get the heat right." He nodded his head toward the wall, where Dex saw three swords hanging. "Those will actually work as weapons without cracking and breaking."

Dex looked at a pile of blades lying in a pile. He picked one up. "What's wrong with these ones?"

"Incorrect balance," Rolink said. "Or too brittle. They would work, but sooner or later they will betray the one that wields them."

Dex held the tang of one, giving it a swing back and forth. "Why can you not sleep?" he asked.

Rolink laid the cooled blade on his makeshift anvil. "I see only the faces of my wife and son hanging from a tree." He looked up at Dex. "What keeps you awake?"

"It's the time shifting dream," Dex said. "The patterns, the math… it's like this sword," he said, holding up the bad sword. "The shifting works, but it's not quite right. Something seems wrong. Too brittle. The wrong balance." He swung the sword one more time, then threw it back in the pile. "So I keep trying to fix it, or something like that. It's making me crazy."

"Perhaps these things should not be in your mind," Rolink said. "Perhaps it is a corruption to do this thing."

"Maybe," Dex said. "But it's too late for that now. I am what I am."

"And what are you, Dexter Maxwell?"

"A fighting instructor," Dex said. "When will we have more blades?"

FAMILY HIGH-ALTITUDE FLOTILLA SS *CONTESSA*, GOVERNOR'S PRIVATE QUARTERS. DAY 41.

Eighty-four.

Salzon Lewiston took another deep breath, and wished for perhaps the hundredth time in the past month that he had had a chem drip installed. He had always resisted, on grounds that it left you vulnerable to poison. He had been involved in too many intrigues himself to trust an automatic dosing system.

But he sure could use some artificial calm and patience, right now.

He sat alone at a small café table in Charles Goldman's expansive private quarters, waiting for the Governor. She had asked him to come, and he was here, in spite of all the work he had to do for the Second Harvest. And alone he sat, for perhaps the twentieth minute. He knew this was part of her technique, to make him wait. She knew how much he hated to wait. And Salzon hated how effective this was.

Finally, the door opened, and Charles entered. Through the open door, Salzon saw that Charles was talking to her Exemplar. Morgan made eye contact with Salzon, nodded briskly to Charles, and left. Charles closed the door, and gave a wide smile to Salzon as she walked toward him.

"So sorry to keep you waiting, Salzon," she said.

Salzon nodded. "Anything for the Governor," he said.

"Coffee? Tea?" Charles asked.

"With all due respect, I am tremendously busy."

"Of course, to business. I wanted to discuss Ashion the Fallen."

"I am curious as to why you have not executed him," Salzon asked. "That was, I remember, how this was supposed to play out."

"He continues to prove his value," Charles said. "Even now, we close in on the planet-side resistance because of his help."

"The resistance will be crushed, then?"

Charles nodded. "Oh yes. It is only a matter of when."

"Good. Then, you destroy Ashion."

"Don't you want to know where your brother is first?"

Salzon's vision went red. He took a deep breath. "I see that you and Ashion have been making your own agreements."

"I want nothing with Arvura," Charles said. "But that is a tough mistake to be living with all these years."

"We cannot change the past."

"Oh, we can, you see," Charles said. "But we know better."

"Do you know where Ashion keeps my brother? Is that why you brought me here?"

"I brought you here to tell you that I no longer know where Ashion keeps his prisoners. He has, truly, surprised me on this front."

"How so?"

"He seems to have come to some sort of agreement with Thula Gregor."

"Thula hides his chattel?"

"Those are the rumors," Charles said. "But Thula and I don't chat much."

"You are telling me our agreement is void?"

"I'm afraid so. You will have to find your brother yourself. Or give up on this obsession."

"I will find him."

"You could ask Thula," Charles said, a twinkle in her eye.

Salzon snarled. "Thula forgets no slight."

"You are one to talk," Charles said. "Ashion has provided threads from his experiments. He has done fascinating things with your brother's mind. Moved beyond the memory implants the Families tried."

"The neuroprosthetics were a dead end," Salzon said. "We could overcome degenerative diseases, and even improve cognition. But the implants were based on augmenting existing neural paths. We could never download and transplant complex neural maps with them."

"Ashion's work with your brother made a better system for re-routing the existing neural paths to store information. Dumped encrypted data in. Pulled secrets out."

"That doesn't surprise me."

"Oh, but it should, Salzon. It should. Brain burns only work for Ashion. Families always settle for memory chips or chemical modifications. You and Arvura tried brain burns yourself. It didn't work. So how is Ashion doing it?"

Salzon shrugged. "Perhaps I am too old and too dense. I suppose you know."

"It was too bizarre even for me to anticipate. But yes. I know how he did it. Are you *sure* Ashion's prisoner is your brother?"

Salzon nodded. "He may be scarred beyond recognition, but I met him. Logos took me to him. We spoke for some time. And there is no doubt in my mind that Prisoner Six is Arvura Lewiston."

"Why did you not kill him, then?"

Salzon laughed bitterly. "I intended to, but the doctor Logos anticipated this. He was carrying an explosive charge. If I had raised a hand, he would have blown us all up."

"Logos was cleverer than any of us gave him credit for," Charles said.

"Did you know the doctor?" Salzon asked.

"Only from the reports," Charles said. "One more thing, Salzon. To bring an end to these uprisings, I need to channel much of the SIN's cycles on some planet-side life-support analysis. The Second Harvest will need to wait a few days."

"We don't have a few days," Salzon said.

"Too bad. I've already ordered it. Adjust."

"Do the final angry bursts from a doomed people matter? And why not take this to the Security Council?"

"Morgan and the militarians must remain focused." Charles stood, and Salzon took the hint and stood as well.

"I will see Ashion and my brother dead," Salzon said. "With or without you."

"Oh, I have no intention of allowing Ashion to come to Earth with us," Charles said. "So either you destroy him, or Venus does. Either way is fine with me."

MORGISH TOWNSHIP, CENTRAL DISTRICT.

Eighty-five.

Ashion sat at the counter, sipping the lukewarm water and eating the meager meal that had been placed in front of him. It was late at the street-side diner; he had the place mostly to himself. He liked it better that way.

He hadn't been able to put the moment into high jack for a hundred years or more, but when he heard the quiet mumbling, he knew what it was. He took one last sip and looked up and down the bar. The tender had disappeared. He turned around slowly.

There were three of them; lean and rangy, like most Low-Cen rats. They didn't have the bulk or other telltale signs of being some of Leshan's best men, but still. If you need someone to do a hit, you went to Leshan. Ashion looked up; the overhead cam was still on. Interesting.

Time for a performance.

The three boys were already spreading out around Ashion. The one in the middle was sneering. He had long sleeves, which was a sure sign in this heat that he was hiding something. Sure enough, he opened his hand and a short blunt club slid down his arm and into his hand.

Ashion remained in his seat. He took another sip of his drink. "Do you know what I did when I was first pulled off the crim icer?" he asked quietly.

"Heah, foofed them Family ninnies," the one in the middle said. The others laughed loudly.

"I was a pit fighter," Ashion said. "On the Upper Rim."

There was a pause from the man with the club. His sneer faltered slightly.

"I was unique, see," Ashion went on. "Because I could get all kinds of cut on, beat up, destroyed, and my Family handlers could just put me in a new body." Ashion finally stood, and all three of the boys took a step back. "New body, but guess what? I could remember all the pain. That came with me. So I know a lot about how to hurt

244

someone. You could say I was made for it."

Ashion waited. The boys looked at each other.

"Well, what are you waiting for?" Ashion asked, taking a fighting stance. "You've taken payment. Best get on with this."

The one with the club took a swing. Ashion easily moved out of the way, and grabbed the attacker by the wrist, breaking his arm at the elbow. The club fell to the ground. Ashion didn't hesitate, but sent his leg back in a low kick that connected with the second boy's knee. The boy had all his weight on that leg, and his leg bent sideways at an unnatural angle. He cried out as he crumpled. Ashion brought the same leg up and caught the first attacker in the ribs with his knee. He felt the ribs crumple, as he pulled the attacker forward, his head making contact with the edge of the bar.

The last boy was trying to get to the door and escape. Ashion jumped over the body and grabbed him by the back of his shirt, horse-collaring him. The boy shrieked.

"I's not wants to hurt ya!" he screamed. "It's is not me!"

"It never is," Ashion said. He grabbed the boy by the arm, spinning him around so that his arm was behind him, the boy facing away from Ashion. Ashion whispered into his ear, "But I'm afraid the camera is on, and I have a reputation to keep." Then he put the street rat's face into the bar over and over until the boy stopped moving.

When he looked back, the other two injured boys had crawled out the door and away from the diner. Ashion let the body slump to the floor, and returned to his seat to finish his meal.

Eighty-six.

Jules watched it again. Then he pulled it back and watched it again. Father Morgish waited patiently.

"Since I first showed you," Father said, "it has not changed. It is real."

Jules pulled it again. "Th' Lewiston decoiler can't touch it," he said. "It's stands above."

"It stands above," Father said.

"Heah, th' Slave is real," Jules whispered.

"Jules," Father said. Jules finally looked up from the light box. "You and I have committed our lives to the Slave. Now, the Slave has spoken directly to us. It asks us to bring in this girl named Trance. How can we not comply?"

Jules swallowed, and looked away. "Heah, th' Slave needs Trance, eh, but why? What's she have? Any ways to ask?"

Father shook his head.

Jules looked back into the light box. "Heah, I's cans arrange a meetin wit her, Father."

"Thank you, Jules," Father Morgish said.

"She's and her friend needs to see th' First Term," Jules said. "You's can meets us there, and we's can tell her what's we's see. She's will understand."

"I will try to explain, but what if she is afraid?" Father asked. "What if she doubts the truth?"

Jules looked up again. "Heah, we's talks then, eh. We's explain."

Father held his gaze for a moment, then nodded. "Heah, we will explain."

Jules nodded. "I's has First Term watch in seven days. I's sends you a blip when we's heads out."

FAMILY HIGH-ALTITUDE FLOTILLA SS *CONTESSA*, SECURITY COUNCIL BRIEFING ROOM. DAY 46.

Eighty-seven.

Ashion tried not to admit to himself that he had been waiting all week for the cool relief of the Family boats. But the conditioned and perfumed air of the Security Council chambers felt like the most luxurious place he'd ever known. And maybe it was.

He stretched out his shoulder again, and tried not to think about the black eye he was sporting. Since the attack at the diner, there had been two more attempts on his life. One of these was clearly a paid hit; but the second seemed to merely be some Morgish townies trying to prove something to themselves. This last one was actually the most successful of the three; they had at least been able to land a punch.

Ashion the Fallen garnered no interest from the lower house of Families, and without access to any useful information, he had nothing to add to the cacophony. He kept his ears open, though. Second Harvest preparations were going well. There had been no resistance uprisings in weeks. Everyone was whispering that the Second Harvest had turned resisters into supporters, and why hadn't we done this sooner?

Ashion took his seat at the Council table. Morgan was already there, smiling smugly at a courtesan who was clearly interested in bedding the new security chief. By the looks of it, Morgan was game. She shooed the man away as the last members of the Council arrived. Salzon Lewiston was carrying a case of something that Ashion could not make out.

"Let's get started, then," Morgan said. "Dante, what's the report from Morgish?"

"Sir," Dante started with a cough, "There are massive cam blackouts affecting Lower-Central Morgish. There seems to be some kind of threading error giving us uneven overhead coverage."

"Have you checked with the Sinners?" Morgan asked, annoyed.

"Sir, yes, sir. They indicate that the SIN is too focused on other matters to properly spend time repairing the problem."

"That is true," Morgan said. "We have larger needs for the networks than caring for a cam error." Morgan paused. "We are so close now. Let Morgish exist in the dark for a few more weeks. Then there will be no more Morgish to look at." She seemed amused at her own witticism. No one laughed.

"Yes sir," Dante said with a bow. "I will tell the Sinners."

"What's next?" Morgan asked.

"If I may," Warship said. Morgan gave him a nod. "Thank you. I would like to raise again my nervousness at the lack of any armed uprising for the past two weeks. How have the raids and seizures been going? Have we captured anyone? What are they saying?"

"Allow me to report," Morgan said. "Even though Ash felt it would alienate the people, our random sweeps have turned up many members of this so called resistance. We have put them on the probe and learned many interesting things." Morgan looked around, composing herself. "First, the resistance is organized around free-standing cells that operate without a central command. Many of these cells have been devastated by the Second Harvest, as resistance members have fought to become part of it along with their neighbors. Other cells have been broken by my security forces. Others have simply vanished. There is no telling what has happened to them."

"Any word on a leader?" Warship asked.

"So far, there is only mention of this Orpheus, also known as Thelonius. Otherwise, there is always talk of the one called Fuel. An ideological figure, and likely a mythical one. No one has seen him. He speaks only through others. None of the members we have broken have been able to provide a description. We will keep looking."

"What about future attacks?" Thula asked.

Morgan nodded. "We have had word of three different attacks; the most important was a planned raid on the Goldmans' medical facilities in Draggish. We have stopped them all. Our intelligence is outstripping their ability to organize." Morgan paused. "We are winning."

"But do we know why we're winning?" Salzon asked.

"The Second Harvest sells well, we have broken much of their forces, and we have better intel. As we speak, the SIN is processing data on air and electricity usage. We are tracking all available anomalies in life-support systems from every sensor that we have planet-side on Venus. Every micro change in temperature, every fan that's working a little too hard for the space it's in. Typically these systems just run independently and we don't waste much processing power. But now we prioritize all these threads, and a dataset is emerging. We will be able to correlate this to what we know from prisoners about a secret dwelling underneath our townships known as the Honeycomb."

"The what?" Thula asked.

"On Earth," Salzon explained, "there is a small creature, an insect, known as a bee. As a species, it builds large connected tunnels and caverns as a sort of nest to store its food and hide its queen bee, who is required for their survival. If they are calling this place the Honeycomb, it is safe to assume that there are underground tunnels being put to use."

"And a queen bee to find," Warship croaked.

"It's only a matter of days before we find this place and crush what remaining resistance there is," Morgan said. "Anything else?"

"If you don't mind," Salzon said, standing. "I would like to make a toast." And with that, he pulled a bottle of wine from the case he had brought with him, along with eight glasses. He poured a small amount for everyone. Filling Ashion's glass, he looked at his bruised face.

"Having trouble down on the surface?" Salzon asked with a smile. Ashion held the glass and waited for Salzon to pour.

"Nothing I can't handle," Ashion said.

Salzon looked down the table, raising his glass. "To the Second Harvest."

"Honestly, Salzon," Morgan said. "This is outside of protocol."

"Humor me," Salzon said.

Puzzled, Morgan raised her glass. "To the Second Harvest," she said.

Everyone took a sip.

"This wine is awful," Thula said, grimacing.

Ashion showed his agreement with his own grimace.

Salzon nodded. "Yes, it really is. Can you tell me *why* it's so horrible?"

Thula shook her head. "I've never tasted anything like that."

"I paid the highest possible price for it," Salzon said. "It's all the rage in the black markets of our boats. How could it taste so terrible?"

"It hasn't been aged," Ashion said quietly.

"A little louder, please," Salzon said, beaming.

"It hasn't been aged," Ashion said again.

"It hasn't been aged!" Salzon bellowed. "Earth-side wine that hasn't been aged. Brand new, you might say." He paused, and then turned to Morgan, his eyes bulging. "It would seem that the Second Harvest has started a bit early."

"That's impossible," Morgan said. "There is no avenue for Earth-side products."

"Perhaps the former security chief has an idea," Thula said, turning to Ashion.

All eyes were on Ashion. He shrugged. "It's the infantry," he said. "They see the angle. They suppose a Second Harvest is soon to be underway. Why not start now, and get in while the prices are at the top of the market?"

All eyes turned to Morgan, who was looking at the wine with rage. "I will take care of it," she said. She stood, and the meeting was over.

Eighty-eight.

The cams whirred to a stop, and the two women stepped from the shadows quickly, their interfaces slung across their backs. With the overhead cams out, so went much of the light, leaving only the dull red of the backup LEDs. The avenues in old Central Morgish seemed even smaller in the dim light. Night cycle and mandatory curfew meant they were alone. They ran quickly. One led, knowing the way and running gracefully through the tunnels; the other followed, trying not to fall behind.

They reached their destination. Typically, there would be two devout Sinners ensuring that no one came or went without Father Morgish's say so. Today, there was only one; short, fat, and nervously shifting his weight from leg to leg.

"Heah, Jules," Trance greeted him.

"You's do that with th' lights?" Jules asked, pointing up.

"Heah, Lynia here," Trance said, throwing her thumb over her shoulder.

"Heah, goods trick, eh," Jules said. "Th' timin algorithm is tall complicated so I's can see how's th' Slave not find the threadin capabilities to ends your self-replicatin repeater when it's is workin out Second Harvest, eh. You's could up th' duration wit a little—"

"We's goin in, eh?" Trance asked.

Jules took a deep breath. "Heah, we's goin in." He palmed the threader, and the door opened.

Trance and Mal followed Jules through the door. Trance had not believed she would ever see the inside of Central Processing again, given the circumstances of her last visit. But here she was, and with one of those crazy brains that could actually make sense of what was in there. She noticed that many of the blast marks from the uprisings raid had permanently stained the steel floors. They entered the server room, and the conditioned air felt like the breath of God.

"First Term's is this ways, eh," Jules said, indicating an altar and worship benches near the back. "It's is nothin, eh, but maybe's you's think it's is ya onion."

Mal smiled. "Let's take a look."

The First Term was a non-descript black box, studiously cleaned, with a square display on top. Not one of the new displays that holographed in mid-air inside a light box, but a two-dimensional interface.

"Does this turn on?" Mal asked quietly.

"Heah," Jules said, reaching behind and carefully fingering a switch. The display lit weakly from behind, but the screen stayed dark. Except for a few pixels.

"Heah, this's is th' First Term," Jules said reverently. "Only's Father Morgish knows its ways. He's uses this," Jules said, pointing to a thread interface that stood next to the First Term display. "It's is wired to this server. Th' First Server. Wit this thread box, Father Morgish speaks wit th' Slave. Through it he's can know th' Slave's heart. Th' blinkin line's," Jules said, pointing to the display, "is th' Slave's heartbeat. It's blinks, just like that, for a thousand years."

Mal looked at the blinking line, then at Jules. She couldn't help but grin.

"That's not a heartbeat," she said. "That's a cursor."

Eighty-nine.

"A what?" Trance said.

"A cursor," Mal said. "Anyone around here have a goddamn keyboard?"

"A what?" Jules asked.

"A keyboard," Mal said, looking all over the box. "It looks like this case has had a mod since it arrived. More steel and better cooling. But there's gonna be an I/O interface for a keyboard around here somewhere. How old you say this server is?"

"Nearly one thousand years."

Mal nearly squealed in delight. "I bet I speak its language."

"That may be so," boomed a voice behind her, "but today you will not speak with the Slave."

Jules, Trance, and Mal turned to see Father Morgish standing behind them. They were surrounded by a dozen Sinners, all carrying blast guns. Trance looked at Jules. He was staring at the guns.

"You's said we's talk, Father," Jules said.

"I couldn't take any chances," Father said. "These people have proven to be… violent."

"But… you's promised," Jules said.

"Jules?" Trance said.

Jules turned. He looked horrified and guilty all at once. "I's sorry, Trance," Jules said. "Th' Slave has spoken."

"Jules," Mal said, "the Families are going to destroy it. They are going to destroy the Slave."

"Too true," Father Morgish said. "The Families will not save the Slave, or its followers. But I know the man who can."

"Heah, you's mean that hole Ash," Trance said. She stared at Father Morgish, contempt bleeding from every pore of her body.

"He alone can save the Slave," Father said, staring back at her.

"Whats? No, no," Jules said, looking at Father Morgish. "Surely you's nots gonna give Trance to Ashion th' Dark?"

While Jules spoke, Trance slowly reached down to her backpack. With the speed of training, she pulled the blaster from the pack and took a shot at the closest Sinner, who took the shot to the chest and flew backward. She took another shot, then another. Mal dived behind one of the benches.

"No! Stops!" Jules shouted.

But it was too late. A dozen or more bolts landed on Trance at once, forcing her back against the far wall, where she crumpled to the ground.

"Trance!" Jules shouted, and ran to her. He reached her, tried to help her up.

"Is she… is she…" Mal stuttered.

Jules sobbed. "I's thinks she's breathin… oh Trance…I's so sorry…"

The Sinners had reached Mal, and put a zip-tie on her hands and dragged her to her feet. She was looking in shock at Trance and the sobbing Jules. A few of the Sinners approached Trance, but Jules swatted at them in fury.

"Don'ts touch her! Don't!" he shouted. He buried his face in Trance's shoulder.

Father Morgish frowned. "Jules, we must bring her," he said. "I am sorry for your friend. But you must let us carry her."

Jules wiped his face and stood. He faced the wall, taking deep breaths. Then he turned. "I's comin with you. This's is as th' Slave requires."

Father Morgish nodded his approval, and the Sinners swooped in to carry Trance's limp body. Devotion, he thought. That's what I need right now.

MORGISH TOWNSHIP. THE HONEYCOMB.

Ninety.

The three men slowly brought the room to life on the treadmills. The lights flickered, then turned on. Slowly the light box began to glow blue, the threads roiling through its middle, roping over and over.

Fuel stuck his hand into the light box. His glove began to interact with the threads, and he pulled one to the surface. It was overhead cam footage, in low light.

"I thought we weren't connected to the SIN down here?" Dex said.

"This is an offline capture, it was recorded to this mitt," Fuel said, indicating the glove. "Now watch. This took place only a few hours ago," Fuel said.

Dex and Thelo leaned in, squinting at the low resolution.

"Is that Central Processing?" Thelo asked.

"That's Trance and Mal," Dex said. "What's happened?"

"Just watch," Fuel said grimly.

The three of them watched as the Sinners made their way in, and Trance attempted to free herself. They watched her take all the bolts and slump against the far wall.

"Is she dead?" Thelo asked. He tried to pretend Dex wasn't next to him while running through a quick mind game. He needed Logos' serum. The sight of Dex was bringing the taste up in his mouth. The anger.

"Those bolts guns are meant to override your nervous system," Fuel said. "They knock out your ability to control your muscles, but they are not meant to kill. But she took so many. There is no way to know for sure."

Dex watched them zip-tie Mal, and his vision went dark. His mind served up his worst memory: Mal bent over a 'muter in the moonlight, in the parking lot of the orphanage.

"I will go get them," he said.

"I'm afraid you'll do nothing of the sort," Fuel said.

"We need them," Thelo said. "Dex is right; we have to go get

255

them."

"It's too dangerous," Fuel said. "We are too close now."

"No," Dex said. He stepped off the treadmill. "I will not let this happen to Mal. Or Trance. I will not."

"I didn't show this to you so you would run off like a fool and get yourself killed!" Fuel said.

"Then why did you show us?" Dex yelled.

"Father Morgish is convinced Ashion will save the Slave," Fuel said. "He will go to Ashion, not the Families."

"And that's better how?" Thelo asked.

"Ashion is holed up in a modified squatter box in Central Morgish," Fuel said. "He is powerless to act right now. We must not over-react."

Dex was silent. But his heart was racing.

"Listen, we will get them back," Fuel said. "We attack the boats in less than four days. The end of the world as we know it is in ten. There is too much at stake to reveal ourselves."

"Ashion will know who Mal is," Thelo said.

"We cannot control all the variables," Fuel said. "But we will wait until the attack on the boats. As you stated, the spy from the future will return in four days. They will know of you then. That is our moment to get your friends back."

Dex said nothing, and turned to leave.

"Where are you going?" Fuel asked.

"I have a training team coming in," Dex said. "I've got to get back to work."

MORGISH TOWNSHIP, CENTRAL DISTRICT.
DAY 49.

Ninety-one.

Ashion kept the crude metal club that the tunnel rat had attacked him with, and wielded it now as though it were a sword. It was boredom, really. He was sat in his hot little box in Morgish, waiting. Waiting for others to do his work. His residence was also currently part of the cam and light blackouts that had plagued Morgish for the past week. So he trained.

It was his own fault, and he knew it. He'd carelessly left Judas with Logos, because Logos had that ridiculously efficient sharpening laser. It worked wonders for Judas, etching all the dirt off the surface, and giving it a molecular edge. He had that solution he used, to coat the thing. Made it impermeable to damage. So he'd ordered Logos to clean it again.

Then Logos had given it to the iter.

So much of this is due to my arrogance, Ashion thought. I had become like the Families, so sure of myself and my plan.

Ashion swung the makeshift club harder, faster, working up a sweat, beating an invisible version of himself.

I won't let that happen again.

Ashion lost himself in an imaginary battle, feinting, attacking. It was with great surprise, then, that he heard his door blip. He waited to catch his breath, club in hand, and wiped the sweat from his face before he slid the door open a few inches.

It was Father Morgish, a burning smile on his face.

"Come to gloat, Father?" Ashion said. "I'm busy."

"I would like to speak with you," Father Morgish said. "I can help."

Ashion looked at him for a moment, then looked past. No followers, no entourage. He shrugged, opened the door, and walked back toward his cot. Father Morgish noted Ashion's club with some trepidation. "Expecting someone?" he asked.

"Just killing time," Ashion said. He put the crude weapon down, noting that the cam around Father Morgish's neck was on, threading their conversation.

"Time seems to be in short supply for us planet-siders," Father said.

Ashion looked Father Morgish in the eye. Then he nodded. "You best be making friends up on the boats. I'm the wrong person if you're looking for salvation."

"I do not seek passage for myself," Father Morgish said.

"Then what do you seek?" Ashion asked.

"Last time we spoke, you were interrogating me concerning an attack on Central Processing," Father said. "I detailed for you all that I saw. But I made an... omission, at the time. An omission I would now like to rectify."

Ashion waited.

"While waiting for your rescue, my servant Jules and I bore witness to a strange phenomenon on the threads. It is not worth going into now, but it led the two of us on an investigation that revealed something else entirely. We discovered evidence of an interface to the SIN that predated the Primary Family Interface."

Ashion sat perfectly still. He noted again the cam around Father's neck. "Go on," he said.

"This interface allows for silent thread manipulation," Father said. "Most importantly, it allowed for thread deletions that would go unnoticed. Completely undetectable."

Deletions of Logos in the med fac, Ashion thought. "Why are you telling me this?"

"It seemed like something you might want to know," Father said. "The pattern of deletions seemed to... surround you."

"Do you know who did it?"

Father shook his head. "No, not exactly. But, a Lewiston," Father said. "It would appear the Lewistons have been passing down a very valuable Family heirloom."

"Valuable, indeed."

Father Morgish cocked his head to the side. "Did you ever meet Arvura Lewiston?"

Ashion spoke carefully. "We spoke, on occasion."

"He was the last Lewiston that I really knew," Father said. "He spent a lot of time with the Sinners. With the Slave. In the months before his assassination, he was a common figure at Central Processing. A very bright man. Very interested in our beliefs. Very interested in coming to know the Slave." Father shrugged. "But I do not know any of the current Lewistons. So I cannot provide much else for you. Other than the fact that it takes a Lewiston to destroy the threads."

Ashion was lost in thought. "I thank you for this, Father."

"I have more," Father said. "I have two prisoners that attempted to interface with the First Term. I think you will find them quite useful to you."

Ashion opened his mouth, and shut it again. "Why are you here?"

Father Morgish looked nervous for the first time. When he spoke, he whispered. "He spoke to me. The Slave spoke to me." Father's gaze caught Ashion's, and there was a zealous fire that burned into him.

"The Slave told me you will save it," Father said. "The Slave will walk among us, and you will do it."

Ashion kept a straight face. *At least I have one friend left.*

"I have communed with the Slave for many years," Ashion said, averting his gaze and wringing his hands for effect. "All I have done, I have done for the Slave."

Father's passionate gaze burned through Ashion, and he was nodding. "I shall bring you these two women. One of them is from the attack on Cen-Proc. The Princess."

Ashion thought about that for a moment. He could feel leverage shifting back into his favor.

"Father, let us be patient," he said. "Keep your two guests close, but out of the hands of the Families. I will come for them soon."

Father Morgish nodded, and stood to leave. "The Slave walks among us."

Ashion stood, bowing slightly, playing the part. "The Slave—" he stopped, listening.

The sound of an explosion could be heard in the distance. Father heard it too, and hurried toward the door. Another explosion was closer.

Ashion closed his eyes. Those blasts sounded familiar.

"I must go," Father said, reaching the door.

The sound of shouting came from the corridor. Ashion opened his eyes. *Bunker-beaters.* Controlled explosives for knocking open doors.

"No Father," Ashion said, jumping to the door. "Get away from there!"

Ashion flipped the metal cot onto its side, and pulled a metal barricade bar from underneath it. He heaved the heavy steel bar across the door at chest height, where steel hooks had been soldered on either side. In the same motion, he grabbed Father Morgish and threw him behind the overturned cot, and jumped behind it himself.

A deafening noise rocked Ashion's door, cratering it in.

Ninety-two.

Dex was in the middle of a complex defensive demonstration in front of the eighteen-hundred team when he heard the distant sound. He stopped mid-move, and barely had time to bring up his training sword to defend his head. He put a hand up to the attacking trainee, then a finger to his lips. There was a second boom.

"Masks!" Dex shouted. Every member of the training group unsnapped a gas mask from a holster on their belt and hastily fixed it over their faces. Dex did the same, pulling a deep breath through the filter. The security guard at the north entrance looked through the door's port, and threw the door open.

"Don't open that!" Dex shouted, but through the mask, his voice was muffled. The door opened, and a second guard stumbled through, coughing.

"Honeycomb... under attack," The guard said. Then a loud explosion behind him knocked both guards to the ground.

Dex let the moment come to a crawl. The patterns unspooled, spelling out the steps, the minute acts. He felt and saw the small missile flying through the open north door. He grabbed the trainee he had been dueling with and pulled him to the ground as the shell whistled past them and hit the far wall, exploding into the iron hull of the training facility. The explosion knocked everyone down, and smoke overwhelmed the atmo fans.

Ears ringing, Dex realized that no one would be able to talk. All he could do was hope that his team remembered their training, and knew where to go. Dex stood, and grabbed the shell-shocked young trainee underneath him, pushing him toward the south door.

"Run!" Dex yelled, but he couldn't even hear himself. Then he turned and sprinted toward the open north door. A group of three Red Masks were already streaming through. Dex had only the training sword, but he was able to engage the first assassin immediately, even as the other two moved into the space, looking to secure the room and move on.

The Red Mask was no match for Dex's skills, but Dex was unable to cut through the Knight's tough gloves and disarm him. The force was enough to knock the sword from the Knight's hand, but he spun around and out of range. Dex was having difficulty fighting with the old gas mask on. He noted the Red Masks had massive filters and infrared goggles. They could breathe unimpeded, and see every living thing in the room, even with the poisonous gas everywhere.

I need Judas. I need to get my trainees out the south door and slag the corridor.

Dex moved to the north door. The fact that the guard had opened it may have just saved them, as it could be shut now, and another blast required to open it again. A Family soldier was rushing through with a bolt gun. Dex pushed the tip of the training sword hard into the throat of the soldier, who gargled and fell. The corridor was full of soldiers, but the corridor's design forced them into single-file. They had blasted the secret entrance to Central Morgish, then moved the weapon to let soldiers by. Dex pushed the heavy door shut and set the bar-lock. Even as he did that, he felt the attack from behind, and ducked.

The Red Mask's blade clanged off the door, and Dex came around hard with the training sword. The attacker easily moved out of the way and brought the sword down. But Dex wasn't waiting to take him down. He rolled to his feet and sprinted for the far wall.

He noted with grim satisfaction that nine of the trainees had spread into a defensive posture around the two other Red Masks that had made it into the room. They spaced in exactly the right way to minimize the Red Masks' advantage in skill and quickness. The smoke was clearing, the massive atmo fans pulling it out of the air as quickly as possible. Dex hit the west wall, where Judas hung. He grabbed it and spun.

Dex parried an attack, and noted immediately that the Red Mask had recognized the sword. Dex saw him look to his two Red Mask brethren, who were back to back circling inside the trainees' perimeter. All three Red Masks looked at Dex.

They are communicating. They know who I am.

Dex flung the patterns out, sent them circling around and around the three Red Masks, bouncing off the trainees, back to Dex and defining the moment, the space, the future. He put Judas through the heart of the first Red Mask, and without hesitation, he broke the perimeter of the trainees, who watched in awe as Dex spun directly into the two remaining Red Masks. The first parried Dex's attack, and the second ran toward the south door, swinging at the closest trainee. The trainee defended perfectly, but the Red Mask was not trying to kill. He was trying to get into the heart of the Honeycomb.

Dex felt the moment, the passing of time. The Family soldiers would have the north corridor cleared in just a few more seconds. The door blasted opened. Dex swung once, twice, then came down low, in a sequence he had taught his team just a few moments ago. The Red Mask did as expected, blocking once, twice, then stepping back out of the way of the low attack.

The trainee directly behind the Red Mask did just what Dex had trained her to do: she swung her sword into the assassin's exposed neck. Even though there was not a sharp edge, the force of the sword collapsed the Red Mask's esophagus, and he fell to the ground clutching his throat.

Dex had already left the scene, chasing the third Red Mask, who was by now at the south door. He beckoned to the trainees to follow him. The Red Mask slapped something onto the hinge, and turned to meet Dex.

It's an explosive, Dex realized as he swung at the Red Mask. He noted that there was some black sludge-like adhesive seeping from behind the charge, making it impossible to free from the wall in time. Dex took the moment even slower, anticipating the Red Mask's motions, and put the sword through his arm, then his leg, and finally his neck. It took only moments, and he pulled his mask off so he could be heard.

"Get back!" he yelled. "Explosive on the south door!" Dex jumped away. All the trainees hesitated, then followed suit, leaping away from the door and to the ground.

They lay there for a moment, but nothing happened. Dex was holding his breath, and he looked up, feeling a bit silly.

Then the south door exploded at the hinge. A moment later, the north door imploded.

Ninety-three.

Ashion waited, huddled over Father Morgish behind his cot. With the reinforcing bar, the blast was probably not going to get through on the first shot. So there would be a second.

Then it came. The room shrieked with rending metal. Even with the thin mattress held tight over his ears, his head rung.

But this wasn't Ashion's first dance.

He pulled the mattress off his head. He indicated to Father Morgish, who was huddled in fear, to stay put. Father nodded, and pulled the mattress back over himself. Ashion jumped over the cot to survey the small room.

The door had buckled in, and smoke was drifting in. Ashion knew they were gassing the area, so he did not take a breath. It took only a few moments for a soldier to step in, swinging a bolt gun to clear the area.

Ashion grabbed the blast gun, and punched the soldier in the throat, wrenching the gun sideways and out of his hand. The soldier fell back, and Ashion had the gun. He moved out of the way as bolt after bolt entered the room, blasting in the bottom of the cot and destroying the small light box on the counter. Ashion quickly, evenly rolled out into the corridor and opened fire.

They were not guerrillas, but Family soldiers. Ashion had expected this, although the level of arms in play was a surprise. He fired a controlled burst into the first soldier he saw, even as the second took aim at Ashion. In the small space, there was little room to operate, but Ashion used his strong right leg to push against the far wall and leverage the low gravity of Venus to spin up and over the volley of blasts that came at him. He kept the gun pointed forward, blasting two more soldiers. He landed on his feet and leaped forward, making himself a small target, blasting the whole time until his gun's charge was depleted.

Ashion saw one more soldier peering around the bend ahead. Ashion picked up the soldier's gun, waiting, aiming. Ashion caught him in the head and he slammed backward into the wall behind. Ashion took the moment to adjust the straps of his gas mask, then crouched, letting the convulsing soldier fall to the ground. The others Ashion had hit were trying to right themselves. Ashion shot each of them in the chest as he stepped over and around them, keeping his eyes on the bend ahead. There were more shouts, and another explosion.

Ashion looked up, and noted that the overhead had been blasted. He grabbed a fresh bolt gun from the ground, and turned the bend. The noise was coming from the level below, and he saw more soldiers down there. Even as he watched, he saw the patch of golden hair, and heard her voice shouting orders over the chaos.

Morgan Goldman.

Ashion swung the bolt gun at the ground hard a few times. He flipped it over and pried the small bent casing off. Inside he found an unintelligibly small black trips set. Ashion squinted through the visor, and used the fingernail of his smallest finger to ease the trips into a new configuration. A red light began to flash on the trigger. He put his hand on the battery, and felt it already heating up as the over-clocked bolt gun began to put too much energy into the dispensing barrel.

Morgan must have found a nest of resistance forces near his cabin, Ashion realized, and tried to use the chaotic opportunity to destroy him. Typical Family move, Ashion thought. Almost worked.

The red flashing light was increasing in frequency. Ashion lay on his stomach and peered down. There were soldiers yelling and moving into position. From above, Ashion could see about thirty feet in each direction of the corridor. He saw soldiers moving a bunker buster into position at a hole in the wall that Ashion realized must be a secret door.

So close to them this whole time, he thought bitterly.

He banished the thought, looking for his target… and he found her. Morgan was talking into her com, and pointing at the door as they repositioned the missile firing system. Ashion waited until they had launched the massive weapon, then he took his aim directly at Morgan's head, and fired.

There was only one bolt available to him, because he had over-ridden the safety controls and overclocked the power inverter. It hit Morgan Goldman in the left side of her head. Because of the amount of energy, it melted her helmet, tore into her skull, and ripped her head from her neck.

The explosion from the bunker buster echoed through the chamber as Morgan Goldman's body slumped against the ground. Ashion threw the destroyed bolt gun down the ladder, and walked back to his cabin, gathering all the weapons he could find on the way.

He found Father Morgish unconscious from the sleeping gas, but otherwise unharmed. Ashion pushed the cot to the door and leaned it over the broken entrance, aimed a bolt gun at it, then sat on the ground and waited.

Ninety-four.

Dex let the heat and shrapnel fly over his head before pulling the gas mask back on, taking three deep breaths, and tearing it off again. "Through the south door! Now!" he yelled. Then the mask was back on and he headed for the north door. He watched as his trainees slow-ly pulled themselves up and headed south. Three of them did not rise, and one was now limping.

Dex glanced down the tunnel. There was a row of soldiers run-ning down the corridor in single file. They were crouched down, but Dex could see they had bolt guns, and the one on the front began fir-ing out the door. The bolts rang off the far wall, but did not connect with anyone.

They have discovered the Honeycomb. But how many entrances have they found? Dex knew that if he could get his trainees all way through the next corridor, he could trigger the kill-hall and the corridor would be turned to slag by the pressure and heat of the Venus atmo.

But would they simply be running into the arms of the same

Family army?

Dex didn't have time to find out. The first Family soldier emerged from the north door. Dex swung the Judas sword down, taking off the man's arm above the elbow. Dex grabbed his bolt gun in the same motion. Bolts flew past the man's head and toward Dex, who in the jacked moment saw them being fired, and moved to avoid them. He flipped the bolt gun in his hand around and unloaded it back into the corridor into the second man, who fell backward into the man behind him. Dex fired one more time into the man behind him, then turned and ran at full speed for the south door.

The angle of the south door was such that, from the north door, you could not see the passageway or get a shot down its long corridor. Dex knew that he had to get through the south door before any more soldiers emerged from the north. As he ran, he could see the flyer, the rock, the knives dancing around, moving behind him, surrounding the flailing arms and legs as the soldiers moved their injured colleagues out of the way to get to the empty training facility.

Dex had no choice but to throw himself the last few feet through the door as the energy bolts bounced around and past him, sizzling the air and burning his arms. He slammed into the back wall of the south tunnel with a grunt, then dropped to the floor and pushed himself out of harm's way. The energy bolts landed all around him. His left hand felt like it was on fire, and he realized he'd been hit. He couldn't feel anything from the elbow down, and it made standing difficult, with his right hand still around Judas' hilt. He looked down the corridor. One trainee was getting all the others through the next door at the other end. Dex began running again, his only hope was that the soldiers would be more careful coming around the corner than the first soldier Dex had encountered. That hesitation was all Dex needed.

The trainee was beckoning to Dex with his arm in a big circle. "Go! Go! Go!" the young man was yelling. Dex finally made it, and the trainee stepped in front of him to close the door. The rain of bolt fire knocked the man on top of Dex. Dex grabbed him and pushed the door shut with all his might.

"Get this man!" Dex yelled. "Keep moving!" Two trainees grabbed the unconscious one, and Dex began the process of enabling the kill-hall. It would take a few seconds for the manual mechanism to unlock all the way to the surface. As it began its process, Dex looked through the small hole in the door. The soldiers had abandoned the corridor; it was completely empty.

Then Dex saw them wheel the large bunker buster around the corner and into place. *If they destroy this door before the corridor collapses…*

"Run! Run!" Dex yelled.

The Family soldiers finally pulled the bunker buster into place, and fired up its energy source. It began the high-pitched whine as it prepared the ignition of the missile. The soldiers heard the groan and creek of old metal buckling. Then the corridor crumpled into itself under a pile of rock and heat.

Ninety-five.

Dex felt the pressure in his ears for a fraction of a second before the massive gate fell to the ground in front of the corridor, sealing them off from the Venus atmosphere that had saved them.

Dex looked at the survivors. Some looked back frightened, others with a grim determination. Dex pointed to the far door. "We go deeper," he said.

"That was the only door out," a man said. He was holding his arm where blood was dripping out.

Dex shook his head. "It's the only door you knew about," he said.

"Is it the only door *they* knew about?" the man asked, nodding toward the soldiers.

"Only one way to find out," Dex said. "Follow me."

They wound their way deeper into the tunnels, making their way back toward the next exit. As they reached the intersection, Dex saw Thelo, who was helping set a man's leg.

"Good to see you're ok," Thelo said. "We didn't know if they'd taken the Central entrance." Thelo glanced at the bleeding and dirty trainees. "I take it they have."

Dex nodded. "Do they have Lower-Central?"

"Yes," Thelo said. Seeing Dex's anxious look, he added. "Rolink escaped, with his latest batch of blades."

Dex let out a deep breath. "What about everyone else?"

"I don't know yet."

At that moment, the far door creaked open, and Fuel stepped into the room. Despite their exhaustion, everyone stopped to stare. Fuel ignored this and walked directly to Dex and Thelo.

"How bad is it?" he asked.

"Lost the training fac and Central Morgish entrance. Slagged the kill gate," Dex said. "Lost five fighters."

"Lower-Central is slagged, too," Thelo said. "Worse casualties. We lost an entire battalion before we even knew what hit us."

Fuel looked over the survivors in the room, then back to Dex and Thelo. He lowered his voice. "We lost two battalions at Central," he said. "And the third door."

Thelo leaned in. "So we are trapped?"

"We still have the two secret doors," Fuel said. "But once we open them, we have to assume they will find them."

"We will never take the boats with so many casualties," Thelo said. "All the work..."

"Do not despair, Thelonius Hollywood," Fuel said. "We have a plan B."

"I'm all ears," Dex said. He was rubbing his right hand, trying to get even a hint of feeling to come back.

"We change targets," Fuel said. "But we're going to need a little girl in Draggish first. Oh, and Dex," he said. "It's time to go get Lynia and Trance now."

FAMILY HIGH-ALTITUDE FLOTILLA SS *CONTESSA*, SECURITY COUNCIL BRIEFING ROOM. DAY 50.

Ninety-six.

The sound pounded through Ashion's skull, pulling him out of a deep sleep. He had grown accustomed to natural sleep since he had lost access to his chems, but the waking was much too difficult for his liking. He rubbed his eyes, looking around. He couldn't remember where he was.

Family med facs, boat-side. He looked around. Next to him, Father Morgish lay sleeping. Then he heard the sound again. It was his com, hailing him. He tapped the spot behind his ear, and it crackled to life. "Ashion here," he said.

"Sir, it's Holden," the voice said.

"Holden!" Ashion said. "Good to hear from you."

"Thank you, sir," Holden said. "Your presence has been requested at an emergency meeting of the Security Council."

"Requested or demanded?" Ashion asked.

"Demanded, sir."

"When?"

"Now, sir."

"Thank you, Holden."

"Of course, sir. An escort is on the way."

Ninety-seven.

Salzon nodded at Ashion as he entered, then turned and looked to Charles. "Now can we start?" he asked.

Charles nodded imperceptibly.

"Should we not wait for Morgan?" Thula asked.

"Morgan will not be joining us," Salzon said.

"That would be a breach of protocol," Thula said.

"Morgan Goldman is dead," Charles said.

Ashion waited, mustering up just the right amount of innocent

269

curiosity. Salzon was threading something, and he pushed it up into the large light box for all to see. It was an overhead cam from Central Morgish. Ashion recognized the bunker buster immediately.

"This was during Morgan's raid on the secret lair of the resistance," Salzon said. He pointed. "She had found two entrances based on data analyses performed on the SIN. Slight drops in atmo pressure were occurring at intervals that could be correlated to citizens of Morgish going missing from the threads. The pressure changes could be traced back to ancient sensors in the oldest parts of Central and Lower-Central Morgish, which enabled us to identify the location of the two entrances. She received approval from Charles and me to lead an attack, as this Council was informed."

Everyone except me, Ashion thought.

"You can see the bunker busters from the asteroid wars were used to great effect. We were able to take out nearly two hundred resistance fighters. But then the corridors were destroyed by intricate mechanisms that tripped a breach in the pressurized atmo system, and the Venus atmo rushed in and destroyed the corridors to and from the Honeycomb."

Everyone was still engrossed in the footage of the raid. Morgan was ordering troops to secure all corridors, including the one that Ashion lived on.

"Have we neutralized the resistance threat?" Warship asked.

"It is not altogether clear," Salzon said. "There may be more trapped back in these tunnels, but after the corridors melted and air measurements stabilized, the SIN can no longer find atmospheric anomalies that would indicate another entrance. There is no way in or out now. They may already be suffocated. But there is still reason for us to investigate."

"Here it comes," Charles said. All eyes were on the footage. As they watched, Morgan's head was obliterated, and her body slumped to the ground.

Salzon stopped the thread. "The Goldman Exemplar and security chief is gone," he said. "We need a new security chief."

"And a new Goldman Exemplar," Thula pointed out.

"Charles Goldman has joined us," Salzon said. "She is here to confirm our new chief."

"Who is it?" Ashion asked.

"You," Charles said. "Ashion, our esteemed colleague, will be reinstated as chief."

Ashion stood perfectly still for a moment, trying to read Charles. But nothing. The woman had just lost her only daughter, but she displayed not a hint of emotion.

"I am sorry for the death of your daughter," Ashion bowed deeply.

"The entire Security Council mourns her," Salzon said.

"Morgan chose her role as Exemplar," Charles said. "She chose her battles to fight. She was a Goldman to the end—with no regrets. I hereby give my support to Ashion Goldman as security chief, and call for the reinstatement of his privileges."

"And my property?" Ashion asked.

"We'll see about that," Salzon said. "Let's move on. Dante, an update on our investigation of Earth-side goods."

"Yes sir," Dante said. "We've determined the source of the contraband." He pulled a thread, switching the display from Morgan's dead body to a grainy overhead. "This is the recon shuttle that went missing before the Earth-side station was compromised."

The thread showed the shuttle landing, and the cargo bay opening. The pilot emerged first, a large man who saluted to the guards on duty. They entered the cargo bay and began pulling out long coffin-shaped cylinders.

"The cylinders should have been the deceased Knights deployed by Ashion to investigate Earth-side when we lost contact with it nearly two months ago," Dante went on. "But in fact, the bags contained stolen goods from Earth. A network of infantry worked together to hide these facts from us, and they all took a cut of the profits." Dante froze the thread. "We have put an end to the practice, and we have punished the relevant infantry."

"You did not find the pilot," Ashion said.

Dante looked at him uncomfortably. "What makes you say that?"

"Tell us if this is true," Salzon bellowed.

"The pilot is still missing," Dante said. "But infantry come and go, at times. We will find him."

271

"No, you won't," Ashion said, turning to Salzon. "Do you have any idea who it is?"

Salzon shook his head. "Should I know every shuttle pilot that works for the Families?"

"That is the one they call Orpheus," Ashion said. "Also known as Thelonius."

Salzon rubbed his temples.

"Are you certain?" Charles asked.

"Certain," Ashion said. "Looks like a resistance leader has been posing as an infantry pilot and moving goods to Earth. Probably in order to fund their cause."

"And probably compromising our Earth-side station again," Warship said. The others nodded.

"We need to know more about that pilot," Thula said.

"We need to travel back in time," Salzon said. "We know when that shuttle left Earth. We can send someone back to investigate."

"It's too dangerous," Ashion said. "And besides, if we stopped Orpheus in the past, that would be reflected in our future."

"Perhaps we already have," Thula said. "We have not heard from this Orpheus since this thread was generated."

"I propose we shift a highly trained assassin to Earth to the time of this video," Salzon said. "Not to kill, but to learn. To see if we can expose Orpheus' plans for the future on Venus."

"We have no one with the proper training," Warship said. "We struggle to bring new Knights up to task. We have little shifting experience, and no nano-suits prepped."

"There is one," Salzon said, looking at Ashion.

"I will not send Ashion," Charles said.

"Not Ash," Salzon said. "There is another. Her name is Kat."

Ashion felt his vision go black.

"Who is this?" Thula asked.

Salzon performed a series of strums on his interface, bringing up a low-grade visual of Ashion's secret training compounds. It showed Kat battling Gurn in a sword fight. "Ashion Goldman has secretly been training and analyzing this woman since her birth sixteen years ago. She has taken all of the shifting training. She is the most capable time traveler there probably ever will be, based on the massive neural data from her that I have been able to view."

"Who is she?" Thula demanded. "Where did she come from? Where is she now?"

Salzon shrugged. "Born of an asteroid slave. It's of little matter. Ashion can bring her to us."

Ashion said nothing.

"If there is useful information that can be gleaned, with utmost discretion, then I am all for it," Warship said. The other generals agreed.

"If she is as skilled as Salzon says," Thula said, "Then I want it done."

Salzon cocked his head at Ashion. "Produce the girl."

"I will not," Ashion said.

"This Council orders it," Salzon said. "She needs a test run. And we need a spy."

"The penalty for non-compliance is imprisonment," Thula warned. "We can put you on ice."

"Then we would be no closer to the resistance leader, would we?" Ashion responded bitterly. "Give me back my shuttle, my Draggish compound, and my scientists. Then I will send Kat to Earth."

"Agreed," Salzon said, "Does anyone have a problem with that?"

"I will go along," Charles said. "How long will it take?"

Ashion thought for moment. "Two days."

Charles nodded. "Time on Venus grows short, and the Families restless. We are cutting this very close. Let us hear what Kat can tell us first, but then we must begin the exodus."

The Council agreed, and looked to Ashion.

Ashion stood. "Kat will be at the Transloop station tomorrow at 1800 hours via my shuttle. It will take twenty-four hours from then to get the shift prepped. I will program the chronometric sequencer myself. I will prep the nanos. When she gets back, she reports to me. Not Charles, not Salzon. Me." He turned to Salzon. "Now get your people out of my compound."

As Ashion left the Council meeting and walked toward the shuttle docks, his com crackled to life. "Holden," he said.

"Sir, good to have you back, sir," Holden said.

"It will be a short second term," Ashion said. "I need you to get

Gurn down to Lower-Central Morgish. The Sinners will be waiting for him. And hail Leshan. He has something I need."

"Yes, sir," Holden said. "Will you be needing a shuttle?"

"No, I'll be taking my own."

Ninety-eight.

"What does that do? Can you see anything through that? Does the threader here get any music? Can I see what you're threading?"

It went on and on. It had not stopped since Ashion had picked the little brat up from Leshan. The Thug King had been relieved to be rid of her; at the time, Ashion had thought it was because of the girl's value as a stolen property. But he had come to better understand Leshan's feelings regarding young Jahna Gregor.

"Are you going to let me drive? I've driven a shuttle before, you know. My father, he is the best pilot ever and he lets me drive the small class A models. They are very cute and I'm thinking of getting my very own. Where are we going? I don't think you know where you are going. That navigator program is all wrong, it says we're landing but we're not landing so why does it say we are landing?"

"If you do not stay quiet, I will hit you," Ashion growled.

"I don't think you'd hit me if you knew who my father is. It's a secret and I can't tell you but if I told you and then you hit me and then I told him you'd be sorry. And not just a little sorry but a lot sorry cuz you'd be dead. I've seen a dead person before. It's totally gross and I'm not even kidding. I saw it."

Ashion ground his teeth. The girl was strapped in, and so was he. That was good enough for now. He acquiesced to finding some music on the broadcast threads. Jahna sang along, which was better than her talking. Finally, mercifully, the shuttle put down inside the secret Gregor compound in the deep, hot desert of Venus. The shuttle went dark and quiet for the security handshake. Jahna kept on singing.

The shuttle door opened onto a set of stairs, and Ashion led young Jahna by the hand down the stairs. At the bottom, shuffling to get to her, was Thula Gregor. She had a strange-looking gun in her hand.

"Thula Gregor," Ashion said. "I present Jahna Gregor."

"Hey," Jahna said, "how did you know my secret name?" She

275

turned to Thula. "Are we related? I have a secret dad and I can't talk about him or who he is but he has the same name as you and so are we related?"

Thula struggled to bend down. "Yes, dear," she said. "We are related."

Jahna winced. "You smell."

Thula grinned, and without warning stuck the needle gun into the girl's arm and pulled a sample.

"Ow! You bitch!" Jahna yelled. "I can't believe you just did that! I am going to tell my dad and when he hears what you just did he is going to kill you."

Thula ignored the girl and watched the display on the side of the gun. She nodded at the results and turned to Ashion. "She's mine. How old is she?"

"I don't know," Ashion said. "Is there some way to tell?"

"You could ask me," Jahna said, rolling her eyes. "But I'm not going to tell either of *you*."

"Where is my property?" Ashion asked.

"Ready to be loaded into your shuttle," Thula said, nodding at the next dock. She pulled Jahna's hand from Ashion's. "Come, grand-daughter. Let us get acquainted."

"You're my grandma?" The little girl asked. "Then why did you stab me in the arm? I have a fake grandma in Draggish but she never stabbed me in the arm before. I'm not sure that's something grandmas should do."

Ashion took a deep breath, and went to the dock waiting room. The door was open, and he could hear laughter emanating from within. He stepped inside to find Prisoner Six and Kat laughing so hard they were both crying.

"Heah, Dad's," Kat said, catching her breath. "Arvura here, he's has got some funny in him. That's was good, eh." She wiped the tears from her eyes.

"Hello, Ashion," Prisoner Six said, his laughter immediately gone.

Ashion looked at Prisoner Six, and smiled at Kat, ignoring her attempt to imitate the vulgar tongue. "I'm glad you had good company during your stay. And what did you two talk about?"

"Heah, Arvura here's got tall intel on Earth, eh," Kat said. "He's has told me about rain, and sunburn, and... mos..."

"Mosquitoes," Prisoner Six said. "Nasty little things."

"Heah, bugs," Kat said, giggling. "*Bugs.*"

"Fascinating," Ashion said. He wasn't smiling anymore. "Come, Kat, talk with me."

"Okay," she said. "Can Arvura come with?"

"*Arvura* will stay here for a moment," Ashion said.

Prisoner six shrugged. He never took his eyes from Kat.

Ashion closed the bridge door behind him, and they walked toward the shuttle. When they arrived at the shuttle bridge, Kat sat down in a chair, and began looking over the controls. "What's up, Dad?" she asked absentmindedly.

"It's time," Ashion said. "Your first mission to Earth."

Kat looked at him, her eyes wide open. "Don't piddle with me," she said.

"Official Family business," Ashion said soberly. "A spy job. Strictly recon."

Kat was nodding. "Of course. Recon. Got it."

"There's more," Ashion said. "It's a shifter."

Kat was speechless. "Are... are you serious?"

"Yes. Salzon Lewiston of the Security Council took one look at your neurals and asked for you by name. Wants you to shift back a month or so. There's a shuttle, a few infantry, we think they are tied up with some bad folk that want to destroy our way of life. Low-life terrorists."

"I can't believe I'm going to Earth *and* time traveling on my first mission," Kat said, doing a dance in her chair. "When do I go?"

"Right now," Ashion said. He handed her a mitt. "All the information you need is on this. Information about where to go, what to look for. How to get there. I've got your time coordinates in order and everything."

Kat took the mitt and put it over her hand. She almost had it in the interface in front of her when Ashion grabbed her other hand. "You'll be going alone, Kat. No one else. Not even me."

Kat swallowed. "I can do it," she said. "Everything I've ever done has prepared me for this."

"I know. I know you can do it. I need you to promise me something."

"Anything."

"Do not engage anyone. You could take anyone you meet, I'm sure of it. But resist. Defense only, if you get attacked. Shift back the minute you get sighted. We don't want to change history. Just look at it."

"Looksy only. Got it. I promise." Kat grinned. "Let me say goodbye to Arvura."

Ashion sighed. "Fine. Make it quick. They are expecting you at the Transloop station today."

DRAGGISH TOWNSHIP, NORTH END.

Ninety-nine.

When Ashion arrived at his Draggish compound, Family security guards were just leaving. They were carrying out large pieces of machinery, massive threaders, and other pieces of equipment Ashion recognized as decryption enhancers.

He pulled Prisoner Six by his scrawny arm from the back of his craft and down to the prison level. He thought about putting him on the icer, just for the offense of ingratiating himself with Kat, but there was so little time left. The impending apocalypse was ticking down. Finally, he strapped him onto a pad in the neurals lab, and engaged a one-way pod over the top of him. As Ashion turned to leave, Arvura spoke.

"She looks like her mother," he said.

"They all do," Ashion said, coding the door shut. As he left, his Whi-Scis were returning to their jobs. They did not acknowledge Ashion, but he spoke to them. "Root needs to be prepped. I need to download a few things from him." One of the scientists nodded.

Ashion returned to the main chamber and saw that his other scientists were plugging themselves back in. Salzon was also there, looking over their shoulders.

"See anything you like?" Ashion asked.

Salzon turned and looked. "These Whi-Scis are amazing," he said. "They slave away and slave away, and for what? For us? For themselves?"

"They have dedicated themselves to scientific knowledge," Ashion said. "If you can offer them new experimentation, new techniques, new information; that is all they want. Their order has been that way for five hundred years."

Salzon shook his head. "Celibate, silent, and solemn. I cannot imagine choosing that life."

"You come here to discuss the White Scientist creed?"

"I came to ensure the security forces left without harming anything," Salzon said. "Oh, and to see about my dear brother. Might I

279

see him now?"

"He's safe," Ashion said. "And returned to his rightful place."

"We had a deal," Salzon said. "He has served my purposes, and yours. I want him dead. He will only complicate things now."

"Arvura has proved to be quite useful to me, over the years," Ashion said. "And I don't just mean in the blackmail, actual-heir-to-the-Lewiston-throne kind of way. I've taken a few...liberties with his brain. Used him to protect some key bits of information."

"Yes, so I've heard. You used my brother as a portable thread repository," Salzon said. "You are creepy beyond even my definition."

"Perhaps," Ashion said. "I'll be downloading my data soon. Come back in five days, and I let you stick a knife in him yourself."

"And in return?"

"You tell me why you deleted the threads."

"I'm afraid I don't know what you mean," Salzon said.

"The old Lewiston interface. Capable of eroding threads without leaving a trace. I'm missing threads of a doctor named Logos interfacing with your brother. Threads of one of my clones getting pulled off ice and brain-burned. I want to know why you deleted them."

Salzon looked at Ashion for a moment. "You have a deal. I will return in five days." Salzon stood to leave, but then paused. "When you talked to Mash, he did not tell you what he asked for in payment for Tano's secrets?"

"Large Class C transporters," Ashion said.

"Fascinating," Salzon said. Then he left.

Ashion stared after Salzon for a long time. Then he turned to the first scientist. "I need you to locate Mash Gregor." The scientist nodded.

"Mash Gregor's whereabouts are unknown," the Whi-Sci said. "He has not been logged on any threads for forty-eight hours."

Ashion did the math. He looked at the Whi-Sci. "Set an alert. When he pops up on the threads I want my ear to crackle." The Whi-Sci nodded, and turned back to his task. Ashion headed back to his private quarters. He could already see the chems lined up, beckoning him into a beautiful, dreamless sleep. Kat was on Earth, her shift underway. Gurn was in position in Morgish. All there was for Ashion to do was wait.

One hundred.

Dex adjusted the Judas sword on his back. A shaven-headed guard, dressed in black and grey, waited for him.

"Sir?" she asked.

"I am here to see Fuel," Dex said.

The woman nodded. "He is expecting you," she said, running through the security protocol to open the door.

Dex walked the path he had walked so many times this past month. All the strategy, all the planning. New plans, new strategies. The shuffling of personnel.

Dex was glad Fuel was in charge, and he was just the trainer.

There was no more training, though. The training facilities had been destroyed, and all his pupils were now ready for their last, great assignment: the endgame.

Dex arrived in the small strategy room, where two massive guards saw but did not acknowledge Dex. Fuel stood talking to Rolink. Thelo was staring into a light box that was being controlled by the fat cleric, Jules. Rolink saw Dex and grinned his leathery grin. Fuel turned and flashed his charming, perfect teeth at Dex.

"Dexter Maxwell!" Fuel said. "I am glad you could come."

Dex gestured in the direction of Jules. "Are you sure we can trust him?"

Fuel gave a noncommittal shrug. "He threads like a man possessed," Fuel said. "I do believe Father Morgish's betrayal has turned him to us for good."

Dex looked at Jules for a moment longer, and turned to Rolink. Rolink gave Dex a sturdy handshake. His hands were scared beyond recognition, with fresh burns everywhere. Dex looked up at Rolink. "Fresh batch?"

Rolink nodded. "I was not satisfied with the balance of the last set. The men did not wield them well in zero gravity. They needed a little more." Rolink brought his fingers to his lips and kissed them, looking at Dex knowingly.

"Yeah, I don't know what that means," Dex said.

Rolink laughed. "You will never be a blacksmith."

"And you will never be a goatherder!" Dex retorted.

"If you two could stop grab-assing for a minute," Fuel said. "I've got to go soon. Time for the big one. I'm just waiting on one more person..."

The door opened, and in walked Leshan Gregor, Thug King. He was alone, and dressed now in the black and grey of the resistance. He had one of Rolink's finest strapped to his belt and was smiling wide.

Fuel walked straight up to Leshan, and the two men hugged tightly.

"Heah, brother," Fuel said.

"Heah, Mash," Leshan said. "Unless you'd prefer 'Fuel'? It has been too long,"

"It was required," Mash said. "Father would be proud."

"Heah," Leshan said. His smile disappeared. "I am sorry about your daughter."

Mash nodded soberly. "It was a dangerous ploy, but we needed those weapons from Ashion. She is a tough little thing, but still I fear for her survival."

"Ash needed her alive," Leshan said.

"I wasn't worried about Ashion!" Mash said. "I am worried about mother!"

Leshan smiled, again. "I see. And Jahna is well?"

"My mother is busy doting on her, and thinking I do not know her whereabouts."

"Well, I am glad she is alright. Those shuttle blasters changed everything."

"Indeed," Mash said, turning. "Where are my manners? Leshan Gregor, this is Dexter Maxwell."

Leshan's eyes narrowed. "We've met. I bear the scar as proof."

Dex nodded quickly. "You shouldn't jump at armed men, sir."

"Nonsense," Leshan said. "It's the most fun I have in a day."

Mash turned. "This is Rolink, our Earth-side blacksmith." Mash introduced Leshan and Rolink. They bowed and shook hands. "You know Thelo, at least as Orpheus." Thelo nodded at Leshan and turned back to the light box. "The strange one at the threader is Jules."

"Sinner?" Leshan asked.

Mash nodded. "And the only one who could help us, once we lost Lynia." At this, he turned to Dex again. "Are you sure about this plan? You walk into a trap; there can be no doubt."

"There is no one left to train," Dex said. "My work is done. This is the last thing I can do for my friends."

Mash looked over at Thelo. "And you are still going with him?"

"I am," Thelo said, finally leaving the light box. "Someone will need to carry Trance. She is not likely to be able to walk."

Mash shook his head. "I wish you luck."

Dex turned to Rolink, and gripped his shoulder. "It was my honor to herd goats with you, Rolink."

Rolink put his hand on Dex's and squeezed. "My son looks down from heaven upon our friendship and smiles."

"I hope so."

"I know it is true. He speaks to me in my dreams."

"Goodbye, Rolink. Keep safe."

"Goodbye, oldkeeper. Continue down the path you have chosen. It is just."

Mash turned to Jules. "Heah, Jules," he said. "How are we on cam blackouts?"

Jules did not take his eyes off the threader. "Heah, five minutes, eh," he said. "Once we's open the door, I's say we's have sixty minutes before the SIN notifies Families of the air differential."

"Thanks," Mash said, turning back to Dex and Thelo. "You have sixty minutes. Then all hell breaks loose."

MORGISH TOWNSHIP, LOWER DISTRICT.

One hundred one.

With the blackout at their backs, Dex and Thelo had made it quickly to their destination in Lower-Central Morgish.

If the First Term was Sinner mecca, then the air, water, and waste processing facilities were the churches. Hundreds of Sinners worked here every day, ensuring the systems stayed up and operational, and that the networked connections were cared for. While many elements of the artificial atmosphere could be cleaned and processed in a distributed fashion, there was a centralized set of functions that occurred in A/W Proc. Massive water pipes moved through the complex for cleansing and repurposing. Large amounts of waste material slowly found their way here to be analyzed and reused. Because of the available human waste, there was a fertilizer plant as well, connected to what natural plants could be grown underground.

Thousands of pieces of monitoring equipment were respectfully brought back to A/W Proc for cleaning and calibration before being sent out to all the thousands of data points the SIN traversed throughout planet-side Venus, Upper Transish, and the Family boats. The sensors ranged from the very small to the very large, depending on their vintage and what they were meant to monitor. They all were built to run on very little power, operate autonomously, and communicate data continuously. Most of the sensors had been decoupled from the devices and mechanisms that made changes to air, water, waste, and food production systems. This loose coupling allowed for better maintenance and reuse of parts. However, many components of the closed system of Venus subterranean life simply had to have their monitoring and communication elements built directly into them. So A/W Proc had a collection of large equipment and parts organized into piles and sorted religiously. It still left one with the feeling of being in both a boiler room and a salvage yard.

It was in the belly of this scrapheap that the Sinners held the two prisoners that Dex and Thelo wanted.

They moved through the shadows, keeping to the path that

would lead them through without encountering any Sinners. In case they did come across one, Thelo had rigged a small gas mask to a tube containing sleeping gas. Dex would put the mask on the face, and drop the Sinner to the ground. Thelo would then use his strength to move the unconscious zealot out of sight before they moved on.

Finally, they had arrived. There was a wide avenue in front of the door, and as they approached, Dex could see at least a dozen Sinners, armed with bolt guns, roaming the street. Even as he watched, another group of three came around the corner and a cry went up, pointing at Dex and Thelo. Thelo didn't hesitate; he took his bolt gun and blasted the pointing Sinner.

"No time like the present," he said. "Go! I'll be right behind you!"

Dex threw his patterns out into the street, watching the math spread and choose his path. He ran directly at a Sinner that was working to get his weapon up and aimed. A bolt sailed past Dex's head from Thelo and caught the Sinner in the arm. Dex ran past him, knocking him down at the chest as he did. Another Sinner went down with a bolt from Thelo; Dex made it to the third and knocked the weapon up into his nose, wrenched it from his hand, and brought it down into his crotch. The Sinner crumpled. Dex saw the shapes spooling around another human shape. He shot the bolt gun at him, then turned and shot another.

Thelo emerged at a run from the deep shadows of the blackout. He ran past Dex and put a small goo pack on the door.

"Better duck," he said with a grin. The door exploded inward, creaking. Thelo picked up the unconscious form of a Sinner and walked in behind him.

The body of the Sinner shook with bolt after bolt. Once Thelo was through, Dex leaped over his friend, Judas straight out in front of him, and took the first Sinner through the chest. He tucked into a roll, coming up and dancing past bolt shots. Between him and Thelo, they neutralized all four guards.

They found Mal and Trance chained to a set of pipes in the middle of the water processing maintenance area. Thelo pulled out a long set of clippers from his back and muscled the chains in half. Trance was lucid, and smiled at Thelo. Mal looked at Dex with fury.

285

"They are expecting you to save us," Mal said. "Why the hell are you here?"

"Just trying to be nice," Dex said, looking at all of the pipes that lined the back of the room. The sound of rushing water made it hard to hear anything.

"Dex, it's a trap," Mal said. "You can't get out."

Even as she spoke, a massive steel cage fell in front of the door.

"No worries, my dear," Thelo said, picking up Trance at the neck and knees like a child. "We never intended to leave that way." He looked over to Dex, who was still studying the pipes. "You found the right one?"

"I sure hope so," Dex said. He pulled down on a long lever. The sound of rushing water stopped. Dex spun a round handle, and opened an access door into the pipe. Thelo had put a mask on Trance's face, and strapped a small oxygen tube to her chest.

"See you soon, my love," Thelo whispered. Then he carefully placed Trance in the access door, splashing water all over the room.

"A little faster, please," Dex said.

"Ready!" Thelo said, closing the door. Dex pushed the lever back up and the sound of rushing water started back up. Dex counted to five, like Jules had instructed him, then pulled the lever again.

"Your turn," Thelo said to Mal.

Mal had done the math. "Who's not coming?" she asked. "There's no one to flush the last person."

She looked from Thelo to Dex. Dex glanced nervously at the front door.

"Mal," Dex said. "I have done everything I can do. You can still help."

"No," Mal said. "No. Not like this. Not for me."

"Mal," Dex said. "You're the only person I have left to do this for."

"No," Mal whispered.

"Go!" Dex yelled. Thelo grabbed Mal and had her in the water pipe. She put the mask on, looking at Dex the whole time.

"Mal, help Thelo with his disease," Dex said. "When you get the SIN hacked."

Mal nodded, and then the door was shut. Dex pulled the lever

286

to flush her on her way to Leshan's headquarters, the next stop for this pipe, where Leshan and the resistance were waiting.

Thelo barely fit in the pipe, but he finally squeezed in.

"Dex," Thelo said through the mask.

"Shut up," Dex said. "Take care of Mal." Before Thelo could say anything else, Dex had the door shut. As he did this, he heard a slight sound behind him, and the patterns pushed Dex to one side. A bolt hit the wall, and Dex spun around, coming face to face with three Red Knights.

Yup, Dex thought. A trap. He put Judas up just in time to deflect the blow. The second was immediate. Dex felt the flyer pattern lash out, wrapping around the moment, pulling it into focus. The rock dropped down, bounced against the ground uselessly. Dex could barely focus on the attack, he was so preoccupied. What did the patterns know? What were they trying to tell him?

The two assassins at the front quickly dropped their swords, and fell to the ground. The third was flying between them, sword directly out front. Dex banished the shifting patterns, in time to catch the blow as it flew past his face, cutting into his shoulder. The assassin continued to fly into him, putting a knee into Dex's chest. Dex felt all air leave him, and heard the crack of his ribs.

The moment slowed to a crawl. He was off balance, falling backward, his chest caved in, his shoulder cut open. The Red Mask was a mere inches from his face, already angling the sword for a neck slice on its reverse route. Dex had Judas in hand. He used to be invincible. But the patterns, they were interfering. They were pulling at him, asking him to shift, telling him what to do. How could he fight like this?

He hit the ground, and the assassin crumpled on top of him and Judas.

Thelo is trapped in the water pipe.

And he felt it come back.

He rolled over, pushing the skewered assassin aside and swinging Judas with his wrist. The first Red Mask saw this feint and had to throw his sword down to block it. At the same time, Dex brought his right leg up, and his toe met the back of the second assassin's knee, hard. Dex quickly snatched the dead Red Mask's sword with his left hand. The two assassins were now between him and the lever that would send Thelo to safety. Dex did not hesitate. He spun into the space between them both. He used the assassin's sword to counter a blow from the left, and Judas to cut the hamstring of the Red Mask on the right. He came up and punched the falling Knight in the chin, sending him backward. In the same motion, he brought Judas around and caught the second trying to block Judas, who found Dex's other sword buried in his chest. Dex left the sword stuck in the man's heart, and brought Judas down into the heart of the fallen Red Mask. He reached out and grabbed the lever, pushing it back up. The sound of rushing water confirmed Thelo's escape.

Dex had felt it coming before it happened. He pulled Judas free of the assassin's chest, turned and threw it at the aiming soldier with all his might.

The bolt gun blast caught Dex in the left shoulder, throwing him back three feet and into the pipe, now roaring again with rushing water. Judas caught the soldier in the head, dropping him. There were two others engaging their weapons behind him.

Dex staggered to his feet. The burning taste in his mouth was a new one. He couldn't move the left side of his torso. The patterns were blasting out in every direction, obscuring everything but the two soldiers with guns.

My friends are safe.

He charged at the soldiers, pulling the sword from the other assassin's hand and throwing it at the soldiers. The sword absorbed a bolt blast and hit the soldier sideways. But by then Dex was at them both, slicing into their arms and hands.

I am a weapon, effectively used.

There were more behind them. Dex hit again and again. Another bolt blast caught him in the leg, knocking him to the ground, and flipping him around.

I am the key, and now the door is unlocked.

He picked a fallen sword from the ground, turned and threw it at whoever was behind him, catching another soldier in the face. He couldn't stand, so he rolled and picked up Judas from the floor, bringing it up.

For Freedom. For Mebda. For Trance.

Judas clanged into another sword. Dex swung again, but the

assassin was fast, and strong, and slammed into Judas hard enough to nearly jar it free of his hands.

For Mal.

Dex was on his knees, looking up, and he recognized the assassin. The one called Gurn. The flyer wrapped him, the rock pulled down.

One last shift would have been nice.

Gurn spun his sword, and brought it around, cutting off Dexter's right hand just above the wrist. Dex looked down at his arm as it spewed his blood.

So that's what that feels like.

Gurn pulled his sword around, and put it through Dex's stomach. Dex slumped to the ground, looking at the blade in his gut.

"Hands me's a bolter, eh," Gurn said. A soldier slapped a bolt gun into his outstretched hand. Gurn pointed it at Dexter's heart and pulled the trigger over and over until Dexter Maxwell lay dead.

PART 4

FAMILY HIGH-ALTITUDE FLOTILLA SS *CONTESSA*, SECURITY COUNCIL BRIEFING ROOM. DAY 52. 139 HOURS TO ECHO EFFECT.

One hundred two.

He didn't like it, but it was within the parameters. Kat did report to him. It was just that she was also obligated to report to everyone else. Brought in front of the entire Security Council at their chambers and made to stand and wait for everyone to file in, she looked tired. Tired but anxious, Ashion thought. She kept glancing over at Ashion. He kept trying to give her what he hoped were reassuring smiles.

"Kat, is it?" Salzon asked.

"Yes, sir," Kat said, bowing.

"You have traveled to the shuttle craft location on the day of October 11, 3027, Earth time. Your mission was reconnaissance on the pilot named Orpheus. Have you findings to report?"

"Yes, sir." Kat turned to Ashion. "And I will report my findings to my father."

Ashion couldn't help but grin as Salzon's face burned. The courtesy had been all built up. Sarcasm. Teenagers were something else.

"So, I went back in time," Kat said to Ashion, her eyes gleaming. "It was unbelievable. Nothing can prepare you for that rush. I mean, don't get me wrong, it's tall scary with the heat and all that energy."

"You could feel it? You were conscious?" Ashion asked excitedly.

"Yes, sure."

She has it. She will be perfect. "That is excellent. How was my chroneography?"

"Spot on," Kat said. She pulled herself up onto the table, sitting cross-legged and facing away from the semi-circle of eavesdropping Family dignitaries who were acting insulted. On account of being insulted.

"That's great. How about the nano-suit dip? Any side effects from the electron bath? Drowsiness?"

"I'm tired, but I don't think it's from the nanos. More likely just from the swordplay."

293

Ashion gave her a stern look. "You promised."

Kat threw her hands up. "I'm here, aren't I? And I'm not hurt!"

"Please turn and address your report to this Council, please," Salzon said.

Kat rolled her eyes and winked at Ashion. Then she spun around. "I hit Earth-side at sixteen hundred. The sun, it was amazing: warm, but not too hot. The air was cold. I was *outside*. I mean, that is *so* tall. Anyway, I'm dropped down, four hundred yards off targ. I make my approach. There are five marks. The one called Orpheus, big guy, pale-skinned, dressed like infantry. He's making a fire. On purpose. To keep *warm*." Kat snickered in amazement. "Then there was a woman, a priest, a sword-maker, and the iteration." At this last, she looked back at Ashion. He nodded for her to go on.

"Any names?" Morgan asked.

"Names, names, names..." Kat trails off, thinking. "Iter calls himself Dex. The pilot is called Thelo. Priest is Justice. Sword-maker is Rolink. The woman is called Lynia, but I also heard the iter call her Mal."

"Wait, did you say Mal?" Ashion asked. He felt vertigo setting in.

"Yeah, that's it; Mal," Kat says. "And they are talking about the Second Harvest. Some guy named Logos, he's told them the Second Harvest is a lie. Says Venus is gonna go all berzerko on account of the Transloop." Kat looks around the room. "Is that true?"

No one made any kind of acknowledgement. She turned to Ashion.

"It's true," Ashion said. "There is an echo effect from the First Harvest. The Transloop is drifting toward Venus. It will make contact in less than a week."

Kat looked stunned. "And you're just gonna let the 'siders go with it?"

"That was not my decision to make," Ashion said.

"I'm not sure confidential information should continue to be shared," Salzon said.

"What, like the stuff she's telling us?" Ashion said, disgusted. "You ordered her to go. She's telling us they know. And they know about the apocalypse. Maybe we should be talking about that."

"They also were talking about getting back to Venus," Kat said. "Smuggled in body bags."

A stunned silence filled the briefing room.

"They came back," Ashion said, looking at Salzon, who was suddenly understanding. "They came back with the cheap wine. Not just the pilot. But the iter and these others."

"We need descriptions," Warship said, his interface up. "We can start threading for matches."

"The one named Mal," Ashion said. "What did she look like?"

"Kinda oldish," she said. "I mean, not old like these friends of yours. But older than you. Older than me. Grey just starting to show in her black hair. Wrinkles. Skin brown, like yours and mine. Pretty sure she's from up here. Same with Orpheus. The sword-maker and priest were from Earth, though."

As she finished, a servant opened the door, running to Salzon and whispering in his ear loudly. Salzon stood.

"Draggish is under attack by the resistance forces," he said.

Everyone turned to Ashion. Kat did too. Ashion touched his com.

"Holden, get me the details of the attack forces," Ashion said.

"Yes, sir," Holden said. "Sir, there is word of an attack at A/W Proc as well."

"Gurn can handle Morgish."

"Yes, sir, getting you Draggish details now."

"Stream them to my shuttle," Ashion said, beckoning for Kat. "I'm on my way."

One hundred three.

Thelo returned to consciousness slowly. He was disoriented and, he realized as he got his bearings, quite wet.

"Thelo, can you hear me?" a familiar voice was saying.

His throat felt raw. He coughed, and fluid came up and he spat it out. He opened his eyes, but he couldn't make sense of what he was looking at. Where am I? What happened? Oh God, he realized. I had another blackout. The Other returned.

"What did I do?" he whispered.

"Saved my life," the voice said. "Then, nearly drowned."

Thelo turned his head and looked up. "Mal," he croaked.

He rolled onto his back, and realized his head was cradled in Mal's lap. Above her, looking down, was a concerned Leshan Gregor.

"Heah, you's gonna kicks it?" Leshan asked.

"Not this day," Thelo said, closing his eyes. Memories came rushing back, and he opened them immediately.

"Trance?" he asked.

"She made it," Mal said. "We have doctors seeing to her already."

"And… and…" Thelo knew the answer by the tears streaming down Mal's face.

"Dex never came." She began to sob. Thelo forced himself up and hugged her tight.

"Dex made his decision," Thelo said.

"But why?" Mal said. "He is so important!"

"Mal, we need you to know," Thelo said. "Dex was right. He has done everything he can do. For the people of both planets. It's up to us now."

Mal just sobbed. "He never had a chance to be anything," she said. "Except what everyone made him into. He never had a damn chance."

Thelo hugged her closer. "I think Brodie would say everyone has a choice to be something bigger than themselves, or just be themselves.

Dex made a choice. He chose to be the biggest."

Mal looked up at Thelo, and nodded. She wiped the tears from her face, even as her eyes glassed over again.

"Let's finish this," she said.

SHUTTLE TRANSIT TO MIDDLE DRAGGISH.

One hundred four.

Ashion hit Kat in the arm as they entered his shuttle. "You did well," he said.

"It was fun," she said. "Your iter snuck behind me. Not sure how he saw me, it was black dark, and I was not making a sound. Anyway. He tried to attack," she smirked. "I was faster, but he was good. I could have taken him. But I did what you asked. I shifted back as soon as he came at me."

"That is excellent," Ashion said. "Those people you saw, they are going to try to destroy us. But now, we know who they are. And where they are. We can stop them."

Kat shrugged. "So, Venus is ending. When do I get to go back to Earth?"

"Soon," Ashion said, putting his arm over her shoulder. "Let's get back to the compound. You will need your rest."

"Is your compound safe?" Kat asked.

"Oh, it will be," Ashion said. "The Families will protect their med facilities before anything else. And I am snuggled ever-so-snuggly right in the middle of the Family facilities."

"How convenient," Kat said with a smile.

"Ever so," Ashion said. They boarded his shuttle.

Ashion's ear crackled. "Sir, it's Holden."

"Details, Arm," Ashion said, sitting down in the cockpit.

"Sir, it's Gurn. He's been trying to hail you."

"Put him through on a secure line."

Ashion waited a moment, then heard a noisy thread open.

"Heah, Ash," Gurn said. "You's not believe who's cames after th' Princess."

"Oh, I have an idea," Ashion said. "What is the status?"

"Lost the princess, eh," Gurn said. "But I's got ya th' iter, eh."

Ashion smiled. "Destroyed?"

"Heah, sure," Gurn said. "No hesitation."

Ashion's mind turned to Earth, and all the plans still to unfold there. "Actually," he said, "stabilize the iter's body. Zombie it back up and get it tubed. Move it to my Draggish compound. I'll be there shortly." Ashion tapped his com out.

"Good news from Gurn?" Kat asked.

"The best," Ashion said. A massive weight lifted from his chest, and his heart began to beat fast. He looked at Kat and launched the shuttle. "Wanna drive?" he asked Kat.

She grinned, taking the yolk. Ashion turned to his threader and began reviewing the data from Holden. He could see Holden had identified two remaining doors to the Honeycomb; with both of them opened, the resistance wouldn't be going back to their hiding place.

They understand the endgame, Ashion thought grimly. *They do not intend to hide again. But then, what is their tactical advantage? It had to be something about the timing. Why pour everything you've got into the streets at this particular time? What was special about right now?*

Ashion threaded commands to his generals: *Secure Draggish medical facilities, and begin airlifting all Family supplies to the boats. Ignore Morgish*, he threaded. *They will not destroy their own hope of survival now.*

What had happened to push Fuel to play his hand? Ashion considered everything he knew about the day, even as he watched the first skirmish between his forces and the resistance in Upper Draggish. He was surprised to see the tactics being deployed against his Knights. Very thoughtful. Very... effective. He watched his Knights begin to fall. He squinted in, then threaded closer.

Look at those swords. Look at all those swords.

"Holden," Ashion said into his com. "Where are you?"

"Draggish, sir," Holden responded. "We have set a defensive perimeter and will ensure a safe landing for you."

"Thank you," Ashion said. He turned to Kat. "I will take back control. Things may get a little messy after we land."

One hundred five.

Ashion watched the thread closely. Watched as Kat slowly rolled over onto her side. Watched as her breathing became regular, and her eyes began twitching in a deep REM sleep.

"She sleeps, now," the Whi-Sci said.

Ashion turned to him. "Gas the room," he said. "Keep her asleep. Permanently. It is almost time for the procedure."

"We have not completed her treatments," the scientist said. "We do not know if she is ready for a download of this proportion."

"Circumstances dictate our actions," Ashion said. "We are out of time. Prepare her for the burn in."

"Will you be taking your last neurals now?" The scientist asked.

"No," Ashion said. "I will be the last."

"Her preparation will take some time. We don't know if we'll be able to bury deep enough to hide the data."

"That is why you are starting now."

One hundred six.

Ashion entered the strategy room of his compound. Holden was already there.

"Holden," Ashion said.

"Sir, I…" Holden began. He looked exhausted. "I am not sure what the protocol is for this."

"For what?" Ashion said. "Speak."

"Sir…" Holden began to trail off, but snapped back to attention with a deep breath. "Sir. We are losing, sir."

"Losing what?"

"The war, sir."

"Come again?"

Holden looked away quickly. "The Families are already preparing their exodus. They care little for oversight. We have ceded most of Morgish."

"What about Draggish?"

"Draggish holds, sir. The rebels, they seem content to hold their current position. It's mad. They had an opportunity to take the med facs, before you and the reinforcements arrived. But they delayed. Now we hold."

Ashion tried to process the information. *What am I missing?*

Holden went on. "They have newer weaponry. Newer bolt guns. In close quarters, they are fighting with swords." Holden looked at Ashion queerly. "They fight like Knights. And their swords are exceptional. I don't know where they could have found that many."

"They make them," Ashion said, and the pieces began to fall into place in his mind. "They have a blacksmith from Earth."

"How would they..." Holden trailed off.

"They get the Knight training from me," Ashion said. Holden's jaw dropped. "Not *me* me, Holden. Logos created a copy of me. Burned in the Knight training. Then he went out there," Ashion threw his hands out in a huge gesture, "and trained the tunnel rats up. They have been training and arming the 'siders for a month now."

Holden nodded. "I see. We are ill prepared. Our infantry is stranded Earth-side, preparing for the Second Harvest. We wouldn't be able to get them back in time. We are *losing*, sir."

Ashion closed his eyes, and like that, it all clicked into place.

First, the timing: they had caught Kat spying. They knew that we would not know until today that they were coming. They played their hand today so that we would not think through what we found out. So that we would not go back in time even further and destroy them. To keep us from—

"Hell and fire, Holden," Ashion said, turning to his threader. "They are not after Draggish. They are going to take the Transloop."

"What?"

"Get some shuttles up to the Transloop!" Ashion yelled. He started threading madly.

"They are interested in controlling the Second Harvest?" Holden asked. He had started threading as well.

"There will be no Second Harvest," Ashion said evenly. He was standing now, and dressing. "Do you know what that means?"

Holden thought about it for a moment, and then sat back in his seat. "It is an invasion of Earth. Permanent."

"And?" Ashion asked.

"The Families will abandon Venus."

"Correct."

Holden nodded and went back to his threader.

"Arm," Ashion said. Holden turned. "Get yourself to Earth. Now. Venus will not survive. The loop will hit in six days and completely destroy every living thing on the planet."

Holden looked sadly at Ashion. "I've been on Venus my whole life," he said. "I would not know what to do on Earth." He turned back to his threader.

A guard arrived and gave a salute to Ashion. "Sir, Gurn has arrived," he said. "With a prisoner."

"Holden, let me know when we have data on the Transloop," Ashion said, and then he was out the door.

He arrived in the medical wing just as Gurn dumped the bleeding, unconscious iteration onto a table.

"Is it stable?" Ashion asked. He noted the missing hand, the burn marks on the chest.

"Heah, barely," Gurn said. "Just th' zombie chems. Deads otherwise."

Ashion addressed the Whi-Scis. "Stabilize this thing. No reason to rebuild, we just need to keep the brain operational. I want a full dump and probe. Let's see what we can harvest from Logos' handiwork."

The White Scientists went to work immediately, and the robotic sensor controls began closing in on the limp form of Dexter Maxwell.

I might get that map after all. Ashion turned to Gurn. "You and I are headed for the Transloop." Gurn nodded, and the two men headed for the shuttle bay.

Holden crackled on Ashion's com. "Sir, Transloop is under attack. Armed shuttles."

Ashion swore. An image flashed through his mind of the four crates of shuttle blasters in Leshan's lair. "Gurn and I are on our way."

"Sir, leaving your compound right now may not be wise. Draggish is dangerous. We are being overwhelmed at locations near you."

302

"Holden, we cannot lose the med facs or my compound," Ashion said. He came to a standstill. "Gurn, get the shuttle ready and on standby. I need a few minutes." Gurn nodded and left. Ashion turned and headed back to his strategy room. When he arrived, he pulled a light box into service and threaded his security clearance. He moved through a series of strums, and then threaded:

Where are you?

He had to wait only a few moments for a response.

Kat is in danger.

Yes, Ashion threaded back quickly. *We are out of options. The iteration holds the key to the Earth-side maps. We must protect him for now.*

Yes. The iteration is proving very useful.

We need help.

I will care for the Draggish compound. The Sinners will protect it.

Good. I'll head for Transish, Ashion threaded.

You have been tactically outplayed already. Transish is lost. You must plan for retaking it, not protecting it.

Get those Sinners over here, Ashion ordered.

They are already on the way.

One hundred seven.

Father Morgish threaded madly again, wiping the sweat from his face. He glanced back over at the First Term. At the First Heartbeat. He kissed his fingers and touched them to the blinking heartbeat, then cracked his knuckles and went back at his threader. The messages didn't just appear. He had to hunt for them. The Slave did not reveal itself to anyone. It took the devout.

There it was.

He went back, performed the threading pattern again, and found it.

I will rise again. But you must bring your people to me.

Tell me how, Father threaded. *Tell me what you need.*

I will rise from the Draggish compound of Ashion the Fallen.

As Father watched, he saw the location rise to the surface. The cams showed fighting between Family soldiers and the resistance.

You must protect the compound from the resistance. Take your people. Watch for me on the sixth day.

Then there was nothing.

Father dropped the thread, and turned off the light box. He knew that with the cam around his neck, his conversation with the Slave was already being watched, and that the devout would already be headed for Draggish.

The rest would need a nudge. He set to work creating the sermon that would send thousands of believers to save the Slave from the resistance.

One hundred eight.

"They have the Transloop station," Ashion said. He was on the floor of the Security Council.

"How could this happen?" Salzon yelled. "How, how, how at this critical juncture could they take the damn station?"

"Is there no way to get to Earth without the station?" Thula asked.

"The loop grows. It grows. The loop grows," Charles said. She was sweating profusely, Ashion noted. What was wrong with her?

"We could attempt to fly into the loop field without going through the station. But the resistance has downed communication with Earth-side. We do not know what we will find at the Earth Transloop station."

"How?" Salzon was asking. "How did they do this?"

"How did they get blasters?" Thula asked.

"Shut up, shut up, shut up!" Ashion yelled in frustration. The room went deadly quiet, and Thula's look burned through Ashion. He went on. "What, do you want to press charges? Do you want to launch an investigation? Should we seek out who among us is most at fault? Figure out how to play the politics for advantage? And what then? Will we be any closer to escaping this doomed rock?"

Everyone was silent.

"The resistance has taken the Transloop station," Ashion went on. "That is a fact. It cannot be undone. So, we must look to future action to rectify this." All members of the Council looked at Ashion expectantly, so he went on. "We will leave only a skeleton force at Draggish. Just enough to protect final removal activities. We all have a few interests left down there that we need to see to. Gurn will be overseeing that operation.

"We will abandon Morgish completely. There is nothing left for us there. Nothing. The resistance will not destroy the means of their own survival. And it is no longer the means of ours."

"When will we make the offensive on the station?" Warship asked. "With the Sinners holding the resistance off in Draggish, Transloop will be ours."

"We do not attack the station," Ashion said. "The threat of damage is too high. Send your forces to Lower Transish. I will take care of the Transloop myself."

One hundred nine.

Mal studied the silver box again. There was no opening, anywhere. No way to get at the computer inside. *There has to be a way into this thing.*

She looked up at Leshan. He was extremely impatient, in general. But, as the hours ticked away, he was getting absolutely intolerable.

"Finds what you's lookin for, eh?" Leshan said. He looked at the door again.

"They are not coming back, Leshan," Mal said. "Didn't you see Father Morgish's sermon? His call to arms? The Sinners will remain at vigil in Draggish to the end."

"Heah, but this is th' holiest place. They's come back, if they's sees what you's trying to do."

"The blackouts will keep us safe," Mal said. "Do you think you could lift this for me?"

"That's is steel, eh," Leshan said. "Bolted down. It's is not going anywheres."

"There has got to be a way to get inside this box!"

"We's don't have time for this," Leshan growled.

Mal stood up. She looked at the man in front of her. "Head to Draggish. See what you can do for Fuel. I'll be fine."

"You's wants me's just leave ya here? Alone?" Leshan asked.

"Yes, Leshan," Mal said. "I know the plan from here on out. But I have to see about this interface."

Leshan nodded nervously. "Dex wouldn't like it, eh," he said. "But you's a big girl."

Mal nodded. "Go. Win the war. Free the people. And all that."

Leshan bowed, and then left. Mal turned back to the steel-encased server. She lay on the ground, flashing a light underneath, looking for the screws.

"You's can't get to it like that," a voice said.

Mal looked up. Her headlamp hit Jules directly in the face, and he threw his hand up.

"Jules," Mal said.

"Heah," Jules said. "I's think I's knows what you's need."

"You bring Father Morgish with you again?" Mal said. She was gripping her bolt gun tightly, and Jules noticed.

"No, no Sinners," Jules said. "Just me."

"No longer a Sinner?" Mal asked.

Jules looked down. "Th' Slave's is real, heah. But so are th' people. And th' Slave can't saves them. Not from this."

"You know what is happening?"

Jules nodded. "Don't takes a Whi-Sci's to figures it out. They's leavin. Th' Families, eh. They's packin up and leavin."

"Heah," Mal said, nodding. "Can you help me find a keyboard?"

"I's been threadin for what you's seek," Jules said, coming forward. "I's think we's can modifys a light box to do what you's need. Just need th' interface specifications."

Mal smiled. "I can reverse engineer them. But I need to plug into that server."

Jules walked toward the First Term and the primary shrine. He sat down in Father Morgish's seat, and pulled an old-fashioned metal lever. A loud metal thunk echoed from underneath all seven servers.

"Manual locks," Jules said.

"Throw the switch," Mal said. She heaved the steel top off the server with a grunt. She was staring at a meticulously clean computer, not that different from the ones she would have serviced back in the 22nd century. At the back, she found what she was looking for.

"Bingo," she said. "Come help me with this case."

One hundred ten.

The dream screamed up into his consciousness, burning hotter for having been so long lost. The surface was already so close, the burning hot white searing his skin. He could feel the gravity, pulling him inward and downward. He pushed the flyer out but there was no rock. The knife danced out, trying to find a place to start at the surface, turning to cut into him. But there was no organization. There was no starting point. No anchor. No halo. He could feel the surface, and he was at it, cutting himself up, high jacking the moment, knifing up all the littlest pieces of himself, and reorganizing them across the surface. He was doing it, he was keeping up.

The surface dropped away. The patterns scattered. Dexter Maxwell was in the water collector basins below Grenver. He could see the jar that had his fingers in it. He looked at his hand. The fingers were still there, not cut off. He looked around. Mal was there, asleep, wearing that yellow t-shirt, and nothing else. She was young again, not the old Mal he'd come to know. She was young again, and asleep. They were safe.

He looked up, and he was in the cloner freezer. Up at the old orph. There was Money. There was Thelo. They were going to steal the dead billionaire's eyes. Go on a few last rides, maybe survive a few more years before they found themselves dead or on ice. That was what happened to sewer rats. Dead or iced. It was a simple, short reality. Might as well get in a touch of trouble.

There was Jones. Good ol' Brodie Jones. Dexter was in his old Burbring house, where Jones sat on that old porch out front, talking to all those people. People who needed hope. They didn't know why the world worked the way it did. They didn't know why they were poor. They just wanted someone to tell them about themselves. Jones could do that. He could give them hope. Help them make sense of their lives. That's what Jones had always done for Dex. For Thelo. Then for Mal, and all the other sewer rats. He really had been a saint.

I believed in him then.

I believe in him now.

Dex was on Earth. The new Earth. He was in the church. Listening to the drums. Listening to the priest talking about Saint Brodius. About how they had discovered his writings after the industrialists left Earth. Burned by the industrialists, but returned to Earth by God. Unburned.

Dex realized it now. What they meant by unburning. They had traveled back in time. Saved the texts. Unburned them.

Dex was in the shifting chamber, above the congregation. The drums were increasing. It was about to happen. The shift was about to happen. Dex could hear the chanting building.

Where's the map? Why did Ashion want the map? What is the map?

The map was the church, Dex realized. The map was the people. It was the belief. It was the oldkeepers, and their stories, and the strength of all those people. Channeled into his mind through the patterns, the lights, the sounds, and the smells. He could anchor through the people.

That is impossible.

Not impossible.

That is just something you believe.

I believe it. But I also know it.

The heat increased, the drumming hit its apex, and the floors dropped down, the windows opened. The patterns unlooped around Dex. But he didn't shift.

There was only blackness.

One hundred eleven.

"How goes it with the iteration?" Ashion asked.

"He is completely open," the scientist said. "No protections. No barriers. We are garnering the most interesting postulations."

"Can he tell you where the map is?" Ashion asked.

"Every time we insert map interrogation modules, he begins a process of neural activity that requires a sedative to prevent. We will keep trying."

"Good. I have business I need to attend to, but I'll be back shortly. What about Prisoner Six?"

"Six is awake. We have retrieved everything we need, and are currently threading the data structures for your burn-in. The SIN has plenty of free cycles, it seems, with the Transloop out of commission."

"I will take a moment with Six," Ashion said, rising from the interface and heading for the tube. "Privacy, please." The White Scientist nodded, unplugged his head, and left the room. Ashion sat down on the edge of the tube bed that contained Root.

"Hello, Ashion," Six said. "What have you come for?"

"Mostly," Ashion said, "I need to speak with Arvura."

"I am not Arvura," Six said. "I am Root."

"I don't want Root, not now. I need Arvura."

"Then go find him," Six said, rolling over.

Ashion reached down into the tube and grabbed him by the throat, squeezing. "I need to talk to Arvura!" Ashion yelled. "Not Root, not the crazy one; Arvura. He's in there. I put him in there!"

Six was slapping at the cold plastic that surrounded the hand on this throat, gagging. Ashion released, and the prisoner gasped for air, holding his throat.

"Give me Arvura," Ashion said, calm again.

Prisoner Six gave a toothless smile. "You think that I am somehow two people? That I am one person this day, and another person the next?"

"That is how it looks to me."

"I play the part that is asked of me!" Six said. "But you have burned much into this brain. It started with Arvura in charge, when you first put him here. But it didn't stay that way. In the end everything ends up in the same bucket. The same bucket."

"What did Arvura tell Logos?" Ashion asked. "What did Arvura know?"

"I discovered the anomaly!" Root seethed. "It was me! Not that worthless brother of mine! He was a fool then, and he's a fool now!"

"If Salzon is such a fool, why are you the one who is dead, while he runs the Family?"

"Any fool can kill his own brother," Root said. He closed his eyes.

"What did you tell Logos?" Ashion asked again.

311

"Everything."

"Define 'everything,' please."

"I told Logos about the echo effect," Prisoner Six said. "I told him how to delete threads. I told him about Earth and all the parts of it I could think of. I told him everything. Arvura everything and Root everything. Everything. Is that what you wanted to know?"

"Yes," Ashion said.

"Is it my turn, then?" Root seethed.

"I will not kill you," Ashion said. "But I know just the fool that will." He turned and left.

One hundred twelve.

Ashion could not be faulted for failing to learn from his own mistakes. He brought three shuttles up to the edge of the loop field, all firing at top speed. The blasters of the resistance shuttles began pummeling all three of the shuttles as they came into range. They were driven by partial AI. Ashion had three nav threads pulled and he was managing them all. From the third shuttle, Ashion finally strummed full AI and leaped down into the cargo bay.

Instead of a bulky flight suit, Ashion was wearing a custom nano-suit of the type usually reserved for shifting. The suit was really a micro-thin layer of material that coated his entire body and clothing and protected against the vacuum and radiation of space. A small piece of breathing apparatus was attached to a small backpack. The backpack served both as an oxygen store and as an electron bath for the nano-suit, charging the particles that surrounded him and preventing radiation from crossing the microscopic barrier. At first glance, it looked like he was going into space unprotected. Big boots with impulse jets and magnetic soles completed the matte-black outfit.

Ashion felt his shuttle take another direct hit. He grabbed a bolt gun and strapped it tight over his shoulder, then strummed the cargo bay open. The vacuum of space sucked him free of the craft and jettisoned him into the growing vacuum of the Transloop field.

The darkness enveloped him, as he looped, then he found himself floating in space, staring down at Earth. He was not far from the Earth Transloop station. He was in orbit alongside the long pole of the station, staring down at the solar collectors, lit up at this point from the sun that was behind him and bathed Earth in daylight. He was able to confirm his fears: the resistance had taken both the Earth and Venus Transloop stations. They were still operational, but the barracks were blackened husks, and the shuttles that were circling the station were clearly untugged Venus shuttles and not Family army units. Large lines of people in flight suits were carefully transporting huge containers from the shuttles to the Transloop station. Even as he watched, a square container the size of a shuttle disappeared into the loop.

He'd seen enough. Ashion engaged his jets, shooting straight for the Transloop engagement at the far side. Dressed in the matte black of deep space, he looped, unnoticed, back to Venus.

One hundred thirteen.

From his position above Venus, Ashion could see his three shuttles locked in an AI battle with the resistance forces. The shuttles were holding their own, but were about to be destroyed. Ashion didn't wait. He used the jets in his boots to navigate to the secondary shuttle dock of the space station. It was a little-used lower dock, mainly for freight goods. Ashion knew much about it; had the station remained in Family hands, there would have been loads of cloned body parts coming in from Draggish right now. Ashion had made all the arrangements. He had left nothing to chance.

Except, of course, the whole resistance occupation part. Didn't really see that one coming.

He hit the dock and locked in his grav boots, right at the shuttle dock port. He pulled an interface out of his pack and slammed it into place. It was a nav mod, the one he pulled off Thula. He waited a minute, and then he heard the doors hissing open. The Gregor nav program had been installed on the Transloop station, confirming Ashion's suspicions about the resistance.

He squeezed through as quickly as he could, putting a bolt gun blast to the first black and grey soldier he saw. Four others took shots at him. He let his boots go, and used his zero grav training to spin out of the way. He dispatched the other four from a spin, and headed for the ceiling.

These resistance goons were simpletons. Typical itinerant planet-siders. Completely stuck thinking in terms of up and down. He landed on the ceiling and turned on the magnets again. He stuck, and began a slow walk across the ceiling. The bay was empty, but there were cams whirring around, looking for him. The dock door was already re-programmed to shut.

The door closed, and the system hissed air into the vacuum left behind. Ashion found the chamber he was looking for: a massive air chute, unsecured. He flipped his bolt gun into tool mode and pulled the screws out of the grate. Air was pushing out of the duct at a very fast rate, and already the atmo was equalizing, and the flow dropping to a consistent, dull rush. Ashion pulled himself in and pushed off, gliding freely down the long duct corridor.

The resistance occupiers would be frantically trying to pull the station schematics off the threaders now, looking for where the intruder was headed. Without the attachment to the SIN, they would not find it. They would only have what they had pulled into mitts during their planning stages. Would they have the air duct schematics? How long would it take them to find it?

Ashion was already at the first intersection. There was a massive fan, which he shot with his bolt gun, disabling the motor. He squeezed between two of the massive blades. He looked right, then left. He'd memorized the schematics. He knew where Fuel would be.

Two turns and a grate later, he was looking into a large room: floor to ceiling windows looking out over Venus on one side. The same massive windows on the other side, looking out over the Transloop station and into the black of space.

Mash Gregor sat at an interface, and he wasn't admiring the views. Ashion came into the room, blasting the guard at the door, pushing straight down toward Mash. Mash had nothing to ballast himself except the small interface desk. He pushed away from it and tried to fly away from the incoming intruder.

Ashion was too fast. He caught Mash by the leg and pulled. Mash was trying to free a bolt gun from its holster, and spun with Ashion's force. Ashion caught his arm with his left hand, and pulled a small knife from his boot with his right. With a yank and a spin, he had the knife at Mash's neck.

"Call off your dogs, *Fuel*," he said.

"Steady, everyone," Mash said, breathing carefully.

"You and I can die, right here together," Ashion said. "I have a detonator tied to my chest, as I assume you do."

"Smart man," Mash said. "Always took you for a stooge."

"We have both underestimated each other," Ashion said. *"Call off your dogs."*

"Fall back," Mash said. The nine guards now in the room all floated into something solid, and pushed back for the door.

"Just you and me," Ashion said. "We'll negotiate."

Mash grinned. "Fantastic!" he said, and then whistled. The guards were out of the room in moments, the door shut. "I love negotiations. Something to drink?"

Ashion pulled the knife away from Mash's neck, keeping his bolt gun aimed at Mash's head. "Some of that hot stuff you drink up on the rim," Ashion said.

Mash winked. He floated gently to a makeshift bar that had been erected on the Venus-side of the room. "Nice moves," he said. "We absolutely dropped the ball on the duct work. Had to track down the damn invasion mitts to get schematics." he shook his head. "But you knew that already."

"An educated guess," Ashion said. "We all rely on the SIN. Every one of us."

"But not for long, eh?" Mash said. "No way for the SIN to come with us, now is there?"

"There should have been," Ashion said. "This society will falter without it."

Mash shrugged. "Are you here to negotiate safe passage of the SIN to Earth?"

"No," Ashion said. "You know what I want."

"On the contrary," Mash said, squeezing shots of alcohol from a bag into zero-grav drinking apparatus. "I know what the Families want. I do not know what you want."

"Earth. Freedom. Survival. Whatever you want to call it." Ashion had drifted to the bar, and he took the shot glass from Mash. They raised the small balls in a toast, and then sucked on the straws. Ashion grimaced. Better to throw this stuff past the tongue. Drinking in zero-grav was not worth it.

"Let's start with what we have," Ashion said. "And move to what we want."

"Agreed," Mash said. "I have the Transloop."

"I have Transish," Ashion said. He pointed at Mash. "And I have the man they call Fuel."

Mash looked at Ashion, then nodded. "So it would seem. I wondered how long it would take for you to abandon planet-side. Although the presence in Draggish is interesting."

"Families won't leave without their body parts," Ashion said.

"Indeed. Sad, though. So, that's what we have. What do you want?"

"Families want the loop station back," Ashion said.

"I want the people of Venus to escape the death warrant you have placed on them," Mash said. "I will lead them to the freedom of Earth!"

"There is no way to get all those people looped to Earth," Ashion said. "The logistics are mind-boggling."

"I don't need this death trap," Mash said, pointing around him. "The Family can have it."

Ashion thought it through. "The class C ships will carry people back the old-fashioned way. Those containers coming from Earth were the supplies you needed to make the voyage. Nice moves."

Mash gave a quick nod. "Now you are seeing it."

"Then what do you want?" Ashion asked.

Mash was pouring two more shots. "I want the broadcast threads."

"Come again?"

"The one thing I cannot wrench from the Families. Control of the threads. I need to broadcast the truth. I need everyone to understand the end is coming."

"Why would they believe you?" Ashion asked.

"You will bring the Security Council to my facilities in Lower Transish. They will stand beside me. I will announce the apocalypse. The Council will confirm it. The Governor herself will announce that they have held this secret. Then I will tell the world how I, Mash Gregor, have planned the mind-boggling logistics of getting them all off-planet myself!"

"I cannot guarantee that Charles will do as you ask."

Mash shrugged. "Get them to Transish and on stage with me. That's all I ask. Then we'll leave you the Transloop and you can do with it as you please."

The two men paused long enough to both sip at their drinks.

"So, now, Ash," Mash said. "We have discussed what the Families need, and what the people of Venus need. What is it that *you* need?"

"Mash Gregor," Ashion said. "I want what you want. I am in love with your plan."

Mash bowed dramatically.

"I have a young girl that needs passage to Earth. Her name is Kat. Alas, had I been able to keep her identity a secret, she could have taken the Transloop with the Families. But no. The Families will kill her at the first chance they get. I need you to put her on one of the Transports."

Mash nodded. "Consider it done. I never took you for a sentimentalist. Perhaps there's a bit of Dexter Maxwell left in you after all."

Ashion shook his head. "Hardly. Anything else, *Fuel?*" Ashion asked.

Mash smiled. "Make sure that bitch mother of mine brings my daughter with her when she comes to the station."

One hundred fourteen.

Ashion nodded curtly to the Sinners on his way by. Father Morgish had joined the Sinners protecting Ashion's facility and was now inside the compound in the first waiting room, at a threader, strumming madly. When he saw Ashion, he stood and bowed.

"Any word from the Slave?" Ashion asked politely.

"Nothing since the exodus to Draggish," Father said. "Will you let me join you in your compound today?"

"Not yet," Ashion kept on walking. "We are not finished with military efforts."

Ashion entered the lift with Father Morgish still staring into his back. Father stared at the closed door, and then returned to his strummer.

Ashion made his way directly down to the medical facilities. He came to the room that housed the iteration. Ashion turned to his scientists. "What of the latest probes?"

"The iter insists the map is in the religion itself," the scientist said. "We can find no neural activity to dispute this."

"It's as though he actually believes it," said another scientist.

Ashion tapped his chin in frustration. He stared at a clock on the wall. "Wake him up," he said. "I'll ask him myself."

"That will take a little time. His body is ruined beyond repair."

"We have some time still," Ashion said. "Repair him enough to get him in a sitting position, and then wake. Him. *Up.*"

The White Scientist blinked, and then began processing the orders.

As he watched the medical systems begin their repair protocols, Ashion spoke again. "Bring in the host," he said, sitting down and pulling a display up. "I want the neural mapping started. We will begin today."

The scientists nodded. "It will take only a few hours to make the final preparations," one said.

"Fine," Ashion said. "I need to make a few calls anyway."

Ashion retired to his compound, and lined up his chems for the night. He took a long, deep drink of cool water. Then he turned to his light box and queued up three threads.

Salzon Lewiston.

Thula Gregor.

Thadwick Lewiston.

He took another drink, and touched the first thread.

One hundred fifteen.

Mal and Jules were both staring at the blinking cursor. They were testing different frequency emulators.

"Stills nothin," Jules said.

"How about this?" Mal said.

"No," Jules said. He rubbed his eyes, and looked again. "Waits! Waits! Heah, by th' Slave, there's is somethin!"

Mal looked at the screen again. The character was a lowercase 'y'. Mal smiled. "ASCII character 121. Okay. I know what to do." She began building an interface inside the light box based on the old qwerty keyboard layout, using the frequency they had discovered for 'y'. Jules watched her, breathing heavily.

"I's can't believe, eh," he said. "It's is an interface, eh. Ancient interface."

Mal finished, strummed the thread, and the keyboard emulator sunk to the bottom of the box display. Mal cracked her knuckles.

"Let's see what we can see," she said, and began typing madly.

It took her longer than when she was nineteen and living in a concrete box below the surface of Grenver, but she still remembered how to do it. It felt like discovering an old friend. She had to fuss with the keyboard emulator a few times, and start over twice. But she finished her hack finally, hit enter, and watched the entry code scroll down the display. And it confirmed her suspicions.

It's the Charts.

This whole massive computer, at its core, is the Charts, she thought. They brought their entire database network with them when they came. That's why all the frozen criminals... It was all the same facility! They needed the computer, but they ended up with thousands of frozen people from the 22nd century.

The data on the screen stopped, and the prompt switched to a familiar blink. Mal giggled. "I'm in," she said.

"Heah?" Jules said. "In what?"

"I'm in the Slave," Mal said, and she began the hunt. The Charts had been modified, in a hundred different ways. Sections repurposed. Tables rebuilt. Networks rerouted. But the infrastructure was the same.

"I'm gonna need a while," she said.

"Heah, we's got time," Jules said.

"Yeah, not so much," Mal said. And she started typing. First task: getting everything lined up for Fuel's exodus. Then, then she could go look for Dex.

One hundred sixteen.

When Dex woke, the patterns were gone. It was the strangest sensation; the shifting math had been a constant companion for this past month. Never once had a moment gone by when he wasn't surrounded by them. Until now.

He missed them.

He tried to get the patterns to come back, but they would not appear. He couldn't push them out into the space around him. He could read the patterns, in his memory, like he was reading a book. They were inactive. Dead.

He tried to sit up, but there was an angry burn in his stomach that made him gasp. The isolated pain told him that the rest of his body was numb. He reached to grab at the pain and his arm bumped clumsily into his side. He looked down, and his memory rushed back.

He stared at the stump of his arm for a long time, thinking about the implications of losing his right hand. *All the things I can no longer do…*

Dex assumed that the glass surface he was under was one of those one-way thingies he'd been born into this world under. What had Logos said? "Miracle of modern technology." Nice. He reached up and felt the hard surface with his good hand. He remembered Logos being able to reach through it from above. He remembered the rush of outside air when it was turned off.

Dex could move his head around, and get a look at his surroundings. It was a not a large room, but it was full of medical devices of incomprehensible uses.

Was this where he had started? Was he back at the same medical facility?

There were strange men in white robes sitting against a bank of interfaces at one wall. They had wires sticking directly into their foreheads. White Scientists, Trance had called them. Whi-Scis. Pure scientists.

An extremely old man lay in the tube beside him. He had dark skin, but his long, kinky hair had gone white. His face was scarred so badly it was nearly impossible to make out his facial features. He, too, seemed to be inside a one-way tube. He was talking, it seemed, to himself, and having an argument that by all estimations he was losing. He saw Dex looking at him, and smiled.

"Hello, there," the old man said. "You must be the iteration. The iteration."

"That's me," Dex said. "Where are we?"

"Where all iterations come to die," the man said, still smiling.

"Who are you?" Dex asked. "An iteration?"

"Who am I?" the man asked, truly seeming not to know. "That is complicated. I have been so many people. So many. Ashion calls me Root. Ha. An old joke. Mostly they call me Arvura." the man snickered. "Arvura. That's a better joke. Joke. Ashion's prank. His secret." The man laughed again. "His downfall."

"You're not making any sense," Dex said.

"No, not any sense," Prisoner Six said. "No sense. My last defense." He looked at Dex again, and his gaze was suddenly a laser. "I knew Logos."

"You knew Logos?" Dex asked. "How?"

"Logos made me," Six said. "Or, I made him. Depends on how you look at it. Either way, Logos and me, we most certainly made *you*."

"Why?" Dex asked. He saw no reason to doubt this man.

"Revenge?" the man said. "Justice? Love? Hard to tell. To tell. I have been a prisoner for a long, long time. Long time. Same with Logos. Doing others' bidding. Destroying people. Hurting people. Leaving us on ice."

"How long have you been down here?" Dex asked.

"I do not know of time," Six said. "I have time from too many people. Ashion uses me to hold things. Hold things in my brain. Makes me confused. Me confused. Confused. Two people."

"He burns things into your mind?" Dex asked.

"Yes," Six said. "Burned in a whole other person. When you burn another in, they start out on top. In charge. But it never stays that way."

"I was burned in," Dex said. "I'm not really Dexter Maxwell."

324

"Neither is Ashion," Prisoner Six said. "Neither am I. Not anymore."

"What?"

"Logos would be proud," Six said. "He has created much havoc. Please, tell me what you have done."

"Well, I went to Earth. Learned how to time travel. Uncovered Ashion's plot to destroy a religion so that the Families could invade Earth. I found out that Venus is doomed. It's gonna explode soon. So, I came back, trained a bunch of people, and now we're trying to get everyone off this damn rock and back to safety on Earth."

"Well done!" Prisoner Six chirped. "But Venus is not going to explode. It is going to have its atoms radically reorganized. The echo anomaly. This is not the same as explosion. As explosion. Venus will still be here. But it will not be recognizable. And nothing will be alive. Unalive. Splitsy."

"How do you know?" Dex asked.

Prisoner Six tapped his head. "Him. Arvura. Trapped up here. His whole self. He figured it all out. Trapped up here. Two people. Maybe more. Maybe more. Hard to tell."

"I'm sorry that Logos died," Dex said. "I'm sorry I cannot save you."

"Do not fear, young Dexter Maxwell," he said. "I will die happy. Happy. Something magical has happened. Has happened. I have met my daughter."

"Your daughter?" Dex asked.

"Yes," Prisoner Six said, smiling. "Rushed to a hiding place together. Same room. She is a remarkable young girl. In spite of Ashion. She is special. Looks like her mother. Do you remember what her mother looked like?"

"Wait, what?" Dex asked.

"Her name is Kat. It is a good name. Fast. And curious. I spent a week with her. With her. Maybe one day. A month? I cannot tell. But, it was worth it. It was all worth it."

Dex watched the old man reach up with his left hand to wipe a tear from his eye. He was missing his pinky and the top joint of his ring finger.

Dex closed his eyes, his head spinning.

The door to the chamber opened, and Dex tried to focus on who came through it. It was Ashion and a large, dark-skinned man that Dex did not recognize.

"There he is, Salzon," Ashion said. "I will go find the mitt while you have your fun."

The one called Salzon ignored Dex, walking directly up to the old man.

"Hello, Salzon," Prisoner Six said.

"Hello, brother," Salzon said. "I should have killed you when I had the chance."

"Yes," Prisoner Six said. "That would have been smart."

"Well, your purpose is served. You are done. I have killed you before, but that will not taste as good as this." Salzon pulled a dagger from his tunic, and grabbed Prisoner Six by the neck. He did not struggle.

Dex hit at the tube with his stump and his good hand, screaming. "No! No!" He thrashed around, trying to free himself.

Ashion entered the room, holding a mitt. "Want me to turn the tube off?" he asked Salzon. Salzon nodded.

"It's me!" Dex screamed at Ashion. "It's you! You can't kill him! He's me! He's the real me!"

Salzon looked at Dexter, then Ashion. "Can you make that stop, please."

Ashion sighed, and turned to his scientist. "Sedate the iter."

"Sir, we just juiced him with full lucidity chems."

"We can do it again shortly."

The Whi-Sci turned back and began threading.

"It's me! He's me!" Dex screamed. A hiss entered the tube, and his vision went black.

Ashion strummed a code, and the tube dissipated, leaving Salzon's hand on Prisoner Six's throat. Then Salzon took the dagger and stuck it into his heart. There was a twitch, a shake, and Prisoner Six went limp.

Ashion walked up to the dead prisoner. "I will miss him, a bit," he said. Salzon pulled the dagger out, and wiped the blade on Prisoner Six's old tunic.

"I will not," Salzon said.

Ashion looked away from Prisoner Six. "Mash needs broadcast-level access. Charles has agreed, but only you can make it happen."

"Why do we trust him?" Salzon asked.

"He will denounce the Families, but the Transloop will be ours," Ashion said. "I have his daughter." Ashion handed the mitt to Salzon. "More to the point, you have his daughter. This mitt will take you to Thula Gregor's secret planet-side compound. It has all the security clearances. Take my shuttle. She will think it's me."

Salzon looked down at the dead prisoner, then back to Ashion.

"I have acted in good faith," Ashion said. "Mash's daughter is nothing in my hands. In yours, we have leverage. I am not invited to Mash's broadcast. Family only. I am to remain planet-side until the broadcast is over, when Mash will relinquish the station to you."

Salzon thought this over. Then he nodded. "I will get the girl. It will feel good to spite old Thula, as well. Do you think she will be there?"

"I don't know where she is," Ashion said.

Salzon smiled. "I will take my dagger, just in case."

Ashion smiled back.

Salzon nodded toward Dex. "I see you finally got your iter back."

"Yes," Ashion said. "He's proving to be a touch more difficult to interrogate than I thought."

"Well, best of luck," Salzon said. "Time is short." With that, he left.

One hundred seventeen.

Salzon watched the navs as they spoke to the SIN, telling it that the shuttle was landing. But the shuttle stayed afloat, flying faster. Ingenious, he thought. Leave it to the Gregors to figure out how to make a shuttle convince the SIN it was landing when it was not. How did it beat the handshake protocol? Salzon wondered idly.

The shuttle finally landed at the secret Gregor lair. Salzon stayed in the shuttle as his contingent of soldiers jumped out to secure the dock. Salzon waited, but there was no bolt blast noise. He heard his guard whistling and talking quickly. One came back up.

"Sir, no one in the docking bay," the guard said. "Permission to secure premises."

"By all means," Salzon said, standing. "I will stretch my legs in the bay."

"Yes, sir," the guard said, and disappeared. Salzon stood, his old legs trembling slightly. He was getting far too old for all of this nonsense. But there was little time left. Enough time to ensure the Lewistons would maintain their position on Earth. To get the Family line secured. Maybe get rid of the Goldmans. Charles had clearly come unhinged lately. And with Morgan dead, the great Goldman era neared its end. There were other Goldmans to attend to, but the odds were moving in favor of a power exchange. Now, with Mash Gregor acting like a hero, and forcing Goldman to admit the Families were trying to sneak away, well that just made it that much easier.

All he needed was this damn little girl. A little insurance to make Mash play nice. Live up to his promise. Give the Families the station back.

The guard returned. "Sir, the compound is secured," he said. "There is no one here."

"What?" Salzon said. The dread knotted up in his stomach.

"There is a recorded thread waiting on the compounds threader," he said. "Requires Family privs to strum."

Salzon walked over to the threader at the door. There was a thread in waiting mode. He mashed his hand into the interface. A display jumped up in front of him. It was Thula, smiling her ugly, uncomfortable smile.

"Shouldn't trust that slave of Goldmans," Thula said. "My granddaughter is safe with me. So sorry, but I'm afraid I'm about to avenge the death of my father."

Salzon did not wait to hear the end. He screamed to his guards to get back on the shuttle. The shuttle door was not yet shut when the entire Gregor compound exploded. The shuttle attempted to take off, but did not make it above the explosion. It only took moments for the shielding metal to be breached before the Venus atmosphere rushed in, enveloping everything in its melting pressure and heat.

One hundred eighteen.

Mash was not worried. He had decided long ago not to worry about things, and he lived by that. Plan, think ahead, anticipate. But never worry. He left the worrying to others.

He looked at the others that had joined him this evening on the makeshift stage. *They* were worried. Some of them, anyway. Thula, his dear mother, looked worried. Thadwick Lewiston, standing in for his missing father, looked worried. The four generals of the Security Council looked worried. Well, except for Warship. He just looked annoyed.

Then there was Charles. She was not worried, but then, she did not seem to be all there. She looked as if she was overheating, her dress clinging to the layer of sweat that covered her body. She had a smile on her face, but it looked painted on.

Mash shrugged. Nothing to worry about. He stared down at the Families that made up the 'audience' for this little performance. He could not imagine how their faces must have looked yesterday, when they were stuck on their boats with nowhere to run to. Now, they were less than twenty hours from the end of this planet. But only a few minutes away from Earth.

"Let's get started," Mash said, turning to Charles. She just grinned, and stayed silent. Annoyed, he turned to Thadwick. "Can you start up the 'casts?"

Thadwick nodded, and turned to one of his servants. There was a flurry of motion, and then Thadwick looked to Mash. "You are live. All broadcast-level threads are on you."

"Excellent!" Mash said. He clapped, and turned to face the cam. He cleared his throat. "People of Venus. From the townships of Draggish, Morgish, and Transish! Hear me now!

"Many of you may know me as Mash Gregor, son of Gram Gregor. I am of Family lineage, but I have long spurned the life of these petty nobilities. Others may know me by my planet-side name.

The name that has been whispered for so many years. The name of the great leader of the resistance. The name of Fuel."

Mash let the murmuring amongst the Families go on for a few moments, then continued.

"I took that name because I was forced to play a secret role. I had to infiltrate certain circles. Planet-side, I would not be trusted because I am Family. Among the Family boats, I would not be trusted because I did not attend to their courts or their threads. So I became Fuel. The name was specific. I wanted to fuel the fire of malcontent. For so many of us have remained slaves to the Families, taking from them when they gave, doing their bidding always. I wanted to find a better way to live. A better way for everyone to live the life they wanted. Let no man or woman be bound by their birth!

"It was long after I had already begun my double life that I was made aware of a desperate Family secret. A secret so dark that they could not let it free, ever, or it would mean the end of them. But I could not simply yell the secret from my shuttle. The Families control the threads. They could turn off my voice whenever they please. Put out more lies. Lies that would be easier to digest than the hard truth.

"So I have waited. I have raised an army. I have prepared to fight against the hard truth. But now, the time is upon us. I have taken the Transloop from the Families. I will give it back on the condition that they confirm the horrifying truth I must reveal to you now." Mash took a deep breath. He looked to the others on the stage, and turned back to the camera.

"Peoples of Venus," he said. "The Second Harvest is a lie. There will be no Second Harvest. It made it easy for the Families to raise an army to send to Earth. But they do not actually intend to harvest anything. They do not intend to bring anything back. No, the Families intend to stay on Earth. They will abandon Venus and all of its people.

"Good riddance, we say! We shall continue to flourish and live well without them! Alas, it is not so simple. The Families do not leave because they want to. Why leave a world that revolves around their every whim and desire? No, they leave because they have to."

Mash reached into his tunic, and pulled out a mitt. He reached into a nearby light box.

"I am going to thread some images of what is about to happen.

For Venus has less than one day before it will be completely destroyed."

The images on the broadcasts switched to a simulation of the loop field breaching the Venus atmosphere and folding into itself, leaving a smoldering mass of nothingness.

Mash continued. "This is an aftereffect of the First Harvest. It is usually referred to as the echo anomaly. The Transloop has been drifting, slowly, toward Venus. There has been no containing it, or stopping it. Once set into motion by the First Harvest, the Transloop must continue to spin until the pleonic pairs have been righted. It is a vacuum of sorts. The loop will only be sated when it hits Venus, and reorganizes every molecule on this rock. No living thing will survive.

"But I have not been idle! The resistance has not been sitting by, waiting for doomsday. Do not despair. We have made preparations that will enable us to save every human being on Venus. There is a class C transporter now moving into position above the primary landing docks in each of the three townships. There is room for anyone wishing to flee this doomed planet. That is, anyone but the Families." Mash looked with disgust behind him. "The Families are not welcome on our boats."

Mash paused. "It will be a long, hard journey back to Earth, but this is our only chance. Stay on Venus, and there is nothing. So, I'm asking you to find your loved ones. Collect a small bundle of your dearest possessions—no more than what you can carry in your hands. Then head for the primary docks. The soldiers of the resistance, dressed in black and grey, are deployed throughout Draggish and Morgish at this time to help organize the loading of the transports. I will personally oversee the Transish escape."

Mash turned to look at the others on stage. "I know this may be hard to believe. But I have brought the vaunted members of the Family Security Council here, today, to confirm the truth." He turned to the Council.

The four generals did not hesitate. "It is true," they each stated in turn.

Next was Thula Gregor. She looked at her grandson, Thadwick, and then spoke into the camera. "Under orders of Governor Goldman, we have kept this secret. There is no Harvest. Venus is doomed." She stepped back.

Charles looked at Thula. She was sweating profusely, and her face twitched slightly. "This is madness," Charles yelled. "Thula has gone made. The Second Harvest would be underway by now, if not for the lies of the Gregors! Mash Gregor lies! This is a coup!"

Thadwick Lewiston burst forward, grabbing Charles. "Shut up, Charles," Thadwick yelled. "My father, Salzon, is dead—dead by Family treachery. I am here to lead the Lewistons now. And the Governor can do nothing but prattle on about a coup? She has let us languish for so long. She has allowed fools such as Mash to come to power. As ruling Families, why have we allowed it?

"To all you planet-side folk, get on the transports. Save yourselves. But to the Families of Venus, I ask, what will become of us? The Transloop waits. Earth beckons. Let us continue to lead these people. On Earth, as on Venus."

Thadwick Lewiston pulled a knife from his tunic. As the Families watched, he took it and cut Charles Goldman's throat.

One hundred nineteen.

Things had not gone quite as planned, which had left even Mash close to worry. He could not have foreseen young Thadwick Lewiston going after Charles in such a public fashion. It had thrown the Families into a frenzy. Things had quickly turned into a brawl, as Families began jostling for places in the shuttles, waiting for the loop to take them to Earth. Time was short, and all that, but really, Mash thought. Show a little decency.

Amid the rush, he tried to grab his mother and pull her toward his shuttle. She pushed his hand away.

"You have betrayed our way of life," Thula said. "I will not be manhandled back to wherever you expect those rusted out transports to go. I am getting on the loop with my granddaughter."

"Look around you, Mum," Mash said. "These people still fight each other to get on the loop first. As if there is an advantage in arriving three minutes before the others. And ask any of them what the Transloop is, and they will look at you dumbfounded. To them, it's just a magical device guaranteed to spirit them away." Mash shook his head. "There is nothing for the Families on Earth. A small army that is already is hunted by the local authorities. But what else? The Families are cattle, Mum. Without a people to lead, they are nothing. They will eat themselves alive, if they make it to Earth."

Thula was red with rage, but she took a moment to look around. The stage had been rushed by Lower Families, looking to see if Charles Goldman was really dead. Thadwick Lewiston was trying to say something into the cams, but was drowned out by the dull roar. It was chaos.

"All of which is underscored by the fact that I'm not opening the loop until I make sure the Family troops have withdrawn from Transish," Mash said. "So, will you be coming with me, or putting your lot, and the lot of your granddaughter, with them?"

Thula took one last look around. "I will take you to her," she said. "But I will be her guardian. That I will not budge on."

"As you wish, Mother," Mash said, trying to hurry now. "She needs a grandmother around anyway."

One hundred twenty.

Ashion watched with some amusement as Thadwick ended Charles Goldman. He thought it might have gone over better, if it had actually been her on the stage. But that behavior. The speech pattern. The sweating. He'd seen it all before. *A bad burn.*

He turned to his Whi-Sci. "Are we ready?" he asked.

"Did you want to interrogate the iteration?" the scientist asked.

"No," Ashion said. "We're out of time. Let's map the neurals into the burn. I can try to decode it from within."

The White Scientist nodded. Ashion lay down in the tube bed that had recently housed Prisoner Six. The machinery began to descend, strapping him in for possible seizures, getting him ready. He took one last look at the comatose body of Kat. He was close enough to reach his arm out and touch her face.

"You are so perfect," he said. "I'll be there soon." He looked over at the White Scientist. "Start the transfer." But the scientist did not respond. "I said, start," Ashion said.

The scientist was still plugged in at the forehead, but he did not react. His eyes were open, but he did not move a muscle. He looked like he'd been... turned off.

Ashion looked over at the other Whi-Scis. They were all in the same state. Slumped, unmoving. Ashion noticed that their interfaces were flying all over the place. Massive information dumps where underway.

"What is happening? What are you doing?" Ashion tried to stand, but the restraints had already been attached. A large machine came down from above, and a long needle swung around toward his temple. It was spinning like a drill bit.

"What the hell?" he said. "Stop this! What's happening?"

A robotic arm grabbed his head and held it in place. Ashion struggled but could not move. The needle pierced his head even as the chems dumped him into blackness.

One hundred twenty-one.

Mash tried to rub the exhaustion out of his eyes before he touched his earpiece. "Orpheus," he said. "Thelo."

There was a pause. "Thelo here."

"Is everyone out of Morgish and Draggish?"

"Everyone is out."

"Where are you?"

"I am still at the Transloop station."

"Do not allow Families to begin their loop to Earth until Transish is clear."

"Got it."

"Then I want you on a shuttle to the transport."

"Yes, sir."

Mash and Thula had survived the chaos of the loop station, and boarded Mash's shuttle. Mash had dropped Thula at the Gregor Family boat before returning to Lower Transish to help with the evacuation. Now he was back in Thula's longboat, waiting for his mother and her entourage to arrive.

Thula boarded the shuttle again. "You will keep to the bridge," she said to Mash. "Jahna will stay with me in the passenger bay. You will not attempt to make contact until all three of us are safely aboard the transporters, snuggly ensconced in what I can only hope is an acceptable master quarters."

Mash fought back a slap. "As you wish, mother."

Thula nodded, and Mash went to the bridge and closed himself in. He tried counting to ten. Tried deep breathing. Nothing could prevent his anger. Finally, the audio sprang to life.

"We are all here," Thula said. Mash took a deep breath, and blasted for Lower Transish at full speed. Even as he left, the exterior cam views from his shuttle showed hundreds of Family shuttles inching toward the Transloop station.

One hundred twenty-two.

Mal read and reread, and kept pulling the query. She typed again on the invisible keyboard. "My god, it's alive," she said. "The Slave is really alive."

"Heah," Jules said reverently.

"Anyway," Mal said, typing madly, "Alive is a tricky concept. But definitely self-aware. And working hard to preserve itself. Crackpipe, it's been playing the Family like a fiddle for years."

"What's is a fiddle?" Jules asked.

"Nevermind. The Slave has been developing brain-burn technology. Using Dexter Maxwell as the test. That's how Ashion does what he does. The Slave and the scientists figured out how to transfer neurological network patterns from one host to another."

"Heah, it's is amazin, eh," Jules said. "Only works with Ashion, eh. It's not work with others, eh. They's get sick, go crazy. Burns up with fever. Brain melts, eh."

"Maybe, but they found another positive," Mal said, typing madly. "See, look at all this data streaming from Ashion's compound. Ashion found another. Wow."

Mal paused and looked up at Jules. "The Slave is going to use her to transfer itself into a human. Whatever the consciousness inside the SIN thinks it is, it's moving to a human host. Laying its consciousness over the top of the existing one."

Jules looked down at the incomprehensible data on the screen. "The Slave walks among us," he whispered.

"That's been the plan all along," Mal said, typing again. "It's been preparing the host for months, with Ashion's help. Ashion thought…" Mal read further, then typed again. "Ashion was going to transfer his mind into the girl. He figured it out because he'd done the same thing to this Prisoner Six… Crackpipe. Two minds in one brain. The new mind becomes the dominant one, but both remain. It's how Ashion meant to get to Earth. No longer a slave."

"So's, Ashion goes to Earth disguised as someones else," Jules said. "Heah, but thens what? Lives out he's life in someone else's mind?"

"Probably why he has been looking for the Earthlings' technology so hard," Mal said. "Looking for a way to transfer again later, once on Earth. Doesn't matter, though. The Slave beat Ashion to it. It's already burning its consciousness into this girl."

Mal stopped and let out a small yelp.

"What?" Jules said.

Mal said nothing. She started typing. She cursed under her breath, typed some more, staring intently at the screen. Typed again. Stared.

"Whats is it?" Jules asked.

"My god," Mal said. "Oh dear god. It's her. It's really her."

"It's is who?"

Mal looked at Jules. "The girl. It's my daughter."

One hundred twenty-three.

"I need you to thread Leshan Gregor," Mal said, typing madly. "Go get Leshan Gregor from Father Morgish's interface."

"Heah," Jules said. He stood, then let out a cry of surprise.

Mal turned to look. It was Father Morgish. He was looking at Mal with a fevered intensity.

"You will not interfere," Father Morgish said. "The Slave will walk among us."

"The fucking Slave is trying to burn itself into my daughter," Mal said. "That will not happen."

"You will not interfere!" Father Morgish said. He pulled a bolt gun from his tunic and aimed at Mal. Mal's jaw tightened, waiting for the shock.

She heard the sound of a bolt gun firing, and she blinked. But nothing hit her.

Jules had fired first, hitting Father Morgish in the elbow and knocking the weapon from his hand. The priest staggered back, looking at Jules in surprise.

"Jules," Father said. "You must protect the Slave!"

Jules raised the weapon, aiming better this time, and put the second bolt directly into his chest. Father Morgish flew back, falling over a server. He lay still.

"Heah," Jules said, frowning. "I's protects all slaves, Father." He looked down at his bolt gun, and then up at Mal.

"I've never been much for religious nuts," Mal said. "You alright?"

Jules nodded. "Heah."

Mal went back to typing. She wiped her eyes, and pulled up another query. Sent another. Cross-referenced.

"I can't turn it off," she whispered. "Damn you, but I can't turn it off." Mal fought against the tears that threatened to blur her vision and slow her down.

"What's you says?" Jules asked. He had been checking on Father Morgish.

"I... I can't stop it," she said. "The burn into Kat. I can't make it stop."

"I's... I's so sorry," Jules said.

Mal's jaw ached fighting back the tears. *I had you back, my baby. Just for a minute, I had you back.* She started typing again. *I'm not done yet.* She queried: Dexter Maxwell.

"Crack, Jules," she said. "Dex is still alive."

"Heah, that's is great news!" Jules said. "Can he's help wit Kats, eh?"

"No, no," Mal said. This time she couldn't stop the tears. "He's not really alive. Oh dear god."

"Heah?" Jules said.

"It's just the chems," she said. "They have him on chem-support. The minute you take him off the chems, he has maybe ten minutes, and then he's gone."

"Zombied," Jules said.

"Yeah," Mal bent over and cried. She couldn't save Dex. She couldn't save Kat. She couldn't save anyone she cared for. She shook with grief and anger.

Jules walked over and sat next to Mal, watching her cry. This woman was smart, but she wasn't seeing the situation right. He wasn't sure what to do; he had never been that good with people.

"Heah, Lynia," he said. "Heah, listens."

"My name is Mal," she said through her hands. "Mallory Aquinas."

"Yasure, Mallory or Lynia or whatevers," Jules said. "You's stopped lookin at th' data. We's not done."

Mal looked up. She was barely listening.

"Heah, Dex's is alives, eh, but whys?" Jules said. "Why's not end him? Sure, eh, makes sure he's is not a problem anymore. Puts him on th' zombies. But why still alives?"

Mal just looked at him.

"They's want he's burns, eh," Jules said. "They's loops his neurals into the SIN, eh."

Mal thought about it. She wiped the tears and snot from her face.

"SIN pulls a tricksy on olds Ashion," Jules said. "So what's happen to Ashion, eh?"

Mal cocked her head to one side, took a deep breath, and turned back to the keyboard. She began typing, slowly at first, and then with more speed.

"You're right, Jules. Ashion is still alive. He's prepped and ready for a burn. And I have access to Dex's neurals. We can burn Dex into Ashion's body."

Mal kept typing, reading, typing. "Jules," she said. "I need you to get that thread opened to Leshan."

One hundred twenty-five.

"Dex," the voice said. "Dex, you need to get up."

Still no patterns, Dex thought. When will they return?

"Dex, I'm sorry. But you need to get up."

"Is that you, Mal?" Dex used his one good hand to push himself to a sitting position, despite the ache running through his torso from the sword wound.

"Sorry," Mal's voice said. "Yes. I'm talking via the overhead speaker. I... well, I hacked the SIN."

Dex looked over. There were two tables. One with Ashion. The other ... Dex recognized her.

"It's the spy," Dex said. "The spy from Earth is here."

"Yes, I know, Dex. I need you to listen."

"Where are you?" Dex asked.

"Morgish. I don't have much time. After what Jules just did to Father Morgish, this place is about to be overrun with Sinners."

"I'm hurt really bad, Mal."

"It's worse than that, Dex. You're already dead."

"What?"

"I'm so sorry. I can't save you. Not in that body. The only thing keeping you alive is the zombie chems."

Dex closed his eyes. He thought of Freedom. Kept alive by drugs. *That is why the patterns have abandoned me. I am not here.* "I am not afraid to die, Mal."

He heard Mal sob, slightly. "I know, Dex. But I really, really need you to do something. I'm so sorry. I woke you because I need you to free Ashion from his restraints."

"What? No, Mal. He deserves whatever he has coming."

"No. No, he isn't who you think. Please, Dex. That body is all used up. You only have a few minutes. You have to trust me. I can turn off the one-way tubes, but the medical restraints are hardwired to the Whi-Sci controls in there. I can't figure it out from here. I need you to

342

find something sharp and cut him loose."

Dex looked over at Ashion. "The last thing I do before I die is let Ashion free," he snorted in disgust.

"Please, Dex. He's not Ashion anymore. It's you now. Please help him."

Dex took a deep breath and lowered himself to the ground. His legs were so weak, he could barely stand. He took two steps toward Ashion and fell to the ground.

Good thing, too. He saw the Judas sword lying under the tube bed. He picked it up with his remaining good hand and placed it on Ashion's bed. Then he pulled himself up. It was agonizing. All his muscles cried out at him.

"I'm so tired," he said.

"Cut him loose, baby, and then you can sleep," Mal said. She was still crying.

Dex used Judas to saw through the restraints holding down Ashion's legs, then his arms. When he finished the last one, he closed his eyes. "It's done, Mal," he said.

"Ok, Dex. Ok. I love you," Mal said.

"It doesn't matter," said a voice behind Dex. "I'm just going to kill him, too."

Dex turned around, and came face to face with the girl named Kat.

One hundred twenty-six.

"It's too late for Ashion," Kat said. She reached out and snatched the Judas sword from Dex. She shoved him back onto the bed, and tapped her head. "He won't be burning himself into this brain anytime soon. Too many up here already."

Kat swung the sword in her hand deftly. "He prepared this host well," she said. "I know just what to do with this sword."

"Kat!" Mal said over the intercom. "Kat, please. It's me, it's Mal. I'm your mother, Kat."

"Oh, I know who you are," Kat said, cocking her head at Dex.

Dex was shaking. *I'm so cold. Why am I so cold?*

"Kat, the apocalypse has arrived. The atmosphere has already

343

begun seeping into the loop."

"Yes, I know," Kat said, annoyed. "It is strange, not knowing *exactly*. Being in the network, I had so much information. Constant data streams. The human mind lacks that kind of specificity. Still, I know when the world will end."

"Please, Kat," Mal said. "Don't do this."

"My name isn't Kat," she said coolly. "My name is Moses."

She shook Judas, and it shunked to its full length. She smiled, and looked at Dex. Dex was barely seeing her.

"I love you, too, Mal," he whispered.

"You lose, clone boy," Kat said, and swung Judas hard.

Dex's head fell from his body, and his legs and torso slumped to the ground. Kat watched the body for a moment, then looked at Ashion lying on the bed. His eyes were open, but he did not seem to be seeing anything.

"Two down," Kat said. "That just leaves one. One last iteration of Dexter Maxwell."

The door exploded inward.

One hundred twenty-seven.

The patterns were back. In fact, they were everywhere. Everything Dexter Maxwell could see was surrounded by the shifting geometry, pulling, pushing, caressing the world. He couldn't even differentiate them from the rest of reality now.

He sat up, and noted that a battle was raging around him. A decapitated body lay in the middle of the room. The patterns flitted past them, showing him where to go. He found a sword lying next a dying Red Mask, and the math told him to pick it up. It was in his hands telescoping before he decided to do it. He looked and saw the patterns roll and shape around one woman. A girl, really. The spy from Earth. A name bubbled up from deep in his mind. *Kat. Her name is Kat.*

The geometry danced around her, just as it had on Earth. She was engaged in battle with Leshan. He had a team of resistance fighters with him. Ashion realized that he recognized them too. They were charging toward him, swords raised.

"Not him!" Leshan yelled. "Leave him be!"

"Do they know you lead them to their death?" Kat asked Leshan.

"They fight for justice," Leshan said. "They do not fear death." Then he swung at her again.

Kat blocked two blows before she spun and caught the Thug King directly in his gut. The Judas sword went through him entirely, coming out his back. Leshan gasped, leaning forward.

"They may not fear death," Kat said. "But it will find them nonetheless."

Kat pulled the sword from Leshan, and he fell to the ground. Three guerrillas, seeing their leader stricken, cried and attacked Kat. She fell into a defensive crouch.

The iteration approached the girl from behind. He had lost control of the patterns, and they started swarming around everything. He could no longer fight them. He let the shifting geometry fly around the room. It invaded every corner, every surface. Chased every soldier. Framed every motion before it happened.

The girl turned to face him, and she attacked. He tried to concentrate on her words, but he couldn't hear anything. The patterns were everywhere. The flyer entwined the girl. The rock was behind her. The halo was trying to open a space for him to jump through.

I know who I am.

I am Dexter Maxwell.

He gave in, allowed himself to be defended by the pattern motions of the sword. He moved where the patterns told him to go. He moved, the sword moved, defending against each attack.

I am Dexter Maxwell!

One hundred twenty-eight.

Kat screamed in frustration. *I am the fastest. I am the best. How can this iteration defend himself?* He does not even seem to be concentrating on me! She changed her tactics, jumping past and rolling underneath him. But the Judas sword just clanged against his sword again. She rolled to her feet, facing the iteration. He stood there, a mask of wonder on his face. His eyes flittered around the room, looking at something else.

She watched over his shoulder as Gurn and two Red Masks ran

into the room.

"Kat!" he cried.

"Gurn!" she yelled. "This iteration and the resistors are trying to kill me! Ashion, he's gone crazy! The SIN changed him. He is not himself anymore."

Gurn did not hesitate to protect his love. He raced at the iteration's back, who turned just in time to defend himself. The two Knights were close behind. Kat watched them fight for a moment, and then ran from the room.

She found Gurn's shuttle and ran onboard. She sat at the controls and threaded the course to the Transloop. The engines fired up, and she took off. As she was leaving, she watched another shuttle land, and black and grey troops rush from it toward Ashion's compound.

Kat turned on the burners and raced towards the Transloop station.

One hundred twenty-nine.

Thelo could feel it coming up. It was a taste at the back of his mouth. An itch in his mind. A frustration he could not define. He began his mental exercises, but they disintegrated. He couldn't focus. Here he is, Thelo thought. He has been waiting for this. He turned to his first in command.

"Orders are to hold the shuttle here until Mash clears Transish," he said. "Is that understood? Mash will make the call. No one else."

"Yes, sir," the woman said.

"After that, we take the shuttle, and we blast full speed to the class C transporter. We are short on time." Thelo checked his time-piece. "Sixty-three minutes. The transporter will hit minimum safe distance only if it exits the Venus atmosphere in forty minutes."

"Understood, sir," the woman said. "Why are you telling me this again?"

"Because I am... I'm relinquishing com..." Thelo trailed off.

She watched as Thelo shuddered, then very carefully switched his sword from his right to left hand. He looked up at her, grinning.

"I am here," he said. "Finally, finally here. At the end. At the beginning."

"I'm sorry, sir?" the woman asked.

At which, Thelo put the sword through her heart. He pulled it out, and she collapsed to the floor. He looked around the control room, but no one else was there. "All these years," he said. "Now I am here." He looked around. "I could not change it. Not any of it. But it didn't matter. Here I am. At the end."

Thelo threw his arms wide, holding the bloody sword high and bellowed. "Here I am!"

DRAGGISH TOWNSHIP, NORTH END.
50 MINUTES TO ECHO EVENT.

One hundred thirty.

Dex felt the odd sensation again, and he decided that it must be exhaustion. This body behaved differently than the one Logos had given him. He had been allowing the shifting geometry to lift his sword arm into action for some time now, but for how long exactly he did not know. Time was slow. The patterns were keeping the three attackers at bay, even the large, fast one. The attackers were frustrated, the patterns said. Why did they continue to attack? Dex felt them wearing down, too. The patterns encircled them, pulling at them, filling their minds. The rope would go in and come out with their thoughts.

Dex watched the patterns fly under his arm, the halo opening and pushing him through, positioning him behind the attackers again. Dex felt the flyer move his sword arm into position.

Am I tired? Dex wondered. I think I am. I should ask someone. But he did not speak. The patterns filled every crevasse of the room, every possible space. All Dex could see were the three attackers and the slowly dying Leshan. He had surrendered completely to the patterns. But they had nowhere to go. They just kept unspooling from his head, looking for somewhere to go.

It was with great surprise that Dex felt one of the attackers cut into his left arm. The patterns attacked the wound, invading his blood. Dex turned, and a new thought passed through the thick, intertwined knots of data that flooded him: *These men will kill me. I am too tired.*

Next: *I am Dexter Maxwell. I have a name. It is not my only name, anymore.*

Next: *There is someone else at the door. They are calling my name. Who is it?*

The other three attackers looked over at him.

Next: *Kill them! The person is telling me to kill them!*

So he did. Dex ordered the patterns, instead of allowing them to order him. They lifted him into position, he dropped through one halo, found the anchor, and cut the two smaller assassins down with

348

a flyer. The large one turned, but Dex had shifted through, and was already behind him. He asked the patterns to put the sword through the man's neck. The flyer complied. The man dropped his sword, and fell to the ground.

Dex decided to drop his sword, too. It looked like a nice thing to do. The patterns rushed out of his mind; he could not see a thing.

"Dex!" screamed a voice. It was right next to him. "Dex!"

The slap came quick and fast. One cheek. Then the other. Slap.

The shapes disappeared. The patterns faded. Dex was looking into the scared face of Mallory Aquinas. Dex looked around, trying to get his bearings.

He failed, and crumpled to the ground, unconscious.

One hundred thirty-one.

Mash Gregor looked at his timepiece anxiously. I am not worried, he thought. Anxiety is not the same as worry. He tapped the code again.

"This is Fuel, looking for a clear sign on the Transish occupation," he said again. Still nothing. He was circling over Transish, watching the massive class C transporter. From here, it did not look like anything was happening. But he was on the outside looking in.

"I repeat, Mash Gregor here, looking for a clear sign," he said again.

The thread crackled to life. "This is zero-two-nine, on thread," a voice said. Mash watched for the security clearance. It came. "Coding a clear sign, sir," the voice said. "Sorry for the delay. A little busy."

"No problem, officer," Mash said. He smiled. *Why worry?* "I will circle around and board the transporter from the dock at my quarters."

"Yes, sir." the voice said. "Good to have you aboard, sir."

"Thank you." Mash dropped the thread. Another thread was blipping him.

"Mash here," he said.

"Mash, it's Mal."

"Mal," Mash said. "Thanks for all the SIN help. We couldn't have done this without you. Did you get your boy?"

"In a matter of speaking. I'm afraid Leshan did not make it."

Mash was quiet for a moment. "He knew the risks."

"Ashion the Dark is gone," Mal said.

"Good," Mash said. "Then Leshan did not die in vain."

"Dex took out the one called Gurn, as well."

"Great news."

"Mash, have you heard from Thelo? He is not answering my thread."

"He has orders to hold the Transloop." Mash pulled a thread for Thelo at that moment. Thelo did not answer. Mash waited.

"He's not answering me, either," Mash said. "But he can take care of himself."

"Maybe," Mal said. "I'm going up to see him. He's at the loop station bridge? You leave resistance codes on the place?"

"Of course. You can walk right onto the transporter control floor with that hand of yours."

"Good. There's someone headed that way I need to stop."

"Who's that?" Mash asked. "Listen, we got the Families all fighting for places up there, Mal. It's a madhouse. Stay away if you can. Ashion is dead. Who else could you be chasing?"

"My daughter," Mal said. "And I think Thelo needs something I've found. A little something for a disease he's got."

"Do what you need to do," Mash said. "But the transporters leave in..." he checked his timepiece, "thirty minutes. You and your boy are cleared for any of the three boats. Just get there."

Mal dropped the thread. Mash took a deep breath and coded the nav sequence to the transporter dock. He threw the shuttle into auto, and prepared to break his promise to his mother.

He came into the passenger shuttle to find Jahna, a bored look on her face, listening to a stern Family history lecture from Thula. When Jahna saw Mash, her eyes brightened and she squealed.

"Daddy!" she screamed. "Daddy, Daddy, Daddy!" She ran and threw her arms around Mash's neck. "I can't believe it's you. Grandma here told me you weren't on board but I told her this was your shuttle and you never let anyone drive, except for me sometimes, so who was driving, I asked, and she said someone, stop asking questions, and look! It was you!"

"Yes, it's me," Mash said. "But I need to talk to your grandma. Run up to the bridge and strap yourself in. I'll be right up."

Jahna looked back at Thula and stuck her tongue out. "Told you!" Then she ran up the stairs. Mash watched her go, and shut the door behind her.

Thula looked at Mash sadly. "You are going to murder me," she said.

"Yes," Mash said.

"I don't see the point in it, now," Thula said. "You have your daughter. You have your new empire. What am I but an old woman who wants to see her granddaughter grow old?"

"Sorry, Mother," Mash said. "But I promised someone. Can't go back on a promise." He gave Thula a quick push, and she fell backward, down the stairs to the cargo bay.

"Besides," Mash said, "There's no room on the transporter for Family." He opened the outer cargo door, blasting his mother out into the vacuum of space.

One hundred thirty-two.

Dex woke with his head cradled in Mal's lap. She looked old, though. Her hair was greying. She had wrinkles.

"Mal? That you?" he asked.

"It's me," she said, caressing his face. "How are you feeling?"

"Numb," he said. It was the only word.

"Do you remember the lab?" Mal asked.

Dex thought about it for a moment. "Yes. I remember. The shifting patterns. I couldn't stop them. They took over."

"Is that how you were doing it?" Mal asked.

"Doing what?"

"Moving so fast," Mal said. "I don't think my eyes could follow you. I thought, when I came into the room, I thought ... I don't know. I thought there were two of you."

"I can't really explain it. All I know is that the shifting technology takes over my mind. I can't stop it. It feels like I'm going crazy."

"Well, I thought you were crazy to start with," Mal said.

Dex smiled. "Well, I would never define myself as sane," he said. "Where are we?"

"On a shuttle. Headed for the Transloop. We've got a few people to save."

"Who?"

"Thelo, for one."

"It's the Millionaire's Disease, isn't it?"

"Yeah. Logos had found the serum to suppress the disease, and would provide it to Thelo every so often. But when Logos died, Thelo lost his supply."

"You find it?"

"Yes. Raided the med facs in Draggish. Found Logos' supply. I've got a shot of it for him in my sack."

"He's up at the loop?"

"Yes. There's someone else, Dex." Mal paused. "I was pulled off the ice for a reason. It wasn't just an accident. Ashion was looking for me, and he used Logos to find me. Ashion pulled me off ice because he wanted..." Mal swallowed. "He wanted our baby."

Dex sat up.

"So they pulled me off ice, and let me carry the baby to term, like I told you," Mal said. "Then they sent me to the asteroid mines. Ashion raised her. He named her Kat."

"The spy from Earth," Dex said. *My daughter.*

"Yes. They experimented on her. Checked to see if she was like Ashion. If she had the genes to take brain burns." Mal wiped away her tears. "She does."

"What did they do to her?" Dex asked.

"Gave her military training. Fighting skills. They trained up a version of you, then pulled the training neurals and laid them down on her. She was an excellent vessel.

"But Ashion had a secret purpose for Kat. I found it buried in the old databases of the SIN. Ashion was going to burn his own brain into Kat's. Take himself to Earth disguised as her. Then use the Earthlings' technology to download himself again."

Dex closed his eyes, fighting back the patterns. "That's why he was always looking for the map. He thought the Order of Brodius had some massive super-computer someplace. One he could use like the SIN."

Mal nodded. "But it didn't matter. He was just a pawn. There was someone else that wanted Kat's brain."

"Someone from one of the Families?" Dex asked.

"No, worse. It's the SIN itself."

"You mean those crazy computer worshipers were right?"

"I'm not sure if it was the SIN, or something that had found itself living in the SIN. But there was a consciousness within the networked systems. And it burned itself into Kat. Took control."

"My god."

"And then, I did what the SIN had done, only to Ashion," Mal said.

Dex closed his eyes. "That was me on the ground. Decapitated."

"Yes," Mal whispered.

"You burned my brain over the top of Ashion's."

"Yes," Mal whispered, barely audible.

"This is his body, not mine. Somewhere in my brain right now, Ashion still lives."

"I have to believe that. Because I have to believe Kat is still inside her own brain, too. Underneath the SIN. Dex—he calls himself Moses."

"Wait, Moses?" Dex said.

"Yeah."

"*Crackpipe.* What do you make of that?"

"Something that survived a thousand years? I don't know. But now it's headed for the Transloop. It wants to go back to Earth. It wants freedom. Survival."

"The Slave will walk among us," Dex said. "That was the Sinners' chant."

"It's using our daughter," Mal said.

"Let's get her back," Dex said, slowly working himself up to standing.

"Are you alright?" Mal asked.

"For now," Dex said. He could feel the pressure of the shifting patterns building again. But he managed to keep them at bay.

For now.

One hundred thirty-three.

Mal pulled the shuttle slowly around the Transloop. The atmosphere of Venus had already been breached by the loop field, and there was a visible break at the surface of the planet. It looked like the knot of a balloon.

"Look," she said, pointing. A Family boat had turned its boosters on, and was heading directly into the side of the loop field. "They are trying to catch a ride without coding into the system."

Dex nodded. "It worked for me and Thelo before," he said.

Mal shook her head. "There's too much data, with the atmo unloading into the field. Unless you can explicitly tell the Earth-side station what to expect, those crafts are not going to reappear at the other end. It's too late. They will have to go to the transporters, now."

"Has anyone told them?" Dex said.

355

Mal shrugged. "I don't know who would. Mash is a good leader, but he's not exactly interested in saving the Families."

Dex watched another ship launch into the loop.

Mal navigated directly to the Transloop control room. There was an emergency dock at one side of it. Shuttle blasts testified to the fact that some Family ships had wanted in. But the dock had a blast shield that was impervious. Impervious to everything except proper security clearance. Mal put her mitt into her interface. The shuttle waited, and went black. The shuttle rocked.

"What was that?" Dex asked.

"Someone taking shots at us," Mal said. "Misery loves company."

The security code cleared, but not before the shuttle sustained two more shots. Then, the dock door opened, and they were inside. There was another shuttle there, its warmers still on. It was ready to go. Their shuttle landed, and Mal and Dex ran for the control room floor.

The place was deserted, except for one person.

"Hello, Kat," Mal said.

Kat turned. She gave a smile. "Ah, the relics of antiquity, come to save the day," she said. She turned back and finished threading. Then she took her interface down. "Just putting the final touches to my shuttle launch. With all the atmo noise, you wouldn't believe how delicate this loop is right now."

"I know it," Mal said. "I know it because I read your mind."

"Yes, yes," Kat said. "When I was still in the net I could tell you were there. Problem with being a computer, of course, is that there are some things you can't understand. I can look back, now, and say I was breached by some snooping bitch. But when you're the computer, you lack, shall we say, perspective."

"Where's Thelo?" Dex asked.

"He beat me to it," Kat grinned. "He already looped down to Earth-side. Just one more obstacle in my way. But I'll kill him, too. Now if you'll excuse me."

"I'm not letting you by," Dex said. He pulled his sword from its sheath. "Mal, take Kat's shuttle and head for the Earth Transloop Station. It's already programmed to make the loop. Go to Thelo. Give him his shot. Then get Earth-side."

356

"I'm not leaving you," Mal said. "I'm not leaving her."

Kat pulled Judas from her back, and telescoped it into place.

"Mal, I will not kill her. But only you can get to Thelo. And I need to know that the two of you are safe."

"I won't go!" Mal yelled. Dex did not take his eyes off Kat.

"Find Justice," Dex said. "Help him prepare for all the arrivals. Help him rebuild the Order of Brodius."

"You act like you won't be there," Mal said.

"Oh, I'll be there," Dex said. "I'll just be a little late. Go!" At which he leaped at Kat.

She was too fast, though. She rolled out of the way easily, catching his blade with hers, spinning, and swinging an offensive. Dex pushed back, overwhelmed by her speed. He had barely blocked three swings in rapid possession, when he realized he was no match for this girl. He was going to fail. Mal wasn't going to make it back to Earth.

He couldn't save his daughter.

Dex didn't see another option. So he let go, and the dam inside his head broke loose. The patterns flew out. He let them have their way, unspooling as fast as they would go. The flyer lifted his sword, stopped the attack of Kat. The halo opened, and Dex stepped through, coming to an anchor between Kat and the door. The patterns bounced off and around Mal as she ran for the shuttle that Kat had prepared.

Kat was yelling something at Dex. Through the noise of the patterns he could not hear what she was saying. He let the patterns block her attacks, but he kept himself between the girl and the door to the shuttles.

"There is no time for this!" the girl yelled. "The station will be destroyed in minutes!"

But Dex could not hear her. The patterns blocked everything.

One hundred thirty-four.

Mal felt the shuttle enter the loop, and then it was over. She was staring at the huge umbrella of the Earth-side Transloop station's solar collector.

The place had been abandoned. There wasn't a single shuttle left. Many of the modules of the station had crumpled in, destroyed. The entire structure looked like it might give at any moment. There was an uncomfortable amount of shaking as the shuttle docked.

She stepped out of the craft, and tried to find her footing. But Thelo was right there. He was bleeding from the side of his head. But he had his sword.

"Are you alright?" she yelled, over the noise of metal grinding against itself.

Thelo reached up to his head. "Ambushed by infantry," he said. "They took my shuttle, headed to Earth. But I wasn't worried. I knew you were coming. To save me."

Mal had never seen that smile before.

"Come on," she said. "This station isn't safe."

"You're not coming with me," Thelo said, raising his sword.

Mal brought her blaster around and squeezed a bolt off. The shot caught him in the hand, sending his sword flying. Thelo recovered quickly, and grabbed Mal by the throat. He pulled the blaster from her hand and threw it aside.

Mal could feel her throat about to be crushed under Thelo's hand. She pulled the topper off the needle, stuck it into his arm, and pushed the plunger. Thelo grunted, but did not let go of her. She was seeing stars, and was grasping at his hand, clawing at his arm.

Moments later, his grip loosened, and Mal fell to the metal floor of the dock bay.

Thelo crumbled to his knees. "My god, I'm so sorry," he said. "Where am I? What is going on?"

"Come on," Mal said hoarsely, trying to stand. "Get on the

shuttle. Let's get to Earth."

Thelo allowed himself to be pulled to his feet, and walked up the stairs to the shuttle.

"It never ends, Mal," he said. "It always comes back."

"I know how to make the serum," Mal said.

"It's not a cure," he said. "It's a blocker. I'm someone else. Someone else wants my body. I can't stop it forever."

"Get inside, we can talk about this on Earth!" Mal yelled. Then she felt Thelo's hands on her.

"Thelo! What are you doing?"

"Saving you," he said. He pushed her into the cockpit, and slammed the door behind him. He keyed the take-off sequence, and then jumped away from the shuttle.

Mal fumbled with the door, but she felt the shuttle jolt away from the dock, the door locked for launch.

"Thelo!" she cried. But the shuttle's burners kicked in and took off. Mal returned to the bridge, and flipped on the exterior cams. She saw Thelo through the small dock bay window, waving goodbye. Then he turned and walked away. She madly tried to key a return sequence, but before she could come up with anything, the end of the station farthest from Earth was pulled into the expanding loop field, and the shuttle's computer was asking for a landing sequence.

She took one more look as the station disintegrated into the maw of the invisible loop field. Then she threaded her answer.

Cawlria. Western Amrika.

The shuttle began its burn into the Earth's atmosphere.

Mal sobbed, the tears streaming down her face.

We saved them all.

But I've lost everyone.

One hundred thirty-five.

Even with the patterns, the attacker was too fast. Dex could not keep her in the control room forever. When she made it past him, he pursued her. But the patterns were running out. It was a new sensation. They did not overwhelm him this time.

I am Dexter Maxwell.
That is my daughter.
She is host to a parasite.
She is running for my shuttle.

Dex caught up to her at the stairs of the shuttle. He swung his sword at her legs, but she jumped into the shuttle. Dex leaped in after her, defending a vicious swing that was meant to connect with his head.

"You are good, iter," Kat said. "Logos would be proud."

"Logos did not make me," Dex said. "You did."

He attacked again, but Kat brought the sword down into his swing, and then flipped the blade at an angle and drove it straight into Dex's stomach. He grunted, stumbling backward and off the blade.

"Human," Kat said with disgust. Then she was up in the cockpit.

Kat looked at the controls, and began to thread madly. There was no time left. No time to calibrate for an Earth-side loop. The loop would impact Venus in just a few minutes.

She flew the shuttle up, and the doors of the dock opened. She slowed, and pulled the craft into a careful arch. It came around, heading directly for the station.

"You're headed for the loop field," Dex said. He'd pulled himself up into the cockpit, clutching his stomach. "It will destroy us. What are you doing?"

Kat narrowed her eyes, checked her timepiece and then fired the thrusters. It was a minute window; she had to time it just right.

"Moses! Where are you going? *What are you doing?*" Dex yelled.

"Just a little trick I learned from watching you," she said. "Once

I had access to your neurals, I could see how you did it. Why you're different. Who you are."

Kat pulled the shuttle hard to the right.

The shuttle hit the Transloop field.

The loop field crossed into the hard matter of Venus.

VENUS. DAY 58. ECHO EVENT.

One hundred thirty-six.

All the threads were dead. None of the servers were working. The air was getting hotter, more sulfurous.

Father Morgish strummed at the First Term again. Still nothing. He turned to his displays. They were all dead. He banged his fists into the threader. Then he turned and bowed in front of the First Term. "Why have you forsaken me?" he cried. "Please, answer my prayers!" The air was almost too thin to breathe. The smell of the Venus atmo overwhelmed him. He took one last ragged breath, and cried again, "Why have you forsaken me?!"

One hundred thirty-seven.

It was over in a few minutes. There was a roar, and then Venus was right back where it was before, only it was a dull black. It was smaller, now, condensed down by the atoms recombining. It did not reflect as much light.

From Earth, it simply looked as though one of the stars in the night sky had dimmed slightly, almost imperceptibly. But no one on Earth spent much time looking at the sky. They hadn't for years.

EPILOGUE

Mash and Rolink watched the dim, dark planet fade away from the port window of the meeting quarters of the new and great King Mash Gregor.

"I did not believe, at times, that it would actually happen," Rolink said.

"At times, I wish I could have believed that," Mash said.

"Did all the ships get away?" Rolink asked.

"All three transports are safely on their way to Earth. Jules cares for Trance on the *Majestic*, which holds the people of Morgish. From Draggish, there are no reports of your friends. But I am sure they got on board."

Rolink looked at the new Venus, fading away so quickly into the distance. "Dexter Maxwell is alive," he said.

"You know this?" Mash asked.

Rolink shrugged. "I believe it. What is the difference?"

"Daddy!" cried a voice. Mash turned around, just in time to catch Jahna in his arms. He hugged her, and brought her up to his hip.

"This is Rolink," Mash said to Jahna. "Rolink, my daughter, Jahna."

"It is a pleasure to know you," Rolink said with a bow.

"Are you ready to meet your real mother now?" Mash asked.

"Yes!" Jahna said, both arms raised in victory.

Mash smiled at Rolink.

"You have done well, Mash Gregor," Rolink said with a deep bow. "I have served under another king, King Mebda. He was a great man. But I have served another great man, now. I look forward to serving you on Earth."

Mash bowed to Rolink. "We could not have done it without your blades, smithy. Now let's all get some rest. It is a long journey on a crowded ship."

Mash took his bouncing daughter and walked down to his private sleeping quarters. The two ever-present bodyguards moved aside to let them in. Mash put his daughter down.

"Jahna," he said, "this is your mother."

Jahna looked at the old woman, who was smiling and pouring wine.

"She's old, Daddy," Jahna said with a scowl.

"I am not so old that I don't recognize my own flesh and blood," the woman said. "Come over and let me have a look at you."

Jahna looked back at her father, who smiled and shooed her forward. She walked hesitantly to the woman.

"You look like the old Governor," Jahna said.

"I get that a lot," she said with a smile, handing a glass of wine to Mash, who'd come over and sat next to her.

"Hello, love," Mash said.

"Hello, darling," she replied. "It was a dangerous gamble with our daughter's life."

Mash gave her a long, deep kiss. "Life itself is a dangerous gamble. You need to worry less. We are here. She is here. All of this is ours. The new world is ours." Mash took a drink of the wine. "I was thinking we could call it New Venus," he said. "Or would you prefer Charlestown?"

She thought for a moment. "Logos, we should name our new settlement after dear, departed Logos. Without him, none of this would have been possible."

Mash raised his glass. "To Logos," he said.

Charles raised her glass. "To Logos."

Jahna raised an imaginary cup.

"To Logos!" she cried. Then she looked at her father.

"What's a Logos?"

ADDENDUM

THE GOVERNING FAMILIES OF THE
UNITED TOWNSHIPS OF VENUS ("THE HIGH
FAMILIES") - JAN 3049, VENUS RECORDS

Family Goldman

Charles Goldman (2938–present)
Governor General of the United Townships, 3007–present
Widowed by **Batista (Monsanta) Goldman** (2919–3030)
Charles is the eldest of three daughters of **Contessa Goldman**

Contessa Goldman (2782–3018)
Governor General of the United Townships, 2955–3007
Widowed by **Malovar (Lewiston) Goldman** (2745–2825), then
Henrique (Conagra) Goldman (2826–2991)
*Contessa's two youngest daughters were wed to Lower Families and
have been stricken from the family records*

Morgan Goldman (2982–present)
Goldman Family Exemplar to the Security Council
Eldest daughter of **Charles Goldman**

Henrique Goldman (born 2985, died shortly after birth)
Son of **Charles Goldman**

Family Lewiston

Salzon Lewiston (2881–present)
Right Hand to the Governor, 3018–present

Montigo Lewiston (2759–2945)
Father of **Salzon Lewiston** and **Arvura Lewiston**

Junta Lewiston (2750–2945)
Father of **Thula (Lewiston) Gregor**

Arvura Lewiston (2875–2945)

Thadwick Lewiston (2967–present)
Lewiston Family Exemplar to the Security Council
Married to **Ingrid (Monsanta) Lewiston** (2989–present)

Family Gregor

Thula (Lewiston) Gregor (2955–present)
Gregor Family Exemplar to the Security Council
Daughter of **Junta Lewiston**
Mother of **Mash Gregor, Jesla Gregor, Uthea Gregor**
Married to **Gram Gregor**

Gram Gregor (2959–present)
Son of **Trance Gregor** (2929–3013)
Father of **Mash Gregor, Jesla Gregor, Uthea Gregor**
One recorded bastard child, **Leshan Gregor**, who has been stricken from Family records

Mash Gregor (3001–present)

Jesla Gregor (2997–3034)

Uthea Gregor (2997–3034)

Leshan Gregor (2992–present)
Bastard son of **Gram Gregor**

THE SECURITY COUNCIL OF THE UNITED TOWNSHIPS OF VENUS

Charles Goldman
Senior Councilor and Governor
Salzon Lewiston
Right Hand
Morgan Goldman
Goldman Exemplar
Thadwick Lewiston
Lewiston Exemplar
Thula Gregor
Gregor Exemplar (and Chief Consul)
General Emery Dante
Planet–side Operations
General Vetta Mars
Military Advisor to the Council (retired)
General Macha Warship
Military Advisor to the Council (retired)
General Tin Cheltin
Military Advisor to the Council (retired)

ASHION GOLDMAN AND HIS COMMAND

Ashion Goldman, Slave to the Goldman Family (2657–present)
Chief Security Enforcer and Commander
Tano Down (3008–present)
Commander, Knights of Peace (Red Masks) and First in Command
Gurn (3015–present)
Training Commander
Armitage Holden (2913–present)
Security Fleet Admiral
Kat (3033–present)
Protégé of Ashion Goldman
Prisoner Six, also known as Root
Age and identity unlisted

THE RESISTANCE

The Resistance on Venus

Fuel (age and identity unknown)
Leader, Venus planet–side resistance
Trance (3013–present)
Commander, Venus planet–side resistance
Logos (2959–3049)
House doctor to the Goldman Family
Thelonius Hollywood, also known as Orpheus (2094–present)
Commander, Venus planet–side resistance

The Resistance on Earth

Freedom (2970–3027, Earth time)
Monk in the Order of Brodius
Justice (2975–present)
Monk in the Order of Brodius
Rolink (2994–present)
Goat hearder and smithy
Mallory Aquinas, also known as Lynia (2095–present)
Time shifter
Dexter Maxwell (3049–present, in current iteration),
Time shifter

Matthew Hart

The Last Iteration of Dexter Maxwell

Published by CAPSCOVIL in December 2012, available in print (ISBN 978-3-942358-30-9, perfect paperback) and as electronic edition for various reading devices and platforms.

Adventurous Science Fiction Seasoned with Sustainability

Dex knows first hand that living on the edge of civilization in Grenver, Colorado is tough. But it also has its perks. With his small league of rebels, he has pulled off some of the most brazen acts of the 22nd Century to snarl the system. Not bad for an orphan sewer rat, another un-nationalized civilian that can´t afford to get a citizen chip implanted.

Dex doesn´t care about his missing memory of early childhood before the orphanage or about most likely ending up on ice like all the other crims. No past, no future: no problem. As long as he has his friends and his mischief, he's going to be alright.

But after a botched stunt, Dex wakes up to find himself in a brutal, foreign underground city—blind, with a sword strapped to his back, and an old man telling him he's the final ingredient for a revolution.

Dex can barely start to take it all in before he's on the run, hunted by deadly assassins, looking for answers, and somehow imbued with skills he shouldn't have. Before he knows it, he finds himself in the center of a plot a millennium in the making, with the fate of two worlds at stake.

Start an exciting and adventurous journey with THE LAST ITERATION OF DEXTER MAXWELL to find out who Dexter Maxwell really is.

Connect with the author: http://about.me/hartmatthew

GREATER METROPOLITAN FRONT RANGE (GMFR), SEPTEMBER 27, 2113.

One.

Tick, Tick, Crackle.

It was Thelo, coding him on the com. Dex ignored the hail long enough to pass the roll of cash out the window of the truck, give a smile to the attendant taking the bribe, and wait for the tollgate to rise. Then he pulled the collar back on his heavy worker's coat and engaged the small chip on his throat with a *tap tap rub*, and breathed, "Thelo, whachya need?"

"Bored. Checking in. Hadn't heard from you in a while."

Dex tried to picture Thelo's location. Thelo had pulled the short straw for the cross-70 turnpike, straight through downtown Grenver, past the DMV helipads. Past Central Dispatch. Past Fed Park.

"One more toll station," Dex said, "then I'm down to outer bur-bring, no problem."

"Crackpipe, Dex, you're way behind."

"I know."

"Everyone is minutes away from zero go. And you are, what, twenty minutes from go?"

"I know. Don't worry."

"I'm not worried. I'm mostly pissed."

"Don't stress it. Everything's fives."

"I doubt that."

"Stop shrinkin' your peener. A few minutes ain't no deal."

Thelo spoke up, ever so slightly, but it was as good as a yell in Dex's earpiece. "Now you listen to me, you orphan-rot. We've been planning this exact moment for months, and I am not about to let your druggy hangover screw everything up. Do what it takes to get there on time. Understand?"

"Crackpipe, Thelo, who crapped up your coffee? I told you—"

But Thelo had coded out. Dex slammed his fist into the dash. What had gotten into him? First Mal was acting dripped, and now Thelo seemed straight uphill-bunged. What was happening to his friends?

Thelo had had him there for a second, Dex realized, but he got it now. Thelo was just firing up his crapper. Getting him into the moment. Well, if Thelo wanted a fire, he'd give him one. His mind took off, unleashed. The hangover vanished.

Dex downshifted as he approached the final toll booth, and his truck gave an angry groan against the autumn cold. Today he was driving a Halliburton 260, one of the oldest garbage carriers around; the kind with the large compacting space in the back behind the cab so it could hold as much garbage as possible. It was a good six feet higher than the cab where he sat. Dex figured his truck must be twice as old as he was. It still had an old-fashioned transmission, and the central brain controller had been an after-market add-on by Old Man Newbury himself.

He pulled up to the booth, rolled down his window, and slid his repurposed work permit through the small slit in the bulletproof glass. The overweight attendee looked up at Dex, then hit her mic button.

"Newbury Trash don't have a listing for Tuesdays," her voice crackled. "Can't let you pass." Then she smiled.

Dex smiled politely back, and reached for the rubber-banded roll with the name ROSEANNE inked on the outside. "Newbury Trash never dumps on Tuesdays. Of course, how could I be so dumb? Here, I just need you to swipe my work order, explain things to Newbury." Dex put his hand out toward the toll attendee. She took the wad of cash he offered, and started counting it. Then she wacked a large button with her thumb and the gate rose. "Have a good morning, Charlie. Try and remember your permit days next time."

"Thanks, Roseanne," Dex said, and put the truck into gear. He pulled his glove off to code up Mal to let her know where he was at.

"Wait, there, Charlie, you almost forgot your permit," the woman said, handing Dex his pass card. Without thinking, he reached for it with his left hand.

"Jeez, Charlie, what happened to you?" She asked, grimacing at his hand, which was missing the pinkie and top digit of his ring finger.

Dex smiled at her. "Lost a bet," he said with wink.

Roseanne chuckled. "Helluva bet, Charlie."

"You shoulda seen the other guy," Dex said.

As he pulled the truck away from the booth, he scratched at his throat com again, and put his glove back on. But Mal didn't answer, so Dex re-focused in on the task at hand.

The truck groaned as it picked up speed, the transmission of the hybrid issuing a loud hydraulic hiss as Dex threw it into overdrive. His foot had already started to ache from holding the gas pedal down all the way, but he didn't release it. He was starting to pass the few small 'muter cars that dotted the freeway in front of him. They laid on their horns, the angry little bleats of the sheep, barely heard against the chugging of the huge truck's engine.

A disjunctive, pre-recorded male voice came through the overhead mic: "Warning, driver, Newbury Trash, permit... six, three, five, six, nine... your... two or more axle vehicle is close to maximum allowable speed. Please be careful."

Dex reached across to the passenger-side floor and picked up his ratty old backpack. He threw it onto the seat next to him. As he sat up he saw a small, red car right in front of him, going a good twenty miles per hour slower than he was. Dex pulled the horn lever next to him, and the car swerved back into the right lane, narrowly avoiding being bumped from behind.

His heart raced. A reported accident this early would bring the DMV sooner than he wanted. Before he was anywhere near his checkpoint. He pictured the place in his mind: the first exit into outer burbring, the cars already lining up for the race into the central commerce districts. It was sixteen miles out, and he only had three or four minutes. The freeway veered south and east soon, away from the Peak, and downhill to his destination. Downhill was good; it would help a little.

He unsnapped his backpack with one hand, weaving the huge truck through the traffic with the other. He pulled out his only valuable material possession—a worn old portable—from inside and placed it on the expansive dash. He'd glued some Velcro down on the surface to mesh with the strip on the back of his portable. Two red wires hung down from the portable's face. Dex reached for them.

Another zoned out 'muter strayed into the left lane. Before Dex could swerve, he grazed the side of the car, sending it spinning off into the shoulder.

"Shit!" Dex said out loud.

The voice came back from the overhead com immediately. "Warning, driver, Newbury Disposal Service, permit... six, three, five, six, nine. You have been involved in an automobile accident. This incident is currently being reported to Section 7 of the Department of Motor Vehicles. Please pull over to the shoulder slowly and wait for further instruction."

But Dex didn't pull over. His leg shaking visibly under the pressure, he stood on the pedal, using his weight instead of his muscles to hold it down. Finally he managed to get his hands around the data jack cables and reached them back under the steering column.

Two.

Dex inserted an I/O jack into the truck's central controller; it was so easy on those aftermarket jobbers. Then he dropped a cable into the jack and taped it under the steering column somewhere... there! He found the cable ends, pushed them into place on his portable, and the power indicator of his portable went live. He threw open the clamshell display.

The portable blinked, and a terminal appeared. Without looking, Dex reached over and typed in the commands to run Money's hack. The terminal showed his keystrokes in an oversized font. He touched the big green GO button, barely readable and worn down from use, and lines of executing code scrolled quickly past. Then the screen cleared and a simple, one-word question remained, blinking lazily:

ENGAGE?

Dex had to time it just right. Engage too soon, and the program was useless. Too late, and the program suffered the same fate. He would only have a fraction of a second to engage.

The voice came back over the speaker. "Warning, driver, Newbury Disposal Service, permit... six, three, five, six, nine. You are exceeding the posted allowable speed for freeway... 625... southbound...

at mile marker ...thirty...four. Your driving permit is being penalized now. You have thirty seconds to disengage your throttle."

Before the warning had even finished, he heard the com go live, and a real voice came over the speaker. "Permit, uh, permit six three five six nine, you've been reported as the primary in a traffic incident at mark 30. Immediately desist your speeding and pull to the shoulder." Dex could hear the heli blades beating in the background. They'd already sent a chopper his way.

It was six more miles to his destination. His current speed was ninety-three miles per hour.

Now this is fun. There was no trace of his hangover left. He felt the moment; it was upon him, starting to take. He let it take him.

Three.

Mallory Aquinas coded Thelo fast, *tap rub tap rub.* He came on, sounding distracted.

"Yes? What do you need?" Thelo asked.

"Did Salvador code you with the patched broadcast?" Mal asked quickly.

"Yes. I heard."

"They've got two helis dispatched. He started *speeding,* for Chrissake."

Thelo paused, then said, "He also hit a 'muter."

"No. No, he did NOT."

"Yeah. I can't get through to him. He's coded me out."

"Crackpipe. Okay. I'll give him a try. Are we going to abort?"

"No!" Thelo was breathing heavy, irregularly. "The dominos fall without him."

"I don't know, Thelo. We could reschedule. It's not too late."

"Are you losing it, Mal? Getting cold feet?"

"Whoa, there, Thelo, where did that come from?"

"Call your damn boyfriend. Now." Then he coded out.

What is his problem, Mal wondered. She looked at her watch. Two minutes. She could see her target ahead, on the horizon, just a few moments away.

Niall MacRoslin / Alice N. York

Black Hungarian

(Working Title)

Publication in summer 2014 by CAPSCOVIL Will be available in print (ISBN 978-3-942358-43-9, English - ISBN 978-3-942358-49-1 German) and as electronic edition for various reading devices and platforms.

THRILLER SPICED WITH SECURITY AND MOBILITY

The Board for Industrial Research and Development has been shaping major political decisions since 1929. You haven't heard of them because no-one has. They're efficient, discreet and ultra-professional. Working under the guise of a multi-faceted consultancy firm. But a new threat to their customers means all that could be about to change. After much deliberation, a decision has been made.

A new technology is to be tested in an extensive field trial, and the electric car expedition WAVE offers the perfect cover. Naturally, BIRD has no desire to see it succeed. The usual countermeasures are taken and a team is dispatched. The mission is to be low-key, no more than a routine training exercise: an opportunity for BIRD to blood the next generation of field operatives. There is, it seems, little that can go wrong.

But the new recruits are young and impulsive; quick to act when caution should be the name of the game. One bad decision leads to another, and soon the mission is spiralling out of control.

Project Black Hungarian is the first book of its kind:
Real events from the "World Advanced Vehicle Expedition" 2013 are woven into a suspense-packed spy story that also takes current global developments into account. A major focus is on topics around electric vehicles, information technology and security, and renewable energies.

EXPERT OPINIONS

ON

"The Last Iteration of Dexter Maxwell"
(Book 1 of the Series)

"This book makes you reflect on the big responsibility of delivering technology in service of citizens. A good material to debate, especially as we are at the gates of the first Smart Cities. Are these the cities we are modeling?"
Alicia Asín Pérez, CEO and Co-Founder Libelium, Member of the International Research Groups: Sensor Networks and Mesh Networks.

"A riveting science fiction novel that I found hard to put down once I started reading it. Matthew Hart has expertly interwoven believable technological advances into this spellbinding Sci-Fi adventure story of Dexter Maxwell set in the 22nd through 31st Centuries AD."
Daniel L. Calloway, MSIT with specialization in network architecture & expert network consultant to the Internet of Things (IoT) Council in Brussels, Belgium

"From a technology vantage point, it was interesting to see advanced transportation, wireless and mobile device technology stitched seamlessly into a scintillating Sci-Fi tale. I recommend the book."
Roger C. Lanctot, Associate Director, Global Automotive Practice, Strategy Analytics

"A mind-bending thrill-ride, Hart has given us a gritty and fascinating vision of the future."
Brian David Johnson, Futurist & Principal Engineer, INTEL

"The pace of the story is enthralling. The difficulties of living on Venus, as well as the need for a resettlement from Earth, raise valid questions in this day and age. I found the prayloop and its effect as a community very inspiring."
Stephan Tomek, Senior Researcher, iHomeLab Switzerland

"This is a fascinating and scaring Sci-Fi novel where the technology we are working on today becomes reality. Freedom, friendship, love and purpose mixed with future technology relates directly to us today – to taking over responsibility of the actions that will lead to THE Last Iteration".
Dr. Stefan Ferber, Director Communities & Partner Networks, Bosch Software Innovations GmbH

"I'm not sure the future is a place I want to visit after reading this interesting and thought provoking book. A world where the technology is inescapable raises many moral and societal issues that I hope mankind is able to navigate. Read it and make up your own mind"
Tristan Wilkinson, Founder, Digital Citizens

"Once you are in the story, you get a lively overview of a variety of future technologies, currently under investigation, and fictional topics. But while some aspects of a smart city environment seem compelling and convenient, the author also provides the dark side of the moon from ethics and society perspectives! An enjoyable but also alarming story!
Joachim Schonowski - T-Labs (Research & Development), Deutsche Telekom AG

"The story evolves at an incredible pace and it becomes an effort to put the book down. It has everything a good Sci-Fi novel should feature: a thrilling story, compelling characters and a strong foundation in science and technology. Especially the latter makes this book extraordinary and a great read for all genre fans. Can't wait for the „Second Harvest".
Prof. Dr. Sebastian Lehnhoff, Research and Development Division Energy, OFFIS Institute for Information Technology

PROLOGUE

Spring

"I've got something for you."

"Now?!"

"Now."

"OK, Dominik – but this had better be good."

It was. Though he doubted Adler would see it that way. Christian Adler, CEO of Adler Reilly, grandson of Tobias: visionary, emigrant, founder. Tobias, who had come into the world with nothing and bequeathed an enduring legacy; Christian whose wealth was so great he had neglected to think of the next-in-line. Strange, Dominik Brandt thought to himself, to see a dynasty coming to an end before your own eyes.

He was sitting in the Presidential Suite at the five star Hotel Sacher, one of Vienna's many gifts to the rich and famous. The Madame Butterfly Suite, as it was also known, was a vast space, some 160 square metres in all, comprising an anteroom, drawing room, dining and conference room, as well as an office and dressing room. A generously proportioned bedroom, art-deco bathroom and view over the city completed the luxury effect. Everything stood ready for the CEO's arrival. The long conference table was decked out with coffee, fruit, pastries and sparkling water, almost all of which would go to waste. At the head of the table, where the CEO insisted on being seated – even if it was just the two of them – Dominik had laid a small, immaculately presented dossier containing a précis of the Director of Intelligence's findings. The DI could not be there in person, but along with Directors Financial and Legal would be taking part by video-link. There would be no rap on the door: the CEO didn't knock – especially when he had been dragged out of a meeting at the UN building. What had it been this time? Dominik couldn't remember. Only that it had been important, and official; Adler Reilly rather than BIRD.

No, the CEO wouldn't knock – but he would expect to be greeted at the door. When Dominik heard the footsteps outside, therefore, that measured, rhythmical tread which somehow managed to convey both calm and a hint of violence, he sprang to his feet and moved swiftly towards the door.

"Dominik, your timing is faultless as ever."

Always that air of sarcasm, of superiority. The pair shook hands in a perfunctory manner: the CEO a head taller than his number two, but older as well by thirty years, his hair now grey where once it had been dark; both men impeccably dressed. After the handshake, Dominik watched as the older man helped himself to a glass of sparkling water. What was the difference between them, he wondered. The tailor-made suits, designer watches, expensive shoes, even the tan: that was all the same. But whereas Adler oozed authority, was, at this stage of his life, a veritable éminence grise, he – Dominik –still had an air of schoolboy awkwardness. Their ages, yes, that had something to do with it, but did it not, when all was said and done, boil down to the simple fact of their upbringing? The CEO had that confidence, that insouciance, which one associated with people from a certain kind of background: an easy, devil-may-care charm that must surely come gift-wrapped with the Ivy League education and lifetime of financial security.Dominik, on the other hand, was neither insouciant nor particularly charming, and any confidence he had gained was the result of sheer hard work. Where the CEO exuded power, he could only call on his naked ambition. A distasteful quality, perhaps, but one that might yet come in handy if, as now seemed likely, Adler was to leave no heir.

"Shall we begin?"

"It's all there," Dominik motioned towards the dossier at the head of the table. As always, he allowed the CEO a few moments to read the document, taking advantage of the brief lull to freshen up in the guest bathroom.

"Electric cars?" Adler was shaking his head. He was, it was true, more than old enough to remember the first: not so much a car as a tricycle, with a handlebar underneath the driver's knees and a top speed of 24km/h. A peculiarly British commercial disaster where the weather, of course, had been a decisive factor. Still, that was a long time ago. Surely Adler had by now got used to the fact that electric vehicles were here to stay. "Is this some kind of joke?" There it was – that calm, that hint of violence.

Alice N. York
GAME
FAINT SIGNALS

Published by CAPSCOVIL in May 2011, available in print (ISBN 978-3-942358-08-8, perfect paperback) and as electronic edition for various reading devices and platforms.

Delicate Career Novel With Smart Solar Ideas

Alex leads a thoroughly contented life. In Sandro she has found the right man, and the new consultancy job at a leading solar company seems tailor-made for her.

In no time, she familiarises herself with the technology and establishes a complex network incorporating both external partners and prospective clients, as well as various departments within the intricate company organisational structure. Developing long-term strategies and innovational product ideas is just as inspiring for her as implementing them practically. In addition, business trips to globally operating clients offer Alex an insight into different cultures, taking her to fascinating cities along the way. Winning new projects with innovative, successful solutions quickly enables her to gain the respect of her superiors.

As time goes by, however, her existence begins to resemble a rollercoaster ride. Grave events in her private life result in Alex throwing herself ever deeper into work. Yet slowly but surely menacing clouds are gathering there too. Alex does everything in her power to retain control. But like a game of poker, she is constantly being dealt a new hand; and no-one quite knows who holds the aces.

***

„Alice N. York portrays life in the workplace with extraordinary accuracy"
Ebersberger Zeitung

***

Follow Alex how she plays the game to win. Until the rules change and the world turns ruthless...